The Hanging o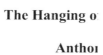

Anthor

FOR PAULA

CONTENTS

THE HANGING OF WILLIAM DODD

PROLOGUE

Perhaps, if it is a long time after I have been released from this mortal coil, the following pages are taken from the iron banded chest and read by curious eyes, let not those eyes weep for the words therein. Nor yet let there be tears for me for I am a long time dead. If your judgement of me and my sins is too harsh to call for your pity, waste not that pity. Neither do you pour out contempt. Give all your compassion for the living who step or run full haste into impropriety or to cardinal sin. Look only into the whole value of their lives and take lessons. For every mistake confessed in life gives both you and others a chance to avoid deeper footfalls. As I should have done. Also will you please:

"When you shall these unlucky deeds relate
Speak of me as I am: nothing extenuate. Nor set down aught
*in malice"**

William Dodd
November 1792

* Othello's last speech Vol. ll p175, Act V Scene X in William Dodd's own anthology: *The Beauties of Shakespear*

1

CHAPTER 1
THE CASKET IS OPENED

*The story begins with Mary, The Reverend
William Dodd's wife, writing to Sir Philip Thicknesse
exactly to the day one year after the
hanging. In it she asks Dodd's friend to come
again to Voirons.*

Mrs Mary Dodd to Sir PhilipThicknesse
Chateau de Voirons
27th June 1778

Dear Sir Philip,

It is now a year exactly since the Fatal Day when you and
we – my dear husband William and I set off for the safety
of M le Blanc's home here in France. Please do come to us
again when you can, for I begin to feel a new uneasiness
for William. His dreadful injuries from the hanging and
perhaps the revivification after it are barely abated.
Everything has been done as you directed, yet I ponder still
whether he should now be told all that took place on that
Fatal Hanging Day – one year ago today. How long will it
be before William remembers everything? Your advice
has been set so strong against this that I will hold back such
history until you come and consider for yourself how
matters lie with us now.

Our day is much the same – William has no speech –
nor do I think he will ever speak again. He hears sharp
enough and has I think more understanding but mind and
passion are all pent up within him – yet fade again and
again from whatever causes I know not.

Yet still my first concern is for the pain that William
has. Sometimes as he turns his head his face contorts and

his good left hand grips his neck as though to press all pain from it. When I told Monsieur le Blanc of this he offered tincture of laudanum – which he takes he says for the gout. William, proffered this, released his hand from his neck and waved me away. On such occasions I put hot towels on his shoulders and then soothe his neck with my hand.

After the meagre breakfast that is customary in these parts, he will take sometimes a walk – but with me always by his side. He will not venture out as long as there is even only but a hint of rain or the slightest wind-blown shower. If it is dry and the air is still he likes to walk on the "English Lawns" as I call them, for these are better tended than any I saw on my journey here and generally are as sparse as French breakfasts are said to be. But, neither bird-song nor the dappled sunlight breaking through the poplars please William. Drooping, he moves at snail pace and the more the throstle sings and the sunlight plays with shadows, the more likely a tear starts to his eye and he turns to me to take him inside again. Then, as has been the custom since you first advised, I sit William in his chair-with-arms and push him close to the writing table. (He does not recognise any of these pieces of furniture – given as a present on our marriage. Nor does he seem to remember when you brought them strapped to your coach on a visit to us from England.) I lift up his lifeless right arm and hand onto the writing table where they remain stiff and wasted and pale and blue mottled against the walnut surface. He lets me put a quill into his good left hand and I fuss to arrange the table like a mother with her child settling the things that shall lead him to read and write and be a scholar within a day or two!

I must come to the point – if not you will charge me with being as William did – a prattler. I would wish neither you nor Lady Ann to think that and so to look down on me. How is Lady Ann? Well, I hope? Is her music still thrilling *the ton* at The Haymarket? And does she still play the viola da gamba and sing English airs to the guitar or accompany herself on the musical glasses? Forgive me asking so many questions. Better than I do so, will you bring Lady Ann when next (very shortly I hope) you come to us here in France?

When you were here last time I understood quite clearly – although you spoke only in hints – that your good wife felt that there was some impropriety in your unaccompanied presence here with me. Does she not know that I barely leave William's side? That I am his burr that cannot be pulled from him? I cannot suppose that Lady Ann, as young and beautiful as she is, and in despite of your wit and brilliance and being constantly a magnet to her loadstone, should find cause to be jealous of me. If only William could speak – he would have the words and many of them – to explain so easily what I stumble over. Let Lady Ann accompany you, please. She shall see again how poor a taper I am compared to her chandelier of candles and thus she will bring perhaps a smile again to the slow and sad face of my dear William.

I must come to the point. I do all that you directed. From his table William can see through the windows to the driveway running across the park between the poplars, and see where the drive gains the cobbles and paving stones in front of the house to reach the stone staircase to the portico flanked by urns – soon, M le Blanc says, to be filled with flowers. I have done everything as you direct, but so many things seem to trouble William now: the approach of loud voices, the rumbling of M le Blanc's carriage, and something else he senses – I know not what – that causes him to tremble. Then he looks up to me, beckoning with his eyes for comfort or seemingly for understanding or for what? I do fear for dear William. How I long for him to speak: to tell me what is his hurt, to tell me, to talk.

You will remember that I prepared and laid William's desk with those things which you said might make strong and fond memories for him – that he might recall himself, and find his past. You said that I was to comfort him –

which is all my happiness to do – but you charged me not to speak of or tell him his history, but let him recall it if he would as it were best for him to do. I mind well when you told me of a dear uncle of yours who returned to full recollection of himself a year or more after an apoplexy. You said that the promptings of memory are like ink blots that drop onto the parchment of the mind and spread large and gently where they will. If enough ink falls you said the whole parchment will be filled, all memories recalled. So on William's table I have put some of the things you brought on your visits to us this last year.

At his right is his dear father's Bible. What else might one day draw William's useless right hand towards it – the stiff and knotted hand that however many times a day I lift carefully onto the table and prop there with a small cushion from his mother's sewing basket. Yet it never moves. There is his book – the book he wrote – *The Beauties of Shakespear* bound in best Morocco. I set it straight upon the table; I speak the title words and point to him and to his name. His good hand repeats the gestures. Now for some days there is, I think, an understanding – overlaid by misunderstanding – and he sighs and then trembles. But why does he tremble? Have I been hasty? There is the inkpot, and the quills in the rack beneath it on which his eyes have most frequently settled.

Great joy for me – and yet I fear it as well – just this very day he has taken up a quill in his good left hand and on the paper before him, at first scratchily and crossed out many times, but now with a shaking but flourishing hand has written as though his schoolmaster has told him:

'William Dodd. Cogito ergo sum.'

Then he writes it again and again but each time more fair than the time before. And now he writes:

'William Dodd. I think therefore I am,'

And he writes that out neat, takes pains and writes it again as if the movements of the pen have re-opened some well-springs in his mind! I have put with this letter some other of the first scraps of his writing, so you shall see that I do not make much more of this than there is to be made. Take regard of this he wrote today, with pain and taking him over an hour:

'I know I am, but until what point in my life? What is, what was, beyond or indeed before the day which Mary calls "that fateful day"? Perhaps I shall find more when this man Thicknesse comes. Please may that be soon.'

As William pleads, so plead I. Come quickly Sir Philip, I beg of you.

In distress, Your friend, Mary Dodd

Post Scriptum (as William would say)

Did you not tell me that you had – or others had given you – a written account of events that took place later in the evening of the fateful day – the "revivification" I think was your word for it? If I might have knowledge of this my understanding and my task in helping William would be easier burdens for me to bear. Whatever you tell me shall be for my eyes only. I vow I would not show any of such to him if you say not; nor give any hint of my owning it, for to do so would be a great offence to his sensibilities. M

Sir Philip Thicknesse to Mrs Mary Dodd Bath
25th August 1778

Dear Mary,

Your letter of 27th June arrived last week. The French I think do not hurry much with their mail when it is to be sent across La Manche.

Firstly, I must caution you not to be more free than you must be with undersigning your letters. Particularly do not be free with your husband's name when writing. Prying eyes will always look upon letters when their seals are broken open and even the ignorant and stupid may recognise a name or signature by its shape alone. For this reason I will be my own postman for this letter and will bring it, as you say "for your eyes only", when I come in a short time (two or three weeks from now for certain).

It is right and proper and I hope wise, to do as you ask and give you an account of the revivification – the action that brought The Reverend William Dodd – to life. Even though the reading of it may trouble you, it may not do so more than did the actual events before-hand which you know about. Shall you depend on other accounts you will have less idea of all the matters which befell your dear William on the fatal day. The report that I saw some months ago, which was the doctors' – Mr Hunter and Mr Pott's – account of the resuscitation, is a dry document. It says little – and it has as you shall construe, good reason for saying little – but it will suffice for William if even in the years ahead he shall pluck up heart and mind to read that report and learn from the doctors about an occasion in which he suffered so gravely from the efforts to revive him.

No one had such a close-hand sight and experience of the events as I; and now, while the detail is sharp in my mind, is the time to relate it. But Mary, though it may serve your needs as a nurse now, you must allow the nasty and brutal scenes to fade from your mind in the passage of time. What is more, you may never let your husband even glance at these pages. No man of sentiment willingly and without other reason than the prurient desire to gloat, would wish to read the descriptions that I shall give of the savage, vile, loathsome and most horrid scenes in which, as William's friend, I was compelled to take part.

Of the hanging itself, Mary, perhaps one day William will tell you himself. Then you shall cradle his dear head against your bosom and let the tears carry the story on their flood. I cannot conceive what grief and what terror he felt. I cannot comprehend what was in his mind when he was dropping into the eternity from which he should have risen

– and will on a better day.

You remember that I spoke of the poor lad Joseph Harris, barely fifteen years old, who had been condemned for stealing two half sovereigns and some silver? He was lifted out of his father's arms and onto the gallows first. William had dropped to his knees when the noose was put around Harris' neck, and he stayed kneeling, eyes shut.

The crowd had not come to see yet another boy hanged. They had regard only for The Reverend Dr William Dodd, a famous man, high in popular estimation. On him the crowd fixed their eyes, not just drawn towards him, but also in utter silence to turn their heads I believe in guilt away from the other sight – a stripling boy taken from his father's arms to be hanged. The sound of Joseph's cart jerking away from the scaffold was lost in his father's single cry, a crescendo as the hangman for a quick death put all his weight on Joseph's legs. Briefly then the crowd's heart fixed on that puppet figure dangling at the end of a rope, and on his father as that old man tumbled down to take his boy away. But one hundred thousand eyes were turned again and fixed on the kneeling figure of your husband whom they had waited so long to see yet did not want to see hanged. It was he alone they thought who was to stir their emotions. He alone they thought could penetrate them by a look, by a movement of his lips, or even perhaps if it was their lucky day a speech – a sermon soaring high above them as it had been from his pulpit in days before; but now, at last, a gesture of his milk-white hands raised in supplication on the sudden brink of finality sent electricity into every present heart. But then nothing further happened.

Yet I doubt if Joseph Harris will ever be entirely out of that crowd's mind.

In a while, the silence and the stillness were ended for a few moments. To shake off the cruel image of the hanged boy the multitude stirred. By slight fidgeting at first and then by coughs and voices breaking the quiet, movements became more obvious: pickpockets moved in the crowds, relieved that their work had not been longer postponed. Elderly gentlemen clambered down from their boxes to urinate beneath. Women in the crowd pointed their companions to look at something yonder while they bent at the knees to relieve themselves. Two boys no older than Joseph started to fight over their branch in an oak tree and fell to the grass, the one without doubt as he fell breaking his leg on the shoulder of a man below, and being roundly cursed for it.

All activity stopped again. The crowd settled. The hangman approached William, who stood up from his knees and continued praying. He cannot have completed his prayers, for what completion could there be but another Amen. There was murmuring in the crowd; it was nervous and restive again, finding uniform difficulty in continuing to wait and be respectful. If William realised this and wanted to hold the attention of such a congregation as even he had never had, it may never be known; but he stopped praying and spoke to the hangman and put something into his hand. The noose was put over William's head and adjusted.

I did not see all the hanging. I moved the undertaker's hearse tight up against the scaffold cart to be sure that we could make a quick departure. I held our horses' heads tightly against any startle. So I did not see the hanging but heard a whip crack. In an instant the scaffold cart pulled sharply away from under William's feet, its iron rimmed wheels crushing the stones beneath and sighs arising from all parts of the crowd and dying away. I did not see the hanging. Only the soles of William's boots, scuffed and needing repair. By William's order and a purse, the hangman did not come to hug his legs, to pull on them and snap his neck. Soon the boots stopped. Soon like pendulums were still. William was cut down quickly and the rope cut short at the neck.

As ready hands helped me lift him limp into the white

coffin's white interior, the knot and stump end fibres of the rope fell away. Someone turned down a torn flap of scalp behind his ear and, with hearse, coffin and him already moving off, I retrieved his wig from the scaffold cart and poked it onto his head.

Thus your husband, my friend, the Reverend Dr William Dodd lay in his clerical black in the white coffin. His clothes were scarcely crumpled, and with the shade of the coffin sides hiding his face and his wig restored to its rightful place, it was possible to believe that he slept, his head lolling with the swaying of the hearse. We set off for Oxford Street and then Goodge Street to the premises of Mr Davies, the Undertaker.

I must tell you that a week before this, without telling this worthy man of my strategy for revivification but by cajoling (a small part) and with money (a large part), I had persuaded him of my intentions. I planned to deliver Dr Dodd in the undertaker's hearse, to encase him myself immediately and send him off privily next day in the care of Mr Davies to the churchyard at Cowley. His premises, I said to him, would do almost as well as any others which might be bought at less cost, but his were the nearest. The undertaker knew what a good and sound offer I made as soon as it was put into his hand, but while condescending to accept, he strove to have me understand he was of a good family in Wales, members of which being scholars and parsons and such like had served to give him a sound education. However, in short, Mr Davies as a man of business saw sense in complying with my wishes.

There was music in the proposition, he said (I took that to be the musical ring of gold coins fingered in his purse). He volunteered to coffin me, when my time comes, for "A very reasonable consideration if paid now". 'Meanwhile,' he said, 'being relieved of my business for the time being I shall take my neighbour the greengrocer Mr Sefton with me and we shall make a day of it.'

He saw no doubt a glint of venom in my eye that he

should take pleasure in an occasion to be of the most tragic sort – Dr Dodd's impending death turned into a theatrical event. Despite this he said:

'Mr Sefton and I shall make a night of it too, and then your party may have the run of our premises without disturbance until six o'clock next morning. And be sure to lid the coffin and I will take it straight away to Cowley. You will find everything you need at hand. You said the Churchyard of St Lawrence? And the Rector Mr Richard Dodd (brother to the to-be-deceased) will be at hand? Another thing,' he said, and grew more serious – even with a touch of mournfulness in his voice and on his face, which had been previously wiped clean of such emotion as soon as I had mentioned money – 'Be sure to put plenty of quick-lime in the coffin.' He pinched his nose in explanation, 'the lime is in a barrel and easily found.'

(I tell you all this detail Mary so that you shall know that if anyone starts rumours of William being alive and begin to pursue him, they will be assured on the contrary that all matters attendant upon his death and burial were dealt with properly and thoroughly by me and are to be relied upon as a true record).

It was with some difficulty we set ourselves free of the crush of people at Tyburn who were all crowding this way and that intent on finding a place for another entertainment. I walked beside the hearse shouting imprecations at those who blocked our way. Those curious people who pushed alongside us to stare into the coffin I enjoined to move off again into the crowds. So, with our large black-plumed horses breasting the throng like galleons in heavy seas and suffering many a slap and thwack from me and from Davies' man at the reins, we came in not too long a time out of Oxford Street. The crowds thinned and we were now accompanied by some half a dozen men, several of them embracing the waists of young women who were thus easily lifted off their feet when our pace gathered or we took a change of direction. These were all would-be-spectators at Tyburn who, being too far distant at the edge of the main crowd to see other than the backs of others, sought now at least to see the very last of The Reverend Dr William Dodd. We went at a canter into Goodge Street. There was no need for Davies' man to step down and help me with the coffin, for our curious escorts put their women down as necessary, waved away all help and lifted the coffin onto their shoulders. They let themselves be directed down the alley which led to the rear of the undertaker's and the greengrocer's premises and into the basement. Davies' man took the hearse away and stabled his horse and made off as fast as he could.

Meanwhile, the surgeons Mr John Hunter and Mr Percival Pott (to whom both an agreed sum of money was also to be paid) were waiting impatiently, cuffs rolled back. They had, they said, over the last two hours been up, many times up, to a window on the top floor to look across the fields to see if they could make us out coming away from the crowds at Tyburn. They reminded me that they had not viewed the hanging itself, for "hangings were only to be witnessed by vulgar minds and the insatiably curious". Assuming that the coffin carriers were of this common kind, Hunter and Pott directed them to lift The Reverend Dr Dodd's body from its coffin, place it on the trestle table and then stand with their fellows and women folk well back against the walls. I was commanded ("commanded" indeed!) to remove William's boots and breeches while the surgeons stripped him of upper garments until he was entirely naked.

Mr Pott set at once to massage William's throat as if to draw stagnant air from his lungs and he pressed his spine at the neck to the same purpose. Mr Hunter took jars of peppermint water, turpentine and juice of horseradish that he had lined up on a shelf close at hand. In turn, their contents were poured onto William's forehead, chest and stomach and rubbed in well as though to pink-up the ashen flesh. Certainly, your William's skin glistened under such treatment but only the surgeon's hands were warmed – glowing red from finger tips to wrists.

While Mr Pott continued to massage, Mr Hunter took a double bellows and pumped air bearing volatile alkalis and spirits of hartshorn into William's mouth and lungs; so breaking his purple lips in several places and contorting his dead face so wildly that indeed it looked as if he were alive and in dreadful pain. Mr Pott called for me to hold a blanket (too small for the task) over William, while hot balsam steaming out of a kettle was concentrated over his chest and stomach. Mr Hunter then took that same kettle of balsam and introducing the vapours into his double bellows put its nozzle into William's fundament. Mr Pott held poor Dodd's knees apart and uplifted. He worked the bellows earnestly and quickly with a flourish, withdrew the nozzle from below and thrust it immediately into Dodd's mouth puffing therein the remaining hot vapours. Hunter was only a short time but furiously at this. He stopped suddenly and nodded to Pott. They stood to either side of William and after the intensity of their efforts composed their faces to be now resigned and grave. They held each a flaccid wrist with its tortured thumb; after a long pause let it drop to the table. There were oh's and ah's and mutterings of disappointment from the bystanders; then a solemn silence, each taking in the scene: the white body of William, wig off, flap of scalp turned up behind the ear again, face suffused and purple veined – the mouth bloodied and lips firm, the blanket wet and clinging over his manhood. Stabbed into the woodwork beside William's other arm, a small blade caked in blood pointed its handle to the crook of his elbow where a clot of blood like a dark red-skinned plum lay in the slit of an open vein. This had been Mr Pott's last action before joining Mr Hunter for their consultation.

Both surgeons stood on a dry part of the floor well away from the urine dripping through the trestle table, the excrement mixed with it and the balsam, dried herbs and blood. Hunter spoke:

'It was not to be. He is dead. Nor would I wish this man to return to life now in such circumstances that are presently upon him and with the prospect again of that miserable and guilty life which was his recent fate. It could not be borne by any man – least of all one who also had the censure of so many people upon him.'

Hunter turned and said quietly to me so that the others should not hear:

'We have business with the living that has waited too long. Kindly send the sums due to me at St George's Hospital.'

As he beckoned to Mr Pott again I put a purse in his hand and gave him thanks which, if not expressing outright anger, fell far short of fulsome gratitude.

'You shall have that now,' I said. 'I am fully conscious that the needs of the quick are more pressing than those of the dead, and I am also not sorry that you cannot have The Reverend Dr Dodd for your anatomical lectures. Thank you and good day to you gentlemen.'

The bystanders realised that there was nothing more for them to see, and the women, like rabbits at last released from the lantern's glare, bobbed up the steps after Mr Hunter and Mr Pott – except for one woman, her features obscured by a veil and the hood of her cloak. She seeming only to have eyes for William stayed quietly on the steps. The Physician and Surgeon did not wait to collect their bottles and instruments but said that someone would come for them on the morrow. Before I could stop him, one of the onlookers had stolen William's breeches which I had cast onto the coffin standing on its own trestle legs against a wall.

And now I was left alone with William. It was unlikely to the point of impossibility that Davies, the undertaker and Sefton, the greengrocer would return that night. Like the surgeons, they had both been signatories to the great petition to the King begging for a reprieve for your husband. But unlike Hunter and Pott, they saw no harm in joining the twenty thousand petitioners who gathered with the one hundred thousand more at Tyburn. Furthermore, Davies had let me know that part of his fee for renting out the basement would purchase one of Mrs Proctor's pews on the highest part of the scaffolding at Tyburn. I knew that whatever coin remained would be passed into the hands of The landlords at the Bedford, The Rainbow, The Shakespear or The Rose – or all of these in turn – taverns that your William knew when he first came up to London.

I hope you do not tire for my letter is not finished. As William has often reminded me, I am not of a religious cast of mind. Therefore, I surprised myself when a prayer of sorts formed on my lips and I laid a priestly hand on William's brow. It was warm. I put my hands on his chest and belly and they were also warm. It was no rational thought that compelled me next, but anger that such a life as his was ended and that all the plans which I had made had failed, and that the journey from Tyburn to Goodge Street was in vain. Had not I, who was once an apothecary and reckoned even at twenty to be a better physician that others who claimed that title, had I not failed my friend? And had I not paid off Pott and Hunter before every measure had been exploited to the full? Was there nothing I could do now but beat my fists on the table, on my temples, and the foetid air itself?

I took courage and seized the double bellows Mr Hunter had dropped.

Forgive me for this Mary and never, never I charge you, tell William. I poured still hot balsam into the bellows and with one arm holding his knees up towards his chin I turned to the veiled and mute woman on the steps to indicate she should not look at what next I did. I inserted the nozzle of the bellows truly into the ring of his fundament and pushed and worked it in a frenzy until I heard fibres breaking. Then there was a great and mighty shout from William and clear spheres of bubbles appeared at his nostrils and burst and he breathed. I took out the bellows at which William gave another sound, a piteous wail and was silent. And has been silent since; but breathes.

Dear Mary, I swear William was not alive until he cried out, and all his senses that were dead were shocked into life and he breathed. I think I trembled with all sorts of triumph surging through me and yet my legs felt as weak as grass. I leaned against the table, witness to a miracle, watching the rise and fall of William's chest. For the best part of an hour I stayed thus transfixed. Yet the motion did not cease as I feared and at last I dared stir myself to stretch William's shirt over him.

I turned to the quiet woman whose veil had dropped again and now was raised so that there were tears seen in her bright blue eyes: 'Then Madam. Hurry quickly to Charlotte Street where you will find Mrs Mary Dodd and tell her of all that has happened. She must come here to accompany Dodd and I to his safety. Let no one else know anything of this.'

It was now become dark; I looked for other candles to light from those that still warmed the kettle of balsam, and set about finding the wherewithal to fill his coffin.

From Sefton's backyard I took old turnips and parsnips, carrots and beetroot – all roots withered but some sprouting green caps; they all joined rank cabbage in the coffin. Large stones laid on a bed of leeks, small stones in limp lettuce leaves were pressed into the compacted vegetables beneath. Great roots of parsley dug and levered from the edge of one of Sefton's rotting heaps found their places – two at the feet and the largest root at the head of the coffin that was to go to Cowley. Lime from the barrel by the steps covered the vegetables and was in its turn covered by William's cloak thrown down from the scaffold cart. I put with it what I had not seen before – a well-worn multi-coloured waistcoat that had been stripped of its buttons when William was made naked. A final dressing of quicklime spilled over the coffin sides when I nailed down the lid.

You know all the rest, Mary. Fearful lest he should waken and I was not with him, I had asked the woman I shall now call Hannah to hurry round to Charlotte Street to find you and Lady Ann and bring you in a carriage to Goodge Street with travelling cases and female clothing for William. You said later that Hannah, who had attended this last part of the drama, had heard crowd rumours that you, Mary, were out of your mind and to be looked after in an asylum far distant from London; that you were worried that it would not be believed unless you were seen at least departing in an Essex coach from London. Hannah had then seen the great distress of Mary if her real whereabouts were known. Saying that her love for her was as great as her love for The Reverend Dodd and she would now if Mary permitted, go instead of her and make her intended journey to the appointed asylum. We know now that is what she did. And I wonder greatly at her love. Was it inspired by Dodd at the Magdalen?
Or was it of longer and more substantial Christian love? Would William have remembered Hannah, perhaps by another name, from earlier in his life?
How shocked you were to see your husband's face and how you wept at his torn scalp and his powerless arm. How we struggled to dress Dodd in his old woman's dress and to lift him to the carriage. Our journey to Dover, and then with "our sick sister" on a rough sea to Boulogne will not be marked as the most pleasurable passage. Even as William partly recovered consciousness, we did feel relief at that, yet dismay and fear at his utter silence. Perhaps it was as well he comprehended nothing. When his eyes opened on occasions there was no light of recognition in them.

I have now confirmed – but then only hoped that – that "other Mary" who consented to be in your place and to be confined as a lunatic in Colchester, really has come to believe that she is you Mrs Dodd. She wails at William's hanging and refuses to see anyone from your past. The physician at the asylum would not let me beyond the porter's lodge when I came a few months ago. He said that since she came two days after the hanging (brought by a man called Bulkley) this "Mary Dodd" was reasonable at times but would see no one unless it was her revered husband whom she says she has known since childhood. I pressed the physician to take good care of "that Mary" and eased his task by tendering him a substantial sum of money, which it is indelicate to say but truly has left me substantially poorer.

Guard all this carefully. We shall speak when opportune.

Yours most respectfully,
Sir Philip Thicknesse

CHAPTER 2

I TAKE UP MY PEN

William Dodd takes up his pen for the first time.
Thicknesse arrives with Lady Anne and they leave after
Thicknesse has given even more advice.

Chateau de Voirons
12th September
1778

I think. I write. I cannot speak. Mary says only write. Anything. Of now or of then. Start. Start. Start again. Start at this morning. But Oh God please let my left hand learn what my right hand once did, to write without effort and be tireless.

Thicknesse has been much in conference with Mrs Dodd. What converse has filtered through to me, as they stood in the hall shortly after his arrival, was muffled; it was disjointed and beyond that appeared to be the tail ends of an earlier discourse held elsewhere. All that I heard for certain was Mary saying to Thicknesse:

'I would have been glad with less gory detail Sir Philip, and wish my mind as empty of it now as was my stomach when I read your letter. I would not ask Cook to give me a full account of everything done to the food when I enquire what is for dinner. It is always my wish that she shall not tell me how the cockerel was plucked, or the capon stuffed. It is enough to know that they have been prepared and come to the table ready cooked . . . but you spared nothing.'

I heard Mary's voice trail away. Thicknesse expressed some regrets and then they both fell silent and came through to the great room where I spend my days.

Mary says Thicknesse is a good friend, although I do not recall much of our first meeting or whether it were in

19

this last year or many years ago. However, old friend or not, he is all powerful here today, and will tomorrow be gone with the same flourish I do not doubt as when he arrived and as dimly I recall came and went before. On this occasion, Thicknesse is accompanied by Lady Ann – a beauty far superior to any description I could give of her. It is also to be supposed, but sadly, that she too will be gone tomorrow.

But now Thicknesse speaks – loud so that I shall hear and *very* loud because he presumes deafness accompanies my lack of speech. And *very, very* loud since he thinks that my blank half-face hides an even blanker mind behind it – obvious evidence of imbecility to be overcome.

As soon as I had picked up my quill and the consequent tremor was still, I wrote in a big and simple hand – to be read easily by one whose sight or reasoning may be impoverished:

'Sir, I beg you lower your voice. For Mrs Dodd tells me that no-one in England must know that I am here.'

He laughed, just as loudly as he spoke, and clapped his thigh and smiled; and Mary smiled, showing that there is some conspiracy of understanding between them. He dropped his voice by a little:

'Good Reverend,' (this is more title than Mary had led me to believe

was mine, for up to this time when I signalled to know my name, she had pointed merely to the words William Dodd on the title page of my *Beauties of Shakespear)* 'here you are to be called Mr & Mrs William Farrier, my erstwhile servants. From now on, you should not use any of your other names or titles – "The Reverend" and "Doctor" and "William". You are, and are to be, plain "Farrier" to everyone though as your wife may find that impossible, she may call you William when you are retired to bed to avoid thoughts of infidelity if imagining conjugation with Farrier.'

I do feel a scruple of hurt pride in being given the name

Farrier – enough insult to be called a servant – but Farrier! A horse-doctor! How does he think that lies with a man who but a few breaths before was styled "The Reverend Doctor"? Yet I must consider that I owe some debts of gratitude to Sir Philip Thicknesse, and in the future more hopefully perhaps to Lady Ann? It is not wise, therefore, to kick against the pricks of his choice of name for me.

Thicknesse continued:

'The Reverend Dr Dodd,' (I raised an eyebrow) 'now renamed Farrier, will you baptize yourself?'

Here he poured a glass of water over me and lifted my useless hand to make the sign of the Cross.

'Farrier. You are here to be saved from the gallows again by Divine Judgement and by my Good Offices.'

There was a certain bombast in his voice and I would have raised the other eyebrow if it had the power. However, for all his manner, he held me fast in his attention. He spoke on these lines:

'You have given proof to Mrs Dodd that not all your past is hidden from you. You still have entire command of faculties of the mind, but recent memory has failed you. Latin and Greek I suppose, the ancient authors and poets and philosophers, as well as everyday people and events which shaped your earlier life – these things may easily be called up and written down. But I do not know why it should be that you can write but cannot speak. Nor do I know indeed why your right arm and hand are withered but your legs, though weak, are not flaccid or paralyzed. I fear it is the events of which we dare not speak that have numbed your mind, shut out recent memories and tied your tongue. My advice, and the plan that I wish to put before you now, is simple: given a supply of paper, quills and ink and pencils, and perhaps some mementoes I may bring from England, you shall write. And you shall write much more than the scraps penned so far. You shall write your history. All of it. From childhood to today.'

Thicknesse added further advice:

'When by your own pen your past is revealed to you, you will learn that some envious people found shocking things to say about you . . .'

He paused to clear his throat and Mary stepped a pace towards him: 'And amazing truthful matters in greater abundance' she said: 'two dozen sermons at least; first heard by hundreds in his churches and then by thousands reading them when printed; charities he founded; paupers and fallen women he rescued from their natural fates; the sorrowing souls he comforted . . .'

Thicknesse held up both hands as though in surrender but went back to his advisory words:

'Shocking things and amazing things, as I was about to say. Just to quote one whose temporary fame gave him the ear of many, the play writer Foote had Dr Dodd as his Dr Simony in *The Cozeners*. And you will recall the actor Jack Bannister? He did not need a stage to broadcast his opinions; they became the talk of every club and coffee house in London. "Dodd" he said "has a diminutive but elegant form, a finished toilette, a glitter of jewellery, a delicate mode of enunciation." (Thicknesse mouthed the word "enunciation" using and stretching every muscle in his face) 'and Dodd makes every gesture represent the true Fop and Macaroni,'

In an unusual soft lapse into quietness, Thicknesse smiled on Mary and Lady Anne and Dodd:

'I retail all this because I do not want any of us to forget that Our Mr Farrier – The Reverend William Dodd – is a fine and great person. He is not as big as I am but his character is above that of men in the common herd. His appearance as a Dandy was to hide his real modesty and more compact stature. Let him not be mocked.'

By this time, Sir Philip had taken the centre of the room and gathered a further audience. The loudness of his speech, now and then modulated by a sprinkling of almost inaudible phrases when he addressed himself, attracted the curiosity of the household. Mary was at my right hand to be proxy for that limb. Lady Ann had distanced herself as far from Sir Philip as possible but had calculated the geometry to be as near to me as needed for me to see her encouraging glances. M le Blanc, always reluctant to intrude, stood hesitatingly inside the door, his eyes also resting gently on me as if I might need defence from Sir Philip's dramatic performances. Cook peeped round M le Blanc. She dried her hands slowly on a well-used kitchen cloth, but otherwise moved neither body nor head as if one twitch of muscle or blink of eyelid would cause her to be dismissed at once. The heads only of Cook's husband and their small son made a brief appearance – the former over M le Blanc's shoulder and the latter between his legs. Then they left. Thicknesse paused, the knuckle of his forefinger at his mouth. He paced silently before my desk, eyes upon me but clearly deep in thought – or the appearance of it. Then raising his head and encompassing me and his audience in his speech, delivered it with suitable mime and action as he thought appropriate to his remarks.

'Consider the good sense and the reason for my plan. As a child when you fell, or caught your fingers in a door, or were frightened by a dog, your nurse adjured you to tell her everything, from the beginning. Thus reminded of ordinary things before the fright and to think of pleasant things that might bring a smile to a stern face, gradually you were brought towards the narration, and memory and tongue were released to tell the final horror. All the truth burst out, eased in its passage by the truths that went before. As a child the story was kept from all but your dear nurse by the apron into which you sobbed.

'You will need no such soft privacy for your own history Dr Dodd.

But it shall be kept from prying eyes. The pages on which you write shall be put into an iron-banded casket I have brought for you. Now dear Dodd, alias William Farrier, take up your quill and start from the beginning. Look upon yourself and your past with the honest eyes of a child. Tell everything. When all is told, your tongue will finally be unlocked.'

'Amen,' said M le Blanc. He nodded to me and to Thicknesse, gave him a little clap which lacked nothing in sincerity, and left the room.

The women fussed about me for a while, which I enjoyed more than Sir Philip's exhibition of his own theatrical talents. Truth to say, I was envious of his movements, of his being centre stage, and of his voice. He had everything in his performance except dancing and I felt dimly that it might have been an aim in my life to be the object of such attention.

Should Thicknesse be told that he has done me some power of good? Is there no advantage to himself or must I show gratitude? Looking to the ceiling as though he now disowned the key to the casket, he handed it to me and promised that it was the only one. Mary took it from me. Slowly a few small fields of memory are becoming populated. I feel more of myself coming into being. Although I quake at the future here at Voirons, I quake more at what memory shall be revealed in my history. I must hold fast to the principle that I shall record my past without making an apology for it, nor an eulogy of it either. The recollection and the writing of the history is proposed entirely to be a balm for me, to heal my wounds and mind and bring back to me the power of speech.

Sir Philip and Lady Ann have gone, suddenly, this morning. Now neither his loud voice nor her seducing eyes will offer distractions to my purpose. I am commanded to write my history and shall start from the beginning where, in the flat lands of Lincolnshire, I the eldest and my two brothers and four sisters, were born into the poor rectory in the even poorer Parish of Bourne...

See! I have started. My pen shall be my tongue!

CHAPTER 3

MY STORY BEGINS

A child in Lincolnshire

Poverty in the village of Bourne was of a worldly sort, but timeless poverty it was, and as permanent as the solid Norman pillars of The Abbey Church of St Peter & St Paul. There too, fading tapestries and the echoing box pews of the absent rich spoke, as did the leaning gravestones in the unkempt churchyard, of unremitting poverty.

My father, the Reverend William Dodd, had scholarship in plenty but it was not matched by wealth. He preached with his eyes closed as much to confine his vision to the richness of the kingdom of heaven as to forget how few and threadbare were the congregation, or to see the spaces of ignorance behind eyes looking up to him when he lapsed into the Latin and Greek he loved so much.

Shortly after he had been lifted from a meagre curacy nearby to the rectory at Bourne, he received a letter from a London cousin, Olivia Orpen, telling of her father's death after a long illness. With a speed not generally noticed in my father's actions, he replied immediately. The letter he wrote was tender and solicitous, somewhat tortuous, sprinkled with Latin and Greek – which languages he knew do not stammer or blush – and finally arrived at a proposition endorsed by the trustees of the school across the churchyard, that she might with benefit apply for the post of teacher. She did so, affirming that she was agreed to the hours of teaching and the salary of twenty-five pounds a year, and was grateful that accommodation had been arranged with Church Warden Drake and his wife.

Within two weeks my father was introducing his cousin to the class of giggling children, who were to be allowed

25

out a full five minutes earlier than afternoon school usually ended so that they might be more quickly the bearers of good tidings to their wider world beyond the churchyard. To the surprise of the young cleric who had responsibility for the school and everyone in it (but not to the surprise of the knowing and nodding heads of everyone else in Bourne) within three months of the start of the scholastic arrangement, Olivia consented to a more intimate arrangement between them. Within another short space of time the bells of The Abbey Church of St Peter & St Paul had rung, and the gossips looking back on those times said that before the last notes of the bells had disappeared into the fens, their Rector Mr Dodd was showing me, a young William, to the gigglers in the classroom and allowing school to end a full ten minutes before time.

I remember now that my father had exact regard to chronological accuracy and justice. In the fullness of time there were seven of us offspring each at their baptism shortening the school scholars' day by ten minutes. For two years after me came my brother Richard, then sisters Barbara and Elizabeth and the twins Sarah and Mary – each of whose added ten minutes gave the scholars beyond the graveyard twenty minutes off school even though, as the twins' shared a celebration, it might have contributed to some economy of time. The school children lost an hour and ten minutes of learning between my mother's twenty-ninth birthday when she left London and the birth of her last child Jacob.

My mother brought little from London – her married sister had the family house and property within it – but she carried with her a love of Shakespear, proved by the well-worn unbound copies of his plays, and a sampler her mother made to mark her daughter's birthday. Olivia Orpen was born on the 10th day of October in the year 1700, letters and figures of such easy symmetry that lent themselves to the needlework riot of flowering O's in the shapes of crowns and garlands, while in the borders fruit of numerical and alphabetical roundness hung with autumn brilliance over sheaves of golden corn. My conceit has always been that this sampler was a metaphor for my mother.

It was her bright mind and laughter that made the schoolroom the liveliest place in Bourne. Here every morning she gathered children from the village who could walk the distance, and her own sons and daughters who all ran or skipped from the rectory across the graveyard, to the single classroom at its edge. There was always help for the youngest member of our family. Jacob was named when still in his mother's womb, which was much swollen and heavy before time and so thought to be bearing twins. But no Esau came. Jacob, much loved for his moon face and gentleness never grew strong enough in his legs nor had breath sufficient to weave his way between gravestones to the schoolroom. Just after his third birthday he died. His grave was made nearest to the schoolroom door. This was much remarked for its sentiment as though he were at last put amongst the babble of his family and friends and was learning with them.

Reading and writing mastered, the catechism well learned, some geography and history comprehended and the rudiments of mathematics understood, the older boys trod back to the vicarage where my father taught, instilled and inspired us with Latin and Greek and more mathematics. Although I made no great show of it amongst my companions, I took delight in acquiring knowledge and, seeing my schoolboy thirst, my father poured his learning into me and taught me how to gain it for myself. Long after Richard had been released to play marbles with his sisters, I was led through leather-boarded volumes – Plato, Aristotle, Cicero – and as the years rolled on, Euripides, Tacitus, Virgil . . . and as further entertainment through Descartes onto firm English soil with Hobbes and then the most favoured of my father's philosophers – Locke.

MY STORY BEGINS

Much more than the habit of rote learning, ideas were planted which formed the mind of a growing youth – "all that vast store of our minds comes from experience and knowledge gained through sensation and reflection upon it. And it fills the storehouse" said Locke. No disputes there, but did my reverend father have the same understanding of it as I? Or was the necessity of pursuing true happiness the "foundation of all liberty"? Or did he advise to my then deaf ears "be prudent in all things so that you ensure pleasure for yourself and others"? I do not think he counselled from his own experience for his was an unworldly life. He spoke with understanding and sincerity – but through the philosophers, the classic poets and dramatists, and The New Testament and prophets of The Old. He rarely touched his pictures of life with real pigments taken direct from nature, but drew with a hard pencil borrowed from authorities he assumed had greater minds than his. Yet in the rectory library classroom he was not remote from us. A cold page of text became warm and alive as he, after one glance, translated the sense of it, and should he wish it, set us to learn the whole of it by heart.

As often as my own inclinations allowed me to leave off study, or was contrived with my father's absence or approval, I escaped from the rectory with a speed and clatter that sent the rooks from the sycamore trees. If the weather was dry and bright, and only then, the lolloping rectory dogs Castor and Pollux tested the air with their noses and followed at my heels with Richard at the rear. In winter we cracked open the frozen white ruts of the track leading to Warden Theophilus Drake's farm and in other seasons blew dandelion clocks in the same direction; or dangled unseen behind the harvest wagon; or reached into the turnip cart and hurled the green feathered globes high ahead of the straining horses. Richard, more circumspect and older beyond his years, kept his feet dry and out of the ruts and restored uneaten turnips to the cart.

If Mr Drake was about his farm he was ready to explain the realities of life – death in the loss of a lamb and its ewe at birth; or conception, demonstrated by his bull Daniel – matters about which the Warden was eloquent:

'It is not of any account where Daniel's calves are conceived, as long as it is on my farm, for I do not wish them to be in any other place. For you, however, Master Dodd, had it been your father's wish that you also would be a clergyman, where do you think conception should have taken place?'

'In church.'

'Exactly. And so it was.'

The Warden would not be further drawn. He changed the subject to tell of sermons preached by my father which were likely to have improved his life.

Next to my mother in dispensing affection in the household was the maid-of-all-work, Tenbury. She, placid and so plump that her clothing and aprons were smooth about her, was called Sine Plica ("without folds") by my father. She proudly accepted the name from us when told that it was Latin and that it paid respect to her good nature and her dress. She was indeed as uncomplicated as Castor and Pollux, who lapped up the milk she spilt every day. They, not as simple as she, would lie in wait for her to come up from the dairy, knocking against her in affectionate greeting and wearing out their tongues on the hard stone slabs of the floor until they grew coats as smooth as Sine Plica's apron

CHAPTER 4
AT LE CHATEAU DE VOIRONS

May 29th and 30th 1778
Dodd wearied with writing breaks off for a while.
Thicknesses come again.

Near on eight months starting and breaking off from my narration. During the first days and weeks of writing I did make some halting progress although my thinking and my writing came in spurts – my left hand struggling to make letters stand up neat upon the page. True images from childhood were broken up and I began to sweat at the effort of telling even a simple story. That I am to be the only reader of my life is no consolation – or perhaps it is, because I need put no gloss on my character or events, for there is no need to tell me a lie. Certainly there is no gloss on my writing – it is as shaky and uneven as the mind that propels my quill. Page after page, however carefully begun, have been screwed up – sometimes before three lines have made their spidery progress across the paper. Crumpled sheets projected towards the grate have alarmed Mary. She has explained:

'It is not penny-pinching William, but there is a lack of economy when half the paper is not written on.'

She soon adopted the habit at the end of every day of harvesting clean paper from my litter. I dare say that it was more than the waste of paper that troubled Mary. She saw my distress and thus my deepening gloom. Her face clouded with concern. No, not my lifeless hand upon the table; no, not pain, I indicated, though it was ever as hard to bear; no, no it was not a disturbing memory that I must deny and wipe off the page. It was my anguish when a word would not come to mind, when a memory, a name, an object would not spring onto the tip of my silent tongue and from there be sent to pen and paper. All my youthful ability, all my manhood joy with words – gone into oblivion sooner than an eye could blink.

When the faltering nature of my progress lessened, and the words began sometimes at last to flow, I showed Mary the day's pages before she locked them in the casket. She measures my health now by the number of lines written and her smile follows mine. Yet still I labour, but less frequently hard, to capture the history of my childhood.

The difficulty of having two lives – the one here as M Farrier in France and the other as William Dodd before this – was made clear to me when I took up my pen again this day. For all my intentions to write and to relive my childhood, and not consider this present state until it was happier, were blown out of the window when Sir Philip Thicknesse blew in through the door.

He gave notice of his arrival – the whole length of the carriageway – of course. I rose from my desk where I had just looped the first letter of the day's first sentence and limped to the window. A two-wheeled cabriolet drawn by a lean-shanked horse turned into the avenue bearing Thicknesse, Lady Ann with a parakeet on her lap, and riding postilion, a monkey in livery. Two whippets loped alongside. Sir Philip with an expressive and attentive grandeur on his face was listening to Lady Ann playing the bass viol; and conducting her music with his left hand nevertheless out of step and rhythm with the tune.

Reaching the stables, Sir Philip climbed down from the cabriolet and handed down Lady Ann toward M le Blanc's courteous greeting. They walked past the green-leaved nasturtiums growing out of and over the urns and stepped into the hall and into the morning rooms where the tinkling of her laughter played above M le Blanc's deeper voice. Thicknesse came along the passageway connecting to our wing. It is unfair to put it as mildly as "came along the passage" because Thickness even in motion was eccentric. In progressing from one place to another on foot, rather than to say walk, he threw the parts of his body ahead of each other independently. When arriving close enough to embrace or shake hands, it was not clear which limb or feature might be presented first, nor obvious what might be expected to happen to whatever part of one's body was nearest at that time. Thus I was grateful for my protection behind a wide desk, though in the event Thicknesse pulled up short of me and stood by the window across the room. I nodded and presented the palm of my hand towards him as though offering him both the window seat and the floor between us. After his usual courtesies and enquiries regarding my health – which needed no reply and indeed left no room for them between his loud greetings – he stood by the window with the fingers of his left hand wound round the curtain cord and pulled it round his wrist 'til it blanched.

Had this scene occurred but two months ago, I think I would have shuddered at the strangling cord. As it was, my still blank face convinced Thickness that my memory had not progressed as far as Tyburn. And indeed, my recollection was dim and confused with regard to that, although I wished to hasten in my narrative to reach that point and beyond.

'You are writing all your history?' he asked.

Mary entered at this point and replied: 'He is writing well and making great progress, but Dr Dodd must not be pushed to it.'

Thicknesse stood with his mouth partly open, at the ready for speech, with the stained and broken keyboard of his teeth open to view. He would have asked how far I had gone with my memoirs, but at that point Mary broke in again:

'Are you going on from here?' she asked.

'Yes,' he replied, 'another Grand Tour is started. My

readers, especially around my estate in Bath require another amusing account of my travels abroad, and this will pay for it. If received as well as before, I shall not want for pence for some time.'

Thicknesse and Mary continued to talk – Mary lending her ear to him while he expanded on previous Grand Tours and the cost of everything in England. Eventually he broke off in search of Lady Ann whom he thought may be "troubling M le Blanc" with her musical talents. He also heard sounds and smelled fragrances wafting in from the kitchens, and hoped that by moving off in that direction he might distract everyone from their present pursuits and elicit an invitation to eat.

Thickness's success brought us all to the table, and he talked all through the meal. Mary could not respond to him as she was occupied with passing dishes to me or cutting meat, and always being watchful and mindful for me. M le Blanc was as ever quiet and courteous and content to smile and nod at Lady Ann when her husband made a jocund or pertinent observation. After the meal Thicknesse, sated with food but not with his own talk, came back to my study with Mary. He continued to engage her particularly in his conversation as she "may not have heard everything he said at table". He cast me in the role of idiot again.
Explaining to Mary the uses of the knife he had brought for her to cut my quills, he expanded in detail, advising her how to hold the feather well away from her.

'Put it on your knee,' he said, 'but protect that delicate limb from harm placing a butter pat on it first. Cut clean and sharp.;

Mary had shaped many feathers into nibs over the last months, for early on I broke more than she could cut since my hand was clumsy and the paper not held still by such a useless hand. But grateful for the "pen- knife", as Thicknesse called it as he folded it away, she did not boast of her prowess but said:

'William finds the crow's feather best for him even

33

though it is reckoned it ought to be saved for fine work. Which is as well for us as swans are rare but crows are plentiful as Cook, who is partial to crow pie, will attest. However, when in joke I asked Cook for only *l'aile gauche*, she thinking I was out of sight, tapped her head to indicate I was mad. Poor Cook, she is not well lettered. The idea that a feather might either slope to or away from the writer, according to its place on the bird's left or right wing, is too fanciful a notion for her.'

Thicknesse was inclined to better this intelligence from Mary. He began to give histories for the grey-lag goose whose feathers were the commonest to make quills but Mary had not mentioned them.

'The lag-goose,' he said, 'is behind all others in going north in winter. Perhaps it is slow in other matters too; for considerable numbers are caught as fledglings on the fens. They are kept in the gooseherds and never leave. You will see them coming down to London, driven in flocks of a thousand or more. They walk together with the white native geese, but lag behind, whereas our native geese go ten miles in a day and the lags fall a mile or two behind.'

Thicknesse continued to expand on the subject of geese, including a description of their frequency in Lapland but their absence (he understood) from Japan. If he were minded to provide stories for every country from Lapland to Japan I was certain that the whole of this day would be lost to my literary efforts and further narrative of the life of The Reverend Dr William Dodd M.A. Though I had struggled up and down from my chair behind the desk several times and limped painfully around, Thicknesse was oblivious of my desire to be alone. I spent some time behind the screen where M le Blanc had arranged a carpenter to make me a box in case of my bowel's urgency. The noises I made there from my nether end would, I bethought me, give Thicknesse some hint of my desire to be alone. There was no such effect. My only consolation was that while behind the screen my half-face was free to make grimaces to relieve my discomfort. Sad there were no mirror there that I might enjoy my performances. Mary did not approve of any part of this and told me roundly before nightfall that she had not believed until this day that I should so far forget my manners that I did not make Sir Philip welcome, and did I have "softening of the brain" to add to my other ills? I fear she may have the truth of it.

Had Mary ventured behind the screen and given her opinion of me earlier, I would not have continued as I did. Thicknesse was describing the plucking of grey goose feathers, which then grew white in their place, and having seated himself in my chair he gave all the signs of taking up permanent residence. I thought to bring on his farewells speedily, as I judged he would not wish to stay and play nurse to me nor have the lovely Lady Ann attending me. So I left the screen's protection and begin deliberately, as I had naturally on many occasions, to start a tremble in the fingers of my good left hand. Trembling turned into shaking and increasing in vigour as it stretched up my arm 'til first the shoulder and then both shoulders and my head and trunk and both legs were enveloped in such a violent seizure that it compelled me to the floor
– as carefully as I could on this occasion. Mary was not fooled by what her fixed look at me told – that she knew my paroxysm was contrived. The same look also gave strong indication – even though I part closed my eyes to receive less of it – that she would take strong reprisals if I dared add urination to my staged performance. I allowed myself only then the further dramatic effects of rolling my eyes like two marbles shaken in a dish, while my tongue popped in and out of my mouth and I let dribble be released over my chin and shirt.

As I surmised, Sir Philip Thicknesse was not of a mood to play nurse or apothecary. He began abstractedly to gather himself and Lady Ann for departure on the morrow as though he had too long delayed himself when pressing matters elsewhere beckoned him.

The room emptied. Lady Ann and Thicknesse went about their business and retired to the apartment put aside for them. They appeared early at breakfast – before I was about – and left a few papers and books on my desk. There was a written instruction to Mary that she should take all these to her keeping; and she should let me have them only when I had reached the time in my narrative when they would confirm my story.

'Otherwise,' said Thicknesse's note, 'poor Farrier would become idle and not inclined to search his memory for the events, the facts and even the feelings that filled his life at that time.'

Thicknesse and Lady Ann had excelled their powers of silence by retiring to bed in silence last night, but now they were restored to their own comfortable habit of noise and chaos as soon as they stepped out of the chateau. The lean horse that had known peace for only a few hours was backed into the shafts to a cracked lullaby by Thicknesse. Lady Ann trilled snatches from Purcell and Arne and Handel as seemed to her appropriate in escorting the whippets, her parakeet and the monkey. This latter was still in livery but now the jacket was stained with the crushed juice of gooseberries, which the hapless stable boy (alias the Cook's son) had fed him. Nevertheless, the monkey was clearly willing to ride postilion and leapt quickly out of the whippets' reach to mount the horse.

M le Blanc wished the party a welcome return and then watched in amazement, the vigour of his farewell wave diminished by his anxiety in case the monkey should fall between pounding hooves or barking whippets. Though Lady Ann was silent, the parakeet raised its beak in an unmusical farewell, and Thicknesse shouted above the din: 'I shall be back dear friends.'

This was a signal for Mary, as she helped me back up the steps, to begin a severe chastisement:

'Your behaviour yesterday, upon which I have yet not properly expanded because my anger is too great' was just

36

the opening salvo and even Mary's "dear Sir Philip" would have me feel again on this occasion how unfair it is that I cannot respond to the wordy attacks of others. I have to suffer everything in silence, only able to squeeze my fingers together in a tight fist and elevate an eyebrow to make it tremble at my discontent.

All the above scenes showed the characters of the actors. Outstanding amongst them was, as ever, the quiet, dignified and pleasant M le Blanc. I know him but cannot yet place him in my memory. Yet I am sure that in time his appearance will be as clear to me as is his open countenance now.

To return to this diary after a day in the heat of Sir Philip's exhausting presence and the hours of Mary's icy chilly and then heated fury, is as pleasant and easeful as convalescence after a raging fever, calm after storms. Yet no lasting ill had come from it. Mary had cleverly parried Sir Philip's questions, and in the end he did not even ask to see the casket where my writings are kept. And though there is nothing written so far that could concern Thicknesse, he might feel put out that my wellbeing and even possibly my recovery are aided by the liberating effects obtained for me by writing insults at him. So be it. However, he has been earnest in seeking my welfare before all else, he says.

It is Sunday and I may permit myself some pious thoughts, some contemplation. For Sunday is a day which has been a day of first importance for so long in my life and from which now I am retired. Mary marvelled at first when I began to write that I did not express a need to attend a service somewhere. Unbeknown to me, she even elicited a conspiracy with M le Blanc for him to take me with him to Mass. I deferred this offer *sine die* on the pretext that the strain would be too great for me. I did not wish to tell him that I hoped all my life to avoid any charges of Catholicism; but my real reasons for not wishing to attend a formal service were otherwise. I felt a distance between congregations and me. If I were not addressing them from the pulpit, but sitting amongst them, I should find the odour of sanctity around me too powerful to bear.

M le Blanc has planted tulips of many different colours in the parterres to the west side of the chateau. In this grove of tulips I perceive a difference in almost every individual flower. Scarce any two are formed or have tinctures exactly alike and each allows a little particularity in its dress, even though all belong to the same family. They are various and yet the same. Thus I thought of Mary and Lady Ann and of M le Blanc and Sir Philip – and indeed, of myself in a former life – of differences between Catholics and Protestants, yet all able to live for a time at least amicably and sociably together. The flowers of the field, lilies or tulips, achieve a greater harmony because they are constant in themselves. We more gifted creatures, within certain constancies, show other patterns of behaviour with no change of dress to warn our fellows. So Lady Ann, so quiet and dignified at one moment, is a magnificent flowering thistle at the next. Sir Philip, voluble and incessant with anecdote and argument in the morning, has in the evening changed in manner to be kind and concerned – only to listen or to read of another's difficulties and to strive for them, to be ready to serve them in all the kind offices of cordial friendship. In one day we complain of the dullness of a companion yet by noon we groan at that volatility. Now being bound in my body as silent as a tulip, I have in humility to call upon my Maker to be united with my fellow creatures. Though we are distinguished by some small circumstantials, let us be joined in one important bond of brotherly love.

So I sermonised to myself and with my left hand lifted my powerless arm about Mary's waist and hooked the crooked thumb through the cord belting her skirt and drew her to my knee. The loss in time measured by the sundial was gained for the spirit and senses by being lifted out of first the dancing agitation and frenzy of our galliard into the restful, graceful, steady steps of a pavane. Such healing promises me more yards for my quill upon the paper. Tomorrow, good intentions shall bear fruit.

CHAPTER 5

MATHEMATICS

Poverty; Advances in mathematics under the eye of The
Rev'd Mr Numerus; I find other advantages in Miss
Numerus and still more in Miss Aphrodite.
My harmonious life continues.

There were few domestic comforts, yet the flowering of
my youth in Bourne was not burdensome to me. That my
parents were almost as poor as the sparrows in the eaves
was a lesson in humility that fitted well with the clergy. It
was assumed without question that to be poor was to be
good – and the reverse of that true. Yet charity and more
so when it carries pity with it, is harder to bear.

Some most worthy souls from the village took occasion
to give us items of apparel for which they had no need.
Touching scenes took place at the back door of the rectory.
When the visitor had been sniffed and licked and examined
for gender by Castor and Pollux, she would hold out
breeches or a jacket "that my boy has outgrown and, he the
last, I have no home for it". My mother conquered almost
every heart with her response that hailed the giver as "a
saint . . . and how clever to judge my son's size so well".
My heart was not conquered. For to me fell the penance,
suffered in the absence of any sin of mine, to wear the
garment in public and in church at every service until the
giver had seen me wearing it. Once, upon pulling on one
such gift – a pair of breeches of too tight a fit – they split.
My whoop of delight did not prevent my mother stitching
them up and passing them down to Richard. He, with more
cunning than decency, became unaccountably ill – too ill
for church attendance at least – for two Sunday's
afterwards. I could not blame him for the breeches were in

40

the first place poorly tailored and forced humility on the wearer, and after thorough use and wear and donation to the rectory even a hermit would have preferred his sackcloth and the ashes with them.

Before my future education was decided upon, my father sought out more teaching in mathematics for me. He said, although clever as he was, he could not put me through the paces needed to lead me to greater learning in mathematics. He was also of the view that Latin and Greek (in which he excelled) fell too easily into my compass. Were I to show any inclination in mathematics, that might be a more proper study for me than the classics. He said that my felicity in those tongues would make me idle, and Divinity 'you could polish off whenever needed, while the complexities of mathematics will consume you more.'

My brother Richard and my sisters let their faces fall in sympathy with me when they heard of the imposition put upon me to learn more mathematics. Yet, in truth, to add to my felicity – since I enjoyed the mind-extending computation of numbers – there were other fresh green leaves within the sad brown outer leaves of the cabbage of my father's decision. He had engaged the services of a clergyman who lived in a nearby village. This gentleman, to whom I shall refer only as The Reverend Numerus, was marked for his great ability as a numerist and as a teacher of the same. The fact that his rectory lay a six mile walk from ours was no sadness to me, even though I should be alone on my journeys to and from, for Castor and Pollux came alongside with me only as far as the wicket gate on the far side of the graveyard. Their wagging enthusiasm failed as a cloud crossed the sun or as the scent of spilt milk in the kitchen wafted on the air to be caught in their flared nostrils. They knew that Sine Plica would have more nourishment for them and give greater exercise for their tongues at home.

But if I lacked the companionship of the dogs, I made

MATHEMATICS

an acquaintance that lifted my spirits. The Reverend Mr
Numerus had a daughter (and may still have) whose
greatest advantage I believe was not her beauty, for she
was (and may still be) plain; but her good and unselfish
character put a tenderness in her blue eyes that was better
than mere prettiness. Her moral virtue, I have no doubt,
was not in question (and never will be).

Some time after this I heard that she had gone to a male
relative's house in London and was lost to her friend. At
that time more important to me was her possession of that
very great friend and neighbour, the daughter of the Manor
nearby. This person, whom I shall call Miss Aphrodite,
who though only thirteen years of age as against the
fourteen years of Miss Numerus, was lavish in her charms.
A few curls from her chestnut hair were allowed to fall
occasionally over her brown eyes and touch her cheeks
glowing softly beneath. Bosoms were pertly apparent
beneath her dress and no costumier could or would hide the
movements of her shapely nether quarters. Had Miss
Aphrodite not been concerned to be more mature and more
serious than Miss Numerus, she would have perhaps been
too coquettish. As it was, her smile, which dimpled only
one corner of her mouth, was friendly rather than brazen,
and when she held out her hand to be kissed, it was
modestly done and gave just a finger-tip gentle pressure
upon the hand that took it.

Miss Aphrodite and Miss Numerus attended each other
at all times that summer and apparently had little other
business than me. While I was intent on matching the
mathematical brilliance of The Reverend Numerus, who
often had his back to the window overlooking the lawns,
the nymph and her companion passed to and fro giving first
a three- quarter view of their faces and then a full view and
then no view at all as they chased each other; whereat Miss
Aphrodite raised her skirts a trifle to give freedom to her
ankles and occasionally more freedom still.

Sometimes they just sat upon the grass and adorned

themselves with daisy chains, although Miss Aphrodite put buttercups in a chain for her dear friend Miss Numerus, which suited her less well.

They knew exactly the time at which my tutorial ended, for while the cleric and I were still seated, they walked arm in arm across the lawn to where a gate through to the shrubbery led to the paddock and the path through the woods to the Manor and five-and-a-half miles to Bourne. The young women's progress to the shrubbery was brisk and with a purpose to let anyone know who may accidentally be observing them that they were going straight to the Manor. Their pace lessened in the shrubbery – no, it ceased to be a pace at all. They lingered there and sometimes sat cross-legged trailing their hands to the ground as though touching moss and crumpling last year's leaves in their fingers were activities of intense interest and importance. If that delay did not give me time enough to break free from mathematics and set off home, while they waited for me to appear they would examine each other's dresses and stockings for stray blades of grass and the petals of flowers and only then set off briskly across the paddock to the woods.

As the summer lilted along and I learned better to time my responses to the earnest cleric, and to strike my exit from the house more particularly, it happened quite regularly that I caught up with the impudent and sedate young ladies just as they had entered the wood.

There, as the path soon entered a wide glade, we joined hands, I with a maiden on either side, but with Miss Aphrodite, by chance and by my endeavour, a little closer to me. With the glade narrowing and the path necessitating if not single file, at most allowing only two to walk comfortably but more closely together, Miss Numerus felt it her duty to walk ahead. Then it would not be unusual for me to press Miss Aphrodite's waist so that her arm had to come behind my back. Such proximity made it natural for her temple to lie against my cheek and, if in stooping forward by chance my lips brushed her forehead and moved a curl from her face as she turned it up towards me in mute enquiry, it was surely natural if not entirely accidental that our lips met. And if Miss Numerus did turn to speak, she turned tactfully away and took greater notice of the blackberry flowers and the clacking of woodpeckers in the trees.

There was no danger in any of this because on arriving near the Manor the path widened again to admit three in line, and our hands would be joined in a companionable way as we crossed on to the road that forked off and in full view of Miss Aphrodite's house.

I asked myself, was there any shame in this? I answered no! But by ill chance appearances were otherwise on the very last day of my tutoring.

Perhaps because there had been a shower of rain and the paddock grass was wet, or perhaps because these maidens were in fact a trifle fond of me and wanted to enjoy the whole extent of our walk on this day I knew not why. But the consequence, whatever the reason, was that Miss Aphrodite and Miss Numerus, this once only waited for me in the shrubbery always seemingly dry and when I reached them Miss Numerus as the host's daughter greeted me first and threw her slim arms round my neck and kissed me. Then in a gesture which spoke of her kindness to me and to her friend, and of her modesty and shy regret at being less lovely than she, Miss Numerus stood back and unnecessarily propelled Miss Aphrodite into my arms. The circumstance of my pending departure, the tender proximity, her lips, her breasts against me, the tip of her tongue meeting mine, her eyes open as though for me to fall into them – all this and more put an urgency upon me that she must have felt as much as I.

At this precise moment the Reverend Numerus realising that he wished me to take a book to my father, had crossed the lawn to call for me as I passed through the shrubbery. Miss Numerus, leaning against a trunk but her senses more alert to the scene that was about to unfold before her father, met him where the lawn ran under the laurels. He at a glance took in his daughter's startled look, the skirt of her dress slightly hitched and crumpled and the few small pieces of lichen and moss clinging to her.

'Where is Miss . . .?' he asked. By this time, Miss Aphrodite and I had separated from our embrace, I silenced her with my finger on my lips and pointed her to leave the shrubbery at the other side and so to continue home; I returned to the shrubbery edge to face my tutor. Then was I submitted to his gaze while he enumerated for himself the evidence of fault to be found about my person. There was nothing more obvious than the passion still swelling my trousers. Poor Miss Numerus who had not at any time been the cause of this excitement was despatched to the house to her mother for them both to wait for the clergyman, who would certainly talk about a conjugation with his daughter that had crumpled her dress and gathered half the shrubbery to its cloth.

He turned to me: 'The book,' he said. 'I cannot trust it to you now.' He spoke as if ravishing his daughter might be excused, but ill treatment of a book could not be forgiven. 'I will take it to your father tomorrow along with an account of your despicable behaviour here.'

Why I should not be trusted with a book after I had presumably sinned with his daughter, was a connection not perfectly clear to me. I remained silent and hung my head – which actions were probably the cleverest of mine that day. He would not have believed that his daughter was not the one in his phrase "taken advantage of". How could I at once both insult her plainness and betray her beautiful friend?

I bowed stiffly, thanked him for his tutelage (at which he hooted) and I set off immediately for Bourne. I came up with Miss Aphrodite on the way and advising her of what she already knew had happened, kissed her respectfully and with restrained passion at first and then . . .

I accompanied her almost to her home. I told Miss Aphrodite that I would explain to my father that Miss Numerus was indisposed and that as it was my last day I had stayed on a little longer with The Reverend Mr. Numerus. There was nothing untrue in any of this. Nor did my dear father take a great deal of seriousness to the facts of the matter. However, he did not let Miss Numerus' father realise this when next day he delivered the book and when also with voice full of moral rectitude he delivered the "appalling" narrative of the day before. Dodd senior was urged never to speak of this ever again except to admonish me in the same vein as wished the Reverend Mr Numerus and also to chastise me for my despicable behaviour towards his lovely, young and innocent daughter, who even if she had been of the age for it, had no inclination to "receive Master William's low attentions."

There was an end to the matter. Yet I did regret the abrupt end of it. Miss Aphrodite was a most beautiful young woman whom I hope (as also for her honest friend Miss Numerus) has made a good marriage. I say now, and not particularly because she will read this, but my Mary combines in herself entire the goodness and beauty of both Miss Numerus and Miss Aphrodite and would not be exchangeable by me for either – or both – ever. Yet still sometimes now I recall their eyes – the sapphire of Miss Numerus and the lovely brown depths of Miss Aphrodite's.

I say there was an end to this matter, yet there was one small consequence for Richard and me. The Reverend William Dodd felt an urge to act towards us in a familiar paternal but pastoral way; to treat my brother and me as members of a flock who needed advice and guidance, particularly in worldly affairs and even more particularly in matters of the flesh. I believe that it was the very vehemence of the offended Reverend Numerus which went some way to prompt my father's action.

In any event a day or two later he called me into the

library, where Richard was struggling with Virgil.

'You are young, Richard,' (it was indeed yet two years before he would leave the protection of the rectory at Bourne) 'but you too must learn to beware of the world. You both have learned from me and from Aristotle that the speculative life is the highest happiness, and that the faculty of intelligence is divine.'

My Father paused for a moment as he sat looking out of the window with the tips of his fingers pointing together like a steeple as lofty as the thoughts he wished to transmit. He cleared his throat and continued with eyes open but never meeting ours. Richard lolled over Virgil and I pulled myself up and sat cross-legged upon the long table that ran the length of the library. I tried to exchange a smile with Richard but he failed to meet my gaze.

'That same Divinity that gave us the intelligence to know the secrets of nature, also gave us the command to increase and to multiply.'

Richard looked puzzled and I stifled a small laugh of surprise at the realisation of our father stepping into a new character in an unfamiliar play; and I wondered if he had serious thoughts that Richard or I might be considering multiplying in anything but a mathematical way. In truth, our clerical parent seemed to have his thoughts suspended between the divine and the carnal and struggled to bring all parts of that conference together. He stood with resolution and dragged the library steps to a far corner. There he ascended and took a slim volume from the topmost shelf and read from the title page:

'*Aristotle's Compleat Masterpiece*. Part I – Displaying the Secrets of Nature.'

He blew on the book and noticed but did not remark to us, that there was no dust on it, whereas companion volumes in this darkest corner of the topmost shelf wanted for neither dust nor cobwebs. Father remained on the steps as far up as he had needed to be and continued to address us there with his face still turned to the shelves.

'This book,' he said, 'which is, of course, not one of Aristotle's works, is compiled by others with some references to Aristotle, yet with fuller details. So you should both read it. I cannot tell you as well as *it* does of the parts of generation both in man and woman, and though you know from your own examinations of what parts your bodies are made, you have yet to learn, I suppose, the unfolding of the plastic power of nature in the secret working of generation – and what makes a woman's parts; or for how in the heat of coition, and in the delights of copulation the conception is determined.'

The Reverend cleric coughed and coughed again which excited further coughing and so he sucked in more neighbouring dust. Then he sneezed and, fearing further tumult in his throat and chest, came down the steps to avoid accident. He laid the book on the table next to me.

'Perhaps we should ask Sine to dust the books on the top shelves. Or has she already dusted there, but only this book?'

My face betrayed nothing. He turned to Richard who had begun again to loll over Virgil. Father looked to me once more with a question mark.

'No,' I said with a horrid smugness that should have made me blush for it. 'No, I would not climb so high for Aristotle in translation. All my Aristotle has been taken in the original Greek from the bottom shelves.'

My Father put his hand on my shoulder, looked silently at Richard, turned and left the room. Far from lolling now over Virgil, Richard slammed him shut and threw him at me.

'I suppose you think it was I who tore out most of Chapter VIII too?'"I picked up *Aristotle's Compleat Masterpiece* and turned to Page 78;
where Chapter VIII "How the child-bed woman ought to be Ordered after Delivery", began. Only the torn remnants of pages 79-86 remained.

'You see,'said Richard.

'How did you know?' I asked and put a father-like hand on his shoulder, looked silently at him, turned and left the room. Certainly both he and Sine Plica had been at the book at different times for different purposes. Most likely Richard had it first and Sine had seen him reading it and followed it back to its shelf to look at the illustrations at leisure.

Dear Richard did not mention it again but I felt he harboured some slight grudge against me even to the end, or at least to my end. Conversation between us thereafter was often conducted with caution on his part, as though waiting for traps laid in anything I said. Richard was a quiet lad and never sought to take advantage of me. I regret that I was not kinder to him.

There was a bond of such strength between our parents that to talk or to listen to either was for us to have the same spiritual guidance. He from the pulpit; she in her nightly prayers for the smaller children; he with the power of learning; she with all the tenderness of her heart; both in their manners and their speech put our hands into the hands of Our Lord Jesus Christ. I remember even now during these last months at Bourne as my childhood ran out, sometimes, though long past the years when my mother knelt with me at night, I would in happening to pass by the door see her kneeling with one or more of the younger children. If their prayers had just begun they would need no further acknowledgement of my presence with them as I knelt, but a slight shuffling of knees on bare boards to make room for me at the bed-side. My mother's prayers were for her family. Since these last few years when she had taken less part in teaching in the school room, the time lost from being with her children at school was gained with them in the later hours before sleep. Still engraved in my memory is what I styled her teacher's prayer with which she began:

"*O Lord please aid me in my earnest endeavours to be*

careful of the souls of these children and to instil into their minds the principles of thy true religion and virtue. Lord give me grace to do it sincerely and prudently; and O Lord bless my attempts with good success."

In withdrawing from the classroom, she had regrets that John Vokes, a clerk in Holy Orders who was master now, had not the same bright mind and deep compassion for "her children"; and he had not a word in praise of Shakespear. The Reverend William Dodd sought to reassure his wife, for she, although denying it, was ailing. The years of carrying six children and teaching five of them and quietly doing the expected work in the parish, and all the unseen labours which would in a wealthier house have been shared with servants additional to our Sine – all these made the yoke of time heavier to bear. Her concern too was for William himself, who thinner as the years passed, ate and drank little. I know not whether this was to allow his offspring to have more, or because of his natural carelessness of worldly pleasures, or because he had the habit of continuing Lenten rigour throughout the year. Whatever the case, I was fatter than he and rarely sought to follow his example. While he grew both more sparing in the flesh and even less given to mirth than in previous years, I grew more roundly fleshed, and learned the pleasures of indulgence.

The summer of 1745 burned brown tracks through dusty grass. Solitary elms in the cornfields turned their leaves golden at the sun's touch. Old dogs lay flat in the shade and panted; sparrows sheltered in the eaves; swallows lifted themselves into the cooler skies to swoop and dive while the larks sang to them. Nettles and poppies and ox-eye daisies wilted in the sun. Mud cracked round shallow pools of brown water – and that was all that remained of the river at Bourne which separated the Abbey Church of St Peter and St Paul and its school from the alms houses.

Children searched in vain for minnows but took instead big

trout stranded on the mud. Older people left their businesses unattended until in the cool of evening and the very old sat in dark doorways and opened the buttons of vestments that had not been opened to daylight since the summer before.

Only my father William Dodd Senior, Clerk in Holy Orders, was to be seen walking from shop to house from farm building to shaded garden, with me quietly beside him. When his enquiries yielded nods of assent, he ticked off names in a pocket book stuck with sweat to his other hand. So he made sure of the presence of the village orchestra and choir for August 1st – Lammas Day – when by custom evensong was a special service at The Abbey Church. My father reported all to us at our evening meal, when as usual conversation was more plentiful than the food, and I was called upon now and again to certify his account.

He related that James Berry, baker of Eastgate was glad to promise to play on his brass horn, but was less hopeful of good flour to make the Lammas Day loaves. His neighbour Thomas Harby, miller, told us he had the necessary first ripe corn in plenty, but the sails of his windmill in East Field had not turned in days; never was a year so windless. And the water-mills for twenty miles up and down the river were similarly idle.

James Berry, when he heard this sorry tale, said: 'I'll speak with Mr Harby. Perhaps he and I and our daughters – we have eight between us, and his three are as big and strong as my five put together but less comely – perhaps these can grind the corn by hand. Leave it with me. Thomas the Miller will not deny us this. There are few who take more of his flour than I and if his daughters cannot put their hands to a millstone perhaps they will save some of their plentiful breath to puff and turn the sails of Mr Harby's mill.'

'Ah . . .' said the Rector, making poor progress in an effort to interrupt Berry.

'He should be mindful also,' said the master baker, warming to his promise as hotly as the day and glad to have the chief part in a conversation with a more learned man, 'he should be mindful that his piece of land in East Field, though only thirty yards long, is Lammas Land, so on the first of August it becomes common land until the spring. We none of us take use of it though we might, for the good man only keeps a cow on it and stacks straw at the end of it all year round.'

'That . . .'

'That is why you may put your mind at rest Mr Dodd. You shall have your five loaves for Sunday fortnight,' and he laughed, 'but it is a fortunate thing there are no fishes needed for blessing, for not even I, James Berry, Master Baker, could conjure those out of the dry river bed, except they were already fresh and cooked by the sun.'

We subsided on to a rough seat in front of the bakery where we were shaded beneath an oak tree that stretched gnarled roots into the road. The Reverend Mr Dodd wished he could remove his wig and be as bareheaded and bald and cool as James Berry: which thought of wigs reminded him he must call on Mark Linton, barber and peruke maker. So, confirming that James Berry would help as baker and musician, my father made his way to that Mark Linton, who was (and may still be) known to roll the wool for a wig as tight as anyone outside London; but had other talents too. He could play the organ or the harpsichord with equal skill and also had some influence on another votary to the Gods of Music – John Allan his close friend since childhood. We never rightly knew what John did. It was assumed that his father had died young, and left John's mother well provided for, and she being more frugal than most had conserved her wealth with great restraint. When widowed, she joined the Quakers when John was still a child, and so he too was a Quaker but rather by adoption than inclination and he had, before there was much more than down on his upper lip and chin, distressed his Quaker brethren by "going to fiddle at a Christening". Mr Dodd let the peruke maker know that John Allan, if he withdrew from the Quakers, would be gladly received into the orchestra with his fiddle if he pleased, on Lammas Sunday. Furthermore, The Reverend Mr Dodd spoke again, not of the practical aspects of faith and the harvest to be expressed in a Lammastide service, but also of the other significance of August 1st at Bourne – to wit a recognition of the patron Saints of Bourne, St Peter & St Paul, and on which day St Paul in Chains was celebrated as a feast.

Mark Linton, Peruke Maker, keeping his eyes the whole time on The Reverend Mr Dodd's wig, (which needed repair certainly and at best a costly replacement), agreed readily to talk with the lapsing Quaker. Mr Dodd urged him not to be prolix in talk with John Allan. It was the heat of the day and his recent experience with the more verbose James Berry, baker, made Mr Dodd cautious about inciting those he met to talk widely (and at length) and to carry about rumours amongst all the good people of Bourne.

My clerical father, the respected Rector of Bourne, was tired and feeling touches of ill temper rising within him. His feet were as oven bricks and the skin was itching above his throbbing ankles. To lift his mind from his own present discomfort, he sought examples and justifications from the Old Testament. Deuteronomy, he mused: somewhere in the torments of Chapter 28 there were words which illustrated his discontent; and if not providing an answer they distracted him for a while:

"The Lord shall smite thee with the botch of Egypt, and with the emerods, and with the scab, and with the itch, whereof thou canst not be healed."

'I have not deserved to be smitten,' he said aloud.

He then remembered that later in the chapter there was smiting with "madness and blindness, and astonishment of heart". Considering as rationally as he might while his brain was being baked beneath his wig, he thought he was mad to be walking in the hottest part of the day. But madness and blindness might not after all be painful when he became accustomed to their effects; and as for "astonishment of heart" he would submit to that and the other curses in exchange for a shady place, a scratch, a glass of water, or for relief at least from emerods. Since for my father the whole of sickness and health was described and defined in the Old or New Testaments, it soon became his opinion that physicians of more recent times – even today – were unlikely to have credence.

The Reverend William Dodd's reluctance to go to see Matthew Clay was more than a normal reluctance to face and to talk with a grieving parishioner. Clay's gloom was, he felt, impenetrable. What is more, Hannah, although considerably older than my sister Barbara, had been often in her company as a friend, each accompanying the other in turn to sing at the spinet, and to mind when at play my younger sister Elizabeth, and Mary and Sarah the twins. The God who had chosen to take Hannah the one daughter, the only child of Widower Clay, rather than from William and Olivia's four, was not a just God in the mind and heart of Clay. The shared sadness and care for one parishioner in these circumstances, my father found oppressive. He warned me that when (in my mind I put an "if" in place of the "when") it was my task as a clergyman to have the care of souls, I might find my presence in silence more affecting than propositions and theological arguments as if I were a schoolman debating the numbers of angels who might dance on the point of a needle.

When we arrived through the heat at West Field, it was uncertain in Matthew Clay's mind whether The Rector was about to crumble like an over-cooked pastry, or melt like butter in the sun, and so he took us in to the coolest part of the house before he gave us water fresh from the well. A quiet scratch while Clay was gone on this errand relieved my father further and he composed his mind to discuss The Chandelier.

In memory of Hannah, to be a light for others as she had been to him, her father had a smithy make a fine chandelier to hold a candle for each year of her life. Hung already over the nave, it was to be lit for the first time at that very evensong at Lammastide for which the Rector was now preparing. The orchestra and choir would be in place, and he asked Matthew would he be agreeable to the chandelier being blessed at this service? He said he was and asked as well if he might provide the candles and the tapers to light them with; and also speak with Warden Drake who came always with tinder box and on any fine evening was to be found sitting before church on a tombstone behind the church drawing deeply on his pipe. Matthew Clay said he thought that the Warden would be happy to light the candles, but that he Matthew would bring confirmation of this before evensong. All was agreed, and with a lighter and cooler step, my father and I returned to the rectory to seek out Sine for a draught of elderflower from the cellar.

Having matriculated with ease at age sixteen, I was to be entered at Clare Hall Cambridge as sizar this Michaelmas 1745. There was, said my father, who was deeply impressed with my mathematical progress, a chance of bursaries and even scholarships to add to my income eventually. Meanwhile, it was no bad thing, in his view at least, that I should have to earn my keep out of the offerings of rich undergraduates paying me as their servant in menial tasks. My father said, quoting from Corinthians I Chapter 9 v.19: *"though I be free from all men yet I have made myself servant to all, that I might gain more"*. I quoted back *". . . what is thy servant a dog, that he shall do this great thing?"* As I was not able to say exactly whence came my quotation from the Bible, my father silenced further discourse. My mother gave it her opinion also that there was no shame in being a servant. She argued – rather to make a point to my father I think – that servants appeared in all Shakespear's plays, and that the plays would not hang together without them.

So it was that Lammas Sunday was to be my last Sunday before leaving on the coach for Ely on the first part of the journey to Cambridge.

Evensong did justice to Lammas Day and its loaves; to the blessing of Hannah Clay's candles; and to the festival of St Peter in Chains. Cast and scenery and effects were as though they had been directed by the Mr Garrick my mother had heard about. Lammas loaves, heaped upon the altar, rose like the mounts of Olive and Sinai, or the stones before the sepulchre. Whichever imaginations were in the minds of members of the congregation, the old and bent gentlewomen from the almshouses saw the loaves as breakfast and supper and midday meals for the next week at least and knew that they would be as hard as rocks before the end of it. The miller's and the baker's daughters saw them as the products of their labours, and were satisfied that they had already tasted crusts from the bread made from the flour that they had milled, and found it good.

From their box pew towards the top of the nave, Richard and I nudged our mother to look round upon my sisters, Barbara and Elizabeth and more particularly the twins further along the pew. Their voices were not heard above the others but there was more motion in their lips than from all the choir. Each word (and not all from the hymn book) was formed completely within the circumference of red lips and white teeth, and had they not uttered a sound the meanings would have been comprehensible even to the weakened eyes of the men and women from the almshouses. Matthew Clay's seat was as near beneath Hannah's chandelier as it could be. Pride and sadness flickered on his face as my father blessed it. Tears glistened briefly before they were wiped away like intruding motes.

As instruments and voices swelled into the roof spaces the doors were opened to allow a movement of air in the crowded Abbey Church. There was no trembling of the earth when Chapter 16 of The Acts of the Apostles was read; but now the skies darkened with clouds as they closed in upon the summer's night and as Curate Voke read the appointed lesson for the feasts of St Peter and St Paul:

"And suddenly there was a great earthquake, so that the foundations of the prison were shaken; and all the doors were opened: and everyone's bands were loosed.

"And the keeper of the prison awaking out of his sleep, and seeing the prison doors open, he drew out his sword, and would have killed himself, supposing that the prisoners had fled. But Paul cried with a loud voice, saying, 'Do thyself no harm: for we are all here'."

I, a young man eagerly searching for heroes, was deeply impressed and marvelled at the courage of Paul who, when he could have made his escape, remained in prison so that he should not bring blame and disgrace and even death upon the keeper.

At the end of the service Mr Clay set off for home with an effusion of thanks to everyone as he left and a firm long shake of my hand.

'Safe journey Master Dodd,' he said.

One of the wardens took the loaves over to the almshouses. The congregation dispersed. The choir clattered home. Members of the orchestra, whoever could, cradled their instruments in their arms, gathered a while beneath the minstrels' gallery and discussed their general satisfaction with the performance this night and their intentions to do better next year when not a crotchet of Handel nor a semi-quaver of Purcell would be released unless it were exact in timing and sound; and how Quaker John Allan had fiddled better than ever before and beyond the realms of genius, at which he blushed and said he was "glad of the chance to be happy in the House of God"; and how the choir too were all angels in everything except – thankfully – for not having angel wings which would have brought out in imitation all the bats in the tower.

Curate and Vicar, Richard and our sisters, all made their way across to the house where Sine was bustling about with a little food and ale for us.

My mother and I sat for a while, silent while others went. She looked at me with that kind, loving gaze that hid all the unrest in her mind and drew out many bursting feelings in me. Feelings – because I was leaving home – feelings that a bridge was being crossed to take me away from my childhood, and my village and my family so that I could never return in the same person and recapture anything of the years before.

When I had unburdened myself, my dear Mother talked quietly and softly with me, her words both soothing me and puffing me up even to feel elated. Her pride and that of my dear father's hidden pride were slid into my mind like draughts of fine wine. Pride she said in my learning and my manhood. She quoted neither the classics nor the Bible, neither Shakespear nor Milton who played no lesser part in her mind's gallery of great poets; but her love even unadorned by any of these was still a balm of Gilead to me. I said so, for then I had no words of my own and could not be so at ease as she in converse. I took the defence of other words from other authors to protect me.

With my mother's arm linked in mine, we crossed to the vicarage.

Later that night as I was retiring my father already in his nightshirt came into the attic bedroom that Richard and I shared. He was holding a worn leather purse; he loosed the strings to show me the gold coin within and handed it to me.

'Oh,' I said, 'Father you have already drawn down money to buy me new clothing.' I looked at the new, but sad, poor vestments laid out on a chair.

'Your Mother and I . . . we want you to have the money

to pay for your return from Cambridge, if not at Christmas nor even Easter, at least at the end of the summer term.'

He faltered as I had seldom seen before. I pressed my hand into his and would have kissed him had he not turned, I think, to hide a tear. He showed nothing more than the stuff of his night shirt and bulbous veins and scratch marks above his ankles as he left.

Richard, who was supposedly asleep, opened an eye and said, 'Who would pay good money to have you come home again?' For answer I threw my old breeches in his face and went to bed, leaving him to put out the candle.

CHAPTER 6
TO CAMBRIDGE WITH LANCASTER

*My friend from Ely; New worlds opening; Laughter and
tears*

The intended short stay at Ely with an acquaintance of my
father was in the event eight weeks long. But now we were
in the coach for Cambridge and making good pace
accompanied by a weakened September sun, which made
silhouettes of the trees and distant town and spires. The
clopping of the horses' shoes had for me classical rhythms
and varied the dactyl and spondee of their beat as they
slowed before, and then quickened after as they rounded
pot-holes and great valley rifts and ruts in the road.

Facing me in the coach, my friend Lancaster of recent
acquaintance looked out upon this same landscape as I did,
but yet seemed to look within himself. A youth of slighter
frame than mine and of lesser height, and pale, with skin
so soft in its parchment it would have tempted all poet-
scribes to write of it and to pen their names upon it to claim
possession. As I looked at him I wondered where I would
put my mark – on his smooth cheek, at the corner of his
mouth, or under the cascade of Titian locks which made a
dark pavilion where his neck curved down to his shoulder?
His eyes came back to mine and we both laughed: he for
shame at his pre-occupation and me for my pleasure that I
was, and we were, at last nearing a great new world for us;
and his friendship; and the friendship of his father.

Lancaster leant across, opened my coat with his finger
and poked my waistcoat. It was very slightly frayed at
some of the buttonholes but brilliant in its rainbow colours.
And its intricate needlework caught the light at every
movement. I puffed my midriff to show my pride.

'Do you like my father?' Lancaster asked.

'Certainly! Not just because he gave me this,' I said smoothing my Joseph-like garment where he had so lightly poked it.

'He is not ashamed to dress well however much others may say it is not seemly for The Rector to dress like a dancing master. I admire him – and his choice of waistcoat.'

'You speak truly of him. When I was very young I asked him if God ever laughed. He was only a moment in replying and said:

"At destruction and famine thou shalt laugh: neither shalt thou be afraid of the beasts of the earth", and, Lancaster added, 'if you have the psalm book – which my father's wife gave to you when he gave you the waistcoat – see Psalm 126.'

I took it and opened it:

"When the Lord turned against the captivity of Zion, we were like them that dream. Then was our mouth filled with laughter, and our tongue with singing; then said they among the heathen, the Lord hath done great things for them. The Lord hath done great things for us; whereof we are glad."

'My father said therefore,' Lancaster continued, 'there is obvious agreement between the heathen and the righteous that laughter is God given.'

'And is the psalm book giver of a like mind?'

'Ah! My step-mother. You know not so. You know how she rarely smiles and she berates me. How she will always correct me if I am wrong and correct me if I am right. There is no laughter in her. I hardly knew my real mother; I was three when she took consumption and it took her. She was a cheerful woman. But father surely was not overcome by laughter when he took my step-mother, Captain Brown's widow, to wife. I think he knew of her wealth – gained from the Captain's profitable sea-trade. Whether or not my father knew of the evil trade buying, transporting and selling slaves that indirectly brought him such riches, I know not. My father is impecunious and not so much greedy, but wishing to enjoy all the pleasures of life that can be had while serving His Maker as parson in a small village. He ever adjures me to do as he says and not to do as he does, but always to keep faith. And he never speaks unkindly of the woman who is my mother by adoption, but he often does not speak of her at all.'

Lancaster was to be a pensioner at Clare Hall which gave him a full four shillings a week with none of the obligation that I was to have to earn my keep by running errands and waiting on other and wealthier undergraduates. Two shillings a week was my allowance as sizar, but this money was anyway to be collected, with any other funds I could raise, and paid to my tutor Mr Curtail. There was to be no room for extravagance for either Lancaster or for me, and the idea of our going to Clare together, was to share some of the tasks of making our rooms reasonable in their furnishing and decoration, and to do this well before the term began. The Reverend Mr Lancaster, when he saw the name Dodd in the matriculation lists that spring, had written to my father whom he had known briefly in their youth, suggesting that if his own son, although only just fifteen, did matriculate straight away, he might join with Master William Dodd first at his Rectory at Ely and then after some short acquaintance could both leave together for Cambridge. This was by both sets of parents considered an idea of great sense, since I had few friends apart from my brothers and sisters, and Lancaster himself had, being an only child, no blood relative other than his father. The arrangement was satisfactorily concluded and I left Bourne for Ely on my way to Cambridge. I think my father thought that Mr Lancaster Senior might still be rich with benefit of the Captain's wealth brought to him by his widow. Sadly however, he had long since spent the greater part of the widow's wealth, his extravagance leaving only just sufficient for ordinary living. The horses he had bought and rode in the hunt, were apparently more extravagant than he; they ate plentifully and were comfortably stabled and cosseted by their stable-men. Each day Mr Lancaster reviewed their fate but decided again to keep men and horses "for another while".

Inside Mr Lancaster's home, furnishings had been brought from London. Many items were of an exotic nature – and cost – for it was thought they would please the Captain's widow, as she had been accustomed to priceless pieces from foreign parts. In reality, she was not pleased. When a wagon came from London loaded with escritoires and commodes and sculptures of strange beasts, she had a mind to have them sent back to London immediately. Fortunately, perhaps, that was not possible without a further great expense. She then withdrew to her bedroom, which was already, against her wishes, lavishly appointed in the French manner as a boudoir fit for a French, and Catholic, Queen.

This boudoir had arrived on a previous wagon-load from London where it had barely waited long enough to catch up with the Rector himself whose journey from Paris and the makers of fine furniture, had been interrupted by three days in care-free company at the racecourse at Sablon.

Our stay at the Rectory at Ely should have been for a fortnight at most. Indeed preparations were already being made for us to make the short journey to Cambridge, when Lancaster fell ill. He was feverish and coughed thinly at night. Rosebuds appeared higher on his cheeks than beauty dictated. The Surgeon-Apothecary was called (another expense) who bled the poor boy so that he was paler than before and I believe also too weak to cough for a fortnight, which was counted as a success by the Apothecary. Despite this, Lancaster began to recover and Mrs Lancaster took aside one of her maids (the one chosen by her husband who was he said rather too pretty for mundane tasks). She was instructed to make hot mutton broth and to add in a variety of herbs. These at least made Lancaster's chamber smell differently; which circumstances made him yearn for fresh air. He was moved to a couch beneath a cypress tree darkening the lawn behind the rectory.

"'*Let me not in sad cypress be laid*",' he joked.

We laughed. We fended off the Widow, the Apothecary and – sadly I thought – the Widow herself fended off the pretty maid who was in my view entirely acceptable company for us as long as she was not bearing a hot-pot of mutton and herbs.

Lancaster and I talked as young men will, of all sorts of matters: and gave characters to everyone we knew. We sought out interesting and salacious stories from the classics; read Shakespear out aloud, taking parts, much as I had done with Richard years ago, and acted them. And we began our affair with Callimachus – translating from the Greek and putting into English verse – first the *Epigrams* and then the *Hymns of Orpheus*.

Although neither of us wished the Captain's widow dead, the fourth epigram struck a chord in our minds:

"A youth who thought his father's wife
Had lost her malice with her life,
Officious with a caplet graced
The statue on her tombstone plac'd When, sudden
falling on his head, With the dire blow it struck him
dead.
Be warn'd from hence, each softer son,
Your step-dames' sepulchre to shun."

Lancaster proclaimed his recovery to me by announcing his improvements with each epigram completed, and as we began the XVth Epigram:

"Half my life I yet possess The other half is flown . . ."
we were reminded that we should be soon on our way to Cambridge. At Christmas we would return to The Rector and his wife, and we did not then put Epigram VI into the context of our memories:

"What mortal of the morrow can sure So frail is man,

and life so insecure. . ."

We rattled into Cambridge and we were certain of the joys of the morrow and certain of all the long days stretching ahead of us as well.

CHAPTER 7
IN CAMBRIDGE

Lancaster;
New acquaintances; Poetry, sorrow and Lancaster

There is an intensity about stepping for the first time into a vibrant city. As the hooves slowed on the cobbled streets and as we lugged our boxes – one on top of the other and we each like tiny Sampsons straining at the pillars of the Temple, our heads turned first one way and then another to drink in the scene and to comprehend the bustle and the noise. In the cool dark street before Clare Hall a tangle of small carriages bearing the sons of the wealthy hindered the passage of porters carrying bright painted boxes with their armorial devices. With boxes held high on their shoulders, they hurried through the gateway to the best ground floor rooms in the first courtyard. We, by this time dragging our own boxes along the ground, were marked down as poor pensioners or at the worst sizars making our way humbly to darker attic rooms above the courtyard. I had barely dropped into one of the two shapeless chairs in our set, when Gascoigne, a haughty youth no older than I, called up the stair well for water,
'. . . that I might wash; and ale that I might slake a thirst worse than a hydrophobic dog.'
He laughed.
   I clattered down on the first journey of a thousand over the ensuing years, to take from Gascoigne – or his friend and room-mate Bulkley – a commission to carry a command elsewhere for:
'. . . the barber to come and shave me and quickly before my beard has grown too long' or '. . . My compliments to

go to Mister, to Sir, to a Fellow, The Reverend So and So and may he accept my regret at not attending this morning because of a distemper'

'. . . Fetch the barber again. He has left several whiskers upon my jaw. Ask him to come quickly or he shall not be paid.'

'. . . Fetch wine for me and my companions.'

'. . . Finish this line of Greek for I must be away to join the hunt at noon and am barely dressed yet and help Bulkley with his boots, he is in the same case as I.'

Gascoigne was forever finding that he should be somewhere else when he had "a line of Greek" or "a morsel of Tacitus" to explain. In truth, it was obvious to the smallest mind that when William Gascoigne Esq. found the going too rough in the classics, he "remembered" he had to see, or ride, or give an urgent opinion on a horse some distance away and:

'Now at once.'

The translation or the explanation of a text was always much less disagreeable to me than chasing downstairs across the courtyard to the buttery and back with tankards of ale or beakers of wine – with the inevitable 'and bring Bulkley one too'. . . So in time, by the effort of slowing my steps and my pen, William Gascoigne Esq. and Samuel Bulkley Esq. began to hold the idea that if they made their own way in leisurely fashion together to the buttery, had a tankard or two each and then walked back to their rooms carrying more "nectar of the Gods" in their own steadier hands, they would find the translation, or the commentary or whatever studies they had, done by me already on their desks. My answers for them would be perfectly written in their own hands albeit with some small and appropriate mistakes that they in my judgement might make. In this way there was some assurance that their inquisitors amongst the dons would suspect no other hands had done the work than those of Gascoigne and Bulkley.

It was a most happy arrangement despite that, early in

the first term, The Reverend Mr Griffiths – an eccentric Fellow of whom I may have occasion to write later in another context, found, he thought, an example of cheating between Gascoigne and Bulkley. I had completed a piece of work which each had to present to the Reverend Mr Griffiths, a translation from *The Aeneid* Bk VI where Virgil describes souls in torment. I translated the line *"suos quisque patimur manes"* as "each one suffers his own ghost". Instead of altering *"manes"* to be "ghost" in Gascoigne's essay and "spirit" or "soul" in Bulkley's, I had put "ghost" down for both. The next day The Reverend Mr Griffiths expressed to Gascoigne and Bulkley his surprise. He said, as a Christian, he expected to see *"manes"* in this context translated as "spirit" rather than "ghost". And even more surprise – and he is reported at this point to have partly opened his study windows either to allow the increased volume of his speech to dissipate, or as Gascoigne and Bulkley said, to call passersby to witness their shame – were not these gentlemen also both Christians, and were they not each individuals with their own minds? He was so led to believe. That Gascoigne and Bulkley should happen both to alight simultaneously upon "ghost" as the proper and best translation for *"manes"* he found suspicious.

Gascoigne and Bulkley did redeem their reputations as far as being accused of cheating however, by saying that it being of great interest they did in fact confer on this point. 'We did,' they said, 'study and discuss the passage for a long time – perhaps too long and late into the night when with the wine being heavy their thinking had not had the clarity, nor had their minds been as swift as that of The Reverend Mr Griffith's.'

Finally, they, scholars Bulkley and Gascoigne, 'had fallen upon each other's shoulders and agreed to agree on all points in the text and its translation,'

The Reverend Mr Griffiths having begun in pretence to eat his hat, which he said he would do entirely if it were true that Gascoigne and Bulkley had been independent in their conclusions, Mr Griffiths gave himself of the opinion that his pupils were now telling the truth. At the same time the tale narrated by his pupils reminded The Reverend Mr Griffiths of his true purpose in life, which was to advise and guide the young men of Clare Hall in particular, but also the young men of the world at large, of their proper behaviour. For, he said, quoting the great Bishop Berkeley, philosopher and preacher, "*The whole world is an idea entirely in the mind of God,*" and therefore said The Reverend Mr Griffiths, drunken behaviour or dishonesty or the corruption of a Latin text or such like worldly crimes could not be countenanced in the mind of God. Gascoigne and Bulkley reported this comment by their teacher, but appeared somewhat nonplussed since their knowledge of Berkeley – so far they declared – was only a name in hunting circles.

The two pupils, affecting a manner of contrition, withdrew from the Reverend Mr Griffith's presence. He was now, they said, fully launched into a sermon and had opened the windows as far as the hinges allowed, so that all passersby, both the begowned and the unbegowned in that street and its neighbouring streets should have the benefit of his moralising. As far as I could divine at this time, The Reverend Mr Griffiths took his moralising texts from Virgil as a poet and Bishop Berkeley as a philosopher. I was, therefore, thankful to be spared the full Griffiths effect, as reported by my tormentors. Instead, Gascoigne rounded upon me to demand why I had made such a stupid error in making a mistake for them simultaneously ("and at the same time" Bulkley added) for both of them. I apologised. I felt that to argue closely with them might be a worthless exercise. Yet I did point out for their consideration that Virgil was supposedly writing about the people of a heathen underworld, and therefore the mind of a Christian God was not present and did not form it. Therefore "ghost" rather than "spirit" was more in keeping with the subject matter of a heathen underworld. I coupled this opinion with the observation that I would be less likely to make a mistake with their studies if I did not have to spend time cleaning their hunting boots when there were more and better qualified people about the college to fulfil that task for them. My point was I think well taken, for after that I was relieved of that and some of the dreary tasks which took me away from their books and my mathematics.

The Reverend Mr Griffiths was seldom out of the minds of the undergraduates (nor indeed the Fellows) of Clare Hall. For bees did not reside singly in his bonnet. He was much exercised that youth should pass by his windows, make their way to the neighbouring King's College Chapel and ignore Clare Chapel. It was partly perhaps because the King's building was an affront to Mr Griffiths. Larger than the chapel of Clare Hall it also had a multitude of pinnacles and little spires about its roof. These facts alone would not have excited our Fellow to open all his windows even on a winter's day to harangue whoever passed by – even if he thought that they were going towards King's Chapel particularly. What he abhorred most was the practice undergraduates indulged of rambling from chapel to chapel to listen to different preachers or different music. He hailed young men in the street:

'Sir, shall you, shall you Sir give preference to that loud King's College organ breaking wind through the chapel doors and drowning both its own choir and the excellent choir and organ in Clare Hall and drowning too our own good clerics at their prayers? Shall you, Sir, give your alms in that place? Shame on you! Yes on you, Sir, who is wrapped in layers of cloak fit to keep out all the arctic winds blowing across the fens! Give your alms and your cloaks to the poor and come into the warm embrace of our small chapel at Clare Hall!'

THE HANGING OF WILLIAM DODD

It was not beyond our Mad Fellow of Clare to give a text and whole sermon through his window. If that season was upon him when the window-preaching became too frequent and to cause a greater disturbance to his colleagues than the organ of Kings College Chapel itself, then the Proctors told the Master, and the Master told all the Fellows. The Reverend Mr Griffiths would be asked by a deputation of a half-dozen of his colleagues, to desist and he would smile: 'Ah, is my method too maddening for you? Shall I not be granted to preach therefore more often within our own chapel?' So they gave way before the agreeable smile, and Mr. Griffiths had the pulpit at Clare Hall for a series of sermons, in Advent or Lent as he wished.

In that first term at Cambridge, at the time and as I look back now, there was a new and powerful binding of minds and, I dare say, hearts too. For Lancaster and me the severance – from in my case family and in his case from his father only – was mollified at first and finally pushed right into the backs of our minds by preoccupation with our daily matters. At the time, Lancaster was always more of the poet than I, and I quicker in reading the Latin and Greek than he. When our studies for the day were complete, he after much labour on serious classical history, and I mathematics, took the volume of Callimachus that we had opened first at Ely and translated it verse by verse and epigram by epigram from the Greek and put each into verses of our own making.

So it was in the first part of that term often of an afternoon we settled under willows beyond the bridge at Clare. The grass sloped to the water, occasionally ruffled by a duck lifting itself onto webbed feet and beating a white path over the surface and into the air. Lancaster sat with his back to a willow's rough bark and looked away from his book and across to the pinnacles of King's College Chapel. I lay on my side with my head cupped in my hand and looked at Lancaster and murmured lines of Callimachus to Apollo which we had just put into rhyme:

"On his soft cheeks no tender down hath sprung,
A God for ever fair, for ever young:
His fragrant locks distil ambrosial dews,
Drop gladness down and blooming health diffuse."

Lancaster turned to protest – I thought at my daring to liken him to Apollo – but no, he had recalled a line of Milton:

"One shaped and winged like one of those from Heav'n
By us oft seen; his dew locks distilled Ambrosia . . ."

'You twisted our translation to your own ends, plagiarist!' said Lancaster, 'You cheat the poets to gain your own rhyme.'

He laughed and poked me in the waistcoat as was his want. Given as an apology, and with a pomposity which sadly I too often affected, I replied:

'Always we add to the creative works of others. If one composes a tune, another adds a song. If one paints a portrait, another adds the varnish. If you sow, I reap.'

'If you buy me ale, I drink it.'

I shook my head and, gathering books and papers we rose and together made our way to the bridge and towards the food and, I hoped, his purchased beer.

In such pleasant ways and ever with affection charging our foolery that first Michaelmas term drew to its close. Blooming health may have diffused Lancaster's looks but he was less strong than before. His letters home had confirmed his desire to return to his father's house for the Christmas vacation despite that by repute it was the only jolly vacation time at Clare Hall. I was to accompany Lancaster to his home and we thought that my presence may somewhat soften the tone of his father's wife. In any event we joyed in the prospect of our shared company, the log-fired warmth of the Rectory, and some cosseting for the frail and lamb-like Lancaster.

To celebrate the expected good fortune, we joined with Gascoigne and Bulkley.

'To dine on the town at my expense,' said Gascoigne.

'And mine,' said Bulkley.

To dine was to drink; to my day-time tormentors to drink was to become drunk – for the pleasure of being abusive and then maudlin but all being forgot next day.

Early in the evening, when the first tankards were still only half- emptied, to my astonishment Bulkley impugned Lancaster for his effeminate manner. This was slightly done, and if by a cleverer man than Bulkley would have caused no offence.

'God you are a pretty chap,' said Bulkley out of the echoing chamber of his tankard. 'No wonder Dodd takes such pains with you,' and he referred to my helping the weakly Lancaster upstairs with my hand in the small of his back – an act of kindness the pair had observed with laughter on many occasions.

'Enough of that, quite,' said Gascoigne clearly disturbed that Bulkley should be rude to one of their friends, or that Bulkley should make notice of Lancaster and not Gascoigne himself. To make amends for Bulkley's insult, Gascoigne said Lancaster should have a glass, '. . . nay, a bottle – of the best Madeira the landlord can find.'

This the landlord brought. Gascoigne and Bulkley made Lancaster drink. They were at pains to make it clear that if he declined or showed the least reluctance to drink all the Madeira they could buy, he was to be marked down as ungracious and unforgiving of Bulkley. Still resenting his remarks, Lancaster drank. He drank more and began to slip down on his bench and rest his chin on the table. None of us aided Lancaster or held the drink back from him. I sat by with a forced smile on my face to which I added a leer as I gazed at the landlord's daughter. Her attributes reminded me of Warden Drake's daughter, but that remembrance I knew was only a poor justification for steadfastly fixing my gaze on her. It was my pretence that I sought to place her in my mind from a previous time. None of this deceived the landlord's daughter because she ignored me and spoke to Lancaster:

'Would you wish to lie down for a while, Sir?' she said and turning to Gascoigne and Bulkley:

'If the gentlemen prefer, you may take your supper into the same room, and stay with your poorly friend until his head knows where his legs are.'

By this time, Lancaster had given up hope of refusing the Madeira or any other beverage with which they were inclined to ply him. I stood up and, making an effort to heave my friend upright, thanked the landlord's daughter for her offer and began to head for home. Gascoigne and Bulkley exchanged glances, tipped their drinks back, corked and pocketed the remaining Madeira and, lifting Lancaster between them as he and I had done with our boxes what seemed now years ago and me carrying his feet like a horse in the shafts of a wagon, we made our way with surprising speed to Clare Hall and Lancaster's bedroom, where he quickly sank deeply into sleep. When I heard the purring of his lips against the pillows, I crept out.

Gascoigne and Bulkley insisted I join them below to finish the Madeira. I did so and several hours later tottered up to my bed and also fell asleep. I believe that I was woken next morning by the silence. Gone nine o'clock and there were no shouts below – no calls for water or barbers, no boots to be pulled on. With relief I lay back for a few moments and then upped and crossed the stairs to Lancaster's room.

Silence. No creaking of springs. No snores. He was asleep; head white on the white pillow, but, oh, there in the valley made by his face, vomitus and blood; I put my hand onto his shoulder and turned his rigid body to face me.

'Send for a physician! Send for a surgeon!' I cried.

A voice from another stairwell answered the urgency

of my call and someone ran out of the courtyard. The man did not know why I called, but only that it was urgent and that desperate haste was asked for. Yet all his speed yielded no better than a long time later a lame apothecary came. This worthy person had a business only two streets away but could not be brought quickly for he had to search for aloes, and for herbs suitable in cases of plague which he said was rumoured to be approaching the city.

'Furthermore,' he said, 'I had of necessity to put up the shutters at my premises for citizens other than university gentlemen were about at this early hour and their honesty was not to be relied on.'

So, breathless and upon a crooked ankle, he stood in Lancaster's doorway holding a bouquet of dried flowers to his nose.

'This is no case of plague,' he said. 'That is bright blood in the vomitus that blocks his nose'. . .The Apothecary approached the bed, talking as he looked closely at my friend.

'Was he turned thus upwards to the ceiling, when you found him?' 'No, his face was in the pillows. Oh my God. Is he dead?'

I knew I need not ask, but I wanted another voice to speak the words. 'Yes, he is dead.'

I waited for the apothecary to tell me more but he asked:

'Has he other illnesses? Has he pains of the stomach? Has he been passing black water? Has he coughed and spat blood? Has he had sweating at night and become more wan and pale as the year went by?'

'Yes, yes,' I said. 'He was thought to have a consumption of some sort.'

'Then assuredly anyway he would have died. But now I think when he breathed his last he breathed his own vomit. Was he drunk last night?'

I could not answer. I was weeping, crouched against the skirting board between the panelled wall and the rough floor boards. Gascoigne, with Bulkley close behind, appeared at my head height as they came up the stairs.

'We hear you have called for a physician to Lancaster. When he has done with him will he come to us? Bulkley's stomach has spent the night heaving its contents into the alleyway outside, and I have a headache cleaving my skull in two. Please have the physician visit us soon.'

They turned and took a step or two down. I lifted my face out of my hands and looked at them.

'My Lancaster is dead. My dear, dear Lancaster is dead. Dead you fools. Lancaster is dead.'

Their eyes only were visible at floor level when they turned to me again.

'Dead?' they said and paused as though they needed further translation and meaning.

'Dead? But please have the physician come to us anyway.'

Curious faces watched from their windows as the apothecary led two college servants with Lancaster on a litter towards the chapel. Lancaster would rest there until his father made arrangements to have him brought home. Mr Curtail, tutor, ascended the stairs to speak quietly with me.

The Reverend Mr Griffiths came, Bible in hand with texts on pages for my attention marked with brown willow leaves:

"Let every soul be subject to the higher powers.
For there is no power but of God."

He read more lines and closed the Bible, hesitated, and I thought started to speak, but he hesitated again and turned and hurried away as though to hide tears and his regret that words of sympathy flowed not as easily from his mouth as did his imprecations to youth.

At evensong in the Chapel prayers were offered up for the soul of John Lancaster. For the moment I did not recognise his name when it was given, for I always thought of my friend, and addressed him as Lancaster and he addressed me as Dodd. The name John, given by his father reminded me that my grief was not as great as his father's would be, and after Chapel I wrote a letter to go back with him: to tell his father and his stepmother how much John was loved; how he had no sins upon him; was ever at peace with His Maker; and his blameless life was a perfect preparation for death and a heavenly life thereafter. I wished to put more and better words into the letter, but my tears were already washing the ink into small lakes on the paper. I concluded stiffly by saying that my presence at Christmas without their son, would magnify their sadness, and so despite the generosity they had so freely shown towards me, would they forgive me if I also indulged my great sorrow alone in Cambridge?

In truth, I had looked so forward to the Christmas weeks at the Rectory with Lancaster, to be there without him would be intolerable. Besides which, I had started that day to gather all that we had already done towards *The Hymns of Callimachus,* and to have it put in print when I was freed to that task. Meanwhile, each midday I wore Lancaster's bright waistcoat under mine, and huddled under the willows with those pages we had completed. Saffron autumn crocuses still pierced the lawns; saffron it was that coloured and perfumed Apollo's hair and "clothed the morning in a saffron robe"; but the God of this Autumn festival was gone.

"Half my life I yet possess
The other half is flown –
To Love or Death –
I cannot guess But certainly it is gone."

On some days Gascoigne and Bulkley made occasion to pass near me on the backs. Briefly and each on different occasions, they expressed their sorrow at Lancaster's death. They said they had paid the Apothecary for his attendance on Lancaster (£4.4s.5d.) and were engaging the sizar on the next staircase to satisfy their urgent needs so that I should be relieved of all demeaning tasks for a while.

'However, please would you Dodd continue for the moment to give us guidance on all matters Greek or Latin as those are beyond the compass of the new sizar, at least to any satisfactory degree.'

They also said, 'We would be obliged (as we have heard rumour of your intent) if at any time we might contribute to the costs of publishing your literary efforts.'

Lancaster, in praising me, as was his habit, must have spoken of my intention to follow a literary career. I did not know then how occupied I would be amidst many other avocations, but their promised kindness was sealed in my memory, and did make me regularly mindful of their gratitude for crumbs from my table-full of knowledge of the classics.

When iron frost gripped the fens and winds blew snow in direct from the east, I did regret for a while that I had not availed myself of The Reverend Mr Lancaster's hospitality at Christmas. The alehouses were warmer than my rooms but had no more company than the buttery at Clare. Gascoigne and Bulkley had fires in their rooms (and someone else to carry the coals for them now) so I very readily showed my willingness to help them. And when not tutoring there, I found the Library warmer than my draughty attic, and more comfort still came from the kitchens below which allowed some hot air laden with cooking smells of meat and vegetables to escape between the floor boards. Here I wrote my letters and built up an acquaintance with the books which would occupy so much of my time.

A letter home drew a long letter from my mother, full of advice and affection and sprinkled with quotations from Shakespear – these as much I think to taunt my father as he read her letters – as to illustrate points in her epistle. His letter was brief – not read by her – and largely concerned with her declining health, which, he wrote, 'may somewhat excuse her preoccupation with William Shakespear although the Bible is a better source of spiritual guidance and of serious medical advice.' As I remember it, the letters I received from both my parents were always much as recounted above, except that before long my mother also had occasion to show concern for my father's health:

'He is,' she said, 'no better than he has ever been, and thinner by far; he has like Hamlet ". . . *lost all mirth, forgone all custom of*

exercise . . ."'

Later there was news of Richard going to Oxford and my sister Barbara travelling to London to stay with her aunt, 'where she may make a match more suitable than any to be made here in Bourne, and have a chance to see something of the theatre which but for occasional itinerant players we never see in Bourne.'

Retreat to the library did not merely provide an escape from thoughts of my well-loved Lancaster, indeed it was here in this first and subsequent vacations that I took so strongly to those literary diversions which became part of my life.

Yet endeavours for the Mathematical Tripos came first with Kederman's *Mathematics*, Barrant's *Euclid*, Wilkin's *Mathematical Recreations* – each taking turns to be a prop while I read from their fellows, and also from Sir Isaac Newton's great tomes. As the daylight faded and the guttering candles sank into the hollows of their sconces,

tiring of numeration I turned again to a line or two of Callimachus. I put all into verse, not that I was ever a great versifier and certainly not as gifted as Lancaster nor claimed to be; but rhymes supply a stretching of the language and a greater sense of the original and so put my lines out of reach of the hurtful charge that I was aping other translators.

Furthermore, in verse I easily applied the love stories to the ladies, rather than to boys as did the original, since in the love of boys I could see nothing but what is shocking, detestable, diabolical, and did with sorrow behold the gross state of those heathens who could think such practices so honourable as to be renowned in song.

I say already in these library hours I was forming the ambition to follow a literary career.

CHAPTER 8

I AM A POET

Suitable clothing; Top in The Mathematical Tripos;
Farewell to Cambridge.

In my college years I discovered in myself some talent
which natural modesty forbad me to declare. Yet others
than Gascoigne and Bulkley were forthcoming in their
praise. The first slim volume of poetry that I produced,
particularly in their minds, was the earliest of this juvenilia
– a skit, a parody on commonplace pastoral poems. By the
summer of 1745 a cattle plague had arrived in England
from across the channel – proving that not all that comes
from France is as welcome as French wine. This distemper
of beasts that have horns and cloven hooves laid waste to
thousands of cattle in their herds.

Countrymen recognised it by its effects while
confirmation, if needed, came from scholars in their
villages. For, had not my father said in a letter, as no doubt
a variation from accounts of my mother's health and her
snippets from Shakespear: 'had not Virgil himself
proposed the diagnosis of the self-same disease? And that
some few years before Christ was born?' And now it was
visited upon the cattle in grazing grounds in Essex,
Lincolnshire and Cambridge and swept up to the last fields
bordering the great city of London.

Soon the wagons on country lanes were white with lime
carried to the pits where the dead cows and pigs were
heaped, while rich farmers and poor cottagers suffered
alike. My lament on *Diggon Davy's Resolution on the
Death of His Last Cow* would not today be seen as a fitting
commentary, but its gay and witty lines were never meant
to mock Diggon and his worthy fellow bumpkins. My

facetiousness was directed at all those literary pretenders who so larded their ballads with sentiment
that if properly affecting their readers as intended would have made them weep until the seas filled over and there was no more dry land.

My pen, encouraged, moved on to an *Heroic Poem* which told the story of the Arab Sheik of Zanzibar. This friend of an English sea- captain entrusted his son and that son's friend, to the captain to be transported to England. (I wondered if this sea-captain could have been Lancaster's step-dame's first husband?) It was I think, in *The London Gazette* that the story was related – the captain sold the boys into slavery, but they were released by the endeavours of the Earl of Halifax in his capacity as Commissioner of Trades and Plantations. The Earl persuaded the Government to bring the "Arabian Prince" to England at last, to be baptised and educated and dressed in finery and to be shown to polite society. It was the craze amongst ladies of *the ton* to entertain the Princes, and the Earl of Halifax received many congratulations for rendering so signal a service to both humanity – and to *the ton* – which indeed in any event regarded itself as the best part of humanity. With strains of Callimachus in the lines, my verses affected to be a letter from one Arab Prince to his betrothed, a maiden called Zara. I should not now have remembered this epic poem, had I not dedicated it to the Earl of Halifax – hoping that therein might lie for me an advantage sometime in the future.

Certainly it was not chance or an idle thought on my part that I picked Zara and Halifax her benefactor. The second Earl of Halifax had much to recommend him. His wife Anne was descended from a family of great clothiers – men of consummate commercial instinct and thereby of enormous wealth. A part of the wealth – it is said £110,000 – was brought to her husband on marriage and the only price he paid was to take her name – Dunk – a four lettered name that I would gladly have exchanged for the name

Dodd, in a bargain far less than that which Halifax obtained. To add to those riches the Earl of Halifax was in about 1742 appointed to the post of Lord of the Bedchamber in the household of the Prince of Wales and soon after placed at the head of the Board of Trade. None of these were as significant in the eyes of Gascoigne and Bulkley as the Mastership of the Buckhounds which Halifax still retained and in which function he made their acquaintance.

Now, having convinced myself by the offerings I had made so far that I had the soul of a poet, it was imperative in my mind that I attire my body as splendidly and lavishly as might be that there should be poetry in my habit as in my soul. But how and what the where-with-all? I laid plans to borrow from Gascoigne and Bulkley, if I could provide them with a bond. It was not seriously to be doubted that this could be achieved – but as they were not bankers, an arrangement was not to be contemplated unless they and I were equals. They had made it clear in the plainest and grandest way that we were not. This was before the first summer's long vacation.

As they fumbled about filling their boxes before the morrow's journey home, they crossed to and fro each other's room saying could one take a pair of boot trees which might better fit a space so . . . and could the other take stirrups and a gun which would be better fit in the other box. They fiddled and poked as they tried to close the lids by jumping on them. They paid no regard to damaging the emblazoned coats of arms while paint was chipped off by their jumping heels. The sleeves and legs of garments hung like emptied corpses over the sides of the boxes and valuable items still littered the floor. I rose from Gascoigne's desk where I had been "getting up" some of "his" writings which he said he might show to his father as evidence of academic prowess. Bulkley, with a cunning which passed as wisdom on this occasion, declined to offer samples of his own work to his father.

Bulkley was proud of his father, particularly in any similarities he felt there were between the two of them. It was no sorrow to either that Bulkley senior boasted along with many of his hunting cronies that he had "no Latin and less Greek," and that "if you offered me a page of one of these I would be hard put to it to know which way to turn it up. But if you offered me a horse on its back, I would very soon determine which way it was up – with the least difficulty of all if it had balls."

Bulkley stuttered the words out and thanked me for the papers prepared for him. He rarely spoke at such length, but I sensed that he was making amends. Meantime I suggested that they both sat down while I refilled and tied the boxes, leaving nothing on the floor which they wished to take away. Bulkley's good-natured face broke into further smiles as I finished his box. Gascoigne whose face at any time was leaner and more thoughtful, had used the time of my employment on his box to resolve the question on his mind:

'We thought to ask you Dodd if you would divide the long vacation between Bulkley's home and mine – and travel with us. But then we thought you would be discomforted as our ways of life are not as yours.'

'Yes,' said Bulkley, 'you would be uneasy in our homes.' He added: 'And we have plentiful help – Gascoigne in London and I in Hertfordshire.'

Gascoigne's face clouded momentarily as he heard Bulkley's reference to their plentiful domestic servants. I had my face turned to attend to the last knot on Gascoigne's box, and gave a double tug on the rope as I realised their opinion of my station in life.

'Your goodness overwhelms me,' I said, removing all traces of sarcasm or bitterness from my voice. 'You are right. I need the tranquillity of a quiet vacation here to master higher rules of mathematics, and to pursue the lonely paths which poets are bound to tread. I shall be staying here at Clare Hall for the long vacation, and will greet you again at Michaelmas.'

'I thought you had already packed.'

'No, a few things I shall not need are put away and I shall have new garments soon upon my back.'

They looked curiously at me as they thanked me and I left, and I had surprised myself too. As we had been talking, the vexed matters of vacations and clothing were resolved for me. I decided on the instant to use the money which my father had pressed into my hand on the night before I left Bourne. I would not spend it on a coach journey home. I would stay at Clare Hall and possess myself with clothes and all the finery I might want. Writing home at once I explained, with all affectionate greetings to each member of the family, that there were new tasks that I was putting upon myself. I was contemplating a text book *Synopsis Compendiara,* a compilation in Latin of the works of Grotius, and Clarke and Locke, to save the likes of Gascoigne or Bulkley the pains of reading the originals, so allowing them more time for those pursuits to which they were more happily accustomed and suited. This long vacation and others too would be fully occupied, and I must be at Clare Hall for the library, for its books and solitude with them.

I put my letter on a coach that day knowing that it would be delivered in two days' time.

Solitude was a property of the vacation which I did not find unwelcome and my head was ever occupied with great schemes for literary accomplishments. The few gaps in my head between the plans for those noble works were filled with trivial verses, the composition and the recitation of which were a restful antidote to the pains of grand creativity. They also, like a tune hummed in the dark, filled the emptiness of loneliness in the silent, deserted college courts of the vacation.

One of my poor poems at this time was *A Day in College in Vacation*

It recalls for me those days when how empty was the silence; how empty the silence of the great dining hall below the gallery beyond the library, when I sat alone at commons. It seemed that the bread and cold meat which a silent servant put onto my trencher board were only the forgotten leavings of a fatter company warming itself in the kitchens.

Cooks and gyps, gardeners and porters appeared not to laugh or even to speak during the long vacations. They slipped soft footed about the kitchens and corridors as though afraid to make any noise that would not now be drowned by the hubbub of sizars, pensioners, scholars and fellows in the full term frenzy of their scholastic lives. Yet at the first dawning day of the Michaelmas term when all the sounds of academic life began again, college servants released from their respectful vows of whispered speech and soft foot treading raised voices again and walked or ran with firm and heavy feet on the boards and flagstones of Clare Hall. I put none of this in my letter home, but only repeated my determination to work on and not come home.

As for money, it would no doubt be a struggle, but it was to be hoped that I could survive on the coins which would have otherwise been spent on the coach journey to and from home. My mind eased by the letter, I rubbed my hands at the thought of what the morrow might bring in the way of new clothing – and if there was money to spare, what other delights? And I blessed my night-shirted father for the purse he had pressed into my hand.

I was up and about early – breaking my fast so quickly that I had barely planted my nether regions on a bench in Hall than I was up again with dry brown crumbs sticking to my teeth and slopping the water I had gulped to wash the crumbs down. It was my intention to arrive early at Dunkerly Tailors & Outfitters while Dunkerly's man was still sorting the term's unsold stock. Rumour had it that all costs fell when the gentry departed and then bargains might be obtained. Even so my purse was very nearly to be emptied.

In the shop every unfashionable item I determined to discard; garments hanging too long on the tailors' dummies 'til the shoulders were faded by sunlight or discoloured by dust, I handed back to Mr Dunkerly's man. A good coat showing darker blue cloth when the pocket flaps were lifted, received such a merciless sneer from me that Dunkerly's man retired for a moment into an inner recess to recover or to summon help, I supposed. Therefore shortly, bowing and smiling, Mr Dunkerly himself appeared:

'To be of service, sir. How can I best provide for you?'

He waved his man away to the further recess and commanded him:

'Bring back the London clothes.'

Then, coats and waistcoats and breeches and stockings and shirts of finest lawn, neck cloths prepared from exotic materials, gloves, a hat – 'as worn by the finest gentry at Newmarket' – and finally a pair of fancy buckled shoes brought in 'from the most skilled boot maker in Cambridge, Sir.'

'These are all clothes to match and fit a gentleman as fine and elegant as you, Sir. You must try them on if you will step this way.'

A "step this way" meant two paces to the left where an ornamented gilt screen was ready to hide the undressing and dressing up again.

'My man will take your garments, Sir.'

It was clear that he did not want my clothes mixed with his, and indeed, they looked pretty sorry remnants compared with the new. His man took the old clothes holding each garment between finger and thumb to allow as small a contact between cloth and flesh as possible. His nose, the while, had just the slightest wrinkle of distaste, which wrinkle disappeared as I came out from behind the screen dressed in my new finery.

Mr Dunkerly, with his hands poised just so and his head very slightly inclined to one side, submitted me to his admiring gaze. I waited for some remark, some point of criticism. Eventually and very gently with his head making slow movements of denial from side to side, Dunkerly spoke:

'No. You could not have made a better choice . . . Wonderful . . .'

He slid a hand round to the small of my back:

'Certainly a tuck here however; the waistcoat is just the tiniest bit loose but my man will do it in an instant.'

In fact, my man was already circling me with needle and thread. He lifted the frock coat and pinched the waistcoat backing together and stitched it. Dunkerly watched intently and I thought with a little of envy in his eyes.

'Now,' he said at the instant the tailoring was completed, 'the waistcoat is tight and smooth over your stomach Sir, and if I may be pardoned Sir, shows the fine embroidery and the glorious colours to their full effect.'

He passed the flat palm of his smooth hand over all the parts of me that caught his fancy or where he thought he should draw attention to colour or fabric 'of this most excellent outfit, Sir.'

When I thought that I was dressed, adjusted, admired and all done Dunkerly had his man bring out The Wig.

'O,' he said, 'this is tight curled indeed and of the finest wool.'

He allowed me to set it on my head.

'O,' he said with his mouth as rounded as the hole drilled by a woodpecker, 'most wonderful. The crowning glory Sir, if I may say so without counterfeiting the phrase.'

He clapped his hands once and then held them apart in amazement at the effect my "elegance and manhood" was making upon him.

'But here the tricorne hat,' he said and reached up with a flourish to place it on my head, 'the ribbons so and so . .

.'

He touched them into a variety of positions until he was
satisfied: 'They add another touch of mystery to you,
Sir – and if the brim be
set a trifle more jauntily – so – the ladies of *the ton* will be
sent ecstatic, swooning in your presence. That caps it all,'
said Dunkerly. 'Another crowning glory,' and fell into the
silence that the emotion of the occasion demanded.

'The matter of cost?' I said.

He made a dismissive gesture as to say the cost would
be a trifle compared to the value of the clothes.

'We shall accommodate you Sir to your entire
satisfaction.' Then changing from the vulgar subject of
financial considerations he said,

'London shall have to wait.'

'What mean you Sir, "London shall have to wait"? I
thought all this finery came from London?'

'O Lord, no Sir. O Sir, Lord no. O Sir, your Lordship!'
He was I think cunningly tangling his titles.

'My tailors make all these garments for London – well,
that is to say for the famous *Tailor of Hanover Square.*'

He lowered his voice at this mention and I dared say if
he could have put his voice in an even lower and more
devout register he would have given me further and fuller
details of this Tailor of Hanover Square, who was
"providing for the most fashionable people of the day
every day of the year."

Mr Dunkerly bowed me into his inner recess where he
became the firm and decisive man of business. Figures
were totted up and Dunkerly's man allowed to check them
twice.

'You have not included the wig,' he said.
There was a pause while Mr Dunkerly examined the
figures again.

'For you, Sir,' he said at length, turning to me, 'the wig
with my
compliments, Sir and furthermore for five shillings we

shall clean and dye it for a year.'

'Most kind. Most kind,' I murmured and began to count out gold from my father's purse. An amount adding to perhaps two sovereigns was left for me when the transaction was complete. Dunkerly's man's eyes grew wide as these two coins were poised at the mouth of the purse and disappeared inside again. It crossed my mind that now dressed as a man both of "elegance and substance" I should be expected to give a florin at least to Dunkerly's man. Had there been more change I might have done so, but greater sums were needed for other matters, so the coins stayed out of sight and his eyes became narrow slits once more.

I left Dunkerly Tailors & Outfitters as a new man. No longer a drab sizar, in my dress at least I was an important person: a person with money, who dared show a brave face and stomach to the world and owe it nothing. The stiffened skirt of my coat flared out as though winging me on air. My large beribboned triangular hat darkened my face to give it, I did believe, an air of mystery. I was well pleased and strode back to Clare Hall, where shortly a voice came from a window above.

'What fop is this? What effeminate creature is this coming into these courtyards?'
I realised with some horror, which reason I will divulge in a moment that The Reverend Mr Griffiths had not gone down for the Long Vacation. I slowed as I walked through the gate and archway. As I came out on the other side, a window opened onto the courtyard and The Reverend Mr Griffiths stood at it with a book in his hand – reading from it and comparing me with what he pretended to read, like a man on the Grand Tour with guidebook in hand:

'Yet they'(*sotto voce* "Dunkerly's I suppose?) a beauteous offspring did beget;

'Bred only and completed to the taste . . .'
He had raised his voice on this line and louder still for: 'Of lustful appetence, to sing, to dance . . .'

Now louder still because I had very nearly gained the far side of the court and nearly out of earshot:

'. . . to dress, and troll the tongue, and roll the eye.'

As he spoke and rolled his eye I escaped into my staircase and for an instant had a tinge of regret that I had not brought my old rags from Dunkerly's, for I realised that the one Fellow who had nowhere to go for the Long Vacation was The Reverend Mr Griffiths, and assuredly I could not appear before him now in my new fashionable wear. As the only sizar in college, I should be answering his needs, as the servant – to dance upon him at every day-break at least.

My discovery was also that he would be dining with me – albeit at another table where the Fellows dined. As a Fellow, even though the only one at dinner, The Reverend Mr Griffiths would be at high table raised on a stage in the dining hall and I would be also alone, but on a lower table for Commoners, and I would be all in finery, now the only clothes I had.

With no regard to economy we had one servant each to bring to table our identical food – except that his man brought wine to him and mine brought ale. At the start of our dining arrangement we were each at either end of the dining hall, and he with his back to me. As the days went by, with mutual consent we placed ourselves daily to be nearer to each other. As at first our progress towards greater proximity was sluggish, our waiting servants soon contrived each day to set our places nearer as we entered. By this means when as the new term approached, The Reverend Mr Griffiths and I were facing each other and only across a divide of two tables' width and a foot or so difference in height. Then conversation between us could be conducted without loudness and with a very minimum of neck movement.

I need not have feared for anything in my part as servant to The Reverend Mr Griffiths. I knew it as soon as I crossed the courtyard on the first morning of my servitude.

He stood at his open window in the psalmist words *"as a sparrow alone upon the house top"*. He smiled and beckoned me close beneath the casement.

'Fetch Forster and come take breakfast with me.'

I set about the first matter immediately. Forster the Flying Barber made it his business to be a legend during his lifetime at Clare Hall. He earned his epithet not because of any speedy response to a summons – for, in fact, when called he moved slowly and in majestic progress between the beards he shaved, adding an impression of importance which his huge bulk had already marked. (It is said in later years sizars were assembled to squeeze him up the stair wells to the rooms of his hirsute subjects.) His reputation and title as the Flying Barber was gained for the speedy execution of his shaving. Chins pulled up were lathered from ear to ear with a stroke of Forster's left hand and woe betide he who opened his mouth to breathe. Then leaping back and at arm's length, he fixed the gaze of his victim upon him while the right hand held the open razor high above his own head and flashed it down to perform its office instantly – down the left cheek and across the lip in one sweep – "say quickly Sir if the moustache is to be kept" – and down the right cheek in another sweep. With the momentum remaining in the barber's hands, razor, brush and bowl were quickly removed and Forster set off for the next beard.

It is said that in Forster's early years, when he had developed speed in advance of skill, many men of Clare grew moustaches for fear of losing inches from their noses. In later years, to the alarm of his subjects, the Flying Barber developed a tremour in his hands. The left hand holding the shaving brush caused some tickling only but the right hand that held the razor glistening and trembling overhead produced absolute eye- shutting terror. Then, it is said, beards as well as moustaches became commonplace in Clare Hall amongst Scholars and Fellows alike.

This was in Forster's good years and The Reverend Mr

Griffiths remained clean shaven of lip and chin and suitably glad to have need spare so little time on a duty to his complexion. In fact also, the time so spared meant that the good man relied little upon me for those tedious domestic tasks that servants usually perform, but shared them with me, talking all the while, glad not to be alone.

'Is this finery the only dress you have for library or chapel? I suppose that you will be dancing next?'

One affirmation to both was all I had time for before he was speaking again:

'Tell me, do you know Master Parkhouse who is a freshman with you? He too has inclinations towards the Church I believe?'

One answer, this time a denial, had to suffice.

'Are your parents alive? Were you intending to follow an academic pathway? Did your father?'

Question upon question poured out and was not delayed for a second for reply. It was, therefore, a surprise to me when The Reverend Mr Griffiths threw himself at last silent into a hard chair. Its timbers squeaked like corks being forced from their bottles – evidence I thought that the chair had been loosened many times before by such sudden sittings.

'Well,' he said 'you are singularly quiet Mr Dodd – even monosyllabic may I be permitted to say? Will you speak now?'

Presented with such an opportunity I hardly knew what to say and stood clutching a cloth with flecks of the barber's froth upon it and shuffled from foot to foot in my shiny buckled shoes, all the time attempting to point my feet in a fashionable way.

'Sit there,' he said, indicating a similar wooden chair on the opposite side of the breakfast table, 'it is less damaged than mine. Tell me all.'

I did. I told him of my literary ambition; of Lancaster; of my struggle to be equal with my fellows in material things – or better if I can be. He listened when I disclaimed effeminacy or dissoluteness, and only raised his eyebrows when I said that I had sacrificed a safe and quiet sojourn with my well-loved family, so that I could work in the library.

He did not press to know where came the money for my finery and asked no more questions. That, I felt, was because his sharp intelligence had apprised him of some of the answers without my need to speak, and for other questions he had no need to have answer, for they were thrown in merely out of courtesy.

Gradually and on many other occasions we fell to talking together about many matters – the state of religion, the writers and philosophers and poets of our day and of earlier times. He told me how, when the time came, I would be able to make the acquaintance of men who would help to forward my career. There were many names, some of whom remained names only, and others, like Samuel Squire, who were to play a significant part in my life.

The Reverend Mr Griffiths sought me out when The Reverend Samuel Squire, lately Fellow of St John's College and appointed four years before to the Vicarage of Minting in Lincolnshire and to further livings since, came back to preach on two Sundays at Great St Mary's. Being a man most able at finding preferment he was, very shortly after I made his acquaintance, made Chaplain to the Bishop of Bath and then Archdeacon and then also Prebender at Wells. It was, however, his appointment as Chaplain to the Duke of Newcastle, who held many other appointments in his gift, that did more to excite the envy of his fellow clergy than to add to his own riches. Even so, grinding poverty was a thing he never knew. He was despised by many in Cambridge and it is said hailed openly as Sam Squirt, an unkind, indeed a vile reference to both his small stature and his brown complexion – likening him to "a squirt" of thin excrement. Such obvious declarations of the dislike in which The Reverend (and shortly Dr) Samuel Squire was held may have been prompted at first by envy. To rise above that envy, I surmise, was later the cause of his frantic climb to high position in the Church where he would be at a distance from the vulgar tongues! It is a probability that Bishops in Convocation are unlikely to refer to each other as squirts or any other euphemism for excrement. For my part I think Dr Squire a kind man and, like The Reverend Mr Griffiths, much different from the common herd and therefore more certainly to be abused by lower animals of that herd.

My own small advancements were at Clare Hall before I became the beloved servant of The Reverend Mr Griffiths – else he would have been charged with granting me unfair preferment. I was awarded in 1745 a Lord Exeter Scholarship of two shillings a week and later the same year, also to mark academic achievements, the Robert Johnson Exhibition of just over one shilling a week. The emoluments did not meet the costs of maintaining my peruke this year in a pristine state. Yet I was grateful, for with the few coins left from my travelling purse I was able to arrange for tuition, not in fencing – as did Gascoigne and Bulkley – but in
dancing.

Mr Joliffe presided at the dance. He was the son of a recently deceased Mr Joliffe, dancing master, who had in turn succeeded his father in the same arts. There was a gap in the Joliffe dancing succession during the Commonwealth, but that break in tradition apart there has been a Joliffe directing scholars' feet since 1326 when Clare Hall was founded and none left off dancing until great age itself brought life to an end. My Mr Joliffe charged £1.10s per quarter exactly, which was tradition has it, the regular fee exacted by every Joliffe who tapped his toe in Cambridge since 1326. We never sought confirmation of what part of that fee secured the services of the respectable ladies – generally the daughters of Clergy – who would take the appearance of being led by us – when in reality it was us they were leading, lumbering votaries of the dance. It may be said that I became an elegant and skilful dancer and more than that, well practised in the arts of conversation with the fair sex, to charm them while putting one foot in front or behind the other as appropriate, and all in time to tunes bearing little resemblance to the psalms and hymns of my life so far.

The Epigrams of Callimachus stood me in good stead again. The XVIIth – adapted for my purpose – became a favourite. By replacing Berenice (the wife of Ptolemy, a Grecian lady, and the only person of her sex as I believe ever permitted to see the Olympic games) with the name of my fair partner in the dance, I could – if I withstood the temptation to use it twice on the same occasion – bring approving blushes and a downward glance even to the lady who suffered most from my misplaced feet:

> *"Four are the Graces; with the former three*
> *Another lately has obtained a place:*
> *In all things blest, bright Berenice;*
> *Without whose charms the Graces have no grace."*

What maiden could fail to give a delicate fluttering to her eyelids as she moved away in the quadrille? Nor later refuse to lend me her hand to kiss? What joy! Verily I danced back to my attic room after those hours at the dance. Though my chest heaved too – but with exertion my recall was ever of those white bosoms heaving with passion as I spoke poetry to them. If all this were my imagination, yet it did no harm to a student who could not afford to fence or ride to hounds.

And so in days of earnest study and fine discourse; in the pleasures of the dance and dalliance with ladies of virtue and pleasure, the time at Cambridge came to an end. I passed my degree with distinction – placed as a "Wrangler" in the First Tripos List – honours in mathematics. How that did please my parents despite my dear Mother's suspicion that I had neglected Shakespear simply because he showed little skill or interest in mathematics!

Perhaps the last and greatest pleasure for me when the lists were published, was the Wrangler's privilege of taking a kiss from every girl met in the streets. I added to my finery a new waistcoat purchased from Dunkerly Tailors & Outfitters after the Lent term had ended. Every year it is said the girls who put themselves in the way of the Wranglers did so in the hope of being seized away to good marriages, and I dare say at one time that happened. In my year the kisses I demanded and received were long and well requited but sadly that year of 1749 was the last year for Wranglers' kisses. Authorities ruled that there should be no more kissing since it would in their opinion lead to immorality and the dissipation and final corruption of the gilded youth of England. Had such nonsense been the rule before my year as Wrangler, I would have left Cambridge with less reluctance.

As was not unusual with the gentry, Gascoigne and Bulkley had gone down a term before me without taking their degrees. The vulgar business of working at their books and then being examined in the Tripos was not likely in their minds to be pleasurable even if the Tripos stool had been replaced with a saddle.

For me there were partings of some pain – The Reverend Mr Griffiths being foremost in my mind:

'Give me news of your endeavours,' he said, 'and if the world and particularly the world of letters does not treat you kindly, come back to us, for we will treat you kindly.'

I thanked him well, but thoughts of failure were never in my mind.

The lure of London was too powerful, and all the unknown it might contain drew me like a gaudy moth to a brilliant flame.

CHAPTER 9

AT LE CHATEAU DE VOIRONS

December 1779
I pray for myself. Mary attempts to release my tongue.

Every day I drop to my knees to pray. Or if that task has been too great on rising, I wait until I am sitting at my desk. Then, in a ritual that has little of the gravity of a high communion but to me has quite as much importance; Mary laces the fingers of my useless right hand with the fingers of my good left hand. She sits quietly at her own prayers while I make mine silently as I must with all the fervour and richness of language stored up within me, but which cannot now sound for anyone but me.

Always the subjects of my prayers are the same: I thank God in his mercy for my life, and since its present paths were not of my choosing, I pray for his strength to live it. I ask also in humility if I may learn what my life's purpose is now, for I am nothing but a burden and an object of pity to those around me. The changes that have come upon me I ask to be altered, but pray if there be only one prayer granted it is that I may speak. In times past my tongue in full flow led to ideas in my head. Now some see me as an idiot because I have no tongue.

O Lord please help me. Amen.

In the first days of my incapacity Mary attempted surgical methods sworn by the doctors – but unproven – to release that organ. To the inside of my mouth she applied well-wiped coal tongs from the hearth. Mercifully these were not red-hot as some advised, but even without heat, caused sufficient pain when they gripped on the root of my tongue and tore at it. To Mary's disappointment the only sounds produced by this manoeuvre were the clicks and clacks of iron against my teeth and a sort of groan. I begged her with my eyes to desist and clasped my left hand as if with another imagined hand in prayer – to achieve by that what iron in my silent mouth could not – and end my agony. Mary stopped and wept.

I pray therefore, O God in Thy mercy grant me once more the gift of speech: and let my tongue sing again in your praise only. My hope or consolation is that prayer, even when it is silent, has power to make effect. And my silent prayer is a dialogue within myself – a chance to confess. This history is a confessional too, but ornamented with details which give me pleasure and help to recall the day-to-day events of my life. That I have in this way a conversation with myself is not entirely an indication of madness, but an expression to satisfy the absence of speech. I hope that I include nothing that is without relevance, nor fail to mention matters which my God may think to be of no small moment.

I am, therefore I think.

Descartes' full circled argument is ever a chorus in my head. By thought and by prayer, each aiding and being aided by the other, I have some hopes that speech will return to me.

Without Mary I would long ago have sunk into a drowning despair swamping the last cries of my deranged and damaged faculties. Indeed, without Mary I would not be here to have any thoughts – Cartesian or not – and she is, she says, entirely happy that I shall strip the flesh off all the past to reveal bare bones.

Mary looks to my slightest need, and has taken every care to spare me from the indignity and madness of my speechless state. She comforts me in pain and soothes me when I show anger at my frustration of speech or movement. To these ends and to obviate disturbance in the rhythms of my writing, she has left small what she calls "morning notes" on my desk before I begin the day's first paragraphs. (Sometimes it is truly nothing more than a paragraph I write all day.) These small morning notes usually contain a line or two perhaps questioning my choice of fish or meat to be taken at supper, or asking if a pillow on my seat may give me more ease. With the passage of time Mary has sometimes put the morning notes in French which she learns mainly in the kitchen and in her forays to the servants' quarters to ask for help with me or in some domestic matter. The virtue of this for me is that those in English call my attention to considerations of some importance which require more Solomon-like judgements than to decide merely between "*des poissons ou des viands ce soir mon mari?*"

So it was this morning, in place of a morning note written on a torn piece of page rejected by me, a whole sheet and a half was filled with Mary's neat hand and addressed to:

Dear William,

You will think me a numskull if I speak my thoughts. However, you will not so dismiss them if they are carefully written out, (and crossed out and rewritten a dozen times, you would not be surprised). Do not take offence at what I write. Anything I write, however bold, is just a question seeking reassurance. The matters most in my heart are about your history. Sir Philip has impressed upon you the necessity of recalling everything that has happened in your life. This is to reconstruct the whole of yours, The Reverend Dr William Dodd's life, to lead you to understand your present state, and to restore to you the power of speech. I am not clear how these twin offspring will arrive, and I think you have some doubt yourself about Sir Philip being the midwife in this case.

I am concerned that there be a perfect outcome because you are a perfect man – not always in the eyes of the world

– but in my eyes. It follows therefore, should it not, that you might with advantage leave out some of the stained and broken bricks in the old structure? Are these not trivial to the main task and may safely be discarded?

You will have realised I refer largely to your recent admissions and on occasion to the language you use. Mr Dodd at Cambridge does not always shine out as the Mr Dodd I knew. I fear greatly that the Mr Dodd at London straight after will not shine out either. Nor do I say this because I have care for me. If you shall think it proper or so important to relate my history and as to how it changed, improved, spoiled or was bundled with yours – then so be it, and use whatever words you care to describe it.

But for you dear, dear William, have care. Regard it not merely as a wife's silly fancy that I hold you in such high regard – that were it not blasphemous I would say that you are a God for me.

Such openness is only possible in our correspondence because it is unalterably private. Equally unalterable is my love for you. Even if it is the fashion to be disdainful of such things these days, I will be out of fashion. That is no hardship nearly as great as any I would bear for you my husband.
Mary

I asked that this letter be put in the casket and also copies of any letters from Thicknesse or Mary, for a letter written privately – not as for publication when there is always a covering layer of humbug – but for one reader only, can expose the very soul of the writer. By the same token, my reply, given immediately before my daily task of writing began, is here below and is to be read and casketed before night fall:

O Mary, O Mary, O Mary. . .
I do all as you ask and weep at the sentiments you express. No "stained and broken bricks" will without reason be

included in my re-built structure.

If my judgement fails, God will be my witness that it is not a deliberate act, nor ever my intention to wound anyone – least of all someone whom I love beyond life itself. O Mary, you know that I am struggling in the dark. Why does not Thicknesse tell me all? Why don't you? No, I need no answers yet – I may find them for myself – but bear with me. If I do wrong now at any time, tell me yourself what is the truth – if I have or do make errors it is the malady, the injury that forces itself upon me however I may wish and plead otherwise. And if I use language that is as vivid as the subjects I describe, and that offends you, if you cannot believe it is true – put it down to my malady as well.

Hold tight in your heart my love, my dear, dear wife, and hold also there in your head the certain knowledge that I am always,
Your William

Post Scriptum: Your concern about the "London" history to come is understood. But you know already everything vile about this city from first hand, and since there are no other readers but you and I, however bright the pigments I use, the finished picture cannot shock you.

Be reassured,

W.D,

CHAPTER 10

TO LONDON BY COACH

*A voluble woman and more attractive ladies in London;
at the Porters' – home of my sister and her husband*

The coach from Cambridge made its intended terminus at
The Coach & Horses at Bishopsgate Street at noon. I had
indulged myself by travelling within the coach, which was
unfortunately in the latter part of our journey too well
sealed from the outside world. This was brought about at
the request of a lady of uncertain age travelling with us
from her home in Epping. She affected a great sensitivity
with regard to London air which she maintained came up
this far north and possibly further out of London. It carried
all manner of diseases she said and begged us to pull up the
windows tightly in spite of the heat.

We were all gentlemen apart from the Lady from
Epping and not one of us was prepared to be so sensible
but so lacking in charity as to deny the request. Though the
June sun only occasionally and then at a bend in the road
burned directly through the dirty glass, our carriage was
already a cauldron before the windows were closed. As the
air became thicker in the carriage, so she became more
voluble. If ever a face was turned towards her, she
addressed her commentary to it. More cunning passengers
established early on a preoccupation with what they could
see of the outside world and fixed their eyes on that so as
not to encourage her. But had all our eyes looked
elsewhere, our lady from Epping still would not have been
silent. The diseases always came up from London, she said,
and never in the reverse direction and set about giving us a
complete catalogue of diseases making their deathly

journeys from the capital.

'Remitting fevers of several kinds, the measles and, O Heavens forbid,' she exclaimed, 'the Small-pox, the Chin Cough' (by which I guessed she meant the Hooping cough) could be entirely fatal'.

I wondered then what form of death might be "not entirely" fatal and curiosity on this point made me turn towards her – a stupidity which encouraged her to more loquacity but gave no explanation.

'Chin Cough,' she said 'is often entirely fatal to children but occurs also in ladies of a delicate constitution.'

She indicated that she was of a delicate constitution and thereby laid claim to a position at least in the middle class of society if not quite the aristocracy. Anyone of lower estate I surmised would refer to "sickness" or "poor health" which descriptions were equally poorly defined but carried also the idea of vulgarity with them.

Our valetudinarian companion did not stick to an alphabetical order in her classification of diseases from London, so there was no possibility of us guessing what might be the next scourge brought up on the south west wind and included in her list. The Common Cough preceded the Bubonic Plague, but not before she reminded an old man jammed in directly opposite her that even the Cough could and did carry off the elderly with tiresome frequency. Her warning was not however sufficiently frightening to stop the old man giving a trial cough which happily had no great length or coarseness and satisfied him that he was still some distance from appearing before his Maker, and would certainly have the satisfaction of seeing his lawyer son in London before the day was out.

Her repertoire continued with inflammation of the eyes, the brain and the skin but surprisingly skipped lightly, all things considered, over cholera and The King's Evil, which latter she might easily to have supposed to be a metropolitan complaint.

It may be that the Lady from Epping's hurrying on with

her catalogue and leaving out many other illnesses she might have included with as little justification, was because of an anxiety to mention before the journey ended some of the fashions coming out of London which carried maladies in their train. She made a particular condemnation of the practice of cold bathing. Indeed, whereas a lady with less enthusiasm for maladies might have avoided too many personal confessions, our travelling companion told us if we cared to listen, that she thought cold bathing to be dangerous in the extreme and that she herself avoided bathing of any kind, cold or hot, in case it stirred up diseases that otherwise would lie dormant and safely fade away.

Further fashions were decried, particularly where they touched upon morality; loose clothing that exposed more parts of the body than was decent could not be recommended for either man or woman:

'Covering up' she said, 'is one secret way to perfect health.'

The air inside the coach was by this time hot and thick. Some of us who had travelled furthest, felt that the air of London, however laden with noxious matter, was likely to be preferable to the atmosphere in the coach, in which malodorous breath, rank bodies and clothing almost combusting with the heat and sweat gave me at last a headache. All of us had parched and sore throats which ever afterwards I would think of as "Epping Illnesses".

Therefore, as we rattled through Bow I leaned forward to put my hand on and lower the window on my side, the woman (I could not think of her any longer as a lady) gave out as though she would swoon and put her hand on mine to stay it. We were carried along then suspended in a malignant atmosphere, a vile cocoon of humanity, trapped in a dark coach. Shortly beyond Bow we ran onto crude cobbled streets which made the wheels rattle and shook us like pebbles in an avalanche and took away our hearing with its noise. Mistress Epping's mouth was still moving but with what dread complaints she listed now I did not know, although I had the suspicion that I read on her lips the words "venereal" and "gonorrhea". We did not wait to hear. The coach had not properly stopped in Bishopsgate Street when we threw open the doors and ejected ourselves from the stinking prison.

No one handed Mistress Epping down, and if one of our hats was doffed it was only to fan the ruby face beneath it. I opened my mouth and took in a great breath of different air even if it should be already on its way north with every disease imaginable and I choked and held my nose tight against these new insults, many of them arising from the gutter running along the middle of the street and steaming and stagnant as far as the eye could see. Somewhat out of the shade of the inn, and posted just to catch the eye of demanding travellers, a young woman with a heavily pock-marked face was crying her "Posies, fresh posies". She offered one up to me – firstly smelling and rejecting another that I was led to believe was less satisfactory. The penny and half penny that I gave her was well spent; the posy passed the next two days until its scent declined, clasped beneath my grateful nostrils every time I went into the streets.

Thus at the very end of the journey, all my senses were engaged to take in all that London had to offer. For when the carriage door was open, not only were all the smells altered, but the sounds too. The volume I dare say was greater than that in any other city in the world. The sounds of Babel filled the streets with voices from north and south and east and west of our own temperate clime and from the hot lands of India and Africa. Hard Scottish tones mingled with softer English rustic voices and vowels while deep-throated Dutch and German voices were audible clearing their throats of verbs at the ends of sentences like dirty gobbets. Latin tongues romanced with words to make songs with them, while French men slid whole paragraphs down their nostrils and waved hands and arms and shoulders as if such gesticulations aided the passage of speech.

I stood for a while before The Coach and Horses Inn and then entered to secure a room for the night.

I charged the landlord with two letters written the night before: one was to my father in thanks for the money sent to my sister Barbara (now Mrs Porter) in Covent Garden; the second, to be delivered this same day was to this self-same sister to say that I should be arriving on the morrow (Sunday) and hoped that she had heard from our father.

The landlord was a surly man finding that his trade was all thrust upon him as coaches were awaited or emptied out on his doorstep. He had no choice of customer and only a few he ever saw again. The bowl of soup he served was good and the tart tolerable. But the beer was warm and tasted as though made up with thick brown mud. The serving maid was plain to the point of ugliness but when I spoke to her she brightened and revealed good teeth with her smile. Impatient though I was to be abroad on the town, I delayed a while and made a point of remarking about those features – and her eyes and hair. It was my wont, learned I think from my mother to lift the spirits of those who were downcast.

Indeed it is not difficult with pretty members of the other sex, but more rewarding with the plainer. And if they should think my manner flirtatious, they might keep it to themselves and warm their hearts with it privately.

So I was delaying, putting my patience to the test while taking stock of myself. Here was I come to London fresh from Cambridge. I was come to be an author. I had an idea for a play, and *The Synopsis Compendiara* was already at the press and had yielded a small advance – a very small advance – which sum purchased two pairs of stockings and a new wig.

As for my health, it was good; my appearance I judged to be just right for an intending author wishing to make an impact on the town, but not over confident. The gay waistcoat was always upon me and my breeches as well as my shoes were adorned with good silver buckles. For a while I was in the habit of leaving my wig off during the day and when at my writing desk, but powdered it up to go into company. I had a plan for further embellishment of my person as soon as my financial circumstances were improved, but now London was to provide for me the experiences and knowledge of the way of the world to illuminate both my life and my writing. It was said – and I quickly came to realise the truth of it – that London was in every way greater than any other city. The jostling crowds, the theatres (O, there I would spend some hours), the coffee houses and taverns and the gaiety and the intelligent conversations to be had within them were by repute all the best in the whole world. Churches in plenty, and preachers more famous than those in other towns took their place on a Sunday at least in instructing and even entertaining those persons with religious inclinations. London was and is a ferment of mental and creative activity for writers and poets, musicians and actors and all manner of men and some remarkable women.

Ah! The fairer sex. How I longed to know it better, to have intimacy and intrigue happening around me and to be able at last to taste those delights.

With such considerations and estimations of myself I soon rose from the cool of the inn and set off to walk from Charing Cross to Whitechapel and thus to see for myself what travellers said was the best series of shops to be found anywhere.

All was true and more surprising than I had bargained for. The shops were splendid – even the humble pickle shop made more display of its pots and bottles and bunches of onions than a whole town full of shops in other parts of the country such as Lincoln and Cambridge which I knew. Peruke makers, saddlers and shoemakers offered their wares next to tailors and milliners, and the spectator or customer wanting to be away from the jostle and to be in peace for a while had only to stretch his legs a few yards to find a coffee house or tavern to welcome him.

The streets bore all manner of people, of all characters. Very fine gentlemen in fine clothing stepped out of their sedans to enter their choice of tailor, perchance to exit after a time in even more finery – a new frock coat with lace dripping at the sleeves – or in fancy breeches or a new hat and gloves. Sometimes the fine gentlemen were accompanied by black servants in livery not much less fine than that of their masters.

Visitors (and I was most like marked for one of these) were noticeable and picked out from the crowds because they so often stood stock still and gazed and gaped at all that went on around them. I gaped at all the black faces – and noted that more than one in twenty of ordinary shoppers had a deep nut brown or ebony complexion. Some of these I had seen at Cambridge, but precious few and none at the university had faces darker than mine.

Comely women in the ordinary way of life were plentiful, and very occasionally one of the smart set came with her maid discreetly to enter a milliner's shop or an apothecary's establishment. Drawn by the beauty of one mistress and her maid, I followed them into an apothecary's at a decent distance and looked upon the shelves to find an excuse for being there. Madam flashed me a haughty look as she departed and the maid an even haughtier one – she clutching a pretty pot of white lead cream and a packet of powders too quietly demanded and served for me to be able to learn the contents. A frock-coated and slightly severe man approached to satisfy my requirements. I presumed from his manner and dress that he was a professional man, and it was another who had attended Madam and her maid. I had failed to find anything upon the shelves that I needed.

'You are come up from the country, Sir? For a few days?'

I was irritated by his assumption but decided to ignore

it and settle upon something quickly. My eye caught the label on a white porcelain barrel which stood with its fellows in a line, taps turned up on a shelf at waist height behind the counter. "Carminative and Restorative" was the legend. Every other label I could see carried a more serious looking title – liquids containing salts, sulphurs, antimony, mercury and frightful sounding decoctions of liquors. Our Cambridge apothecaries never carried so wide a range of curatives; they filled their shelves with syrups and herbs – the latter often hanging from the rafters to be made up on the spot. This London Apothecary waited while I peered anxiously at other shelves. Here the writing was small to fit small boxes containing pills. I had some experiences which told me that small writing on small boxes meant high prices for the contents. Even without considerations of economy however, I had no knowledge what any pill might be advised for. The Apothecary was ready to help me, to run through a whole shop full of illnesses and their treatments, but partly because of the tiresome lady from Epping I was in no mood for more medical matters, and furthermore I was beginning to feel foolish. No one ventured across the threshold to take the Apothecary's mind off me, and I wondered for a moment whether he had locked the door so that I should not leave until I had bought all his stock. He then saw the first flickers of panic on my face and decided to put me into further misery and then out of it again.

'Will you have the excellent Carminative and Restorative, Sir? Is it not a marvellous feat of the apothecary's art to relieve you of undesirable wind and at the same time if you are exhausted by the efforts, restore you to full health? I should suggest if you are not staying long in London that I should let you have a large bottle for you will not obtain the same medicine elsewhere.'

I had no wind but that which I could already dispel unaided at either end. As for a restorative that was the other last thing I needed. Since arriving this morning, once released from the odorous prison-with- wheels, I had urges of a powerful sort distracting me from the consideration of anything but images of beautiful, exciting womankind. Racy was my condition, racy was my state and needing no correction.

Mr Apothecary had witnessed and indeed taken part before in scenes such as he and I were enacting. Fearing the arrival of other custom before he had clinched a sale with me, he repeated his suggestion of a large bottle of the Carminative and Restorative.

'Sir! Three shillings is the pitiful sum required.'

'No!' I said made brave by the cost, 'Give me a small bottle as I have no need for the restorative part of your medicine.'

'Very well, Sir. That will be one and sixpence if you please. A bargain for a gentleman, Sir' and he continued while he was corking my wind reliever, 'Will you be "going on the town" tonight as they say?'

'Why yes, of course.' I said, thinking he was to recommend me to a play or rout in town.

'Then certainly,' he said, 'a fine, lusty and clever gentleman as you will need something for your comfort and protection, I have no doubt.'

He lifted a length of intestine, dripping in oil, and which was closed with neat stitching at one end and as pink as the day the pig was relieved of it.

'One and sixpence,' he said, and he wrapped it immediately in a waxed paper and winked and holding a finger to his lips stretched across the counter and slipped it into my jacket pocket and gave it a tap to see that it was safely deposited.

'One and sixpence,' he said, and would have no doubt demonstrated the strength and softness of another he had beneath the counter, but tacitly I acknowledged him the victor in our commerce, paid him the three shillings due and quickly left.

I saw again Lady Haughty and Miss Only-Slightly-

Less Haughty disappearing into a milliner's shop but sought not to satisfy my curiosity further as I saw no chance of striking up a flirtation, and the expenses accrued already made me cautious. I resolved to fill my eyes but put no further weight of shopkeepers' offerings into my pockets – nor lighten my purse. At no cost now but eventually to the cost of replacing boot leather, I walked up the Whitechapel Road and down to Goodman's Fields and up again to Leadenhall. It seemed that even the meanest back street had its gin palaces where men and women were aiming to lift their minds out of the despairing ruts of life. Drunkards were everywhere.

"Some . . . were red-hot with drinking;

So full of valour, that they smote the air

For breathing in their faces."

And children, even babes at breast sprawled in alleys while their mothers, if they had such opportunity, sold some unlucky man the transient favour of their bodies. I could not help but feeling a rag bag of sentiment in me – for an instant roused by copulation blatant in a doorway, then for longer time saddened by the spectacle. This act given to men and women of all conditions is sullied by a loveless conjugation. Hapless youth flourishing with ideals! I took it on promise and expectation that intimate connections between the sexes were always intended a glory and delight. Therefore if such pleasures were bestowed only on the virtuous, and only in marriage, what a power of good would be wrought for the whole nation. The streets that I trod now would be empty of sin and carnal lust, and the gin itself would remove the last drunkards of this generation rotting to death inside their own improperly pickled bodies.

Such sadness and serious philosophising could not hold their own in my mind in the reality of nasty, colourful, curious, exciting London. The more things I saw that I had never witnessed before, the more elated I became:

sensations tingled in me, my soul bounded and I walked as though entranced; along Cheapside and past St Paul's, Fleet Street and Temple Bar and down the Strand and Whitehall. I imagined taking lodgings, no – a house – in these respectable western parts of the great city so for the devil of it and to tease my fancies I enquired of a gentleman entering a house advertising rooms, what the cost might be of renting such. His answer detailed sizes and numbers of rooms put against a tariff for the street, but in his area and to his certain knowledge all the way up to Oxford Street and beyond, if the accommodation was well made – £20 a year or more was needed. He offered to direct me to "an establishment that would suit." I declined the offer with thanks and bidding him good-day recommenced my walk by making a large circle back to The Coach & Horses at Bishopsgate Street where the Landlord's wife, doing duty for the serving girl, brought me a bowl of soup again.

She looked likely to fall into a terminal decline of spirits when I rejected the soup and asked for some good beef in its place. Through her good offices, a while later the Landlord presented himself at my table. He leaned over the table to put his face nearer to mine and to gain the confidential cover afforded by the wooden panels to the back and sides of my seat. Quietly and with lips nearly closed he said: 'Do not Sir, I pray you, let others see this,' and he placed before me a plate of cold ham with two crusts of bread by it. 'If others see I am serving food at this end of the day I shall be here 'til breakfast satisfying the hunger of a half of London. I shall bring you ale.'

I did not wish for another mug of muddy ale but understood that I might lose the ham if I declined the beer.

In the morning I rejoiced to settle my dues and leave the inn and its unhappy keeper. I was content also that it was a Sunday for yesterday had proved unsettling to me in one particular way – that is with regard to my lust which I felt would be more readily quietened by holy thoughts and sombre imprecations from a pulpit. Concentrating my heated mind on the gospels while torturing my body on a hard pew – instead of my mind and body with imagined connections – surely that would remove temptations from my mind. For the evening before had presented me with fanciful desires in every elegant square and park where ladies with varying provocations made it clear that I could enjoy them for a shilling. I had touched the armour in my pocket but hurried on as though only business of the most important nature kept me from their charms. In attempted distraction I tried to remember and recite passages from Virgil and then, unwisely. Ovid and Juvenal who, with more poetic beauty than I could summon up, put their carnal thoughts in verse. Had I hoped that these efforts of memory would cool my fever, they were as sorely misbegotten as would be the waving of a flaming torch when attempting to put out a fire.

I was certain Sunday's blessed day would drain passion from me as surely as to bathe in icy water. Therefore I took myself off to St Paul's, a building as grand as my intentions. There a preacher of infinite tediousness took his invaluable time to render soporific, if not quite dead-asleep, a congregation of not even a dozen people. They were seated about the great church like blades of grass in a desert. However, the clergyman had some effect on me, at least enabling me to extend my needed devotions on my knees for another hour after the service was over.

Afterwards I walked again at a great pace to the house in Long Acre, Covent Garden where my sister Barbara and her husband Mr Porter I hope expected me.

Our Mother's scheme to have a good marriage arranged for Barbara had, I suppose it must be admitted, turned out not too badly. Not too badly that is even if the husband of means that Barbara obtained gained those means in a fairly humble line of trade. Porter met that requirement a seller of furniture which was frequently fine and always expensive. (Mr Porter never seemed to have any other name than Porter, either I supposed because of a failure at the baptismal font – which is unlikely – or because his parents one presumes unwittingly, had bestowed upon the baby Porter a Christian name of such abhorrent sound and reference that even they shunned the use of it.) However, he was a good prospect for my sister Barbara on account of his shrewdness and his ability to select furniture that was *a la mode*. Sir William Chambers, Mr Chippendale and Mr Sheraton were "names" in furniture and furnishings that Porter latched upon. He advised their sale when now and then a notable household fell upon hard times – often through gambling debts or the misfortunes of trade – and he was first at the side door. Here he would talk with the most confidential and trusted servants who were anxious to learn of any scheme likely to relieve their distress and the expected dismissal from the house. He persuaded these loyal servants of the erstwhile rich that they could trust Porter and persuade their masters or mistresses to call him – Porter – in for a valuation. He gave an absolute guarantee that he would give the highest value for any furniture, furnishings or paintings or property of any kind that would enable the now impoverished owners to realise profits from their earlier wise purchases. Porter also was emphatic to the vendors that neither their neighbours nor friends would be aware of the transactions taking place. All would be done discreetly and at a time of day when the neighbourhood was empty. The loyal servants who acted as ambassadors (as Porter liked to say) for the vendors, received a "consideration" the moment the last item was lifted on to his cart.

There was a touch of dishonesty in the business because to aid a good sale in selling old furniture to a new customer he was certain (assuredly in a discreet fashion) to advise of the history of the piece and of the pedigree of its former owner. Barbara, if she thought that any of
Mr Porter's actions were not Christian, turned a deaf ear to mention of it. Mr Porter provided a good income and

seldom sailed out on pleasure without Barbara by his side, making certain that those pleasures were as innocent as the theatre or opera house could provide. For this he was forgiven mumbling speech and a habit of spitting on his hands and wiping them on his frock coat, which he did before lifting a valuable piece of furniture, or sealing a deal with bailiff or duke. His wife, however, found it hard to ignore the repetition of his action before putting his hands together before grace, lifting his knife and fork to attack the leg of mutton on Sunday and, worse by far, before putting his arms around her to embrace her with the intention of satisfying his amorous inclinations.

Good people the Porters were. However, Barbara affected now a simplicity quite beneath her talents as condescension to her less gifted husband. He in turn indulged her fancy for the theatre when it was possible, as had our mother at the same age. And now they had both been at great pains to give me a room in the attic with all that I required – a desk table to write on, a shelf for books – a bed – a real bed with box mattress within four stout posts and ornate canopy and curtains. This monument to Lethe was made in fine mahogany. It took Porter and his lad the whole of one day to carry the pieces up the twisting stairs and to cut the post and canopy on one side to fit under the eaves.

I was full of praise to Porter for his kindness and he spat on his hands for an occupation while he received my eulogy. Barbara assured me:

'Dear Brother. While you are with us you shall have every comfort we can supply. And if Porter allows me, I shall be a mother to you.'

I could want for no greater sisterly affection and vowed to be the best lodger the Porters could have and I meant to keep this promise before others. It was easy at the time because I could not think of any action of mine that would cause inconvenience or render unhappy such excellent people.

The next day I began with a discipline of much greater difficulty, but rarely departed from it. I rose early before the cockerels, and wrote continuously until breaking my fast in mid-morning. The afternoons were for visits to book dealers, publishers or theatre managers. The evenings and, too often alas, the nights following – were dedicated to pleasure – to fit me to be a connoisseur of dissipation and everything that London had to offer at the lower end of society. I say the lower end, because unless there was to be a speedy reversal of my financial fortunes, the upper reaches of society would remain beyond me.

However, my spirits were ever raised on crests of optimism.

CHAPTER 11

LITERARY ACHIEVEMENTS

Including The Beauties of Shakespear

Through the second half of that first year in London, I was more industrious and careful than I had promised to be, hardly stirring from my attic until the early evening. Then I did frequently share in tea with Porter and my sister before hastening to the theatre. I hoped that by acquaintance with plays already successful, my own intentions towards the dramatic form would be better shaped.

Garrick was a marvellous man. I saw him three times performing as Benedict in *Much Ado About Nothing*, acting with fresh "business" at every performance. I noticed how his railing and jests against matrimony were received with uncommon applause, even though or perhaps because it was known that Garrick himself had just left the ranks of bachelors and entered the lists of marriage. He soliloquised so gravely and yet put a comic inflexion to every phrase – his: "If I don't pity her I am a villain" brought laughter from noble dames in the boxes. It was as though he did not merely recite lines and exhibit himself on the stage – he created the part. So deceptive and skilful was his art I decided that a play need not be so very good if the actors were greater than the parts they played. I put pen to paper and wrote a review of "Much Ado'", bending my quills under the pressure of exclamation marks and apostrophes. I took the liberty to make this review an excuse to meet Garrick. I did so and he was most kind and listened to my plans to achieve fame with the pen and encouraged me by listening keenly to my scheme for a compilation of what I called *The Beauties of Shakespear*

118

– nearly completed when I left Cambridge. Mr Garrick, with great civility, thanked me for my kindness and promised to send my review off to the newspapers. He was, I think, flattered and amused.

The theatre yielded another happy advantage for me. It is strange that great London Town with its teeming thousands, offers up again and again the same expected faces. It is as though the important people are much about in society, and there are so few of them that they become even more noted. The larger number of people even if they turn up in the same places day after day, are unnoticed and unimportant and to be less outstanding than the bricks of the houses.

It was therefore no surprise to meet old friends Gascoigne and Bulkley in a coffee shop near Drury Lane. We exchanged loud and sincere greetings and gave account of our doings over the last year. Gascoigne, he admitted himself, was severe and serious now on joining the ranks of learned and quiet legal men; he stood stiffly, and when he spoke that was also stiffly putting one word before the other with the care of a dancer stepping on ice. Bulkley, once quiet before the superior intellect of Gascoigne, was an ebullient figure now with all the confidence of the banker that he claimed to be. He knew that money and, therefore, power was at his command. A younger brother, he said, had taken over his father's estates in Hertfordshire while he, Bulkley the senior brother, had been acquiring an education in Cambridge. Now Bulkley had through family links joined the Banking Firm of Coulthard & Coulthard and risen quickly to a comfortable position that might be the start of great things.
Bulkley had "connections", which it appeared, were more necessary than wits and in his case brought him into contact with people of importance and their underlings throughout society.

I had no Greek or Latin texts to review and to improve for my friends – nor had either thought of their Classical

Studies since leaving Cambridge – so the conversation lagged. We summoned the proprietor's daughter to replenish our coffee pot. Then we picked our way through a desultory conversation on music. Both my friends were happy to concur with me on my opinion of Vivaldi, Bach and Handel, but only on the assurance that these composers did in fact write minuets. They argued that the genteel deportment gained from dancing to the minuet improved posture and so the whole behaviour of a man.

I illustrated our discussions with short quotations from the Bible
". . . *singing and dancing with tabors and with other instruments of music. . .*" and "*Thou hast turned for me my mourning into dancing*". This latter I offered in a jocund way to show how pleased I was to see Bulkley and Gascoigne, but they allowed only a little smile and called for another pot of coffee.

I tested them on the Theatre and found that they had little affection for Shakespear or any serious dramatist, but were passing fond of a lower kind of play. This information yielded another fact for me. I asked: 'Where might I see in London the sensuous, and the seedy – purely,' I added, 'to add colour to my writing.' I had to explain something of my endeavours and how, to relieve my hours with serious works, did intend sometimes to employ my pen with lighter novels and plays. Gascoigne and Bulkley were most impressed at my "descent to a more tolerable sort of literature" and wished to help me by referring me to people or places where I should be able to witness the practices of vice and lewd behaviour. Gascoigne called for ink and quill and wrote into my pocket book:
Madam Thomson
Lester House, Covent Garden.
Please accommodate my good friend Mr. William Dodd and make his stay in the Town entertaining.
Yours etc. etc.
Marsden

'Why signed thus with a false name?' I asked.

'Not false,' said Bulkley who had read and nodded his head while Gascoigne wrote. "Marsden is the man who knows every gentleman in town, and acts as agent for all of them. He has told me many times before to use his name thus to make introductions. There is not a Buck in London in want of entertaining – to whatever particular taste – but Marsden can make the connection.'

They both laughed at Bulkley's use of the word "connection" and made signs with their hands to show what sorts of connection was meant.

'We,' said Gascoigne, laughing in the same careful manner in which he spoke, 'do not know the ins and outs of London vice, but assuredly Marsden does. He makes a business of it. Should you require young boys to entertain you, Marsden can procure them . . .'

Gascoigne jolted to a full stop. He had seen my eyes smoking with disgust, so he began again with:

'Entertainment of a different character employs the wiles and sultry concupiscence of our ebony sisters. I gather that Giles Marsden has the knowledge of at least two black brothels which it is said, however, have entirely white skinned customers.'

'So, if black be a colour, and that to your taste, you shall know where to find "the experience" you call it, to add "colour" to your wordy creations.'

Bulkley congratulated himself with a smile at the cleverness of his pun, and I thought this a suitable time to hasten away and make use of the information given to me. We promised to meet again shortly at the theatre.

I had not yet done a proper job instructing myself on the need for experiences to help me to write lighter literary works and to put the touch of veracity in them. Therefore I presented myself at Lester House – which was not as imposing a residence as suggested by the name and introduced myself – without being overcome with embarrassment, as a person who was more of an academic than a rake. Madam Thomson appeared to permit herself the liberty of believing me, which allowed her immediately to relieve me of ten pounds which was four pounds short of all I had on my person.

I was shown into a drawing room that was sparsely furnished but heavily decorated in the French style. The curtains in deep maroon had golden tassels in abundance. An enormous Turkey carpet covered the boards almost to the wainscot. A black marble fireplace gave out a good heat and more brightness than the few fat candles in their sconces.

If there are to be places especially decorated for luscious or loose behaviour, it is as well that the French style is adopted. A sin is that much more readily excused – by the sinner at least – if it can imply and blame a foreign influence that perverts morality. I let my mind digress for a while with these thoughts because I was already becoming aroused by what I saw. Two bucks dressed fashionably and expensively – in the English style – stood at either side of the fireplace. Madam Thomson introduced me briefly to them and easily obtained their permission for me to join in their sport. For "Sport" indeed it was for them, and they had little regard for me, merely waving me to a seat outside the circle of firelight. A young woman whom they called Kitty was standing in front of the fire with her back to it. She was more than passing pretty, with no blemishes on her skin, and curves of flesh both supple and enticing. The slight spoiling of her features I noticed was occasioned by the frown of anxiety

— even fear – showing on her face. She wore white stockings tied with pink ribbons. Apart from these and what might have been a tablecloth to hold in front of her, she was naked. The bucks told her to pose in certain ways, and to turn and pose again keeping the cloth well above her breasts. They called out and clapped a little mockingly if they considered she had not struck the pose that entirely exposed the more intimate parts of her body. They put their hands out, touching and patting her lasciviously.

I was already ashamed and would have made a quiet exit had I not been held in my seat, a spellbound but unwilling voyeur at a spectacle which was, I realised, only just beginning. I could not in any event move until the passion evident in my breeches had subsided. That became an even more unlikely event since the rakes had now ordered the girl to dance first slowly on her own and then rapidly twisting until she tired: at which point they opened their breeches and one in front of her and the other behind presented their members closely and intimately to her. She wriggled and whimpered, which made both these animals grunt and jerk before they separated and leaned back breeches closed again, against the fireplace. One of them took a poker and put it deep into the coals to withdraw it white hot a minute later. They took turns then to hold it close to her breasts and nether parts with the promise given to her of more dangerous intentions if she did not dance again. Kitty did her best and still hugged the cloth around her as well as she could.

I accused myself of cowardice but still made no intervention on her behalf . . . until . . . even now I am revolted . . . one buck bent Kitty forward while holding the poker within an inch of her bottom and demanded her to give satisfaction with her mouth to his companion first and then him second or he would insert the poker into her fundament. The second buck had opened his breeches again and I jumped out of the shadows and struck the poker from the first one's hand and hurled it through the window glass.

'Go. Run. Flee,' I said to Kitty 'and tell your mistress what has happened and that she must make amends by sending these creatures away or I will fetch the Constable. Now. Go!'

Kitty fled in her tablecloth and the bucks giving me sneers and threatening me with their fists, left the room. They stamped down the hall, banged the door shut after them and within seconds one of them hurled the poker back through another window and they departed loudly hailing chairs up from the Strand. I had no words for Madam Thomson and hers were few enough: 'I do not know what. Gentlemen have never behaved like that before. Goodnight Sir, and thank you for rescuing my maid. Oh, my windows!'

I left but was not pleased that Lester House was so close to the Porter's shop. Mrs Thomson (or the maid) may recognise me in the street, or the Porters may have heard the commotion or would soon hear rumours of it. I wanted to walk for I was still in a state of high excitement not lessened by my recalling Kitty's perfect skin and the soft curves of her limbs and breasts. I had not seen the female body in all its beauty since I saw my sisters bathing as a youth.

I was full of lust.

It had been better if I had returned immediately to my attic, for my walk took me to the parks further west; to be particular, directly and without being aware of it to St James's Square, where even though night was settling in, the figures of harlots were easily picked out. Although my loins ached I still made no move towards them. But I was beyond reasoning with myself and when a girl of seventeen years at most detached herself from the deeper shadows and came towards me I held out my arms for her, unbuttoned, put on armour in a few moments and took her suddenly silently and with such passion that I shuddered as I entered and withdrew. She cried out 'Oh Sir', and leant her head against my chest.

When I put a hand up to her face to lift it to kiss, my hand was wet with her tears. I kissed her again and thanked her.

'Why are you here?' I asked. 'What is your name?'

'Sir, you need to know nothing of that.' And then she

124

blurted out her story. 'It is my fault. I loved a lad in Norwich and would have married him but he was by my parents' say beneath me. I came to London, had my child who died stillborn and the lad I loved died too. I cannot get work. I cannot get the money to return to my family where I hope to be forgiven and start life anew. Oh Sir, give me something to help me pay for the journey home.'

The dark had closed in too far for me to be able to see her face or to tell by her eyes what she said with her lips was true, for the story came too glibly off her tongue to be the first telling.

'What is your name?' 'Mary . . . and yours, Sir?'

I could think of nothing to say to fill the silence now as she sobbed. I gave her my name and reached into my pocket for all the coin I had – not so much for her comfort, but rather to pay for my guilt which already creased my brow and made me long to be alone. Four sovereigns I gave her. I closed the coins into her hand and left. Dimly, as I walked away, I saw Mary leaving the park as well. I prayed that what she told me was not an invention and that my payment would settle her into a better future. But I had no hope that I was any better than a guilt-ridden, shameful and sentimental fool.

The Red Lion off Drury Lane was host to players and their nightly audiences – the players to receive plaudits where due and to solicit praises where appreciation of their talents was slow to mature, while audiences hoped to gain for themselves a touch of immortality by conversing with great actors and actresses, and noting the fashions and topics of conversation and gossip that gripped the town that day.

Into the haze of candle smoke and wig powder and ale-house fumes, Gascoigne and Bulkley appeared like guests late to a wedding. I had just thrown a phrase "unbeatable pair" – into a knot of chattering play goers –

'That's us!' said Bulkley elbowing him and Gascoigne

into the circle. 'Possibly, possibly,' I said, 'but Mrs
Pritchard and Mr Garrick were
the persons I referred to.'

We moved away from the people around us whose
excited talk had ebbed on the entrance of Gascoigne and
Bulkley. It was as though their presence blocked all other
exchanges, and useful though they were as friends of mine,
it was no advantage to introduce them widely into other
company. We stepped out of The Red Lion to stand in the
brighter light of stars and moon, and carriage-lights.
Liveried men descended from the theatre gallery to light
torches for their masters, and in their flickering
illumination women stood against the theatre wall,
advertisements for themselves.

From the theatre, more lovely and proud than any of
those, stepped a woman of such wholesome prettiness that
it seemed impossible that she had any relationship to the
ugly bear of a man on whose arm hers was laid.

'Gascoigne, Bulkley, who is that?'

'Why, that is Giles Marsden – your introduction to
some fleshpot colouring,' Gascoigne said.

'Then such a man – of such Esau-like hairiness and
Stygian evil – has a Goddess on his arm?'

'I can account for both circumstances,' said Bulkley.
'Sandwich, The Earl of Sandwich,' and he paused for
effect, 'John Montague, Fourth Earl of the same.'
It appeared likely that Bulkley was bringing to his lips the
whole genealogy of the Sandwiches and to avail me of the
same history whether I cared or not – and I did not. At this
moment all I wished to know was on the subject of Miss
Pretty, the Goddess. Gascoigne took over.

'Do not fret. I will tell you. The lady over whom you
are about to swoon was lately the mistress of The Earl.'

'Why was? Why lately? So fine a creature cannot
willingly have fallen now into the hands – or worse the
arms – or worse still the bed – of this hairy ape.'

'Gently Dodd and keep your voice a little lower and

cover your mouth with a hand, your Goddess has already seen you stare. She shall mark you down as a person of the utmost rudeness if you continue in this manner.'

I did as Gascoigne bid me, though the necessity had passed, as the Goddess had stepped into the carriage Marsden had called for them. Her gaze met my stare as they moved away.

We re-entered The Red Lion which now had nearly emptied apart from a few hardened customers who attempted nightly, play or not, to drink the ale house dry. We sat at a distance from them and I beseeched my friends to tell me everything they knew. Mary Perkins was the lady's name. That name made me wonder if this Goddess could be the same Mary who had received my embraces so recently on a night in St. James. I begged to be told more of her.

'There is not much we can tell,' said Bulkley. 'She comes from Durham and her father there is Verger at the Cathedral. Before promotion to that office he was servant to Sir John Dolben, a prebendary there.'

'Not from Norwich, then?'

'Why should you ask?'

'Ah, no reason.'

Neither Gascoigne nor Bulkley seemed inclined to pursue their question and I was disinclined to answer closely.

'Continue please and tell me more about this Goddess,' I begged them.

'All else is rumour.'

Gascoigne and Bulkley then took it in turns to retell what rumours there were.

'Sandwich,' Bulkley said, 'as a habit chooses a very young mistress, seldom more than fourteen years of age when first admitted into his household.

'It was "known" from one of Sandwich's London grooms, who met on occasion with Bulkley's groom at the alehouse nearest to the farrier they used, that the Earl had his mistresses weighed regularly. The groom himself performed this task on the stable yard scales. Should the mistress tip the scales at eight stones or over, she was no longer fit to be the Earl's jockey in his amatory sport. For he, lying supine, which he preferred to be while she rode him, could not bear a greater weight.'

'Thus,' said Gascoigne who had clearly heard Bulkley's account before, 'and when the lady over whom you seem to drool tipped the scales at one ounce over eight stones, she had to go, and it was no use her to complain that it was the Earl himself who fed her to be as she thinks, as round as a capon.'

Bulkley took back the narrative:

'Sandwich is never mean, however, and has set her up despite her being only seventeen years old with a house in Frith Street – and an allowance. What is more, in addition to the settlement, the Earl of Sandwich has charged Marsden with her care, and instructed him to introduce her to suitable company.'

Gascoigne continued:

'What the Earl considers is "suitable company" for Miss Mary Perkins is not clear, yet the general opinion maintains that Sandwich is not aware of Marsden's thriving business as whoremaster and pimp.

'There is also a ready flow of money to Marsden from those satisfied with the introductions he makes. Sometimes he is given a purse, but more often a trinket or a work of art well above the value of the transaction in question. On another occasion advice at a gaming table, given covertly and over the shoulder of his opponents, puts him in the way of undeserved richness at the distress of the loser who will never himself have nor wish for benefits from the whoremaster's business.'

Immediately, I was troubled that a woman of such attraction should appear therefore to be in the gift of Marsden. I wondered if this Mary Perkins now had something of the aristocrat transmitted to her by virtue of the connection with this John Montague, the Fourth Earl of

Sandwich. Whether or not this was the case I felt powerfully drawn to Miss Perkins, and sought a further meeting.

'You surely do not look covetously on a woman rejected – a woman once another man's mistress?'

Gascoigne spoke censoriously and I surmised he might soon begin to lard his conversation with dredged up lawyer's Latin.

'I took you for a man far above lust and base carnal desires. I remember that when we had you accompanying us to Newmarket, you left us to bring delight to the attendant harlots, while you spoke with the landlord at our inn and recited epigrams and aphorisms for him – from which he may not yet have recovered. Your virtue was unassailable then.'

I did not feel insulted, but I recollected that my virtue at that time was merely the necessity of poverty. But I let the matter pass.

'I need and I am impatient for further acquaintance with the lady,' I said.

'*Necessitas non habet legem,*' said Gascoigne translating it for the benefit of Bulkley into "necessity has no law". He continued:

'I – we – will help you if we can.'

So it was agreed that on this night two weeks ahead Gascoigne and Bulkley would arrange for Miss Perkins to be at Vauxhall Gardens. The presence of the hairy bear Marsden was considered to be inevitable – and possibly even desirable to give protection to the young, the delicate, the overpoweringly beautiful – and although I had not yet any evidence towards that opinion – the very gifted and intelligent Miss Perkins. All these thoughts I held inwardly to warm my heart.

I did almost, and almost religiously abide by my vows to avoid indulgence, but, (how often "but" and "if" mar the paths of virtue) but I yearned all the more for the company of the tender sex because I was denied further sight of Miss Perkins for a whole two weeks. "If" came to my rescue and to my fall. I devised a scheme my father would gladly have owned for himself. In it he paid tribute to the moral philosophy of Locke and to the intellect of Descartes. Yet my father's own principles were of greater practical worth than those; and he had advised me of a method to divert the passions from the body to the mind. Hence it was that: if love was making an unsuitable conquest of my heart, I should write poetry to dissipate the sensation. If lust was fuelled by the enticing body of a sinner, remember that her mind was ugly and awaited re- direction. I should then seek to change that object of my attentions to bring her to a truer path of virtue.

The scheme was easily designed and, alas, clever enough to deceive me of my own body's intentions. I would aid and convert a harlot to make her a new being. Thus she would be put upon a high pedestal. She would relinquish the profits of the flesh, and have nothing but disdain for any man who wished to sully her. The task I thought was easily to be executed, for any dishonourable intentions were abated by my mind's
pre-occupation: and call her what I would, a harlot, whore, or strumpet – she remained a woman – tender and fragile – always to be desired and likely a woman in need. My wealth was insufficient to be of much aid even to a single victim. But if I gave a little money and a greater worth of persuasion, and that moved her towards a finer morality, would I not be virtuous? Would not that virtue in its necessary actions be of greater good in the eyes of God than my miserable abstinence? Nor did I suppose physical indulgence would be a natural consequence of elevating advice and conversation with a whore.

With this fine plan before me I set out for The Angel in Islington. The name was not only attractive to me because of its suggestion of saintliness, it was also as I knew a lure to impudent doxies who might offer themselves as exemplars of the heavenly creature whose portrait and name adorned the inn sign. I was not in the least deterred by the frightening stories of young women who plied their trade in two's; often, it was related, as one engaged her customer in the most occupying rites of passage, the other made the pretext of giving close attention and intimate caresses: 'You find that touching there gives pleasure?' and, 'That saucy business has not come your way before, I'll warrant.' Meanwhile pockets are emptied, purses removed, rings and belts hustled under the skirts of the second sorceress. She gives time for her companion to retire to adjust her clothing with some such ploy as 'My, Oh my, Sir! You are a mighty lover. I will take some time to recover from this and you too, you should rest awhile.' Then with that, the pair retire, at speed, and take the gentleman's breeches to make pursuit less likely.

I, however, was forewarned by these stories and had a ruse to remove all risk from the venture.

On entering the inn and without much difficulty selecting a likely pair of Angels, I showed them privately beneath the trestle table my purse fixed fast in my breeches. I showed them the gold in it – four guineas – and loose change of a few pence in my jacket pockets. They listened to my scheme carefully, which was to come back with me to my room at Porter's in Covent Garden and they should have all the money on my person. (A small amount was also hidden in my chamber – but no moveable valuables there were likely to attract their attention.) My two Angels listened to my proposal, and when I said, 'I wish to talk with you only, to understand your plight and to help you' they exchanged glances but masked their disbelief with admirable restraint.

We walked on only the most busy and open streets – I with an Angel on either arm – and we timed the journey to arrive at Porter's shop when the shutters were up and dark had long fallen. Barbara had on many mornings frowned deeply at breakfast and asked me in the tones of a patient teacher if I would be more gentle in my progress up the stairs to my attic chamber when I came home "unnecessarily" late. She said that I was less careful on my feet than a shire horse and woke the whole household – that is to say she and Porter and their lad on a pallet on the shop floor, (although this boy John was worked so hard by Porter, it was no fear his slumbers would be disturbed unless trodden on twice or more). We therefore carefully negotiated furniture and the sleeping boy. The women removed their shoes to make our treading on the creaking stairs less like a party of woodsmen at work and gained my room. I had every intention to deliver a gentle remonstrance rather than a sermon to the harlots attending me, and asked them questions – first to see how best to pitch my words. The one was nineteen and her companion fifteen, but when I plied them with more and more questions and began to sermonise them they became restive.

'We have a living to earn,' said one.

'We cannot tarry here because even the watch won't light us out to Islington,' said the other.

So I put them at their ease, I hoped, by offering to engage a hackney when they left my apartment. This would not do for long, and I think they were of low intelligence, not able to be still for more than a few seconds.

To receive a sermon or even a mild chiding was beyond their compass, nor did they believe that I would offer up money for their conversation only, so the older began to draw up her skirts about her waist which made me forget the moral and almost priestly function I had started out upon. Then, strong woman that she was, she began to push

me back on the bed – where we had been forced to sit because of the dearth of chairs. She rolled me over and deftly removing my belt, twitched my breeches down to expose the globes of my buttocks and began to whip me.

'This is what you wanted, wasn't it, Sir? Ordinary

congress is not good or bad enough for you is it, Sir?'

More lashes descended and I did mind and it was not what I wanted although I cannot deny the experience offered a certain amount of excitement to my member – but the noise I feared would alarm the house. The other Angel, in the meantime, struggling at my ankles had failed to remove my breeches entirely and therefore helped the older to turn me on my back to look at the canopy, who then occupied my aroused machine with her own less obvious parts – but not before with a caution bred entirely of fear of the pox – I had retrieved my armour from my jacket pocket. The younger woman meanwhile completed her task with my breeches. Subsequent actions were as loud as the earlier ones.

Very shortly – for these ladies were efficient in their business and, assuming that I had received the service I required but had been too bashful to demand – they declared themselves ready to depart. Indeed they were at the door announcing this before I had found my feet. They rattled the door knob and nearly wrenched it from the oak before they realised the door was locked and that I had the key.

Not subdued by what had happened and amused and laughing out loud at their discomfort, I bargained the key and the promise not to call the watch, in exchange for my breeches and the purse, which all were secreted in various ways under their skirts.

Later I was full of remorse for my actions on this evening. I had failed to transmit even one moral precept to the doxies and furthermore I did not aid them in any thoughts of conversion to a good life. But at least I had given them nothing but the few pence loose in my pocket. That night my prayers were fervent that God would grant me forgiveness and a chance to prove myself worthy of the talents he had given me and spare me from the powerful goads of lust: that His commands would be always my joy and not the painful bonds which I deserved.

Not all my contrition had worn off by breakfast, but it had not the force of the night time penitence until I sat down to the breakfast table. Here Barbara and her husband sat uncomfortably as though they had awkward matters on their minds rather than that the seats themselves were discommoding them.

Barbara spoke first while Porter, as he did at every interval, spat on his hands. She frowned more than she had on earlier occasions when displeased by my actions, and sought to set the moral tone of our conversation by opening with a text "*Who loveth wisdom rejoiceth his Father; but he that keepeth company with harlots spendeth his substance*". My sister spoke in the grave tones, even with the inflections used by my father in his sermons. She paused to pass me bread across the table before continuing:

'It is your lack of wisdom that hurts me most. And it is that which our mother and father would find most surprising and regretful; that such a clever boy (Yes, "boy" she called me) would not consider the upset in our household.'

'You had a whore in your chamber,' said Porter who wished to get quickly to any interesting narratives I might reveal. Barbara kicked his chair as if by accident and said:

'It is the noise you make returning and have made every night you stay late upon the town. You are home long after the candles are out.'

'And you bring a whore into the house . . .'

'You strike the furniture and even broke the leg of Lady Porchester's escritoire which albeit is foolishly placed.' She glanced at Porter to see if her reprimand to him had found its mark, or if a further kick to his chair was needed.

'If you paid for the whore you should pay for the escritoire.'

'No,' said Barbara, 'We won't treat our brother harshly, but it is inevitable that he must find other lodgings.'

'I am cat-like in my entries of a night. Granted I may

stumble in the shop and the stairs do creak . . .'

'Stairs creak?' said Porter, mistiming his expectoration and distracting Barbara while she wiped specks of spittle off the oak table. 'Stairs creak? What then of your bed crashing with the weight of two people?'

'Another thing,' said Barbara. 'There is to be another Porter in the house. I am with child.'

Porter, I presumed, knew of this coming event, for he ignored utterly what was news to me and continued, 'Your bed is right above ours; every creak and all the crashes are transmitted directly into the posts of the matrimonial bed . . .'

'Yes,' Barbara wished to talk about less intimate matters – 'Porter needs his sleep. For he is a man who rises early and works hard . . .'

'And so do I.'

'No, but Porter works all day lifting and heaving and carrying. His whole day is filled with action.'

'And your nights, William Dodd, are filled with action. If I am not mistaken, there was whipping going on last night.'

'Let us not discuss that, husband, even if it be true. In short we need William's room. If I am to have a maid, we shall need the attic for her.' 'Perhaps the maid is already there for the noises from William's bed
seemed to be multiplied and continued well into the small hours. Were there two women in your room?'

'William, you do not have to leave straight away – but say one month from now . . .'

'I swear I heard whipping last night. How do you explain that, Master Dodd?'

'No, not whipping.'

'What then?'

'Just some – what, a little slapping perhaps . . .' I cut myself short. I had no intention of giving a full narrative of the night before. Porter was now wetting his lips with tea drawn loudly across the top of the tea-cup as he repeated and sucked in the word, 'Slapping?'

'We do not wish for lurid details,' Barbara interjected

'I have none to provide,' I said, 'none.'

I did not wish to account and apologise for two harlots in my room.
But in view of what appeared to be Porter's approaching apoplexy, I thought it necessary to soften the story a little:

'Although I believe it might stretch your belief further than reasonable, I ask you to understand that I did invite a young lady to my room a lady who has fallen a little from virtue.'

Barbara had left the table and set about her ordinary tasks of the day. Porter sat back now, easy in his manner and allowed the disbelief in his eyes to fade when I said ". . . has fallen a little from virtue". He now engaged me with a wink designed to make me tell more and in confidence as one man to another.

'I brought this lady, not as you may suppose, for a frolic, but to instruct her to mend her ways. Alas, fine and plump she was also well- formed and big. I had never spoken to her before last night and she took exception to my lecturing her. She set about me with her hand, slapping me on the hand and face and shoulders.'

'You kept your clothes on?' 'For the most part.'
I fixed Porter with a glance to discourage him from asking for more details.

'Ah well, I'm sorry.' There was a cadence of disappointment in his voice. 'You'll have to find lodgings. But not at quite the rush your sister said.
I formed my features into the shape of penitence and bowed my way
from the breakfast table.

Barbara did not mention any of these matters again that day. I knew that she would wait until the month was nearly up and then ask me what arrangements I had made for my accommodation. In the meanwhile, I would continue hard with my literary efforts and hope that these might repair some of the damage to my financial state. I had indeed been unwise in seeking to live the life of a voluptuary when I had not the means.

Porter made several attempts to have me repeat – and adorn – the story of the "harlot with the whip". He did this by introducing the creaking bed into a conversation, and even came into my room armed with tools to "fix the creaks". But I told him nothing more, and wished myself to forget an incident which redounded so poorly to my credit.

I decided to put aside for the moment the question of new lodgings. Practical matters were better left until I had seen Miss Perkins again. What thoughts I had of her were fanciful as yet and I applied myself closely to my desk, obliterating her charms from my mind with some partial success. Samuel Johnson had been overheard at The Mitre saying that "a man had no reason to write except for money", and money was certainly a desperate need for me. I laboured with what I did not think so at the time but think now were poor verses, to make *An Elegy on the Death of the Prince of Wales*. The four pounds gained by this was the only reward since, although my name was by this means brought before the King, he made no acknowledgement. I knew that he had no admiration for the Prince in life, but assumed that his dislike would not endure beyond his death. However, it is perhaps fortunate that the King forgot the Prince and me with determined alacrity.

I might have had more success with what was really little more than an extension of Pope's *Dunciad*. To this base lampoon I added a few characters who were of greater consequence at the time but now are forgotten and so mention of them brought me very few pence for my work.

However, the money gained from these compositions paid for my recent excesses with the harlots. It did not leave me well established for the future but at least my attic chamber was for the present secure. For entertainment, fond fancies cost nothing and who if not youth cannot survive on those? My imaginings with regard to Miss Perkins were filling and nourishing, and thoughts of that divine object, lately the mistress of the Earl of Sandwich, were more than sufficient to encourage me in literary efforts and yet allow me indulgent hours in dreaming of how famous I might be for her.

So, honourably set up and prepared, I resigned myself to total abstinence from all voluptuousness. From morning's first chattering of sparrows to the grey doves' cooing at evening-time, I applied myself to the writing of a play. It was a comedy following the course of Sir Roger de Coverley from a life of intemperance and riot in the manner of a man- about-town turned rake, to the time when he was on the verge of descending to be a common wretch and a public nuisance. Sir Roger met his match and his saviour in the person of Miss Nancy Proudheart – a quiet young lady come up from the country. She had but a modest fortune of her own, but all the guile and a greater wit than he to save him and his fortune. There had been no error in her education. Her mind and reason had not been turned by nonsense gleaned from the pages of fashionable romances. For, so far from being harmed by any of these chimerical ideas of romantic love, she possessed a head quite firmly set upon her pretty shoulders. What is more, her head was set on saving Sir Roger's fortune and – he understood at last – that as a secondary consideration she was intent on saving him. The last act contained all the plot and saved the first gems of humour until then so that the public as they might, could see it for free. Such was the confidence shown in *Sir Roger de Coverley* that Mr Jolly, actor manager at The Haymarket, bought the play off me for one hundred pounds, but on one condition. I was to understand that for the play's main importance to start in the third act was to deprive him of half the profit, since custom not arriving until then would avoid the expense of seeing acts 1 and 2 unless the meat of the play was brought into them. It was his intention, therefore, to alter the play to bring much of the third act to the first and second acts. If I agreed, the hundred pounds was mine. Flushed with this success, I shook hands upon his offer and counted myself the most fortunate and possibly the richest man in London at that moment.

There is a value in fine clothing beyond the pence spent upon it. It can give a man the cut to make him feel fearless and secure. Besides this, a playwright should not dress as though he is a legal clerk, unless his object is to deceive a lady into believing he is such. Never did I feel that I dressed to deceive, I was always what I was, clothes and all. So went my arguments for myself. The Strand shops waited no longer for me.

Within hours of my reward for the play *Sir Roger de Coverley,* I was returning to the Porters in red shoes with a very slight raising of the heels; white stockings and white breeches fitted snugly just below my knee (the shape of which were much complimented upon by the tailor). Buckles at shoe and knee were well matched. The waistcoat was a marvel of stitch work – coloured silks and fine gold threaded their ways through a veritable flower garden of exotic plants. The jacket was of a deep violet shade and allowed wide flaring at the cuffs, out of which masses of brilliant white lace sent its delicate billows around my hands – and there were similar matching extravagances at the neck. A modest cambric handkerchief charged with oils and spices from the orient replaced the simple nosegay which had done such valuable service before I was an established playwright.

The wig, the greatest expense of any item, towered majestically upwards and had the extra quality of loose working which allowed my own hair to flourish beneath it.

Did I not deserve all this? And did I not deserve to ride

in a hackney carriage to Vauxhall Gardens when I set off on the due night to see Miss Perkins again? I answered 'Yes', of course I answered 'yes'. Hard had I earned such luxuries. And only a part of my gains was spent. The largest part of the remainder was in a handsome purse to match the jacket and threaded on a belt of doe-skin round my waist.

CHAPTER 12

THE VAUXHALL GARDENS; MISS PERKINS

*From licentiousness to Miss Perkins and sudden
decisions all in a day*

April 1751 was summertime in Spring, and such an
evening as I had chosen was the best of all to take pleasure
at The Vauxhall Gardens. The hackney carriage bearing
me rattled over Westminster Bridge, jerking to avoid
slower vehicles and holes in the road and couples on foot
and dogs who were caught up in the general excitement
and ran alongside. These lent their voices to the noise and
if any other voice was raised loudly, barking was raised
above it.

Once over the bridge the crowd thinned on the wider
road down to Vauxhall. Sniffing, we drew in the fresh air
south of the Thames. Green shoots burst in the hedgerows,
birdsong in the trees trilled above the human babble, and
sheep called to their lambs. My hackney carriage increased
its pace to let me down to return sooner for another fare. I
paid my dues and joined the crush entering Vauxhall gates.
I thought that the mass of people was so great in the first
avenue that I should never make my rendezvous with
Gascoigne and Bulkley at the pavilion we had chosen.

In these crowded circumstances the tight-packed
intimacy of strangers allowed instant friendships and
pleasantries which were over in a moment. A young
woman of more than passing prettiness put her arm around
my waist and squeezed me as though I were a lost lover or
her husband returned from his labours. She smiled up into
my face and asked me if I would care to "go" with her. At
any other time the impulse to respond agreeably would
have been irresistible. In fact, it almost was so then and I

looked around to see if there was some privacy in the yew lined paths leading off the avenue we were in. But I swear this was no more than a whimsical wish. In any event a ruffian – who obviously had a closer tie to this young woman than the attachment so recently developed between her and me – this roughneck, I say, practically tore her away from me. Her pathetic wave as she was pulled into the crowd almost convinced me that she had formed an immediate affection for me. Vain and foolish man that I am; that I was.

I pushed on past lawns where all was gaiety and pleasure amongst the throng of dancers. Large spaces near to the orchestras were covered with boards answering to the purpose of stages on which assembled those who wished to dance. The sight of hundreds of couples in motion at the same time gave a most gratifying effect and it was exciting to see such graceful striving in each dancer to be alert and responsive to the other's motion. The women were light and airy in their movements and their persons in general well-formed for the purpose. The men, dancing, were usually inferior to the women, and made awkward rolling movements in all their steps but performed better and more nimbly on their feet when sent by their partners to fetch refreshment from nearby tents. Had I had not the fixed purpose and desire of paying attention to Miss Perkins – if she were here – it is certain I would have joined in the dancing at once, and because of my well-spent time at Cambridge with Mr Joliffe, I was certain that I would cut a handsome figure here and I would not be sent off to fetch refreshment while an elegant lady rested her crushed toes.

I had more idle thoughts to delay my proper progress but these were quickly replaced when I caught sight of Bulkley and Gascoigne entering a pavilion not far from a superior dancing floor. They hailed me as best they might while their hands were full with tankards and glasses, and pointed out Giles Marsden to me as I threaded my way to their comfortable, dark and secret pavilion. Walking beside Marsden (my heart missed two beats and leapt up and down in my breast and somersaulted four times more) – walking beside Marsden was the delicate and utterly lovely Miss Perkins, she endowed so richly with personal attractions, she the Goddess I had come to worship.

First I was properly introduced to Giles Marsden on whom, since I first saw him, I had hung the epithet "The Bear" – well fitting such an ursine hairy creature. He surprised me by being gracious about the use of his name to gain entry to Madam Thomson's establishment. He enquired courteously whether I enjoyed that evening. I avoided direct answer for I was rooting about in my head for a question that would certify for me that he had no personal amatory connection with Miss Perkins. I was anxious to be introduced to her and to dally in aimless conversation with The Bear was not part of my intention. Therefore, with not even a passing resemblance to subtleness of manners, I asked outright of Marsden:

'Is this your wife? If not please end my suspense and declare it and do me the honour of introducing your fair companion Mr. Marsden before I die with impatience and before I have heard one word from her cherry ripe lips.'

As I turned towards the object of my desires I thought perhaps I had over larded my speech, for Miss Perkins' eyes were steady on me making an evaluation of my character. For all my finery and my sweeping bow, then in that instant I suffered a feeling of nakedness before her, until her eyes dropped and she, stooping with her curtsey, let the topmost curves of her milk white breasts draw my senses to their beauty and left my introspection to another day. Sixteen or seventeen years of age was she? And such a presence, such a Lady.

The Bear made the introduction.

'Miss Perkins.' He waved his hand towards her – a hand which bore no jewellery, unless it were deep embedded in the hair that covered it: 'Miss Mary Perkins, lately much in the company of my uncle The Earl of Sandwich and now on his instruction to be introduced to the best company in town.'

(then turning to indicate me):

'William Dodd, playwright and a gentleman who keeps the best company in Town, and indeed of the *bon ton* as you might say.'

I remarked to myself that Giles Marsden's manners were well above the level expected by anyone who had heard of him and his business but had not met him before. I wondered why he was at such pains to be exceedingly polite to me unless it was that he was anxious to put Miss Perkins – for this evening at least – into my care. This prospect did not, of course, alarm me and indeed if it occurred would be greeted by me with relish and delight. The Bear had called in vain for his flunkey, who had supposedly returned to the nearest refreshment tent with a fresh order. The Bear's shouts were lost in the noise of the music and dancing feet so he set off in search of his man. His mutterings and imprecations were much less elevated than his introductory remarks to us.

We, Miss Perkins and I, joined Gascoigne and Bulkley who were already supping in the pavilion. They rose briefly as we entered and then settled back to stick their forks into the plate of mixed meats in the centre of the table, gesturing to us to do likewise.

'Regrets,' said Bulkley. 'There is a shortage of wine I am afraid, until Marsden's man returns.'

I thought to reply in song that I was happy to drink only the charms of Miss Perkins and would not ask for wine, but I thought better of it. It was my impression that her modesty would not allow her to believe such flattery was in fact sincere and would consequently think less of me.

Before long, Marsden returned pulling the flunkey along by his ear. As his hands were both occupied in holding the tray of bottles he had been sent to fetch, he could not resist or alter the action upon his ear.

I was keen to return to a conversation with Gascoigne and Bulkley or better still to begin one with Miss Perkins. Meanwhile, The Bear with his flunkey – who had the appearance of a Half Sized Bear – had a different play to perform with just that cast of two. Each question from Marsden and each answer that he could elicit from the flunkey was punctuated by squeaks from that Half Bear as his ear was squeezed and twisted.

'Why,' said The Bear, 'did you go to another lawn to get our wine?'

'Sir, because Sir, it is cheaper at that other refreshment tent.'

'But that is at a small rough lawn where common people drink and dance – vulgar country wenches and so forth. Have you a mind to attend to their business and not mine? You realise that no dancing boards are laid there, only bawds with a double "u" put to lie on rough grass.'

As he spelled out the word "bawd" he looked all round for approval.

The flunkey laughed very loud and said,

'No, Sir. O, No Sir! Oh very funny, Sir – bawds – in the rough grass. Very jocund. No, Sir. I say the wine is cheaper there – and the ale – and all from the same bottles and casks as here if labels are to be trusted.'

'They are to be trusted and you are not. And where is the change from the purchase of these cheaper wines? You have pocketed the difference I'll warrant.'

Marsden twisted the flunkey's other ear as well and threatened to spin him by them both. The flunkey put down his tray and squealed mightily causing a few heads to turn from the dance floor. Miss Perkins winced and looked softly on the poor flunkey.

'No. No.' he said. 'The money is here.'

He took coins from his coat pockets letting some fall on the ground.

The Bear made him stoop and return them to him and stopped Miss Perkins from aiding him in the task saying, 'You should not demean yourself so before a servant.'

Gascoigne and Bulkley, to distract us all, began to talk of a larger play than the one just enacted by Marsden and his flunkey. Having, as I remember, seen a performance of *The Suspicious Husband* I remarked on the imagination Garrick put into his part. And my old friends agreed and were as always full of praise for him.

The Bear was now making up for the time lost while dealing with his man, and seemed determined to drink every refreshment tent as dry as the deserts of Arabia. As he dropped out of the conversation his flunkey attempted cheekily to push into it. He had seen the play my friends referred to, from the gallery – as the perquisite of a liveried servant of nobility. He nodded as he agreed with one of us or shook his head vigorously in disagreement with another, while he made sure that his master's glass was filled. There was a touch of improper familiarity about this flunkey which suggested to me that his lack of respect arose from knowledge of The Bear's alleged businesses when not in his cups.

'Benjamin Hoadly, the author of *The Suspicious Husband* is the Earl of Sandwich's cousin.' said Gascoigne. 'He is known to me as is also his father, the Bishop of Winchester.'

Bulkley signalled that he also had that acquaintanceship, and would have interrupted his friend to expand on the details, but Gascoigne had his reins on the conversation:

'He is a man of rich talent is Hoadly – and not so poor in worldly things either, having a rich Bishop for a father who can guarantee an income for his children. But on top of that your Doctor Hoadly – for that medical title is his first claim to public attention – is physician to the King, our King George II.'

The Bear, at mention of the King, attempted to gain his

feet and stand to attention, but his effort failed in a tangle of saluting arms and clicking heels as he settled back untidily in his chair and closed his eyes.

My face must have betrayed some displeasure when shortly Gascoigne had finished his praise for Dr Hoadly, which was a recommendation rather as a wealthy man than as a physician or playwright. Miss Perkins, who was drinking very little but observing us all closely, leaned forward and said to me:

'Did you not like the play Mr Dodd, or is it the author of whom you disapprove? You are very silent.'

'No to be sure not. I like the play and think its author has a great talent. No, may God forgive me, I suffer from envy. I cannot but think that just a trifling talent harnessed to royal, or even only to an aristocratic connection, cannot fail to succeed beyond expectation. Though I may hope to be regarded as rising in the world of literary endeavour, I have no connections.'

I then allowed myself what I feared would be thought a great liberty.

Emboldened by the almost recumbent body of The Bear and the susurration from his lips which seemed to foretell a deeper sleep, and while Gascoigne and Bulkley were continuing on their own the conversation about the play and about Hoadly and were still distracting the flunkey with errands to recharge their glasses, I said quietly to Miss Perkins: 'I envy other people's connections, and Mr Marsden's most of all.'

'Why so?' she asked. 'He has no close connection with the King even though he has been in his presence once. Why, as for that, so have I!"

'No,' I rejoined patiently as though to a child who would not understand, 'I do not envy any connection with the King, neither Gascoigne's nor Marsden's. It is the latter's connection with you that I envy.'

The dear lady did not cast down her eyes or permit a

blush to be encouraged up her cheek; her tender eyes rested steadily on mine, and – it must have been my imagination – her lips parted very slightly, O so imperceptibly slightly, and formed into a kiss. Gascoigne and Bulkley returned their attention to us and Miss Perkins turned to them:

'Do you think Mr. Dodd has talent?'

'Most decidedly.'

Gascoigne was emphatic and he chose his words carefully:

'Dodd has golden talents as a teacher. His knowledge of Latin and Greek and all the classics is beyond compare. The poets and philosophers he knows as well as you and I know our friends. The Scriptures are open to him in all their parts; and he has withal a silver tongue. It may be argued also that the gold and silver of his talents are purified by the furnace of his intelligence. Certainly Miss Perkins, I would guarantee that I speak the truth.'

My eyes widened in surprise at both the rhetoric and the compliments being paid to me.

'I would not gainsay any of that,' said Bulkley, 'and would add more. He should not let his literary powers lure him into striving for success in the glitter of The Haymarket or Drury Lane. It would be wasted. It is in the Church he should seek his fortune, for he is a good man. The others we have discussed have talent in plenty but, to my knowledge, their opinions are not allied to goodness.'

Bulkley seemed taken-aback with himself for making so pointed a recommendation, and Gascoigne likewise for his own untypical hymn of praise of me.

Miss Perkins looked at me steadily again, but let nothing be given away except by her melting tender eyes and provoking lips. I was gladdened by the good opinion of my friends, and was a few days later to think more of what they had said now. Meanwhile, to remove myself necessarily but reluctantly from the gaze of Miss Perkins before I drowned in it, I troubled the flunkey to refill my glass, then shortly put it down and as though as an

afterthought rose elaborately to my feet and bowing before
her asked:

'Miss Perkins will you be so gracious to join me in
dancing the minuet?'

'I hardly know how,' she said and I noticed for the first
time and was enchanted by the softly flattened vowels of
her speech.

'But I thank you Mr Dodd.' She hurried on, 'Perhaps
you will teach me?'

She put her gloved hand in mine where briefly and by
accident one or two fingers entwined deliciously with
mine. I was glad of the chance to direct my thoughts and
my heated blood to my feet, which could more ably than
speech demonstrate my terpsichorean skills.

Miss Perkins needed very little or no instruction in the
minuet. In fact, I suspected that where she did make a small
mistake, it was allowed to give me a pretext to correct her
and in the sweet union of graceful bodies, I think given
liberty, we would have danced more hours than the
orchestra had strength for.

Too soon the musicians ceased to call for new candles
and long before we tired the last minuet was announced.
Over our shoulders we saw Gascoigne and Bulkley
indicating their departure. As I brushed closely in front of
my partner, I spared a compassionate thought for my
friends who can have had little pleasure in an entertainment
that did not include at least two fine horses and a pack of
hounds. They waved and at the same time heaved The Bear
into a chaise which had been summoned from where it had
been waiting at the head of one of the avenues.

The idea to call for a conveyance was good:

'Miss Perkins, will I call a carriage for us, or shall I
pursue
Mr Marsden and get you a place in his chaise? I am
ashamed that I did not see his man beckoning for us
before.'

'He did not beckon, nor Mr Marsden either, who is

beyond that sort of nicety at so late an hour. But do not
concern yourself Mr Dodd. Earlier I assured Mr Marsden
that you would see me safely to my house. I hope that I did
not presume too much?'

'Nothing could make me more happy. Will you stay
here while I bring a carriage to the gates? Or will you put
your arm on mine and come with me?'

For answer she put her hand on my arm and at the gate
I called for a hackney carriage which stood with its restless
horse nose deep in long grass at the road's edge. The surly
driver named the fare and demanded to see the money for
it before we stepped in. I looked at him angrily, resenting
his suspicion and his failure to see that a man of my quality
could certainly afford the miserable sum required by him.
Then I recollected that perhaps some of the customers
applying to him or to his fellows, had spent everything in
the gambling hall at Vauxhall and then bolted without
paying when their journey ended. I calmed my anger and
reached for my purse. I reached for my purse again in case
it had slid round my belt. I reached in vain. It had gone. My
belt had gone. Nearly all my worldly wealth had gone. I
was distraught. How foolish to put so much into such a
place.

Miss Perkins stood aside as I chased for the missing
purse again. 'It is moonlight," she said. 'I wish we could
walk.'

Even if I had had no cause to admire Miss Perkins
before this, I had cause now. She said nothing about
money, nor the shocking discovery of theft from my
person. Until we left the coachman's hearing she said
nothing further on any subject but put her arm in mine,
pulled her dress up a trifle to clear the droppings where the
horses waited and walked with me up the long road to
Westminster.

'In the crush,' I said, 'my belt must have been cut.'

'Assuredly,' she said, 'But what a chance this has given
me to spend a longer time with you.' There was nothing

forward in her manner, merely common sense and kindness. She asked no questions and certainly I would not on such short knowledge of her burden her with my stupidity and vanity at my encounter with a Vauxhall harlot, for assuredly I now realised it was she who had robbed me.

So easy was our converse, the journey passed too quickly, although for safety's sake we took no short cuts to Frith Street – that better part of Soho – where the Earl had given an apartment to Miss Perkins.

'The Earl is fond of you?'

'I don't believe The Earl has "fondness"; until he arrives at the bed chamber he is kind, and in his way he is fair and, though an old man full of eccentricities, his generosity is to be counted upon.'

'And his cousin Giles Marsden?'

'Oh. Not a close cousin I think. But do you think I have an obligation to the Earl's cousin?'

She assumed that was the tenor of my question and continued, 'No in taking me to an entertainment he is obliging the Earl of whom he expects other favours – appointments and such like; some gossip says she expects a post at The Admiralty. The Earl, as I say, is a kind man but does not require favours to be returned with favours. If he thought that I needed or would welcome the personal attentions of his cousin Mr Marsden, he was sadly informed. Mr Marsden himself says he has a reputation as a match maker, though there are other words too foul to mention to describe the actuality of what he does. And I have evidence of it from servants' gossip. But if you think he is pimping for me you have him, and you, and me, all wrong.'

There was a little hardness in my Goddess' voice and I feared mightily that I had offended her. But thankfully the moonlight was not strong enough to show my anger at the thought that my Goddess had been sullied by Marsden. She sensed that and slightly changed the subject and her tone with it.

'When you were speaking to your friends – what gallant fellows they are – you referred to Mr Marsden as "The Bear". Why is that?'

I told Miss Perkins what physical attributes were so obvious in her recent companion to earn the name "The Bear".

'O,' she said, 'it is well if you are struck only by his great hairy paws. There is nothing else that I know of. And as for being amorous, as a bear might supposedly be, he is not amorous with me, nor any other thing you may imagine.'

Perhaps Miss Perkins sensed my arm relaxing yet holding her even more closely to me, and knew that I was relieved to learn of the slightness of her attachment to The Bear.

Miss Perkin's door at Frith Street was come upon too soon. For in the last few streets before arriving we were silent and walked closely with our arms about each other. The softness of her hip against mine and the curve of her waist under my hand, and our fingers laced together, were the entire perfection of sensuality and intimacy. Only for an instant did I compare my sensations now with a distant recollection of Miss Aphrodite. Miss Perkins presence with me that night was the summit of all pleasure to be obtained in the innocent company of a beautiful young woman.

'Will you come with me to Matins tomorrow? May I call on you?' We reached the top step at her door and she slipped inside, turning to close the door but leaving it ajar. It was dark in the porch, and as her face appeared in the gap between the door and its post she said,

'Yes Mr Dodd, I will. Good night Mr Dodd.'

And unless l were entirely mistaken she did blow a kiss at me and just for a half a second stuck her tongue out at me and then withdrew it rapidly as she closed the door.

Had any of the clever men of science just then in vogue

observed my progress home, they would not have said that I walked on air. But less prosaic men, poets or priests would have thought certainly that mere roads could not support such a springing step as mine. Nor would they have been slow to divine that I was in that strange state bordering on the metaphysical or mad. I was in love.

To feel to be walking as if on air was not sensible as I negotiated a passage through Porter's emporium. I had happily few collisions and those only gentle ones before reaching the stairwell, but there at the top of the first flight my foot encountered a large ewer which then fell step by wooden step until it shattered on the stone floor. I knew at once that Porter's cunning was behind this. He wished to be woken on my entry to discover whether I was alone or taking rude company to my chamber.

The crash of pottery below was greeted by a creaking above and I could hear Porter breathing behind his door. For a moment I considered making several journeys quietly down and more noisily up, whispering in a different voice each time to give the impression of a motley gang of companions ascending to entertain me. Such a ruse would have caused so much anxiety for Porter at breakfast that in charity I could not raise his hopes now of a lascivious narrative only to have it dashed by the truth in the morning. Therefore with admirable quick wittedness I said aloud to myself:

'O Dodd you clumsy fellow! How lucky that was a cracked ewer!'

Indeed, I had recently seen this mock antique pot in various parts of the shop, partly hidden to hide the chips and cracks which owed more to deliberate distress than to real antiquity and *anno domini*. At breakfast Porter made no mention of the ewer or my entry, for if Barbara had had wind of the former she would have chastised him for the careless placing of it and led on about the lateness of my return – which in the event brought nothing of impolite interest to a saddened Porter.

On the Sunday morning, to impress the Porters with my religious frame of mind, I made some show of leaving the house for Church, being wigless but with my hair well combed and smoothed down; soberly dressed and prayer book clasped in my hand. I was sure that I was the picture of a virtuous gentleman in a modest way of life, or even poor. 'Even poor,' I echoed to myself with the realisation already half forgotten that I had lost nearly everything the previous evening.

Barbara and Porter were preparing to attend for morning service at a nearby church and looked up in surprise and then approval at my appearance, although Porter did not pay much attention being much occupied by an inspection of his palms. Barbara – a forceful wife since she felt perhaps she was of a slightly better class – had insisted that her husband wore gloves at least on Sunday for his attendance at the church where he had purchased a pew. Porter's hands being covered created a dilemma for him. Where should he spit upon them? When he did lift one glove at the wrist to spit beneath it on the palm Barbara provided the answer he had been puzzling for:

'You should not spit at all in gloves and not ever spit on a Sunday either.'

Porter shrugged and rubbed his hands together and fierce enough to wear them out before midday.

As if Miss Mary Perkins had received a message from me she also was modestly attired, with a great deal of white in the dress and about the neck. It would not look right if we were richly dressed and then stood throughout the service in a side aisle at St George's, Hanover Square, for only the very rich could afford there the luxury of their own pew. The rest of that congregation, by such definition poor and of a lower social condition, stood the entire time – unless they found a leaning place against a pillar.

The Reverend gentleman in the pulpit, an elderly curate – a Scotsman – announced the text of his sermon as being appropriate to the considerations of the Vegetable Creation. Beginning in the Garden of Eden he might have detained his congregation for a good while by expounding upon the pleasures therein, since I at least felt that morning that the garden of Eden had some kinship with The Vauxhall Gardens, but in his proscriptions he was soon launched onto the high and stormy seas of the dangers of immorality where we and he if unguided by the lights of the prophets might all perish in the consuming fires of Hell.

Like small fish slipping through the meshes of a net, many of the standing poor escaped quickly from the church to the sunshine and pleasures of the world. The wealthy, however, in their box pews were trapped, and only those with the knack of looking to be awake while they slept had some relief from the severe and penetrating admonishments from the pulpit.

'If your pleasures in their nature are so shameful,' he said, and my lovely Miss Perkins began to shuffle her feet, 'in their tendency so pestiferous and treasonous against virtue . . .'

We both in geometric movements akin to our dancing the night before, silently gained the door and heard only as it closed behind us

'. . . such horrible violation of all decorum.'

Miss Perkins stifled her laughter and leant against a tombstone to recover.

'"A horrible violation of all decorum",' I said to her and led her away with just a touch of decorum towards the green fields of Hampstead.

Here our pleasures were simple. We walked and talked. Our imaginations gilded the countryside; even humble cottages with sagging thatch were, in our minds castles and their simple inhabitants Kings and Queens. We supped at one of the many inns beside banks of primroses and scented bluebells. Then home at nightfall with lengthy and sweet departure at Miss Perkins' door, with her yet innocent of my lust. And I home to my attic lingering on the way to pluck a dog rose from the hedge. I was almost into my bed without prayers when I picked up the dog rose which I had laid on my pillow – as sometime might, I thought, so lie the gentle face of my Miss Mary Perkins – if she were my wife!

On my knees I spoke to the rose with it held before me, its pink and white near flesh-like petals holding my gaze in the candle light. To it I argued the case for marriage as a rational being should; and thus:

'Miss Mary Perkins is beautiful and I yearn for her. Tell me rose, is that such a wrong thing?'

'It is not,' I spoke the rose's reply. 'To be possessed of both the good and the agreeable would be an extraordinary stroke of good fortune. What is more, a man is governed by irregular appetites and if they should be directed and controlled by the accommodation of a good wife, so much less imperfect will that man be. Also he will be more healthy and natural for other reasons.

'The Almighty Creator has ordained marriage for the mutual comfort of the sexes and the procreation of children. If on the other hand, lust is to be satisfied with harlots it is to make a coffee-house of a woman's privities, to go in and out and give nothing freely.'

I turned the rose, the humble dog-rose, in my fingers and kissed it.

There are practicalities to be borne in mind should I venture into marriage. A wedding ceremony is a costly affair if wanted, but in reality all that is needed is a Fleet Marriage – the man and woman with witnesses to declare that they are (*de praesenti* – "there and then" as Gascoigne would say) – husband and wife.'

I was up from my knees now, pacing the room and

talking aloud.

'Where money for living? What and where a house? Oh beautiful Mary, for the immediate month the allowance you have and the apartment – both in The Earl's gift, could they be continued? Should you trust me with your person and everything tithed to you?'

In my mind I gave my answer for Miss Perkins, hoping that she could not give a more certain answer to any other man. She knew that my philosophy resided firmly in the equality of all mankind and did not believe as some said that when God made the society of marriage, he made man superior because he knew equality would breed confusion.

My discussions with the dog-rose left me firmly convinced that immediate marriage was the most favourable course for me. A place for my head to sleep and for my passions to reside would be immediately settled if Mary agreed to be my wife.

There was no more need for argument with myself or the rose that night, so we put both our heads on the pillow, I dreaming of a face and a person that have never been out of my mind since.

Porter at breakfast was in a state of high curiosity which he could barely contain until Barbara had left the table.

'You had a man in your room last night Mr Dodd,' he said, emphasising his statement by clapping his ready moistened hands together. 'Is this some new foulness we are to tolerate?'

'Indeed I did not have a man in my chamber. And as for "a new foulness" there have been no old ones – only the careless amusements of a young man. Furthermore with the deepest respect to you Mr Porter, I am surprised that you consider unnatural practices within your experience. Moreover . . .'

I was aware that already I had spoken too many words to find comfortable lodging in Porter's mind, but felt impelled to continue

' . . . Moreover it is my intention today to press my suit towards a regular arrangement with a member of the opposite sex.'

Barbara, who continued to be rarely out of earshot when I was engaged in conversation with Porter, appeared at the door:

'Do you mean *marriage?*' she said.

I wished, I wished I could have taken back my words. They had done no harm in Porter's ears as he had less facility in the understanding and use of words strung together in long sentences, but Barbara caught everything quickly – sometimes before uttered.

'Your father shall know of this!'

Barbara delivered the threat.

'Your mother will be heartbroken!'

Barbara appealed to my loving nature. Porter sat silent, being sure that he was about to be blamed for something but he knew not what. Barbara left the room looking for a sheet of Porter & Company's paper – a clean bill-head – that she might write at once to Bourne.

Mr Porter, by pushing me into my indiscretion, did deserve some blame for my next action. Without more hesitation I left the shop immediately, sacrificing further time at my desk, and hurried straight to Frith Street. I feared Miss Perkins might be too rational, too cautious to accept my proposal, and that I would lose her. I knew that my father would put such objections in my way towards marriage that by the time all that was overcome Miss Perkins would be some other man's wife, The Bear's perhaps, despite her protestations. I wielded the knocker on Miss Perkins' door as urgently as a fugitive strikes the sanctuary knocker of a church. Her landlady, Mrs. Frampton answered and seeing my urgency admitted me at once to Mary.

'Oh, why Mr Dodd? Why so early?' she said. 'Will you consent to be my wife?'

'Of course. Is it so urgent now, this minute?'

'Yes. It is,' I said and could not think of a short way of telling my Goddess the reasons and – despite Mrs. Frampton's presence, could think of nothing better than to drop upon one knee and say 'I love you.'

'That settles it then. But . . . '

'But what?'

But I think,' she said with the most mischievous smile, 'you might drop onto both knees.' I did. I turned to Mrs. Frampton and said quite roughly, 'You will do to bear witness.'

'Indeed I will not. I cannot read or write and in any way the lady you are supposed to be honouring deserves better than that.'

'And what should that be?

'A wedding at least. Some sort of celebration – here if you wish. For a very reasonable consideration I will get it ready for you.'

I felt that I had been trapped on all sides, but my exhilaration at acceptance by the Goddess made me easy.

'Then so it shall be, spend what you will.'

'Oh William,' cried Mary, 'William the Conqueror and William the Extravagant. Will you not always be so wild?'

I greeted everybody who looked my way as I walked as fast as I could to the City to persuade Gascoigne and Bulkley to meet Miss Perkins and me at The Fleet Prison at six o'clock that evening.

And so it was. The clergyman was found. He was a good man though sharp in business and had crossed his Bishop and then not paid his due tithes. Sent by the Ecclesiastical Court to serve four years in the Fleet, he made a good income by Fleet weddings, and Bulkley said, still had income earned for him by curates in his parishes to line the pockets of his own cassock.

The simple ceremony in a bare cell was short. Afterwards Gascoigne was careful to check the register to make sure there were no false names or crossings out –

which he said could invalidate the marriage.

Then we all returned to Frith Street where there was cold ham and tarts and wine taken with a great deal of laughter. Gascoigne and Bulkley left discreetly soon after candlelight and Mrs Frampton hurried us to our room while she cleared away.

I thought I should have let Porter and my sister know where I was, but decided to leave that until the morrow that their sleep should not be disturbed and I now should be that much sooner into the arms of Mrs Mary Dodd.

A very few days had passed before I presumed Barbara had reported everything to the Rectory at Bourne. Barbara was not previously famed for the frequency or length of her correspondences, so our parents will have been as delighted to have a letter from her as they were displeased to know of my marriage and other "foolish doings". For my part, I felt that manhood had put its steadying hand on me. I was twenty-three years old, with all ambitions ahead of me. I had a tender young wife for companion who with her soft allurements would guard me against other temptations and vain distractions. Even the loss of my purse was accepted without comment, when in confidence, I told Barbara and later Gascoigne and Bulkley. For it is a fact that most mortals can bear the misfortunes of others perfectly – like Christians –which helps them to forget, so that they are relieved of any sense of obligation to give aid to the unfortunate and may continue in calm and peace of mind. My state of mind, however, was ruffled for me when I was summoned to the Porters at Covent Garden.

It was Mr Porter's lad who came at speed to deliver the summons. He was out of breath. We could see this from the parlour window as he rounded the corner into Frith Street where I had become lodger in Mary's house as soon as we returned from our brief marriage ceremony. Mr Porter's lad was wearing shoes which quite clearly and properly belonged to bigger feet – those of Mr Porter I assumed. The result of this too large footwear was that every few yards one or another of the shoes fell off and the boy had to stop and hop back to retrieve it. To make up for lost time he then attempted to run more quickly than he had before – so losing a shoe again and sometimes losing both curling into the air behind him like wheeling gulls. He pulled up at the parlour window and Mary reached out to take the letter from him. It was in Barbara's hand and said to come straight forth because her father and brother were with her now and wished to have converse with me, and Mary was to attend.

I realised at once that Barbara's letter to Bourne to tell of my intended marriage had been written in disapproving terms. This had brought my father to London by the first possible conveyance, in an attempt to prohibit a marriage that in his view would be a mistake of enormous magnitude and folly. No doubt only on arriving he found that it was a *fait accompli,* The Reverend Mr Dodd would then have employed his philosophic and religious resources to pour oil on his own and Barbara's troubled waters, although when I had told Barbara that I was married she held her silence and expressed no opinion to me about it.

Mary stepped forth and took my arm with an impish smile playing about her mouth which I thought expressed her pleasure at this prospect of engaging in converse with my father, because she guessed how potent was even so little a part of her as her smallest finger when trying her minx effects on an older man. But since I had referred very little to my sister, and almost not at all to Richard, she was not yet apprised of what difficulties they might present.

Mr Porter's lad led the way, unnecessarily for we knew it better than he, but his reward was to gain our admiration at footwear which I believe he had never worn before this day. Arriving at Mr Porter's emporium we were shown in immediately to the ground floor room and Barbara closed the door to the stairwell and upper rooms. Mr Porter took a stout chair onto the pavement to guard the shop from there. With great consideration and with no doubt much hand spitting, he had arranged a selection of furniture round about him. In view of his business he had to have fine furniture on show outside but none that would fade in strong sunshine or suffer serious damage if the clouds opened. One of the advantages of having a large oak settle outside, together with eight ample dining chairs, was that customers who must necessarily be delayed from entering by our presence within could be seated with relative comfort outside. The second advantage was that there was more room inside for us all together – and there would not have been space for all of us had we been invited upstairs.

Mr Porter came in as we arrived and showed us to our seats, or rather I should say to our positions, for there were only two seats left, one a capacious wing chair in mahogany with red upholstery, in which my father sat; he had his hands folded in his lap and sat very erect with his shoulders not touching the chair back. Next to my father was Richard who had turned a walnut dining chair around so that he straddled the seat and lent forward over the back. He rocked a little forward and back – and I did wonder for a moment whether he had similarly treated the fellow to his chair which stood or rather leaned on three legs in a corner with the broken leg lying across the tapestry covered squab.

Barbara, swelling daily, nodded to Mary to whom she had presented herself and so beckoned her to sit beside her on a well-made sofa. This had a serpentine padded back and out scrolling arms all of which together with its squab cushions were covered in gross and petit point floral needlework. This most fashionable piece of furniture was outside the radius of the moted shaft of sunlight which broke through a fanlight at the back of the shop and directed its beams onto the remaining piece of furniture – this time in mahogany – a set of library steps. I was required to ascend this to where it was thought that I might sit in some comfort on a step, but a step being entirely insufficient to accommodate hind-parts, perforce I ascended and lodged a half of each buttock on the top.

Barbara spoke first presuming that as it was her husband's property which had become the meeting house she should make everyone welcome; but first she sent out the lad who had been putting the finishing flourishes to Barbara's stage direction and who spat finally on his hands in the manner of his employer.

'Thank you John,' she said to the boy. 'We will call for you later.

Father you have something to say?'

She knew well that he had something to say. That is why she had written home to tell about his son, me, her brother William, 'who has,' she said, 'again stepped outside the bounds of common sense and familial duty to marry so young and without a proper profession of any sort.'

Father coughed to claim his daughter's and our attention and silence.

Looking straight ahead of him, and apparently with great effort overcoming the tiredness and flatness in his voice which I had not heard before today, he said,

'William I come in great distress upon this occasion.'

He paused: 'I speak first of this city, this London to which you have come from

the innocence of Bourne and Cambridge. There is scarcely any object in London which presenting itself to my view does not raise my indignation and my anger as a country gentleman. I detest all the follies of the town. The walls are covered with bills for plays, balls, assemblies and an abundance of other diversions.

'I hold the State and my own Church entirely at fault for these and they have not prohibited nor even spoken against, against . . .'

(my Father paused to dry his lips and to take a great gulp of air before continuing)

'against the indecent dress of women in hoops of

immense rotundity while there is a disproportionate littleness of their hats forming only a small circle over their silly heads. All these no doubt are foreign fashions and are we also to be inflicted with these follies and with the language of France? Are we next to import their laws also and to submit to their government? London is nowadays a den of thieves, homicides and barbarians.'

My Father paused and started up again – but in a quieter vein.

'Now I speak of you William. Your family, whom it may be said you have shamefully neglected over the past several years, feel that you are dancing upon a precipice and they are alarmed at your situation. You are without a profession that grants a regular income, you are without connections, and you have taken upon yourself the responsibility of a wife who has no wealth other than that of her plentiful physical attributes.' He turned his head to her and looked upon her, and his eyes softened as they would rest on an innocent child.

I know that my father did not mean those particular attributes towards which Richard, who was bursting to speak, momentarily directed his glance before he said:

'Dear Brother,' – his voice carried the tones of a senior cleric rather than one of the youngest and most recently ordained – 'Dear, Dear Brother you must have a mind to your family, and take a profession. You will have no difficulty – if you are still as ever I remember clever and persuasive – in rising in the Law if you choose to take that, or in some capacity engaged in the government of this great country of ours – or even in Parliament itself if a seat could be bought for you . . .'

Richard's voice trailed away as his father allowed a hand to rise from his lap to flick away his suggestions.

'No,' he said, 'Richard you make most sensible remarks about your brother's ability, but without connections or money the courses you propose to him are not possible. He has a start already with you and me, his father, in the Church. I would that William was also on his way like you to a curacy at Camberwell, unless it is too near the centre of London.'

There, William senior paused again and put a shaking hand to wipe his lips and said in an aside to Richard, 'Perhaps Camberwell would not be a great enough distance to separate your brother from those temptations which now occupy so much of his time and which he may always regret. The course which I direct you towards, William, is that which good and clever men have trodden many times before – and in which industry and application and with reasonable solicitation for your fellow men you could gain lasting satisfaction as a clergyman in this world and finally secure a place in the next. You should be ordained.'

Barbara joined in:

'You should be ordained; it is what our mother would wish. Do you not think so, Mary?'

Mary looked at me with her gentle, steady glance and sought first in my face for my opinion and then turned to my father:

'Ask what does William say Mr Dodd. He may be driven to water like a horse, but he may not choose to drink.'

All eyes turned on me.

'I have not studied what is needed. I have a little Latin and Greek it is true, but my time has been occupied with mathematics rather than Hebrew. I am not fit for the Church of England unless higher mathematics is considered an advantage to count the number of benefices needed to provide an income and to keep count of the patronage available.

My efforts to turn this discussion into a thing of amusement fell like the good seed on stony ground.

'I dare say I could make a lawyer as Richard suggests, but as for Parliament or any part of politics – you know how badly that has been for anyone of a Christian vocation: how the clergy as a particular example have been persecuted within the last one hundred years with punishment, imprisonment and execution by the state.

'But if I do tackle the hurdles of Hebrew and formal theology and take the study of divinity and all such subjects that are necessary to ordination, I would give myself humbly to a parish. I should do that as my father has done before and still does now. Also, I would eschew politics and its affairs with the same earnestness that you would have me relinquish a literary life as dramatist and poet and man of letters.'

In speaking so I realised I had made out no solid case for my literary achievements and aspirations of which I had higher hopes than they had any understanding. I had spoken in tones of humility of my deficiencies rather than my talents. Mary looked at me quietly with a question in her eyes.

While Richard began to speak again with more confidence than usual, I looked at my family gathered here to see if I could find in them the answer to Mary's unspoken question: why was I, the bouncy William Dodd so prevailing over his customary manner to sit quietly and listen.

As they spoke I looked each one in the eyes, arguing like Descartes that the eye is the window to the soul.

The shaft of sunlight had now moved from my slightly elevated and comfortless position on the library step, and fell on my father. He sat stiffly in his chair; there was a tremor in his hands and his face had taken on a plainness in which the furrows and creases did not change as he spoke, nor did his head move except rarely on his neck. At the corner of his mouth there was a slight and shining smear of wetness, while his eyes gained no expression from the surrounding tissues but looked mournfully ahead. Although a mask may hide much, while his eyes remained open I could look into his soul. Dear father, to what sadness I have brought you? And are the anxieties of my dear Mother's declining years weighing heavily upon you?

Sensing my gaze upon him The Reverend Mr Dodd Senior rotated in a single slow movement to look in turn at me and as though from some inner power the first parts of a smile opened slowly a little way on his face. He did not speak again, exhausted by all the efforts of speaking.

Richard next addressed those present directly as though they were his congregation, so that they might bear witness to his speech even if I happened not to be listening. However, I was listening; a man may listen and look and breathe and walk and swallow and I dare say break wind as well all at the same time. I had heard Richard say how easy it would be for me to master Hebrew if it was thought necessary; how from the testimony of other judges that the Hebrew language is as remarkable for the simplicity of its formation as for the strength and beauty of its meaning; and how he Richard when at Oxford had had the tender hearted Reverend Dr John Wesley of Lincoln College to teach him Hebrew, and surely there was at Clare Hall Cambridge a teacher to match Mr Wesley?

Richard puffed himself up a little as he spoke; I was glad of his pride for I thought how shamefully had I, and occasionally my father, compared Richard's dullness unfavourably with my supposed brilliance. Yet Richard had made his way, and more quickly than I, for breaking from the bonds of family and from Lincoln College where he, even further removed from Bourne, had suffered more than I from loneliness, Richard had come clear upon his feet. As neither a libertine nor spendthrift, and having no taste for fine clothing or boisterous company, I saw at once that he would be comfortable with an ordinary life which,

however commonplace, might exceed his expectations. I understood and loved my brother in that instant. He was a good man, with no malice or envy in him and ambition was low in his priorities.

It was apparent on her face that Barbara agreed. Even though there was no shaft of sunlight to put Richard at the front of the stage, she held her eyes upon him whenever he spoke and often when he was silent.

Richard, I learned later that day – when we spoke of other matters – was as it were *in loco parentis* to Barbara as our father's strength declined.

He it was who took care to write to Barbara and she to him when Father's writing became too cramped and small to read and tired him unreasonably. It was Richard who made regular correspondence to enquire about our mother's health: it was Richard who was this repository of all family news. He was certainly a good man. I did not need to wonder if he would be the first to send out news of the birth of Barbara's baby when it happened, and send out for trinkets for it too.

Richard, constant at all times and reliable in every circumstance, was a mainsail in the family and would have similarly graced any family in the land. For my part an advantage, but also providing a further careless pit- fall for me, was the certain knowledge that I need not spring forward to execute family responsibilities: for Richard would be there.

Sunlight had retreated entirely from the hind part of Mr Porter's shop. Barbara and Richard had fallen into the same silence as my father. Mary, some three years younger than my sister, regarded her with respect and was in a little awe of her hugely gravid state, but made polite enquiry without crossing any conversational boundaries that might show familiarity.

I felt that I had been defeated by my family, that they had won a conquest when I had barely entered into the battle. They presumed that I had no thought for the morrow, let alone for the future course of my whole life, and they saw it their duty to determine everything for me. They did not know, and I barely recognised, it had been a strand in my conscience for some weeks that I was already contemplating entry to the Church. If I detract from my virtues I shall do myself disserve. Often concealed from the sight of the world I harboured a need to be of comfort to others: to bring, if I do not put too fine a point on it, some of the light of Our Lord as revealed in the Testaments, to those who are sad:

"It is better to go to the house of mourning,
than to go to the house of feasting:
for that is the end of all Men;
and the living will lay it to its heart."

My father had preached on this text when I was half my present age and I made an argument with Richard as we lay abed in which I preached the folly of misery and the God-given command therefore to be glad.
Recalling this as we sat in the back room of Porter's Emporium, I still recoiled at the unnecessary idea of being miserable to be virtuous.

Could I not, I reasoned to myself, be still and yet a better comforter to the downhearted if I was lifted on occasion above the vale of tears by taking strength in some pleasures of the world. Even following the life of a clergyman, I could in the words of Locke – the foremost philosopher in my father's opinion – "faithfully pursue that happiness I propose to myself – all innocent diversions and delights as far as they will contribute to my health . . . and my other more solid pleasures of knowledge and reputation I will enjoy also".

So my mind was made up. The time was too short to argue or attempt to perfect all sides of the proposition put to me by my family. A conclusion must be brought about at once.

'Decidedly,' I said. 'Decided what?'

The question came from each of them in psalm-like part song.

'I shall be ordained. I shall follow my father and my brother into the Church. I will renounce a literary life. I shall go back to Clare Hall as soon as may be to begin the necessary studies for ordination.'

Various exclamations of relief and of pleasure were exchanged. Hands on my shoulders clapped, patted or shook in accordance with the characters and bodily states of their owners. Mary let herself be seen making a short and silent prayer. Then as Barbara and Richard and my Father stood back, looking now with approval at us, she kissed me and said,

'I will be glad to be Wife to your Parson,' and she squeezed my hand and then when she knew no one could observe, pinched me intimately beneath my frock coat. These acts of piety and private pleasure in their brief contrasting moments were a summation of all that had passed in the hour before.

Mrs Dodd (I remember how I puffed with pride when I used the title), I say Mrs Mary Dodd and I were some good part of the way back to Frith Street when Porter's lad caught up with us. He had tied hempen string around his boots to prevent their wilful projection and held a letter in his hand. Pulling up as we turned to face him, he took a deep breath, and on the exhalation started to deliver something on these lines before he took another breath:

'Mrs Porter asks and hopes to be forgiven what she had quite forgot before and now having climbed up to the parlour hoped she would be forgiven for not putting the letter herself into Mrs Dodd's hands but trusting it to me, John that is,' he pointed his thumb into his chest '. . . because . . .' (breath) 'he is younger by many years and had not so far today earned the money Mr Porter gives him and furthermore Mrs Porter begs to be allowed to entertain Mrs Dodd at another time when she is not heavy with child . . .' The last sentence could only be heard with difficulty as John had no further breath to blow out his words. He handed the letter to Mary.

Mary walked a pace ahead of me reading the letter which was from my mother to her. Lines from it of no importance or that she wished to keep to herself, were spoken quietly and quickly while her head was down.

Single words, phrases, even whole sentences conveying messages that in her opinion I should mark and mark well, were tossed clear over her shoulder and with varying loudness and tones modulated to express her own opinion and to interpret my Mother, as only one of the gentle sex might interpret another. My understanding of the letter was much like so:

'Now I call you Daughter . . . you shall be . . . a good adviser. Let him not dazzle you with his cleverness . . . gold Latin and silver Latin he has knowledge of above most but he gives a poor account at tailor or vintner of the difference between five pounds and five pence. As he has been a good son, so in the same measure shall he be a good husband.'

Mary walked on still reading but in silence for a while. Turning a page and a corner by chance at the same time, she turned her face to me and just in the way my teacher Mother had done years before, said:

'Listen hard William, there are still lessons for you to learn.'

The not too gentle smack I placed on her posterior was remarked by a grin from a Mr Wright, Plumber & Glazier of Frith Street, who was lifting lead pipes into his premises. (I recall now that Mr William Wright was the husband of Mehetabel Wesley, the sister of Mr John Wesley. She was ill at this time and a week or so later her funeral procession brought people to their doors. And it was said that that day was the only day in years Mr Willie Wright had been seen entirely sober and without a grin spreading his mouth apart. Withal it was also said he was a good tradesman and well off.) Mary had not quite finished her letter, or she was taking up lines not uttered before.

Mr Willie Wright stooped over his pipes again. Mary walked beside me and continued to read from my mother's letter.

'William will establish in his own mind whether or not he wishes to enter the Church as his father intends. He will be impulsive in that decision . . . You should guard against his sudden wilfulness in some things, but I would advise take no great caution in this matter . . . if he does decide in the way that all his family wish, he may have regrets for a lost literary future . . . What he can do with your encouragement would pass beyond imagining . . . shall you give him a reminder about a little book of Shakespear that he has mentioned? This would be better than a saucy novel he plans that Barbara wrote of in her last letter.'

'Ah,' said Mary putting the letter away with a final firm fold to the creases, 'no more to be said. And Mrs Dodd Senior and I, the Mrs Dodd you have before you, are entirely of one mind.'

We stepped inside the house.

To this point in my life so far I had rarely been silent, and others – in my opinion wrongly – have judged me to be unwise and too quick and too full of responses. This night at table I kept my mouth almost continuously full of the cold supper Mrs Frampton served, so rending further discussion too muffled to be contentious. I returned as quickly and as decently as I could to the parlour in which the heaps of books and papers turned it from a comfortable room for an unmarried young woman to a much more comfortable study for a young married man who was given over to literary pursuits, albeit now forsworn. However, after supper I stayed in "my study" for moments only: time to pray for future studies and for life subsequently in the service of Hebrew and Divinity, a life in the service of Our Lord. Amen.

But first soon to celebrate the occasion with a visit to Vauxhall Gardens, as a reward for my common sense and virtue and obedience to the wishes of my family, for I was resigned to a future with fewer pleasures, and no chance should be lost now to seize opportunities for happiness when they arose.

CHAPTER 13

AT LE CHATEAU DE VOIRONS

Sir Philip not greatly pleased about many things

May 1st 1780

I have returned to my desk after fallow months of sickness
and disability while Mary, who has quite forgot her
customary charity, says that all my sorrow is brought upon
me by myself. I cannot believe such is the case nor believe
Mary for saying it.

Firstly, early in December, my entrails appeared below
their proper station and being inflamed beyond bearing, put
me into a fever. I cannot tell how many days and nights I
remained on my bed burning as if consumed by Hell's own
fires and wracked with pain. One or the other, or both – the
fever and the pain – together then threw me into a
convulsion. This was no pretence as Mary first surmised
when she said that it was a judgement on me for an earlier
fit which I had worked up and acted out for Thicknesse.
This time I had now no control of my body – nor indeed
any knowledge of it – so I must believe the account that
Mary gave me. The restlessness of my fever stopped and
to her alarm I became rigid and without breath. My face
was purple until choking and snorting I began to flail my
left arm and legs like a windmill in an earthquake – though
how Mary should know of earthquakes I do not know. In
this enormous agitation of the body I threw myself onto the
floor and fell amongst the furniture, watering everything in
my path. I remember nothing of this. Later, it was as if I
was fuddled by drink and for three days afterwards I had a
headache to make me weep. Despite all, and M le Blanc
offering laudanum drops again but which Mary would not
accept for me, on the fourth day I had made it seems a
complete recovery – except that my good arm hurt mightily

if I moved it and at the lower end my wrist had taken the shape of a spoon handle. Since all fever had passed and a copious discharge of yellow pus had relieved the sharpest agonies from my nether end, I was in a good frame of mind to return to my history. I would have done so at once had it been possible to write. But I could not. It has taken this time for my bent bone to mend and for my hand to learn again to form letters and words and to write easily without pain.

When my distress was relieved, instead of finding solace in books, I was driven out of doors by a cursed restlessness. This is no bad thing because my legs, weak as they are and having their strength further diminished by idleness abed, are now recovering and finding more power than they had before. Often during the last weeks I have walked crippled but without help and far beyond the English Lawns into the copses and pasture land behind the chateau.

On this very day, returning from such exercise, I had determined to sit down straightaway at my desk, when Mary hailed me with news as surprising as unwelcome. The Thicknesses had arrived with all their menagerie at the end of another Grand Tour. I hurried out to greet them and on the steps sat a weeping Lady Ann. There was no sign of Thicknesse and I leapt to the conclusion that his absence was in some way connected with Lady Ann's tears. But no. She had Jocko the monkey safely in her arms and the monkey's arm quite comfortingly round her shoulders. The whippets were in attendance and silent – looking upon their mistress as if their gentle gaze would stem the flow of her tears. I looked to see if the menagerie was complete – if the parakeet was nearby – but it was not . . . neither on Jocko's shoulder nor on that of his mistress. On the point of asking after it I saw a few brilliant feathers held in Lady Ann's fingers. Her eyes caught mine and she spurted more tears and stroked the feathers as if so doing would bring their owner back to life.

'The Whippets?' I gestured to them.

'No! No! Nor Jocko,' she sobbed and pointed to far down the avenue where I could just descry the bristling tail end of a cur and beyond it poking out from slavering jaws the tail and head of the lifeless parakeet.

I put my hand beside the monkey's hand on Lady Ann's shoulder and stood over her thus until Mary came out with M le Blanc and shared in the task of comforting the distraught gathering of Lady Ann and her remaining animals.

'The cur ran out from behind us as soon as we pulled up and Sir Philip ran straight inside. He did not know the cur was about, nor does he know yet what has happened,' Lady Ann said.

M le Blanc left the scene and entered the house to advise Sir Philip of the fate of the parakeet and of his wife's distress, while Mary stayed to comfort Lady Ann. I lingered a while before, as I thought, to take a cushion to my chair and start again where I had left off some months before. My hopes were dashed. Thicknesse was at my desk and at a task which brooked no interference from M le Blanc or me.

Without any request or by your leave Thicknesse was sitting firmly in my chair, had seized my best quill in his horse-dealer's hand, and was filling another sheet of paper while earlier editions of a letter lay upon the floor. His mouth moved grotesquely in time with the words appearing under his pen and he loudly articulated each syllable as it was formed.

On occasion his tongue licked out of the corner of his mouth when the lines he wrote found particular favour with him. My questioning glance as I came upon Sir Philip was ignored as utterly as if I had been unseen in another room. He took a further sheet of paper to begin again with his masterpiece – a letter of complaint it transpired to an hotelier who had served him ill near Calais on his way from a tour of the Low Countries.

175

AT LE CHATEAU DE VOIRONS

The letter set out the various causes of his wrath in vigorous terms, and was to be wrapped in crested paper fixed with Thicknesse's own wax seals. Coming to Calais from so far away, the recipient would suffer considerable expense in receiving the letter – or such was Thicknesse's hope.

I remained on my feet, witness to successive versions of Thicknesse's letter, and give here the next to final letter – fully embroidered and ornamented to a high degree – which was left discarded on the floor:

Madame Boulevardier and Your Doting Consort,
I must tender my most hearty congratulations for providing me and Lady Ann with a spectacle, and an experience of the greatest kind. For so unpleasant was our short stay in your establishment we were next day forced to go away and into the town; and if we had not done so we had missed the real soul of that vile city which even surpasses in its evil your own hotel.

Madame, we found the town of Calais the very sink of France and also to my shame found it to be the asylum of whores and rogues from England. Nothing can be more extraordinary than this group of English men and women headed by a Lady Bull – the doxy, I believe, of a Canterbury Alderman who ran away with Pauper's Money. Another twenty geniuses make up the English colony at Calais:
"Whose necks are protected from the stretch of a halter,
By twenty-one miles of Gallic sea water"
I would not spend more ink to extend my rhymes on so pitiful subjects but instead send my thoughts to you in particular, as mistress of a whore house that masquerades as an hotel and names itself the Hotel
Angleterre.

The ancient harlot who served breakfast – very sorry fare and we stayed for no other meals – had a red face and a nose as big as a brandy bottle (proving how her time is spent when you release her from her regular labours of insulting us your guests and tipsily pouring food into our laps) and when she did that she had no better manners than to take our best cambric handkerchiefs to mop our clothing and all around.

Which circumstances – and such anger struck me I was nigh to apoplexy at this time – put us, or at least our cambric handkerchiefs, into the hands of your *blanchisseuse* who has an extra thieving practice to make her laundry pay. For when the part-boiled and unstarched handkerchiefs were returned, they had all been trimmed two inches round to make the lace from it into borders for night caps. Lady Ann wept at such treatment served out to our linen and begged me to remove her from your hotel before all her clothing was similarly treated, and she reduced to near nakedness.

Neither you nor any in your household appear to have any pride in the tasks you have undertaken or in your God-given place on earth. You do not blush or show any other symptom of decent feelings at the shameful failings of your establishment. Were you worthy of my further epistolary attention, I would grant you the opportunity to purchase this letter-copy to prevent its publication widely in the press. I am sure, however, that the Hotel Angleterre will fail miserably of its own despicable character and will not need my advertisement to that end. Furthermore I shall gain considerably amongst my friends and save my own expense by recommending another hostelry – but one of fine quality – near Calais, an hotel which does justice to the honourable calling of "Hotelier" and does not insult, rob and poison the traveller who is at its mercy.

I am and Will Remain, in a Fury of Disgust,

Sir Philip Thicknesse (Knight)   *vide PS* over

. . .

. . . *Post Scriptum*: It is my fervent wish that the carrier charges you highly for this letter – as much or more as the night at your Hotel Angleterre cost .

Mary and Lady Ann had witnessed the last and fully embellished letter which Thicknesse wrapped and sealed with much to and froing for lighted taper and wax and still even at the last moment inserted another piece of invective written as a second postscript into the letter.

The ladies' continued distress over the hapless parakeet had brought Thicknesse to his feet but there was still too much frothing and muttering from him to allow a proper sympathetic hearing for Mary and Lady Ann, who took turns while one told the tale and the other wept over the bird's death. However, there was just enough distraction for me to slip into my seat and begin the task of unbending my quills and removing splashes of ink from the desk and its surroundings. Finally with a gross rudeness I had not thought possible even of him, Thicknesse left the room breaking wind . . .

He came straight back in as if he had only left to save us from the consequences of his rearguard action, or more likely I feared to let a noisy rip in a not so much different way on another subject. It was another subject:

'I have been reminded' Thicknesse said 'by considering the faults of the proprietors of the Hotel Angleterre that it is the characters themselves who are hateful. It is nothing to do with skin colour or any part of their physical appearances but about themselves – their actions – their speech – kind and attentive – or opposite in all things. I learned these things in Jamaica where the whiteness of white men and women or the blackness of black skin is no indicator of quality or station in life or anything other than the deeds to be credited to them. It is the same in London where dignified coal black men and women mix freely with the white *ton* but without matching their pretensions.'

Thicknesse had no more strong gales blowing through

him immediately and glaring at me just once to deny me
opportunity to challenge his opinions, he made his way to
the hall and on to the kitchens in a series of violent
movements which punctuated his further comments about
all manner of vile behaviour in human kind. He took into
account the "Flanderkins" – other people recently to have
received the lashing of his tongue:

'They are a very dirty people,' he said, 'strangers to
sentiment or delicacy; and they all take snuff! All classes
take snuff. Even their cooks and scullions have the tincture
of tobacco flavouring everything they touch!'

His voice could still be heard in the kitchen – he
demanding of Cook did she take snuff and ordering her to
hold her hands out that he might look for tell-tale brown
stains. Disappointed I have no doubt by that inquiry he set
forth on a new tack:

'Show me your copper vessels to see if you are
poisoning us with them.'

Whether it was true or not he said that there was
"verdigris in the saucepan!" and he flung it to the ground
as though he were already tainted by it:

'How many hundreds of people have been sent to the
other world by eating soups and ragouts made in copper
pans poisoned with verdigris?'

'*Pas moi, pas moi,*' said Cook '*Je vous en prie croyez
moi.*'

'Bah! I shall question your master M le Blanc for he
may be in ignorance of your carelessness.'

I imagine Lady Ann had discovered her husband ranting in
the kitchens and ushered him out. Cook's gain was my loss,
for Mary, wishing to distract Thicknesse from insults to the
cook, told him how poorly I had become, so setting him on
an expressive oration on "Doctors, Apothecaries, Diseases
and their Remedies" together with examples drawn from
the "Profundity of his own Knowledge and Experiences".

The speech began at the kitchen doorway but in no

time at all was brought into my study and directed fully at me with sufficient loudness to penetrate my dull wits. Feeling that I was expected to play the part of an idiot and one further handicapped by deafness, I was at liberty to play with my wrecked quills and even to write now and again as long as I put a few mock submissive and respectful movements of my eyes in his direction while he spoke. Thicknesse was so occupied with exposition of his own opinions nothing else entered his mind. Now he held forth at length on physicians:

'They are excellent companions over a bottle of claret,' he said 'but they are odious in the company of a phial of their own concoction.

Whomsoever the physician visits, truly his arrival fills up a space, and he may cheer the patient by a pleasant story – but let him not give you his own medicines – have them instead made up by a diligent apothecary.

Most of these have young apprentices whose eyes are keener to read a doctor's bill and understand his hieroglyphics better, and they know more readily how to put the various drugs together.'

Thicknesse waved his hands to include Lady Ann and Mary in his admonishments, and they felt obliged to stay since it was they who had brought him out of the kitchens and they who judged that he was still in need of guards against his more violent outbursts.

'There is much reason to fear from physicians. In the course of every year numbers of worthy citizens are sent to their graves, not from the disorders they labour under, but from the disorder in which their medicines have been prepared. Therefore . . .'

I was uncertain whether he was about to wind up this subject now, or to lengthen it by a mile or two, for he was in full spate and Mary, seeing my one active eyebrow rise, opened her mouth to say something to Thicknesse, but he put his hand up to silence her and continued:

. . . 'Therefore, there is much reason to fear and it is of

the utmost importance to employ an honest, conscientious Apothecary; whereas if you should have need of surgeons – they also command respect.' He allowed a pause for Mary to speak.

'We have called neither . . .' she said, and was silenced.

'But had Mr Farrier needed calling for the stone, or had he suffered as I did for forty years from gall-stones he would have been wise to call for a surgeon. Though to be truthful I have managed with my own physic and the exhibition of laudanum.'

'Yes,' said Mary. 'Tell us about laudanum.'
This was to stop Thicknesse dwelling as was his wont on his own maladies, for gout in this narrative of epic proportion, would follow gall- stones as surely as night follows day – if he were not to be deflected into a possibly briefer dissertation on this one particular medicine.

'Laudanum,' he told us all, 'has rescued me from the most dire distress. When the great Dr Heberden had failed me with his physic I resorted to laudanum for myself and then passed a stone of such magnitude that Dr Heberden vowed he had never seen a stone so large and begged to accept it in place of his fee.

'If there is something peculiar in my temper – as many of my friends as well as my enemies assert – it is entirely to be accounted for by forty years suffering at the hands of Master Gallstone. Large stones have cracked the chamber pot and small black diamond gravel has sprayed and chipped the edges of the very same pot at the very same time.'

'But do tell us about laudanum,' said both Mary and Lady Ann in chorus.

'Unless you had rather tell Mary more of our Grand Tour of the Low Countries,' Lady Ann pleaded just loud enough for Thicknesse to hear.

'Laudanum,' said Thicknesse again, rolling his eyes around with impatience at this interruption, 'even without an ox bladder of hot water applied to the stomach, laudanum on its own – twenty drops every half- hour – will ease the passage of the largest and hardest stones. Laudanum is the foremost elixir – the cordial for any pain such as gout or colics of any kind.'

'But are there not other necessary measures to be taken along with the laudanum?' Mary asked.

'Indeed. A good wine tends to the prolongation of life – gives a fillip to nature. And before laudanum is administered, in severe cases of any kind, previous evacuation and vomits are strongly recommended. In stones from the gall bladder – provided the aforementioned matters have been attended to and that sufficient of the laudanum has been given – I have discovered that lying on my belly on a table with a heavy person on my back, has caused the stone to pass – or return into the bladder.'

'It is true. It is true,' said his long suffering wife, 'and when I have been the only person to be found to sit upon you, you have chastised me for my lack of weight.' Thicknesse looked kindly upon his wife for a moment and then cleared his throat to begin again:

'In the case of a Venerable Dean at Bath – cousin to the late Countess of Desmond – I told him this cure for his gall-stones and he was so enamoured of my treatment he made me a very handsome present then and at every anniversary thereafter. Then when one day as he did many times a week, he drank a large quantity of Bath Waters and ate a hearty breakfast of spongy hot rolls – Sally Lunns – and dropped down dead and never played the fiddle again.'

Thicknesse has an aptitude for embroidering a great deal into his stories with rarely a *petit point.* Certainly breathlessness, not tact,

and possibly hunger, but not consideration of fatigue in his audience, brought Thicknesse to an hiatus in his discourse just wide enough to permit "His Ladies" as he called Mary and Lady Ann, to encourage him away towards food for them all.

'One more word about gout . . .' said Thicknesse over his shoulder . . .

'I remember . . .'

But the women hushed him, and finally each taking an arm ushered him from the room.

Mary will return in a while to give me some supper in privacy, with no spectators to see the overflow of spittle from the corner of my mouth.

Chateau de Voirons
May 8th.

Thicknesse and Lady Ann have stayed several days amusing us (to his satisfaction at least) with accounts of this and that culled from Thicknesse's various experiences of life. He related with particular relish how before he left England with a Captain's commission he had spent all his income-in-advance in a female coffee house in Covent Garden. Here as the coffee grew cool and he and the serving maids grew hot, for his necessary relief they removed the uniform that they declared had caused all their excitement and allowed him to buy it back after his pleasure was complete. Thicknesse regarded himself as a brave character in the narrative but Lady Ann had a different opinion and said so.

After one evening's account of this and other adventures, Thicknesse and Mary spent time in some other part of the chateau, as my father used to say "as closely boxed together as Will and Mary on the coin". My instant concerns about infidelity were relieved for a short while by the presence of Lady Ann. She appeared to enjoy my company as well as I hers, and I was flattered to have the pleasure of her beauty and close attention. She appeared to me, although I am lame and speechless and with many of the afflictions of age before my time, to look upon me with a very gentle kindness, as if I were the cleverest and most handsome prince alive. To my shame I let my fancy dwell on the ifs and mights of what I might achieve with my one good arm if she were compliant and Thicknesse and Mary remained much longer "boxed together".

I had begun to scratch out these lines when my wife returned to explain her absence. Thicknesse had let Mary know what a fine musician he is. (Oh I do write of him unfairly. He said in my presence that he had only poor talents as a fiddler but I believe later he had dropped any cloak of modesty from himself and declared his talents as a fiddler to be above the ordinary.) Mary, with that quick intelligence that surprised anyone who is in her company for more than a minute, prised out from Thicknesse the real extent of his skill and, what is more, had him promise that the next time he came he should bring his fiddle with him. Then Lady Ann on her viola da gamba, and they adding anecdotes when the music paused, should regale me and us all with an entertainment. For Mary said: 'Poor William has had no frolics in years and no entertainment has cheered this chateau for a long time before that.'

Thicknesse was no less charmed by Mary than I am by Lady Ann, and he readily agreed to Mary's plan but would not give a day for it, nor even a year, but will come again, when he can he says, and bring his Lady and his entourage as complete as it might be. These promises reminded him of other promises he made elsewhere and in his usual whirlwind manner, he was packed in a minute and all assembled for immediate departure –but for one delay. Cook's boy had found some feathered remains and the best part of a wing of the parakeet in the avenue. Thicknesse took these from Lady Ann's hands and announced a ceremony. He sent for a shovel from the stables and precisely measured the centre of the first lawn before the chateau. Here he dug a hole five times as large and deep as needed. He called us all to attendance at the graveside and said a loud prayer in favour of this "beloved parakeet and all other beasts who may receive untimely death by curs", Then he pulled up a young cherry tree in bloom from beside the lawn and planted it fair and square in the heaped

184

up grave. It did not occur to Thicknesse that M le Blanc may not wish for his view or his grass or his trees to be altered in this way, but there was little effective to deter Thicknesse when he had a mind for some plan of his own. Lady Ann gave M le Blanc a tender look of supplication for her husband's errors – a look I would gladly have intercepted on his behalf.

M le Blanc stayed for the customary farewells and to give Thicknesse reassurances about some matter they had discussed. Thicknesse enquired of M le Blanc if all was well in his household and if he could afford to keep Mr and Mrs Farrier for the uncertain future until he Thicknesse, had ensured a good profit (which he is sure will arise) from his published account of his *Grand Tour in the Low Countries.* If M le Blanc was in an easy mind about this charitable matter would he also, Thicknesse enquired, be a subscriber to the intended volume? M Le Blanc agreed.

As Mary said today, 'M le Blanc has finer manners than any other man she knows and seems unaccountably and always firmly in favour of the Farriers.' And I knew M le Blanc to be kindness itself for his present hospitality is a very great reward for some slight favour I did for him on one brief occasion.

It seemed this day again I was not to be entirely master at my own desk even though Thicknesse and his party have gone, for Mary came in when I had just started in a serious way to write. Affecting not to disturb me she tore off a piece from the sheet I was about to write upon and took a new quill and wrote:

'Cook says: "*Le pigeon, et la tarte aux groseilles vertes*".'

I attempted a smile at pigeon-pie and succeeded with a grimace of overpowering sourness at the gooseberry tart which in Cook's recipes was almost always a gooseberry fool made with old gooseberries, curdled milk and burnt sugar, and with pastry afloat like flotsam on the tide. Mary disappeared to tell cook how her suggestion had been received, but before I had done no more than retrieve the new quill, Mary returned. This time she took her place firmly at the end of my desk and with a whole new sheet of paper and another new quill began to write again:

Husband,
You write of such little matters – if the casket offerings you have made lately are considered. How can you hope to "find yourself" again when instead of great matters brought out to reveal your real heart and mind, you mention and make much of trivial things? How shall you remember your own greatness? How shall you explain your passions and warm regard for other people? In what way can inconsequential actions remind you of the good man you are – or were?

Small subjects, the little drudge things form my life it seems. I bear such diminution ill at times. But as a woman I have to pay attention to matters beneath your dignity and, as you would tell me, they are "beyond your capacity" as a man. So please Husband, lay out the grand scheme of your life, not the gossip that fills your pages now. For then when you recover you will regain your pride as well as your speech and again you will speak powerfully in the way you once did – sufficient to fill a cathedral with every utterance.

And Cook says you shall have red currants in a tart instead of gooseberries.
Mary

Wife,
You do not, I think, understand. Such is the fate of every man – to be misunderstood not only by the world at large but also by the woman who presumes to love him. I am not exceptional in this. You Mary, misunderstand yourself and trivialise yourself in the same way that you accuse me of

186

making a smallness of my life. Note that Lady Ann is not so unkind to herself. On the contrary she has demonstrated her talents at every turn. She has done and still performs in public – braving the gaze of a sometimes critical public and being the subject of tavern tittle-tattle because of her masculine deportment. Although I do admire her as a woman for her beauty, she is too manly bold to reside permanently in my affections. You my dear, dear Mary on the other hand, hide unnecessarily your talents of tenderness and domestic skills which are entirely suitable to a woman, and not lessened by your being beautiful and clever to a great degree. It may perhaps be that womankind, your fair sex, has been so reduced and diminished as to what you may or may not do in polite society – all your sentiment and sensibility has spilled out into the daily lives of men about you. As a consequence, we have at the time and in the years I am reaching here in my own history, all around us a bursting into acts of charity and fine feeling amongst the populace. Even though perhaps the greatest acts are apparently done by men, the sentient power that directs them comes from you and your sisters. You dear Mary, please do not groan under the weight of your disadvantages. Rejoice in the great good you do even when you might say you are in chains.

Here is another point in your morning note: the "small matters" that you so despise in my story are told because they are real; they exist and therefore come into my mind. Memory – at least my memory – is quite perverse. It is a sieve which often selects the little easy things and preserves these finer grains for consideration. Large things are on occasion too large to fit into the sieve of memory, and are rejected or fail to make any appearance at all. It therefore follows that whatever edifice is created from my memoirs, these are my confessions and will be recognised as being truly from me by inspection of the individual small bricks that built it and their characteristics of colour, shape, size and surface texture which all put together give the whole structure of me.

Even if that were not so, there is an ease and comfort in recalling trivia. More importantly I do need the ease and comfort of considering trifles, and who should deny me that? There may . . . I hope there will be . . . consequences for me from what I write, but my scribbling has no import for any other person than me and puts no cares upon you, my Mary.

William

Tied up in a pair of knotted garters frayed and faded and on the point of snapping, Thicknesse has left a bundle of papers – letters and books. It is a mystery where he found them. Mary asked him, but he only tapped his nose and winked and said,

'Do not concern yourselves good friends. They shall not cost you one penny although the guineas charged to me lessen my income considerably.'

Then he bowed like a gallant, and changed to many other subjects about which he has no shortage of opinions.

Tomorrow – for today is far spent – I shall direct my pen towards Cambridge for the second time, and shall see if the motes from my memory will make a small beam to shine on my life.

CHAPTER 14

BACK TO CAMBRIDGE

*Advice from Mr Griffiths; The Reverend Dr Squire;
John Parkhurst for Hebrew and an introduction to his
Aunt; Ordination and return to London.*

The Reverend Mr Dodd had never been so long absent
from Bourne and doubted whether his curate Mr Vokes
could be trusted with the parish and the school across the
churchyard without frequent prompting and suggestions
from my father. In this latter's mind it was then doubly
urgent to return as soon as possible to the fenlands. Barbara
needed my room, which my father now occupied, for a
maid whom she intended to engage as soon as possible.
Porter declined to interfere in discussions between his wife
and her father, and although he did not actually wash his
hands of those matters, he spat anxiously on them a great
deal.

My mother's declining health was of concern to my
father. Adding urgency, in his mind was his growing doubt
that I would remain set upon the course towards ordination
to which I had agreed, if I remained open to all the
temptations that London offered .

With these grave worries bearing him down, my father
wrote quickly to his friends at Cambridge to beg them grant
my immediate admission to tutors in Hebrew and Divinity.
As soon as letters returned making all arrangements clear,
my father fixed his return to Bourne by way of Cambridge
so that en route he could deliver me directly into the hands
of my mentors. An early morning departure was indicated.
Mary and I were barely finished our breakfast when The
Reverend William Dodd arrived on foot. Though impatient
to be going again to Bishopsgate, he stood with us a while

189

in the small parlour. He clasped our hands in his and prayed aloud. He did not turn prayers into a litany and then those into a sermon; he only recited slowly as we joined in:

'*Our Father which art in Heaven, hallowed be thy name . . .*'

His sincerity and touching sadness brought a tear to all our eyes. I could not but wonder at his goodness: that he should have his first concern for us who each had a life ahead while his was stiffening into age and death. Mary and I embraced; I charging her with writing a letter to me if at any point she was unhappy, or in danger, or in distress.

Casually, as we stepped towards the door to leave, my father said, 'I have bought back your play,'

'What? "Sir Roger de Coverley"?'

'It is not fit that one expecting to be ordained should have his work appear on stage.'

'Where is it? How much did you pay to bring it back? And how?'

Mary saw my eyes flashing with anger and my father's tremble increasing as he withered before me. She held up her hands as though to protect my parent from the heat of my temper.

'Your Mr Jolly was quite glad to return the play. He said there were difficulties in mounting it and some of the actors who were already engaged proposed after all to be in another piece.'

I quietened my voice – but to a sinister level:

'How? How much? How should you feel it right to take my living

from me?'

'Mr Jolly was satisfied – in view of all his trouble – with one hundred and twenty pounds. So my son, I drew up a draft for that sum.'

And then he cut me to the quick:

'Mr Jolly said he had been too generous before and was as sorry as I that we had both paid above the odds for a work of little worth.'

I, from being on the point of bursting out into a torrent of angry words, sank into stunned silence. Mary, looking over the old man's shoulder silently mouthed, 'Forgive him.'

We began, he trailing behind me, to walk to Bishopsgate with our bags held tightly in my hands. By the time I had reached Bishopsgate my father was some way behind, tottering painfully. I waited and looked pitifully on him – a man who had never loitered in the flesh pots of London – a man whose income was sparse and yet, to save me as he thought from impending disgrace, bought back my play at a cost which could have employed four curates for a year. I hoped The Reverend Mr Vokes would not learn of my father's largesse – a largesse that any curate might envy and that would put debt around my father's neck for as many years as he might live; but I could not let my anger rest on him any longer and found sufficient coin in my purse to allow us to pass time in Mr Bartoli's Coffee House. My father's anxiety to be in good time for the Cambridge coach had allowed us an hour before it should be due at ten o'clock. Warm beer in The Coach and Horses was not to our tastes, but there was comfort in Mr Bartoli's Coffee House and so we sat and shared the pages of the week's *Gentleman's Magazine*. The Reverend Mr Dodd read serious news of books reviewed and notices of church preferments. He examined obituaries in detail to compare the age of the deceased with his own and if there was a given cause of death to dwell upon for like comparison. Youth will rarely tarry on such timely deaths; and I sought out tragedies to read and all the better if those were of a salacious nature. I read aloud to my sad parent:

'On Monday of this week,' (it was now the Thursday) 'a young woman took a boat at Somerset Stairs and when the workman had rowed into the river, he attempted to be rude with her which she resisting, the boat overturned and they both drowned.'

'She will enter into the Kingdom of Heaven,' my father

said, 'but only God knows how it shall be with the boatman even if he was but an instrument in the hands of God.'

He fell silent for a long time then, no doubt conjuring images from past accidents and deaths that had darkened and would still darken his priesthood and how he had comforted the bereaved; for he was a sentient man who ever questioned his purposes and their effects.

Our silence following this was broken by the entry of a weary coachman to our Coffee House. He said that if any of us were expecting to board the coach for Cambridge at ten o'clock we should find some employment for another hour at least. Our appointed coachman had broken his leg that very morning on taking a tumble from the roof of his coach "while fixing a tear with pitch and canvas of which he now had greater need to mend his own leg."

Our companions-to-be on the coach declared their presence by being the ones themselves groaning loudly at the delay. Those who had just eavesdropped on my report of a young woman's drowning were even louder now in their expressions of unhappiness, and only lowered their discontented chorus to listen to further news from the informant that "a fresh coachman has been sent for – but he has to come up from Holborn and it is doubtful whether he will be fully fresh since he was known to be drunk last night and unlikely to be in full command of his senses for another hour or two."

The weary coachman who enlivened himself by telling this tale was asked – even commanded by one arrogant buck – to take the reins of our conveyance himself. He declined with solid reason – he had to take the Harwich coach on the following day – but the groaning and disbelief was hardly abated.

"*O tempora*! *O mores*! How the times are changed,' said my reverend father for the buck to hear and did not feel at all discomforted by the sneer he received in return. The buck then took himself off, acquired a chaise and went down the Cambridge road immediately. Our progress was

more leisurely and required an extra night at Royston
before reaching our destination late on the Friday. Here I
settled immediately into Clare Hall and my father repaired
to The Blue Boar that night and left for Lincoln early next
morning. He left a note for me with the lodge porter at
Clare. It was without heading and written on a scrap of
paper which on the reverse claimed it to be the property of
The Blue Boar:

'Live soberly my son, righteously and Godly. Fear Him
and keep his commandments. Be daily devout in private
and in public. Be penitent, faithful and charitable. May
your studies, as your devotions, lead you to a calm and
good life henceforth.

Your father, who holds you tight in his affection, William
Dodd'

My rooms were grander than before, being also by good
chance immediately below The Reverend Mr Griffith's
apartment. He was not only to be *in loco parentis* – a
position to which he appointed himself – but also was to be
my tutor in Divinity, and the immediate care and attention
to both these responsibilities was aided by the proximity of
our rooms. In fact, I was to spend more time above than
below and able to apply myself most diligently to my
studies. At least for this time, Mr Griffith assumed a new
seriousness. On my arrival he had greeted me from his
window over the street with a shout and a smile that filled
the casement and he caught me stretching my head
upwards and backwards to see him clearly:

'Welcome Dodd – returned, come back as surely as the
sound of your palindromic name predicted – Dodd.
Welcome emocleW!'

'Thank you Sir. Back, but not backward I trust.'

'You are married now I hear? Your Eve has taken you?
Not against your better knowledge, I vow?'

He had made a parody of the lines from Milton and I responded in a like vein:

'No, *"but finally overcome with female charm"!'*

I bowed to him, sweeping the cobbles with my hat. He then saw how modestly I was dressed: coat and breeches of brown stuff with no lace dripping from the neck and wrists; my hair tied with a simple black band – for my wig was in the bag at my feet – silver buckles fastened my shoes and fixed my breeches at the knee but the stockings were of a coarse green wool which would not chime with the floral waistcoat had I revealed it. With no further words exchanged but following a gesture from Mr Griffiths for me to come in and come up, I restored my hat to position and he closed the window, pulling it home with a final tug tightly into the frame. (To my knowledge he did not open it again for the duration of my stay and his copy of *Paradise Lost* stayed shelved, squeezed between the *Lives of Latimer, Prideaux and Grotius* on the one side and a black bottle of claret on the other; which latter was replaced each day and which bestowed a wine red kiss where it stood on the cover of
Mr Milton's *Paradise Regained.*) Neither were my labours at divinity interrupted in any way, for all Mr Griffiths sermons were delivered in Chapel and his apophthegms reserved for the Fellows with him at High Table, where it was a matter of duty for them that each of his sayings was matched by at least two of theirs.

Within days if I had thought my return to Clare signified a life of ease, time to revisit old haunts and bathe in the still waters of academic discourse, I was rapidly disabused:

'Before the letter came from your father,' said my tutor, 'I was sure you would return to us to set upon a new course . . .'

'That is more than I knew then, Sir,' I interjected respectfully.

'Ordination and the church did not appear in my mind before and now I have met with some success as an author where my heart lay more firmly. But I have put all that aside.'

The Reverend Mr Griffiths then enquired in some detail about my writing. When I mentioned my *Synopsis Compendiara* – finished all bar the dedication – he said that The Reverend, now Dr Squire should be consulted. His opinion as to the name to be writ large on the title page was more important than what followed in the body of the book.

Therefore, on his instruction I wrote a flattering letter to The Reverend Dr Squire, reminding him of our meeting a year or so before and his promise to assist me in my advance should I choose a life as a parson after all. Several weeks elapsed before a reply came from the good Dr Squire. The delay was because, on the latest advice at the time, I sent my appeal to the cleric at his fine residence in the palace at Wells where he was Prebender. Whoever forwarded my letter was even shorter of news than I and did not take into account the plurality of Sam Squire's benefices. For it next went to the rectory at Topsfield in Essex. This benefice Rector Squire had left some months before to travel to London for his induction at St Anne's, Soho – which living was in a pair with Greenwich, both crown gifts just granted to him. The latter Vicarage was reputed to be of more than adequate comfort and perhaps even luxury and therefore over the years claimed a considerable number of lengthy visits from Dr Squire. It was not necessary for him to go to another of his livings at Minting in Lincolnshire. (His critics said that was fortunate for "Sam Squirt", because though reckoned to be a scholar in languages – particularly of the Saxon and Icelandic tongues – he had no knowledge at all of geography and was uncertain as to in which part of Lincolnshire Minting was to be found. The reality, which his critics would not accept, was that unlike those less successful at obtaining preferment, Dr Squire had good curates and paid them above the supposed minimum of thirty pounds per annum.) He paid his curate in Minting well to the entire satisfaction of everyone, but even so, there may have been some delay put upon my letter at Minting while the careful curate sought money to pay for its receipt and to enquire where he might send my letter next. No one, it appeared – save Dr Squire himself – was in possession of a complete list of his livings.

In due course, however, a reply came. The tone of it was affectionate and the contents admirably helpful. It suggested that I should put the Bishop of Ely upon the title page and compose as long and as flattering a dedication as the printer allowed room for. The wisdom of this lay in the knowledge that only Dr Squire appeared to have: that my ordination when it took place shortly would be conducted by that very Bishop, the Bishop of Ely. My benefactor also added in his letter that should the Bishop take a like to me and I kept myself unsullied by the world's vulgarities, real preferment may follow early rather than later.

So much good fortune was an encouragement to me to work hard – especially with my other principal tutor – Mr John Parkhurst. He took his
B.A. the year before me and his M.A. and a Fellowship followed quickly after. Early he established his reputation – before he was ordained – for his Hebrew grammar and Lexicon. He rose every morning at five despite being a sickly man – although it was suggested that his early rising and being day-long closeted with his books were the reasons for being a valetudinarian. Whatever the case, my rising habits were little different from his. Together we worked at Hebrew grammar and began reading original texts as soon as I was able. He was a kind man with decided views on punctuation and accents in the language he loved, but he did not insist to me that I should follow him in every line. He brought also the greyest morning to light with colourful descriptions of life in biblical times, and of the

travels of Israelites and Disciples. I sent a message to my father and mother and to Richard to tell him that I had found "my Wesley" and that Hebrew was becoming as familiar to me as Latin and Greek.

My mind was formed with discipline and virtue. Daily bread and water with John Parkhurst before dawn gave way to bread and fruit and claret with Mr Griffiths. My body was kept in touch with my soul by a more satisfying repast in the dining hall – well below the salt – in late afternoon, but I made small beer suffice for my thirst and took the Bible early to bed until candlelight proved no match for the sun's declining rays.

John Parkhurst made himself conscious of my monastic life and my avoidance of all entertainment. Detecting an unfamiliar and unwanted lowering of my spirits, he proposed a scheme of pleasure at the ends of the weeks of September and October. This was to be obtained by paying regular visits to his widowed Aunt Lady Frances Dormer. She was still barely of middle years and had been left well provided for by her husband. He, nearly twice her age, had continued to apply all his waking hours to bringing in a regular harvest from his commercial enterprises – principally of brewing and the manufacture of fine sauces. His businesses and the occupations of such were more suitable to his talents and inclinations than paying constant court to Lady Frances and by dissipating his energies in a giddy life of masked balls and soirees. Other entertainments, hinted at by John Parkhurst, were also avoided by his uncle – principally amongst which was anything of an amatory connection. Scholar Parkhurst suggested, with an obliquity surprising in a student of Hebrew, that he himself only avoided the ardent embraces of Lady Frances by regular reminders to her of his consanguinity.

I felt fully master of my destiny with any of the fair sex, particularly more so when I discovered the real and admirable nature of my tutor's aunt. The distance was too great between the far side of Trumpington and any part of Cambridge where an attractive widow might avail herself of the society of *the ton*. Therefore, the good widow had considered the choices that may be open to her as a clergyman's daughter who had risen into the possibility of good times on the death of her wealthy husband.

She avoided transfer to London – because the "air and the people are unclean", and she declined various offers of marriage to gallants who had arrived at a similar age to herself without making permanent connections. She knew that though their gallantry was not to be doubted, they had produced convincing evidence throughout their lives that their principal ability lay in spending money that was not their own by right. She wished to spend her own money as and when she wished and wisely.

'Lady Frances,' said John Parkhurst, 'despite appearance, had not considered turning her estate into an enormous garden,' although she left her gardeners a free hand to introduce exotic plants and to provide in her hallways and drawing room magnificent displays of flowers and foliage to put amongst the busts and statues.

With modesty and elegance and well controlled passion, Lady Frances hid behind these mass contributions of Mother Nature and Master Artifice. If not there she was at her embroidery, or at her spinette. The former drew very few spectators to watch her nimble and beautifully preserved fingers drive the needle through linen and canvas, while the latter musical prowess seldom attracted more than a half dozen of a pressed audience to listen.

In short, Lady Frances was a woman of refinement, but lonely. My tutor was not for his own fancy inclined to detach himself from Hebrew texts and live beyond Trumpington, but to take me and offer me up to his aunt seemed to him a most excellent idea.

Accordingly every Friday in that autumn, John Parkhurst and I made the journey to Trumpington-and-beyond, shuffling our feet through the crisp autumn leaves and daring each other to mention anything bearing even a remote connection to academic studies of any sort. The Hebrew language was totally banned as a subject for our conversation.

Lady Frances, courteous in the extreme, was anxious to preserve the niceties and not to exceed the most rigid bounds of propriety. She made sure that when we were finished, stuffed full as capons at her table, her maid – who by age could have served as Lady Frances' mother at least – joined our company in the drawing room. This self-same maid had one God-given skill in the same vein as Lady Frances – she could play a minuet. While John Parkhurst, silk scarf around his neck against cough, cramp and quinsey leaned against the spinette, the passionate widow and I danced a minuet or two. The butler and the gardener and two maids of a very humble sort were brought in to dance as the evening wore on.

Whereas a man of less terpsichorean mastery than I may have wilted and been subdued by Lady Frances' energy, she quickly accepted her proper role as a fair but delicate flower in my hands.

Rooks heavy-bellied with spilled grains and beetles from the rich earth flew low over the newly ploughed fields that October and on a Saturday before my ordination, while we took a turn on the lawns, Lady Frances was as heavy-hearted as the laden black birds above her:

'You will, of course,' she said, 'be ordained and leave us shortly.' 'I will, but with many regrets,' I said. 'Your kindness has made the time pass quickly for me – too quickly I fear, for you will have little cause to remember me when I am gone.'

She laughed as if it were a thing of no consequence; but there was in her eyes and in the slightly softened and lowered tone of her voice tinged with the dryness of husks, that suggested my departure meant more to her than it was proper to speak aloud.

'Is there anything,' she said, moving between the palm trees which in great blue pots richly printed with flowers stood in numbers on the flagstones outside the drawing room, 'is there anything I can do for you in gratitude for your visits here these last few weeks?'

'No, surely not. If anything I should make lavish presents to you for you have been and are more than kind to me who has resolved to be a parson and will be permanently poor, no doubt.'

'If only Sir Robert were here . . .' His widow paused then, as if realising if he were here I would not have been. 'He would have had in his power to put you in the way of a curacy nearby. Then I should have had you always near to me.'

My tutor's aunt paused again, knowing this time that she had declared herself too fully.

'What you may help – or direct me towards, is in your power perhaps,' I said. Lady Frances gestured to me to tell her. Now it was my turn to mask my face a trifle with the rich green leaves on their bending stems about us.

'I would I could appear at my ordination in clothes a little finer than this brown stuff,' I said. Then I bit my tongue and blushed and was ashamed to have made such a begging appeal.

'It is done. As good as done, of course. Why could I not have thought of it before? My nephew has an account at Dunkerly's in town. If I am allowed to put a little more than usual there, you may have a suit of clothes and not be ordained in brown stuff with stockings more suitable to a ploughman than to a parson.'

I reddened as much with anger at my own stupidity. While I had been pointing the toe and capering, Lady Frances had been taking note of my coarse clothing – I a bumpkin masquerading as a gallant. Never should I be so dressed again I vowed. If clerical cloth is to be worn it shall have adornments to make, O Lord, this one of Thy chosen people joyful.

To her lasting credit, and to make her saintly in my eyes, Lady Frances with a gentle pressure on my arm and a lowering of her eyes in graceful humility, so inflated my own opinion of myself again that bumpkin or not I danced another and then a final minuet with the greatest skill and smoothest steps of all my dances with her.

On the 21st October, not extravagantly but finely dressed in clerical black with good lace where it would be noted and a new wig and buckles shining like starlight, (Dunkerly's man had dealt with everything), I was ordained at Caius College. The Bishop of Ely impressed upon me the seriousness of my calling and afterwards took pleasure in telling me that I was to be curate to the church of All Saints, West Ham. I bowed deeply at the news, for though the Bishop was only the informant rather than the benefactor, I was sure that gratitude on my part would enhance for the future any good effects gained from making to him the dedication of my work on Locke and Grotius.

The very next day I made farewell to John Parkhurst (who the following year was also ordained and earned the title of Doctor of Divinity), and farewell to The Reverend Mr Griffiths, who had been at my side during the service of ordination and who hoped that I would consider the Bible most often, but never forget Shakespear and rank John Milton always his equal in merit. I made briefer farewells to others – Fellows whose claret I had occasionally drunk – and college servants who had waited upon me. Certain that I would not return to Cambridge during her life time, I gave my gyp a shilling and embraced her for a moment – to give her the illusions of beauty and attraction which, had she possessed, would have prohibited her from serving any of the young men of Clare whose virtue it is supposed must always be guarded from temptation by the ugliness of their gyps.

I left immediately for London. During the term two brief letters from Mary had merely said that she was in good health and was enduring my absence bravely. A letter from Gascoigne on his behalf and also of Bulkley, was intended to give encouragement to me in my clerical studies – "which we always predicted" – and hoped that I had good company to ward off the loneliness of my endeavours. A *post-scriptum* – crammed in at the bottom of the page and consequently of miniscule and barely legible writing – stated starkly that "Marsden was found to be of ill repute and fallen from The Earl of Sandwich's favour."

These letters did not alarm me unduly but I had an uneasy feeling which made me anxious to see Mary quickly. When discharged from the coach into a fine London rain I all but ran down Bishopsgate towards Frith Street.

CHAPTER 15
FINDING MARY

I am Assistant to a Man-Midwife

After Bishopsgate I composed myself in the way I imagined a young curate should compose himself – dignified but with an air of purpose. Purpose indeed I still had, being excited by the prospect of taking my Mary in my arms after nearly six months abstinence.

Despite the drizzle, I opened my coat as I grew warmer and then my waistcoat too. This latter precaution was to hide its brilliance in case it attracted some cut-purse looking for gold in the pockets, for there was as ever jostling on the pavements and rarely any certainty as to who was friend or stranger or thief.

As I came towards the corner of Threadneedle Street, a large crowd was near blocking the way ahead. All to be seen over the craning heads was a pall of smoke; and all to be heard was the popping of charred timbers and the hiss of rain on the embers of what had been a manufactory of perukes. I continued towards St Pauls.

Head down, as the drizzle grew into heavy rain, I contemplated my future beyond Frith Street. By the act of ordination I had given myself to God and to His service. I had, I thought, a purity of heart – and though that had not been tested in the world, I knew I wished with Christian endeavour to labour for humanity. Virtue, honour, benevolence, I had never been at sufficient pains to define – yet they were to support me, I hoped, with the love of God through a lifetime of obligation to Him.

In my soliloquies I did not deny the pleasures of my youth, and my spirits were not yet borne down by white nor even grey hairs on my head. I determined to be honest

203

as well as happy, to be warm in the pursuit of pleasure but not riotous. My prayer again was heartfelt:

"O God make Thy chosen people joyful, and make me always as one such of those".

And as I will ever do, I paid tribute to the effects of my second time in Cambridge.

As my strides lengthened and I approached Frith Street, my expectation of Mary's welcome took precedence over all religious thinking and feeling. In my mind, my picture of her was viewed through the medium of a romantic imagination. Would Mary be at the window looking out for me? Would she run down the steps to greet me and fall into my arms, her kind eyes and open lips telling the warmth of her feeling? Would she swoon right away from the intensity of her passion?

I slowed again to walk with clerical dignity – for my coat was buttoned again now and the white bands of my calling in place at my neck and the trailing coils of my wig wrung out, and my hat balanced for quick removal. But I trod slowly up the steps of the Frith Street house and put a steady hand three times on the knocker. And three times more. And again. And again. And again with a different and more urgent rhythm each time. To the door came . . . Mrs Frampton. She was red faced and flustered, wringing her apron and twisting it as though to tear it into shreds. She hopped from foot to foot – which a person of her plentiful flesh should not do in a narrow doorway.

'Oh, Mr Dodd. Oh, Reverend Mr Dodd, she is not here.'

'But where? But why?'

'Mr Marsden took her, Mr Reverend Dodd. He takes her – or at least sends her – two weeks or more ago. She is went. She is no longer here!'

(Whereas many persons in similar stressful circumstances develop an impediment of the speech, Mrs Frampton developed and demonstrated an impediment of her grammar as well):

'Mr Marsden brings another two women – I should say gentlewomen if I meant it – in place of Mrs Dodd. Aside to me he said, "They are of means and will pay their own way". But I had no money so far.'

'Where is Mrs Dodd now?' '

'Your desk is still here Mr Dodd.'

'The desk be damned! Where is Mrs Dodd?'

'I have the address. I can fetching it at once. The two ladies share the bed – it's the only one I have downstairs.'

'The address?'

Mrs Frampton chose a foot with which to lead off and hurried into the nether-regions from which she had first come. Within a minute the dear lady was back holding a torn off corner of a sheet of my paper. I took the pencilled note.

'It says,' I said, wondering if I were to be made a fool of, 'two penn'orth of best loaf, grapes and apples to make up sixpence.'

'Oh Reverend, I have no letters. I do not read. The note was on the dresser and has been there a fortnight I'll warrant – the last I had before Mrs Dodd left. I'll look for another.'

Even more flustered in her coming and going, the poor woman was back after a while with another torn corner piece of paper. This gave the name Madame Corbiere and an address off Thames Street – further east than Bishopsgate. I cursed under my breath.

Mrs Frampton, unable to tear her apron had removed it and formed it entirely into one large knot which she twisted evermore tightly into its coils.

'When you find her you shall both come back. You should have my room and bed and I will sleep in grandfather's chair in the kitchen where he died five years ago. Oh Reverend Dodd, I am so very sorry. What could I have done?' She twined her fingers painfully in the knot and tears fell on her cheeks like bursts of rain on a poppy field. I could not but feel sorrow for the poor woman

205

despite that my greatest fear for Mary strained to over-ride my every other sentiment. I squeezed the knotted apron with her fingers in it in a gesture of friendliness, and apologised for my oaths, which gestures called forth another spate of tears.

As rain set in again with renewed force, I pulled my hat down over my face and turned back the way I had come to seek for Mary at the sign of The Ship in Tar Alley, Thames Street. I thought for a moment to take a chair, but the cost of that had left me with too few coins and could not in any event carry me as fast as would my feet. So, springing over puddles and small lakes in the Strand and stepping gingerly over the torrent pouring down from the Fleet Market, I passed quickly along between the steaming flanks of the draymen's horses pulling their loads along Thames Street, and so on to Tar Alley. No pickpockets here. They were sheltering in the gin palaces along the route and like all others with sense looking out from the dry rooms inside at the wet world without.

Whether because the rain was greatly reduced in force or could not find its way between the touching roofs in Tar Alley, I was able now to see at what mean dwelling I had arrived. The landlord of The Ship, with reddened haddock eyes and hair stuck lank and flat and black over a white forehead – this Adonis of the Alley – was emptying tankards left hurriedly on the cobbles when the rain fell.

'Madame Corbiere?' I asked. He pointed me to another alley – no more than an aperture – between the timbered walls of adjacent buildings.

'My wife is there now,' he said.

'Thank you kindly, Monsieur Corbiere,' I said.

'I'm not Corbeer,' he responded angrily, 'nor any other Frenchy thing – beer or not. I am Mr Pullen if you wants to know and my wife – Mrs Pullen, the midwife. She is in Madame Corbeer's hutch at this very minute.'

I was hopping from foot to foot now – not like Mrs Frampton with anxiety which properly excludes every other distraction – but in an absent minded and mechanical effort to empty my shoes of water. I was about to ask details of Pullen – to know why a midwife was called to the house where my dear Mary was said to be. But he had returned into the depths of his palace shaking and clanking his tankards and in so far as a haddock may show any expression, looking disdainful and insulted that he might be thought a "Frenchyman".

I therefore put down my coat collar – which when my hat brim had drooped with wetness had acted only as a funnel to pour water down my neck and into my undergarments – and, taking on something of the appearance of a clergyman again, I squeezed my way into the alley- inside-an-alley and knocked on the second door of the evening.

I made adjustments to my frame of mind so that whoever opened the door I should be prepared.

If it were Mary, I rehearsed a smaller play than that imagined at Frith Street, but it still included the first happy consequence of our meeting – kisses and embraces – but fell just short of Mary swooning away and, such is the determining power of language, I was certain that if the door was opened by Madame Corbiere I should see a crow of a woman dressed in black, with a large nose set in a dark face with a bristly sprinkling of black hairs on the chin and cheeks around it. To my surprise the door was in fact opened – at the first knock– by a handsome woman of middle years or above, dressed entirely in red velvet and with features painted to their best advantage to remove unwanted lines and to give the skin a bloom of youth that age denied. But what artifice could not alter was the hard look in her eyes. Nor could it touch the lips up to a smile or bring a look of welcome to her features.

'Oo sent for a clergyman?' she asked in a heavily accented voice and speaking into the room behind her.

'No need to send,' I said. 'I am the Reverend Mr Dodd. You have, I believe, Mrs Mary Dodd in your house?'

FINDING MARY

'Oh, of a certain. Come in. Per'aps a clergyman is no bad person to come just now. For the girl in question is beyond much else I zink.' Thinking she spoke of Mary I pushed past Madame Corbiere into the room. Pallets were on the floor and lying on them was a pale child with a grossly swollen belly. Her head was cradled in Mary's lap as she sat cross-legged on the pallet.

'Oh, come dear William. Come. Do not distress yourself. Sit on the chair next to me . . .While Emily sleeps in my lap I will tell you what I can.'

Mary looked quietly towards Madame Corbiere as if to encourage her withdrawal. Madame Corbiere answered the look as she made her exit:

'I suppose you and Marsden are responsible for all zis and he or you shall pay for it. I am beyond paying for the carelessness of sluts 'eavy wiz child when zey come to my 'ouse.'

The harshness of her voice woke Emily who began to cry and hold her belly as though to contain the pangs arising from it. I looked away from her as much to avoid that pathetic sight as to look at the rest of the room.

Poor candlelight in a bracket on the wall showed another figure squatting on a pile of garments and towels in a corner. This must be Mrs Pullen, the midwife. As if to declare it, she filled the glass she held in one hand from the gin bottle held in the other and took it over to Emily. Mary pushed the midwife's hand away and made no response to her when she complained:

'Waste the very last of the only dregs there is to help this child, would you? What can be done more,' she belched, 'to ease her into eternity?'

'You have done more harm and more hurt than any other shilling midwife off the streets could have done I dare say,' said Mary. 'You have filled her bladder, and sotted her brain 'til she has no sense or strength to push.'

'You are a fool,' said the midwife. 'I have done what I could. She is too small to give birth, her boy-like hips make a channel too narrow to let a full-term babe pass through. I did what I could.'

In a quiet voice, unnecessary now because Emily was asleep again and Mrs Pullen had returned to her corner and was joyfully discovering some more gin left in her bottle,

Mary told me what the midwife had done for her shilling:

'She gave Emily the gin bottle and glass to hold and told her not to spill them. Then, with her filthy black nails and calloused fingers, she groped under Emily's skirts, first making much of "being very orthodoxical, putting mother on her left side"– it was "a side" added Mary, but the right side – and getting her to keep the gin steady and drink some if she would while Mrs Pullen went behind. Emily's feet were used to push her knees up under her belly and Mrs Pullen rummaged into the tender passage to claw back "skin that flaps inside and won't let me get a finger on the baby's head". Emily had cried and her contractions grown more painful but to no purpose. She spilled the gin and angered Mrs Pullen more.'

Mary finished her account with further details at which I blanched and she said to me when Emily was apparently asleep between contractions:

'There is no ease for Emily. She cannot have a live child if it cannot be brought out soon; so in this case her only hope is for the infant to be sacrificed.'

'What do you mean and how should such a dreadful end be achieved?'

'A man midwife will have performed this much many times but none of them yet as far as I know have brought out a baby in the way of Julius Caesar. The French do it often I am told – and so save another child for the church though the mother dies – but a man-midwife could save the mother though the babe would die.'

'And where should we find a man-midwife who will do what you say is needed?'

'Ask the midwife,' said Mary.

'Mrs Pullen,' I said, 'do you know how we may obtain a man- midwife to help Emily further?'

'She is beyond "further help",' she mocked my tones, 'but there is a man-midwife and apothecary who makes much of his skill and may turn out for a fee.'

'We should have him,' I turned to Mary. 'Will I send Mrs Pullen or go myself?'

'Go yourself,' she whispered. 'If Mistress Pullen goes, even supposing her legs won't buckle before she leaves the room, she'll have to take a guinea to bring out the apothecary man-midwife – and she will spend that on gin before she gets past The Ship. So please go yourself. And hurry.'

Committing the man's home and address to memory, I set off into the darkening evening. Mercifully now it was not raining in or out of the alleys although my clothes, already soaked, would hardly have suffered more if the skies had opened their entire burden of rain upon my head. Within half an hour Mr Lloyd was brought back, I acting as his apprentice to carry his case of tools – supposedly his instruments for confinements – and he carrying a more precious and smaller case of medicines and ointments.

Immediately on entering he dropped to his knees by Emily, spread out the contents of his cases and gave her an emetic and a cathartic. He watched the first of these to judge its effect before proceeding to the second. Emily retched and cried in pain and sobbed and retched again. Lloyd turned her on her left side and waited again and hummed and counted the given measures marked in sixpences on the side of each bottle.

With Emily quiet, he raised her outer skirts behind to examine the appropriate parts. One hand rested on her belly and pressed on it from time to time, while the other, not with much less grime upon it than the midwife's, plunged deep into the recesses of the small body, saying he was searching for the "os". Emily struggled and wept for mercy. Lloyd poured four measures of laudanum, handed the phial to Mary to put between Emily's lips and returned his hand beneath her skirt.

Mrs Pullen watched from her corner.

Mary adjusted herself again to cradle the mother's head in her lap. She stroked the child-mother's hair and put a cold compress on her forehead from time to time. With tiny rocking movements and soft lullabies Mary soothed Emily as well she might between contractions.

Mr Lloyd had me on my knees beside him – at first I thought to be at hand for prayer – and indeed I was prepared for that – but now I was to hold Emily's knees up towards her chin with one hand so that the man- midwife had a clear field for his operations. He ordered me to pass instruments into his right hand while his left hand "held the ways open". First he had me pass a small steel pipe curved like a boatswain's whistle which he said he was to put into the bladder. Judging by Emily's screams the pipe never found its mark and certainly no floods of urine escaped, but it did bring pools of bright blood around our knees. By this time sweat had broken out on Mr Lloyd's brow and mine; the fuddled Mrs Pullen found and lit more candles; tears glistened in Mary's eyes and Emily was strangely quiet, her white cheeks even whiter than before and contrasting now with her blue lips. Mr Lloyd called for a "trocar" and snatched it impatiently from the tray when I could not put an instrument to the name. He made a stabbing movement with this piece of steel-tube- and-blade. A flood of dark black fluid spurted to mix with the bright blood about us.

'Ah,' Lloyd said to himself. 'Now the "os"! Spread, spread and let my finger in.'

Apparently the manoeuvres worked to his satisfaction for he put his bloodied left hand back on Emily's belly shamelessly revealing all below her waist. He pushed and pushed with this hand turning on the white flesh beneath it and printing its bloody palm print on the skin.

'Ah,' he said again, 'a head. Here's the softness in it.'

His next movement was so quick, so fierce, that I saw only

the flash of trocar and then as it withdrew and plunged again . . . white matter like

lambs' brains came down in lumps from within poor Emily.

'Ah! Evacuus!' Lloyd shouted, *'cranium infantum de structorum!*

The evacuation is near complete!'

He grunted and twisted the instrument savagely again and pulled.

Then he inserted forceps from the tray and brought down crushed bone. There was no resistance from Emily. I felt her legs slack against my hand and looking at her face on Mary's lap that fair child's head was still; her eyes lifeless behind half closed lids, her small dimpled chin smooth and drooped towards her chest.

Lloyd pulled down hard with a hook taken from its case. Tiny chest and arms and hands and fingers and legs and toes, all perfectly formed came quickly now and lay loose in the blood and dark fluids on the pallet. I hid them from Mary's gaze with some coarse towelling, but her eyes were fixed, blind, spilling tears onto Emily's dead face and all were silent as though this were a sacred moment, a sacrament. I put my hands together and prayed.

We all were still silent there while blood congealed and a distant watchman called "Ten of the clock and all's well", denying the truth we had all witnessed in that dark house that dark night.

'You say a prayer would you, man?' Mr Lloyd asked, 'Aloud for us?'

I did, and with more sincerity than I knew I possessed asked mercy for the souls of Emily and her baby – a son who had neither known or been known to Emily or anyone in the cruel world:

'And may God through the mercy of our Lord Jesus Christ grant us forgiveness for our ignorance and give us the power to make better of our lives in this world.'

As I finished and as Mary and Mr Lloyd said 'Amen'

and after them Mrs Pullen said, 'Amen, Amen, Amen,' Madame Corbiere appeared at the door. She took in all with her stony glare and fixed that glare finally for a long time on the infant body lying headless on the pallet.

'*Peche mortel* – what mortal sin,' she said and left the room.

Half an hour beyond this, Mrs Pullen was senseless on her pile of cloths; Mary was weeping still and I comforting her as she sat now upon my knee like a child with her nurse; and only Mr Lloyd was sufficiently recovered to speak about the ordinary things of life, principally amongst which – when he had gathered all his instruments and medicines together and cased them – was the urgent matter of payment due to him. I thought I might have included some supplications about fiscal matters in my prayers – asking for mercy from the man-midwife, but it was too late for that now for Mr Lloyd was a man of the world again. So I settled his bill

— which my startled eyebrows showed him I thought it beyond the mark: 'The labourer is worthy of his hire, look you upon it that way,' he said

and put the coins I handed to him deep into a pocket no pick-pocket could ever find. He left promising to send an undertaker to Madame Corbiere's on the morrow.

I walked across to The Ship and asked Mr Pullen to have his wife – whom I said had become exhausted by all the procedures – fetched home to him. Pullen's man was given the task. Ancient and creaking, he scarcely had strength to carry himself over the road, let alone the additional burden of his master's wife. He begged me to help him in the task, which done I returned again to Mary.

With great relief I brought Mary away and felt even more ease of mind when we had safely negotiated the dark streets leading away from Tar Alley. I found a link-man to light our way to Frith Street. Here Mrs Frampton, appearing to us as an angel of light compared to Madame Corbiere and to Mrs Pullen midwife, gave up her bed as promised and took up her grandfather's chair in the kitchen.

Before she sank into an exhausted slumber Mary told me that Marsden had been found out as a pimp for clients other than the Earl of Sandwich's friends, and had been dismissed from further association with him. Marsden's last act before Sandwich cut off his income entirely, had been to send Mary to Madame Corbiere's on a pretext and to move his two new "ladies" into Mrs Frampton's house.

Mary fell asleep before I could give her any proof of my ardour, nor release any of the monastic restraint I had suffered over the last six months. I had to be satisfied with the sight of her beautiful face, fresh touched with the pink of roses and with her chestnut hair tumbling over the white pillows. I was thankful for these mercies, for how would it have been had I found Mary not Emily lying in the dark room in the dark house in Tar Alley, and how would I have borne that?

Mrs Frampton, quite recovered from yesterday's anxieties, was up before times. Her crumpled clothes told of the night's discomfort in grandfather's chair, and also offered an explanation for her calling us from our bed long before the pigeons had left Frith Street for the ploughed fields of Marylebone. Mary was likewise full of today's business and one would imagine had no recollection of the horrors of yesterday. She chirped and bustled about the house getting our goods and chattels together.

I had a dull headache and a chill sufficient to turn my marrow to ice. I sneezed and Mary, happening to find the nosegay unused since I was last in London, made a half serious attempt to discover roses on my skin. She laughed and desisted in her role as mock-physician only when Mrs Frampton began to knot her apron and to hop from foot to foot.

'Dear Mrs Frampton,' Mary said, 'The Reverend Mr Dodd is in good health I assure you. Mind you he is a worry to himself. If he does but sneeze or cough just once he will declare that the plague is upon him and that it is too late for physic and that he will be dead within the hour. "Please," he will say "call for the undertaker now that I may make proper arrangements for my burial." Oh! My husband is a worry.'

I frowned to disclaim such cowardice and paucity of spirit. But I did truly feel ill and had rather stayed in the warmth of Mrs Frampton's parlour than to venture out under the black skies casting their dripping sackcloths over London.

It was, therefore, with no great pleasure we left the comfort of Mrs Frampton's house to enter the cold climate of the Porters – or at least the temporary coldness of Barbara's reception for us. She had been at pains between the demands of her present maternal cares, to prepare for the delivery of some admonitory sermons to me. My sister always assumed that she had the licence and authority to act *in loco parentis,* and the more so now when she had matched my achievement of ordination with her maternity; and there at her elbow, shiny cheeked and filling his cradle with the sounds of recent attendance at the breast, was Thomas.

Mary was readily given consent to lift him into her arms.

The conspiracy which then developed between them took them round other parts of the house to admire and name objects that were beyond the interest and comprehension of the babe; from the far reaches of Porter's emporium I dimly heard him told to greet his father who thus let us know that the wonderful son was also named for his father – Thomas.

Barbara was now free to direct all her attention to me. She took a small purse of money from a drawer and gave it to me as a present from my father; and from the same drawer, a set of well starched clerical bands which she, Barbara, had made as a token from my mother and herself. I thanked her profusely, which thanks did not, as I had intended, bring warmth into her manner; but I had to allow that she was perhaps charged by our parents with the serious matter of my moral welfare. Such responsibility could not be faced lightly by a woman younger than I and not regularly given to cleverness.

I settled back as far as possible in a hard chair in the Porter's parlour, and sniffed and coughed and blew my nose immediately to establish in Barbara's mind that whatever noises came from me subsequently were entirely due to my ill state of health and not as commentaries on anything she said.

'William,' she paused and looked at me intently, 'you have I suppose – I hope – given up and have entirely done with all the follies and frivolities of the city?'
The question demanded no answer and as I had momentarily expended the last sniff in my nostrils I felt that a dry snort would be overstating my feelings of insult at her question. I remained silent.

'Your father and your mother, William, expect great things from you.'
Barbara spoke earnestly about their faith in my honesty and my ability to interpret the scriptures rigorously, about my upright character and setting an example to the congregations – avoidance of the wickedness and lewdness of the theatre – about seeking comfort at the domestic hearth not in the chambers of libertines – to be modest and to give my talents in the service of God and not for my own vain gloriousness . . .I remained silent. Barbara smiled a little, self-conscious at the length and passion of her exhortations. Yet she began again:

'William, you have seen a little of the world. Porter has seen more . . .'
I raised my eyebrows, but allowed them to settle slowly as though their elevation had been coincidental and I wiped

an eye to show that I was a man of feeling to be moved by Barbara's words . . .

'. . . Porter tells me that our great city east of here is a hell on earth where the poor – men and women – fall to theft and murder and even young girls are sunk into prostitution. Whatever vice that leads to drink and follows from it, claims the poor. He says on any night however cold, you may see children naked but for a few rags, sleeping huddled in the shelter of walls and even in the gutters; though often those without a parent to protect them, or perhaps left by their mothers as unmanageable and unsupportable, are dead. Dead, William, dead . . .'

Barbara tried to show that she was not affected; but the deceit was only achieved by her leaving the room. Had she seen the tears in my eyes a cascade would have burst from hers. Barbara looked for Mary and Thomas and gave the babe the hug denied to the dead children of whom she spoke.

I did not protest when Barbara came back and took her place facing me again. What was the use of me denying what Porter told her when it was true? What was the use in telling her that I knew all this sadness if I would not raise my voice against it, much less lift a hand to help any one of the gutter orphans of whom she spoke?

'William, now being The Reverend William Dodd, will you as a clergyman have any thought about these things? It is such sadness that it is no-one's particular business to attend to the wants of the wretched creatures, the poorest people of London. But your mother would have you take thought. And I. Your father too, though he has poured all his effort into giving you an education and manners fit for a gentleman. Yet he will say that good manners and *hic haec hoc* cleverness, as he would say, won't feed a mouth or lift a soul from despair.

'William you are a serious man beneath it all, and full of good intentions. Will you be so as the curate in West Ham? Or is the egg still sticking to your head as Mr Porter

217

says?'

This latter question roused me from my silence, but as Porter, Thomas and Mary all came in at the same time, Barbara's sermon was abruptly ended and my rejoinder cut off before it reached my lips.

The next day in Porter's cart Mary and I leaned against the desk-table that had served for all my literary efforts in London. Sticks of furniture – gifts from the Porters – rattled around us as Porter encouraged his horse to make steady progress through the city and to trot more quickly along the flat roads to West Ham and Plaistow.

CHAPTER 16

ALL SAINTS, WEST HAM

However low my spirits after Barbara's gloomy sermons, they were raised by the sound of bells ringing loudly from the tower of All Saints, West Ham. My mind was diverted from the awful scenes visited and retold – of sickness and poverty and of the vile and meagre lives decaying in the blacker parts of London, and each peal reminded me that this was the first of November – All Saints Day 1751 – a day red-lettered in the calendar for the church itself and for me as the day when I was to begin my work amongst the people of West Ham and Plaistow.

It was to the clean, rain-washed cobbles of Broad Street, Plaistow, that we were now come. The Curate's House stood at the corner of Broad and Baalam Streets, which Mary said being named for Baalam must be named for Baalam's Ass as well. And she used some strange phrase pulled out of the language of Durham, which was to mean that I and Baalam's Ass were well suited – but there was no need to stop the cart in mock anger to demand her obedient and immediate descent because we were already pulled up before the steps of our home.

At the doorway stood The Reverend Mr Wyatt – my Vicar and my future friend and mentor.

First appearances, if faulty, do not deceive for long, and in all the years I knew this man he never varied from being a pious and prudent divine; and much more than that, a rare man in whom showed the happy conjugations of civility and sincerity and an easiness and freedom of manner in measures to enrapture his friends and disarm any who would be his enemies.

Peeping round Mr Wyatt was the diminutive Mrs Wyatt, who directed her welcome particularly towards

Mary. They were soon in cheerful conversation, exchanging histories, and oohing and aahing about all manner of things in our home. So engrossed they were, Mr Wyatt had to claim their attention for him to introduce Mr Arthur Semple, Church Warden, to their presence.

This man occupies but little time in my memory and none of it gratifying; and if I shall have cause to mention him it cannot be for pleasure. The good Vicar had brought him to help with arrangements in the Curate's House as soon as we had advertised our coming. However, Mr Semple was clearly not content to be summoned on such a trivial pretext. He was a man so prim that he walked as if he had fouled his small clothes and the look on his face as if he smelled it, and the greatest contribution he gave to this day's welcome was to go from room to room and point out to Mrs Wyatt things that needed attention – some other person to do – "a cabinet dusted there, a floor-board tightened here".

It was, therefore, with a sense of a burden lifted when Mr Wyatt released Mr Semple with thanks and we four were able to find seats and talk together.

Mrs Honore Wyatt was herself the daughter of a clergyman on whose death his widow had been thrown onto the world. Honore's mother was suddenly without income and, since her husband died young, had but twenty pounds capital. She opened a small shop selling millinery and at the back started a "Petty School" and earned a few more pence. Three sons of the widow were taken out of their school at once and found humble employment in the vicinity – one aged thirteen apprenticed to a baker, another (who was quick with letters although only twelve) helped a gentleman's land agent with his bookwork and was accommodated by him; and the third was taken in by a distant relative – a farmer – in Norfolk. It fell to the boys' sister Honore to help their mother with the shop and needle work to supply it, and to listen to the lisping children at their alphabet and catechism. She kept up the school teacher task even after the Reverend Mr Wyatt (then a curate) took her as his wife, and she walked daily from West Ham to Poplar where she taught and then back to West Ham, until her mother died.

While Mrs Wyatt gave out her life history to Mary (and had little time to hear much in return) her husband questioned me closely about my literary endeavours. Correspondence with my father, whose benign but determined shadow still loomed – and was bound to loom over me – suggested that I promised to lay aside all pretensions to be an author; that my *Hymns of Callimachus* was considered a trifle to be forgotten; *Sir Roger de Coverley* an aberration best forgotten. But my mention of *The Beauties of Shakespear* already much advanced, was greeted with applause by Mr Wyatt:

'You are not to ignore this labour – Shakespear has brought more into our language and into our mental lives than all the silver tongues of other poets and dramatists and puts our philosophers to shame for meddling so airily with the principles of life.'

'I will not, Sir, agree your argument about one of our poets – Milton is not to be ignored – nor Locke, nor Bishop Berkeley amongst our philosophers. You may argue that Hume has stepped too far outside the pathways of true religion but even he must be allowed a place – and Descartes too if you care to remember him.'

'I enjoy your contradictions. I see we shall get on famously. And you must follow those paths that God and your inclination lead you to.'

When I told my mentor of my concern for the common run of people and how they were for the most part in London's most God-forsaken places, he said:

'Not at all. You shall find here in the gentle pastures of West Ham and Plaistow both Dives and Lazarus, and both will hear of you. There are as many die of gluttony as starvation; and both have need of understanding and compassion.'

Mr Wyatt then softly questioned me about my ambitions; about my aspirations for preferment and said:

'... *Love and meekness Lord,* become a Churchman better than ambition: do you not think so?'

I borrowed a twinkle from his eye and replied:

'I hope that you will allow one favour to your curate and do not as some ungracious pastors do:

"Show him the steep and thorny path to Heaven for I would rather

Tread the primrose path of dalliance ..."'

So it was to be: beyond that day our conversation rarely omitted quotations from Mr Shakespear, unless it was instead to exchange Greek or Latin epigrams. Our friendship blossomed as we also shared all clerical tasks.

The landscape and the people of West Ham were both congenial. Merchants and bankers, lawyers and men of affairs weary with their labours in the city were refreshed and calmed by the pastoral landscape as they returned home. Marshland bordering the placid river Lea meandering quietly to the Thames, sounded only to the cries of wheeling gulls. Sheep and cattle grazed next to the turnip fields; goats let roam into the village were herded from mischief by simple children trained to that task only; every house had a view of green sward and the billowing figures of elm trees standing sentinel in the fields.

At the beginning I had no ambitions to advance more quickly in my profession than the slowly turning years required and I caught the leisurely mood of so many of the parishioners – men of letters, antiquarians, men of science, poets and musicians – who were either already blessed with sufficient means, or who had profited well enough from their exertions to leave off unceasing occupation in their professions, and to slow to the leisured pace of all West Ham.

Mary of course, although I think sometimes she had quicksilver in her veins instead of blood, earned surprise and gratitude as she moved between poor households dispensing kindness. Occasionally she gleaned clothing from the rich, where she was just as welcome and where she took tea with the lady of the house, and gave the clothing to the poor.

Meanwhile, I had before long satisfied The Reverend Mr Wyatt with the sermons I delivered – which was no great surprise as he was my mentor.

'A good sermon at All Saints," said he, 'has to suit the congregation.
You will preach to empty pews if you upbraid the people here. Rather show them by various illustrations from life and from the Scriptures how they can confirm for themselves that they may all enter the Kingdom of Heaven. Show them how that in the giving of alms and generous but not ostentatious offerings to charity – and with the power of the God whom they understand and whom they fear less than do many inferior mortals – the eye of the needle will be widened so that even our fat camels in West Ham may enter into the Kingdom of Heaven.'

For all Mr Wyatt's piety, he knew as well as did all his congregation that the important object in his life and theirs was money. Beauty and truth and godliness were without lasting effect if they were not supported by a sound foundation of wealth. West Ham and Plaistow and the nation at large were mere useless shadows of reality without the gold – not paper money – but the gold that made England great.

My own contribution to "solidity" – an attribution much admired in West Ham – was to secure the Lectureship at All Saints. Such an advance to my curate's income earned me the right I thought – and I was encouraged by my Vicar – to give some time outside my daily visits to the sick, and to the ordinary services, and baptisms and weddings and funerals – to complete *The Beauties of Shakespear.*

Autumn was exceptionally kind this year as it stretched

into late November. On sunny afternoons I sat in the summerhouse of our garden selecting and indexing all the passages which would in my judgement, when compiled together regularly, be of use to others. Then I rose early and wrote notes upon the text during those hours when the only sounds were of starlings fidgeting in the ash trees and the crowing of our neighbour's cockerel who mistaking the moonlight for daybreak, ignorantly declared his happiness noisily and triumphantly to the world.

Often through the years, Mary stayed until sunlight faded, at one or other of the crowded cottages in or beyond the village, reading to the children and their unlettered mothers from her Bible or from a book plucked – unwisely at random – from shelves already bending under the weight of books in our Curate's House. I know not what her listeners understood or gained from some of the books from which she read. Such a leaden work as Neal's *History of The Puritans*, for instance, must not have given rise to anything other than enduring boredom – while it pretended to offer purity of mind. On the other hand, the replacement for that particular volume – snatched with equal thoughtlessness the following week – was Yorick's *Sentimental Journey,* the half hidden sexual fires of which surely ignited blushes over all the women's faces.

Mary was not then a frequent visitor to our summerhouse, but at first took me engagingly to bed at those times when the old women of the village said were propitious for her intended maternal purpose. But when a year or more slipped by and there was no cessation of those regular woman's flows that prove a child is on its way, Mary hid her sadness in more hurrying to do good to parishioners who needed it, and some who did not. I was also sad for Mary, but for my part the expense of extra mouths to feed and bodies to clothe, would be a heavy price to pay for the honours of parenthood. The marriage vows call for procreation but do not make a stipulation as to numbers; and how much pain and exhaustion my mother, and how much selfless sacrifice my father might have been spared had there been no other child but me – or no child at all – though I was daily glad of the life that God gave me.

Self-denial and sobriety even with regard to my dress – apart from the occasional flashes of silver buckles and glimpses of gaudy waistcoats – were undoubtedly good to purge my soul – as I told myself. Yet however much Mary bore her unfamiliar sadness with stoic fortitude, her health was a cause for concern in her and an unnatural restraint in me. On occasions too frequent for several years, I returned from parochial duties or the excitement of a sermon well received – and found her not with arms open to receive me, but with those self-same alabaster limbs embracing her own sweet form for comfort. Hetty, twelve years old, and our only living-in-servant would be summoned to bring hot towels to apply below the waist and to hold her mistress' hands and comfort her.

Meanwhile I would pace the floor more like an anxious father than an urgent suitor.

Despite the lightness of my purse three or four times I ventured the idea of a fashionable physician to give an opinion. Mary would have none of it. She put her faith in the printed words of *The Gentleman's Magazine* where Physicians and Surgeons (fashionable or not), and Ladies with literary attributes (titled or not) and various Toms, Dicks and Harrietts (without fashion, ability or title) paraded their medical opinions in extensive correspondences. "In a like case . . ." Mary would read, and then followed wisdoms to defeat all doubters "after blistering of the abdomen and giving purges and diuretics to little purpose, the surgeon should scarify the lower abdomen pretty deep and then lay on cataplasms . . ."

My interjection that Hetty could do the scarifying – if that allowed use of a kitchen knife in the bedroom – was not well received by Mary. Nor was I allowed to expostulate when the cataplasms recommended were poultices of "fresh cow-dung boiled in milk".

The Beauties of Shakespear proceeded apace that year. On the third day after Christmas the two volumes were completed and ready for publication. Mary and The Reverend Mr Wyatt marvelled at my speed in writing. Hetty the maid clapped her hands to see me spring so quickly and lightly into the saddle to set off for Mr Waller the printer at The Mitre and Crown in Fleet Street.

My horse Bellows had characteristics peculiar to that dignified breed.

Of course he huffed and puffed, and kept that up between nods which were apparently acknowledgements of his fine career as a hunter in Bulkley's father's stable; but more of a steadying effect was his thoughtful side-stepping motion after a dozen or so nods. It is not right that a big horse should be slow, for the rider, who is in a very elevated and public position on a high saddle, is thus exposed to every passing ridicule. However, if I had allowed my anger or impatience to show and had I berated Bellows as Balaam did his ass, my ire would have been all spent and none left to expend on Mr Waller the printer. Not that it was difficult to find his address, Bellows on his own could have done that, but to find Mr Waller himself was nigh to impossible. He was at the Coffee House his man said. The Coffee House was in The Mitre and Crown itself, but was now doing only a dying trade in coffee and tea and a rising bibulous trade in products of malt and grain and grape. Waller if not here, (and he was not when I called) was said to be "taking a repast" at The Queen's Arms in St Paul's Churchyard, from whence (it was said) he had gone to The Red Lyon in Islington "on a matter of business". Since this business was thought to be a literary matter – and more than likely connected therefore with his patron Doctor Johnson – when Mr Waller was not to be found at The Red Lyon I was directed to The Three Hats in near-by Islington.

Equestrian performers were habitually gathered here

to show their ability to ride three horses at once and other tricks that by perseverance men may do with the co-operation of their steeds. Despite neither Dr Johnson nor Mr Waller being here, Bellows and I would gladly have loitered awhile. However, showing both the meaner and more determined sides of my nature, we pressed forward (and sideways) to Fleet Street. Arriving at each inn I received a cheerful greeting, but departed to surly looks from landlords who had not profited by my drinking even so much as a small tankard of ale. Finally, when night had not only fallen, but also set thick and fast with snow (announced unnecessarily by the watchman), and Mr Waller had not been found, we were forced to stay overnight and chose The Mitre and Crown on the chance that the printer may make it his first port of call (or – forgive me my pun – call for port) on the morrow.

While final preparations were made to put *The Beauties* to the press, during those unnatural delays occasioned by Mr Waller's progress from tavern to tavern, I considered as carefully as I had done the quotations themselves, to whom I should make the dedication. For although a book may carry between its boards all the knowledge and virtue its title may suggest, it is of no avail if the whole work is not hung upon a name already making a great sound in the world.

Sadly, (although fortuitous for the son George), his father Sir Thomas Lyttelton Bart. of Hagley, died leaving his title and all his substantial estates in Worcestershire to his son. I fixed upon this son – Sir George Lyttelton – and he consented to receive my respectful inscription and dedication to him as "One of the Lords-Commissioners of the Treasury". He might also be valuable to me and therefore named on the page as "A Patron on whom the Inimitable Shakespear wou'd most probably have fixed his Choice". Expressing this flattery for him, and describing me modestly as "His Most Obedient and Devoted Servant" at the bottom of the page, and my name William Dodd writ in heavy type below that, I thought to make it unlikely that I should be forgotten by him in the future.

The newly titled Sir George was a mere twenty years my senior yet had made his mark in the country on two particular counts. His performances in set debates in Parliament were more than once described as having "the force and wit of an orator and the spirit of a gentleman". Envious members who opposed him could only find fault with his body "thin and lanky", his face "meagre" and his bearing "awkward". They were forced grudgingly to admit his integrity and strong religious convictions. On this latter point I had been impressed not by his Christian poetry, which was mediocre, but by his well-written book *On the Conversion and Apostleship of St Paul*. That such a spirited work should arise from a member of parliament, a man with a purse well-lined from his family estates would perhaps be a surprise in itself. More surprising was that it had filled my father with admiration and he had recommended it to me in one of his rare letters.

Therefore, when I wrote to ask permission of Sir George Lyttelton, I made particular mention of his work on St Paul, and also apprised him of my father's enthusiasm for it. It was also not furthest from my mind that Sir George was a thoughtful man and was as likely to be grieving quietly for the death of his father and that perhaps within the pages of *The Beauties of Shakespear* he might find some consolation for the grievous loss of his parent.

No lesser person than Alexander Pope – a far better poet than Sir George – had sought patronage from George Lyttelton before he was titled or had a reputation. He had then referred to him as "still true to virtue, and as warm as true". These words were echoed by Sir George's powerful friends the Grenvilles, the Temples and William Pitt – all of whom held Lyttleton in high esteem.

I was well pleased when the two volumes of my Shakespear "collection" were published with its wise dedication. I remembered the delays the book had suffered during the wanderings of Mr Waller and would not call it back for improvements to the print work even though he appeared to have settled on The Mitre & Crown for his printing business (and declared it at the bottom of the title page). Straight away I sent off copies to my new patron and to my dear mother on her sick bed at Bourne. I wrote on the fly leaf to her copy:

"'From women's eyes this doctrine I derive:
They sparkle still the right Promethean fire;
They are the books, the arts, the academies,
That shew, contain, and nourish all the world."

You taught me of Shakespear and you taught me more; therefore these two slim volumes are for you.
Your affectionate son,
William Dodd'

My name was here signed with a flourish – with pride – for I, her son, entertained the hope that a mother so full of other virtues would nevertheless allow this one small sin of pride to herself and to me.

Some weeks after this I had a reply which expressed gratitude for the tender inscription and gave restrained praise for me, which was only muted by my mother being mindful of the promise I had made to my father – and indeed had confirmed in my preface. She wrote:

'For my own part, better and more important things henceforth demand my attention, and I here, with no small pleasure, take leave of Shakespear and the critics; as this work was begun and finished before I entered upon the sacred function in which I am now happily employed.'

My dear mother pointed to a "lack of absolute honesty" in the promise as I had not entirely completed the work when I became a curate. The blow of my mother's honesty showed up my lie and I was compelled to admit to myself that I was even now contemplating further literary efforts, and would break my word again on the pretext of achieving some great project that must not be hindered by an earlier vain and foolish promise. She rubbed vinegar on my conscience with lines taken from my own anthology:

> *"If thou . . . wert grim*
> *Ugly and slanderous to thy mother's womb,*
> *Full of unpleasing blots, and sightless stains , . . I*
> *would not care, I then would be content:*
> *For though I should not love thee: no,*
> *But thou art fair, and at thy birth, dear boy! Nature and*
> *fortune joined to make thee great, Of nature's gifts thou*
> *may'st with lilies boast, And with the half blown-rose."*

To stir my feelings more, my mother's writing was feeble and leaned on the paper as broken willow wands list over water, and the envelope bore the now small and wavering lettering of my father's hand, and inside wrapped around the pages from my mother, was a long letter from him which gave me great concern. It said:

'I have sent the physicians away. No expense was spared to summon them before, nor will there be to summon them again if they should offer a remedy better than bleeding.'

The scribbled lines continued, begging us children – Barbara, Richard and me – not to be angry with him, and setting out in many words our mother's illness and the logic of withdrawing the medical men from her case. My mother had had an issue of blood almost daily for two years at least, she becoming paler and weaker all the time. In his and her view the debility was in some part caused by losing blood and, therefore, to take more from her would compound rather than remedy the condition. He arranged for Sine Plica's younger sister to join her in managing the household and so to allow Olivia to rest. My twin sisters Mary and Sarah were a great comfort and skilled as nurses and wanted nothing in the arts of household management, but – now rising seventeen – were shortly to leave the

230

Rectory to take up residence with an elderly aunt in Yorkshire. Here it was generally believed that this aunt's prosperity and their own high qualifications in domesticity, would attract suitable husbands from the farming fraternity.

My father's letter told us too that Elizabeth – a year younger than Barbara – was now betrothed to a curate presently serving in a neighbouring parish - but with expectations of preferment to his uncle's parish near Lincoln. A wedding for this daughter and her immediate departure, therefore, were both a joy and a sadness anticipated by our parents.

Having dispensed news of all family matters, my dear father took the occasion of the letter to point up one or two defects in me that if stood corrected should proffer benefits to my future welfare. He firstly remarked upon my obstinacy – my capacity to ignore advice from those in a better position to make judgements than me. An instance of this was to hand immediately. Had I not given him the most vehement assurances that I would step aside from the wiles, the craftiness, and the indulgences, which so particularised those who advertised themselves as men of letters? Were there not, he said, enough such in the present Church of England to use up whole seas of ink and yet not to send the gospels into any dark corners that needed illumination? He cited Oliver Goldsmith but recently dead, Jonathon Swift, Laurence Sterne and other clerics whose pens exercised more persuasion on paper than their tongues in pulpits. Then he asked when would I change my ways? He replied to his own question: *'cum mula peperit* – when a mule foals.'

'Your own adventures in the sink of iniquity,' he wrote, *'would provide poor texts for sermons and God forbid,'* his letter ended, *'that you should write on such dismal subjects.'*

What wind of my intention to put my adventures into a

novel had blown towards Bourne? My suspicions were directed at Barbara, but could not be verified without telling her the truth that would raise more sermons from her. Mary, I knew, would not tell of a plan – that was partly made at her request – to write a cautionary tale. For it was clear to us that the more godly a reading is, the more likely to be dull, but a story that has the ring of truth and is shocking, will be remembered long after other tales are forgotten.

If, in writing this fiction, I was to go against the will of my father, his charge of my "obstinacy" would hold true. Yet I did think that the description of obstinacy and his understanding of my purpose fell far short of enlightenment. It was ever my determination to use the difficulties in life, and with my voice and pen attempt to prevent the fall of some and raise a few others from that hell on earth into which any creature may tumble.

So it was that I began *The Sisters,* writing as was my wont in the early morning hours. In the evening Mary would read what I had written, suggesting touches of reality from her experiences and trembling when I wrote "whore" or "harlot".

'These are hard words,' she said, 'hard words for women who are not always hard. They may be the victims of their own vanity, or desire – or worse still merely the trusting dupes of others' lust.'

And Mary wept:

'Such as they are, so was I. The Earl, and him you titled "Bear", had the power to command – but more than that, the power to persuade. If that persuasion used finery and gifts of money to flatter the poor weak object of their attentions, who can say that the weakness is but one side of the counterfeit coin of the exchange.

'So,' she said, 'will you make your story to put a binding spell on those who would destroy us?'

Mary wept again, and nightly when she snuffed the candles. As the day's last page fell to the floor she told me how certain I must be to put the novel to the publishers:

'Not that it is to excite lusts in the reader,' she said 'but to caution those who open the book, and thus maybe just once in a life prevent one of my kind from falling into the abyss.'

My fear of unalterable characterisation as a mule did not prevent me from taking the completed manuscript to the printers, and finally I was persuaded of the entire morality of *The Sisters* and changed the story to relate that the villain Blackwood – who bore a more than passing resemblance to the Bear – went quite rightly to the scaffold and for his crimes suffered in the most abject and pusillanimous manner. This morality was not a sop to vulgar licence; it was a justification for me as a clergyman soiling his quill with the horrors of the nasty world beyond the pulpit.

Publication of *The Sisters* yielded entirely unexpected benefits. It was very widely read – copies exchanging hands amongst even the lower classes who were possessed of reading skills. Certainly in West Ham were labourers and old ladies who asked for passages from *The Sisters* to be read aloud – and Mary was in high demand at the most humble cottages in the hope that she would bring her volume of *The Sisters* in the same hand as her Bible, and forget other choice of reading.

There was particular satisfaction expressed by many people who recognised the Earl of Sandwich in the narration and hoped that he would catch his own likeness when he read it – for he was known – albeit through the *tete a tetes* in the newspapers – as a man with little concern to act towards the fair sex with any restraint. It was said by his peers also that he had difficulty finding the latch to his breeches even when sober.

It was, however, a surprise to me that a work of fiction written by a curate would not only be accepted, but even admired. For a young cleric might be supposed to be in ignorance of lives betrayed and the vile diseases consequent upon those faulty lives. Rumours, however, gain credence; and rumours of my salty days in the sink of iniquity were enlarged to suggest connections with names which were known in the parishes around London. Many of these could tell of one maiden at least who had sought a release from poverty and had like a moth to a candle become drawn to her death in some bright bordello in the city. The tragedy narrated became fact; and planted in each mind it created fears that the same fate might strike a member of the reader's household.

From visiting my parishioners I have my own evidence of the truth of this and Mary also heard the same wherever she went. But Vicar Wyatt frowned when he first learned of *The Sisters* and expressed some disbelief that the novel could have been written by me, and so quickly and in the midst of all the parochial duties he had heaped upon me.

Afterwards, when he had finished reading, he described to me in what way he heard the view of Warden Semple who approached him after evensong one day. Semple whispered through tight lips, and gave his opinion that the book was "an invention – though he truly believed that Mr Dodd himself was capable of all the lasciviousness that was therein."

He also said, 'The novel (this time spoken down his nose as if to block off the smell of such a dirty thing) is a creation to titillate the venereal senses of a few shameless men with time hanging otherwise heavily on their hands, and to shock near to ecstasy the sensibilities of "decent woman kind".' My response was that for any reader to dance with the devil in my pages was to be warned against the devil.

The Warden was reputed to have said also that he thought it incredible if, in my writing of any book at all, I had not closely considered the possibility of financial gain to follow from its circulation. I neither disclaimed nor nodded when Mr Wyatt reported this, but in all conscience I could not have denied the grain of truth in Mr Semple's last remarks about money. I think it doubtful that any other man aiming at publication would fail to calculate profit and loss unless he already had money enough to support his greatest vanities. Semple had also noted in passing that the novel contained quotations from Shakespear, Milton and the Bible – all of which were thereby discredited and sullied because of the connection and the present author was discredited even more so.

Apart from *The Sisters*, of greater offence to the discriminating nostrils of Mr Semple were my advancement by appointment as Lecturer at St Olave's in Hart Street in the City and hard upon that – I was assured truthfully because of the quality of my sermons – my appointment to the neighbouring Lectureship at St James, Garlickhythe. These two pulpits distracted me a little from West Ham – which I thought might have pleased the Warden – but he divined a more subtle reason for my being honoured with the appointments. Sadly his home was at the London end of Broad Street – and because of the frequent departure and late return of my distinctive horse Bellows, Mr Semple divined that I was bound upon business outside the parishes. Mr Semple was thereby able to calculate by an addition of two and two that made twice four at least, that I was up to no proper good and was certainly visiting fallen women – and thereby making their decline more rapid – and bringing The Church into further disrepute. I had no doubt at that time that Mr Semple's proscriptions, whether accurate or not, did not dent my popularity. The good people in the parishes I attended had convinced themselves that there was a blossom on me that made my light shine into dark corners, and they therefore thought little or no evil of me.

CHAPTER 17

AT LE CHATEAU DE VOIRONS

Lady Ann; M le Blanc; Mary and Me

Provided that my ailments do not incapacitate me with pain – for stiffness and tenderness of neck and shoulder, to speak of no other ills, have their effects in rendering every other part sluggish – I let the sunlight lure me onto the lawns. Although my walking is still uncertain and uneven and although I cannot entirely ignore the small scything movements of my wilful right foot, once my crippled rhythm is regular, I walk alone for miles beyond the chateau. Then I can almost effortlessly bring to mind the next pages planned in my memoirs – confessions, anecdotes, descriptions – of me the Reverend William Dodd of West Ham – now still masquerading as M Farrier at Voirons.

This morning all augured well for healthful exercise and reasonable contemplation. Frost whitened the English lawns except where trees hung over the grass and made small green islands to defy it. Mary was at a window watching out for my return, her breath blurring the glass. She saw a hired chaise coming up the drive and wiped the pane clear. I turned also to see who it might be and became as always rigid with fear at the noise of iron-rimmed wheels striking the cobble stones near to the steps. The chaise stopped and then drew away and Lady Ann Thicknesse was revealed alone, her lovely oval face framed by a fur calash, and her breath making a cloud around her lips. Mary rushed out, as much I think to admire her friend's costume as to greet Lady Ann herself. I, more interested in the effects of a costume on a figure within it than its needlework, took time to look into Lady Ann's eyes, and to bow gently and deep, and to remove one of her warm white hands from the muff and to kiss it; and for one moment only forget any other thing but her.

My pleasure at the arrival of this beautiful guest was obvious – and Mary too in that moment was glad that she may have some softer female company for a while. By what strange impulses through the ether M le Blanc became aware of Lady Ann's presence I know not, but he deserted the silent book-lined cavern of his study where it was his wont over the last year to pour over a microscope. He joined us on the steps and encouraged us all into the hall. Here Cook's boy had two days before built a large fire and now was poking a brand into the centre and blowing his own hurricane after it.

For a while, the fire's crackling and explosions of dry pine logs drowned all but the briefest of exchanges, which collected together in one or two sentences, told of Sir Philip and Lady Ann's good health, and of her journey to collect the two daughters of her husband's second marriage from a nearby convent. Here they had been schooling for the last year in an attempt to restrain them in some of the more impudent excesses of their adolescence.

When the fire had settled to a steady level of noise, Lady Ann told us grave news. Rumour had come to England that the good Reverend Doctor Dodd was alive and well and had been seen parading as resplendent in his dress as formerly – and quite openly – in the streets of Paris, Brussels, Geneva, Marseilles and Bordeaux. News carried even more recently put the reverend gentleman in St Petersburg, Rome, Athens and Constantinople but sightings in these latter and more distant cities related to a time two years ago. Therefore, a few questioned them, as old news made stale by the length of time in transit. Those who treated the rumours with more severe scepticism calculated that the Reverend Dr Dodd had acquired a magical talent: for he was reported to be simultaneously in two or even three cities up to five hundred miles apart and

that the day chosen was most commonly said to be a Saints
Day to add a Christian conviction to the story. At this news
my companions sat silent, as I am always compelled to be.
They looked at me to see if I feared. I did not. Rumours so
wide of the chronological and geographical mark were not
likely to be credible except to very simple minds, and their
very wildness set them apart as fantasies. I was not afraid,
and Mary saw the amusement in my eyes and became at
ease. M le Blanc as always took an average assessment
from the moods around him and set his manner likewise,
while Lady Ann having the appearance still of being afraid,
was justified by that and moved closer to me again. Mary,
dear child, put a pout upon her face and looked up to
M le Blanc as if he were a far better man for her to admire
while I was flirting with Lady Ann.

I am capable of dramatic forms, although miming is
difficult to maintain with one hand, an unmoving mouth
and only half a face in motion. But I had little need this
morning to act out deceptions to show that I was not afraid.

I am better in health than I have been the last
twelvemonth. My walking has improved though my right
arm has withered more and my neck pains me sometimes
on rising and again if I have sat for a long while at my desk;
those parts that are wont to painful descent are comforted
by being supported and motionless on a soft cushion.

A further advantage of writing my history is that
memory has returned to greater clarity in recalling far
distant events, and now makes step-wise progress towards
1777. There is some blurring in my mind around and
beyond that, but I have every expectation of more to be
revealed.

The greatest sadness is my loss of speech; the voiceless,
soundless void within is unaltered. I wish when I am
lowered in mood that I were deaf as well, for I am envious
of other's speech when they address me, and I must – like
a religious vowed to silence – droop my head over a scrap
of paper and write words as short and as sparing of ink and

effort as may be to give answer. Mary's morning notes, which she supposes are written to spare me distraction from my toil at the desk and to render me less aware and envious of her possession of speech, get short response from my quill. Often the torn sheet is handed back to her with only a few angry words underlined to give her answer. It is a disagreeable business to be dumb and crippled.

Lady Ann has stayed for two days now. It seems to me that her attention also is greatest when we are joined by M le Blanc. At any time I welcome her company, for she gives me the feeling that I am a mightier man than I am. She ignores the weak half of my body, and talks cleverly giving question and answer for both she and me, and guessing my responses from the slightest movement of my eyes or hand. But still she is drawing M le Blanc to her. He has left his microscope gathering dust since she arrived and each day has had the fire lit in the hall. He and Lady Ann are there now, she telling him of Thicknesse's deeds. Sir Philip had declared himself retired – to be a man of leisure – "as far as funds allowed, if funds allowed" – and had bought St Catherine's Hermitage, a cottage at Bathampton, a hamlet a few furlongs from Bath.

Lady Ann waxed quite eloquent about this and her own hopes for comfort if Sir Philip ever finished the extensions and the ornamentations to the building.

'What he does,' she admitted to M le Blanc, 'is done to perfection and a little beyond. The cave, and a lake and the cottage are linked by magnificent architecture displayed as in Temples, Columns and Porticoes. Statues of *Il Penseroso* and *L'Allegro* divide the gardens and a statue of Eve as real as flesh itself gazes at her own image in the lake, and there are exotic trees and flowers bloom everywhere.'

Lady Ann continued in raptures, but at the end of every exclamation of delight was a cautionary note – of the expense of her husband's scheme and of the need for seclusion from curious admirers. She explained that the already so-called "polite society" of Bath had discovered The Hermitage and spoiled the privacy she craved for and that he said he desired.

'It is only a short walk from the centre of town,' she said, 'and visitors, and the fashionable and the invalid are coming in their scores – not only to enjoy the gardens and the sculptures there – but to peep at Sir Philip and me. The peeping gives great pleasure to Sir Philip but discomforts me his wife, for he strikes attitudes and affects not to know he is watched even though rougher sorts climb up and sit upon the walls to examine him and everything within.'

Without my having any view here into the hall it was apparent by listening only, that there was in this moment a warmth between Lady Ann and M le Blanc for which the log fire could not entirely account.

'My dear Lady Ann,' said M le Blanc, 'you have need of privacy. If there were to be higher walls entirely surrounding The Hermitage, and iron gates locked when necessary, all your needs for privacy would be answered would they not?'

'My very thoughts,' said Lady Ann in such an excited voice that I thought she would break into song. Then *sotto voce*, 'Alas there is no money left for such extravagance,'

Whether the following long silence held promises within it I do not know, nor shall I dwell upon the thought. Without going ahead in my history – for I save discussion of the future like a child with many presents saving the best of them 'til last – but it is the strongest of likelihoods that Lady Ann is an ambassador for her rascally husband and part of her diplomatic purpose is to raise money for his ventures.

Thicknesse retired indeed – with luxury at some other man's expense!

This morning is the third that day Lady Ann has been with

us at Voirons, her eyes just slightly fluttering occasionally towards M le Blanc and less often to me. Mary has hovered at my desk taking pages from me as they are filled, reading them and putting them into the casket with a loud bang of the lid and wrenching the key in its lock. In laying further emphasis on the nature of her feelings she takes up a whole sheet of clean paper, tearing it irregularly until each part of it is of size to fit the words intended for it. Then taking her own quill from a side cabinet (I protested much against destruction of *my* quills and eventually she forbore to use them), she loads her pen from my inkwell, writes and slips the message under my nose:

'Your indecent fancy for Lady Ann is transparent and despicable and ambitious beyond your strength.'

This was her opinion. I shall not answer it. Mary will read here later that I love her and she may perhaps be ashamed to exaggerate my hurt with barbed words that remind me that I have so little about which to preen myself – being only half the man I was and now without speech.

Very early this morning Lady Ann has gone. I saw through the misty glass of my bedroom window that M le Blanc himself handed her into his carriage. Before stepping up Lady Ann turned and offered both her hands into his. They stayed longer than necessary for an ordinary and friendly farewell, and their fingers slipped to and fro passing sensations and language between them I have no doubt. The lips of neither were employed for more than three words apiece and I have been turning the scene over in my mind for an hour since and can make out nothing innocent in the exchange. But M le Blanc is foolish if he did not speak some gallant words as he bowed deeply to Lady Ann.

She did not make her farewell to me. She has gone to collect her daughters and hurry them all back to England where no doubt Sir Philip is planning further extravagances and enjoying the delights of Bath. He will receive the respectful attentions of his daughters; and the embraces of his wife. He is a fortunate man.

Mary may think that I am a man of irregular passions. Not so. If she comes to me today I will show her how constant my feelings are for her.

When I cannot write, or when I cross out and tear up the greater part of what I have written, my thinking turns inwards. Thoughts most often arise from the very memories I have been recalling in my history. As this November at Voirons approached I have been reminded of All Saints Days at Bourne and West Ham – and how these festivals along with Christmas and Good Friday have the very essences of Christianity in them. Guilt has swept in on me, and clouded and shrunk by selfish considerations, I realise I have not followed any course of formal Christian observance since I came to this refuge at Voirons. Before today, the need for regular worship had not made a pressing case on my conscience. Now, perhaps being penitent for some of my past, I should seek religious comfort in attending a service, or having a service brought to me if that were possible. If a day does come when the Thicknesses give warning of a visit to Voirons, perhaps a service, a concert of hymns and sung prayers would lift my sinning soul to heights not felt in years. But let there be nothing Catholic about it.

CHAPTER 18

THE DEATHS OF MY MOTHER AND FATHER

Preaching and Writing on: death; religion; Milton; philosophy from Locke to Rousseau; illnesses (from small-pox to childbed); parish work and sermons at Hart Street and Garlickhythe and now additionally West Ham and Plaistow

My mother died in the May of '56. It was of a sudden, though her decline had been gradual and anxiously predicted. A letter from my father was dated and written on the same day as the funeral and it was full of anguish and guilt.

He wrote that two days before this as he sat at her bedside Olivia became even more unusually pale. In a matter of moments, his beloved wife's face vanished into the white of the pillows and she breathed no more.

Unbidden, Sine Plica's sister had called the same physicians he had sent away, but they arrived too late to do more than close my mother's eyes with pennies from her purse.

Then they set about scolding my father for not summoning them sooner. He in his grief would not reply but hung his head, which the physicians took as a sign of shame and berated him again. Then they spoke of the hot weather – surprising so early in the year – and of what damage to man and beast, alive or dead, the warble flies and bluebottles could do, and how an early funeral was advised. So it was arranged for the Friday of that same week. I detected a note of defiance in my father's letter that the date was to suit my sister Elizabeth's clerical husband rather than to comply with the physician's suggestion.

THE DEATHS OF MY MOTHER AND FATHER

The Reverend John Slater had two strokes of good fortune – the one in obtaining Elizabeth for his wife and the other in being appointed to the parish of his late uncle.

The young Rector and his wife came over to Bourne as soon as they learned of mother's death. He took the funeral next day and since he had no curate to take the Sunday service, and as they had already three children clamouring at home, The Reverend John Slater and Elizabeth returned immediately. Mr Voke, the curate at Bourne, was incapacitated at this time though no cause was given for this.

Many villagers gathered at the graveside, seeking to grieve for themselves and for the absent family members, for Richard and Barbara and the twins Sarah and Mary in Yorkshire had no more notice than I. This would not have displeased our mother. She wished no one to be inconvenienced in her life or at her death.

In his letter, The Reverend William Dodd Senior recorded his wife's request of years ago when Jacob died:

'Let me be next to him, not in "sad cypress laid", but cased in elmwood when I die. If our spirits linger at the schoolroom gate, we shall hear the sound of children as we did, and old men and maids may remember their teacher and her young Jacob and perchance the name of Shakespear too.'

My father concluded with a plea:

'Forgive me if I have not done as I should have done. I did not put my trust in physicians and who can say my trust in the good Lord was sufficient. In the midst of my sorrow I am mindful also of your sorrow William my son. God be with you.'

I composed letters to my father to comfort him for he was unable to comfort himself. My letters may have lacked the power to aid the good old man, for I received few replies and they of the briefest sort and made comment only on small matters of fact and let no part of his feelings show on the page.

A letter of a different sort came within a year of my mother's death. It was written by Esther Boldwood who described herself as the second daughter (now married) of the late Mr Theophilus Drake, Church Warden. She gave news from Miss Tenbury "who has difficulty with reading and writing when she is so busy caring for Mr Dodd Senior." (It was a moment or two before I realised that Miss Tenbury was Sine Plica, and wondered if she was still plump and smoothed tightly into her dress).

However dulled the story may have been by its indirect relation, the true picture of my father was portrayed. He had been unsteady for a long time and took the best part of a quarter-hour to make his way from the rectory to the church. Thinner "than a thatcher's hazel pins and weak and trembling like an aspen leaf," he tottered from gravestone to gravestone, resting and pretending to read the inscriptions, every one of which he already knew by heart. Mr Voke, the curate, had to help my father into his robes and practically carried him into the pulpit. I could imagine him there announcing a few biblical texts and Greek and Latin aphorisms before his brief closing prayer indicated to Mr Voke that he should begin to bring my father down from the pulpit again.

Esther Boldwood's letter added that after evensong on Sunday the reverend old man was standing by my Mother's and Jacob's graves talking to them. Others say he was not talking but only nodding. Mr Vokes took him straight into the house and put him to bed. He had not left it since. Mrs. Boldwood concluded:

'I do suggest you do come if you can. Miss Tenbury says she always did everything for your mother and father and will so until his death. Which cannot be far off.'

Mr Wyatt gave me leave of absence and hastened me and Mary to Lincolnshire hoping that we would not be longer gone than two weeks. He then remembered that a fortnight could be too short a time to be confident of my father's recovery if he made it, and only just enough time there and back, to bury him and settle the estate if sadly he was called to his maker at once. Mr Wyatt had hardly need to put much of this into words. The expressions on his face and the directions of his eyes gave a full explanation in plain vocabulary and he emphasised his intentions by wafting us away on our journey like geese from the dairy. 'Away to Lincolnshire,' he said. 'Away, away.'

We did leave straightway and arrived in Bourne after two days. I sat by my dear father's bedside for two more days reading to him and giving him sips of water from time to time. The Bible was at hand and while he still had strength, tested his memory against quotations I read for him. As he became more feeble and as though to have a rest from me, he sent me off to the library to find a book he would have me read. Towards the end of the first day, each book was found easily and I hurried back to the bedroom: one line of Greek or two of Latin read aloud, I was sent on a journey of discovery again. Time went by. On the second day long silences were filled only with the sound of my father sleeping. When he spoke he named – by his desire I believe – titles I did not know, and on searching I did not find. Then in the mid-afternoon he woke and asked me to bring *The Beauties of Shakespear* that I might read from it. I could not find it in the library; though I searched an hour for it there, nor in my mother's desk in the window bay in the drawing room. I could not find it. I turned lastly to the kitchen where after my mother's death my father, shunning the dining room, had eaten what little food Sine could persuade him to take. There by his place at the table was *The Beauties* of *Shakespear* opened at a page in the second volume:

". . . O, my love, my wife!
*Death, that hath sucked the honey of thy breath Hath
had no power yet upon thy beauty:
Thou art not conquer'd . . ."*

I gathered up the book and returned it to my father's

bedside. There was a flicker of his eyes and his lips unfroze from their stiffness for a longer moment; and he died.

Brother Richard arrived for the funeral from Cowley where he was now Vicar. Mrs Boldwood had not thought to write to him nor had his address, but I had written to him as soon as I set off for Bourne.

Elizabeth came. Sister Barbara could not come because she was again heavy with child. My sisters, the twins, Sarah and Mary had both married yeoman farmers who still lived, almost as neighbours, in the wildest part of North Yorkshire. Though letters eventually reached them, their replies took a week or more to come to Bourne. They did not follow their letters. I and the curate Voke and the Reverend Mr Slater were in attendance when we buried my dear father beside his beloved Olivia and Jacob.

It was understandable that I was greatly affected by the deaths of my mother and father; their deaths gave a conclusion to exchanges of love; wrote *finis* to histories shared; and this bore down on my spirits all the more since their deaths were so close upon each other. I had no fear, but only the certainty that William and Olivia would be received into the Kingdom of Heaven. Their good lives were a surety for their happy immortality. I did not feel the anguish, the physical sense of loss that gripped me when Lancaster was wrenched from me and that has never left me. Anger at the physicians' paltry actions at Bourne left me quickly too – for I was resigned to the effects of their ignorance which, after all, could not be recalled and changed.

What was overpowering in me – more sharp and quick than tears – and for which I had no preparation and no consolation now at hand, was the knowledge of my own mortality. Three score years and ten had been denied to my mother and father. On approaching death they did not wring their hands and weep at it, for to be quitting this earth each in their fifth decade, was they knew commonplace.

THE DEATHS OF MY MOTHER AND FATHER

Unto few is granted a biblical length of life. I did wring my hands and weep for me at the startling acknowledgement of my mortality, for the tombstones of my parents were milestones showing how short was left the journey to my final stopping place if I lived no longer than they.

Parson, undertaker and sexton are rarely offered condolences when they are grieving at the death of an intimate companion or a member of their family. They, it is too commonly assumed, have a familiarity with death and the frequent day-to-day occurrences in their lives of churchyards, funerals and graves serve to harden rather than humanise their minds. The parson, it is said, enters the gloomy chamber where a life is expiring without the least emotion. I cannot say that is never true, but know that the physician and the lawyer who attend at the bedsides of the dying have to fix their faces to command a fee and to make sure that they receive it; the undertaker is anxious to make certain the body will fit its coffin; the sexton relieved of emotion by his labours, turns his mind to other matters as the spade lifts old bones and dust of his fellow creatures from the grave.

Death is common to all – *mors omnibus communi* – but that is only the fact of death. The circumstances of death are not common to all. For each one dying and for each one close to the dying there is rare, uncommon particularity.

I, therefore, in my misery sought out parishioners of all sorts, and their families – people who were weary under the fears of a death awaited, or grieved in the shadows left by their departed. Those also who were unprepared for death did not escape my attention from the pulpit. All these I intended to be subjects for an improving book.

To this purpose I marked out such as Mr Norris – a merchant of no more than thirty years of age who lived only for this world, and had no other view than to amass wealth. His conversation was larded with chimerical schemes – of fine coaches and country retirements – of brilliant gaiety and envied splendour. Bored in church, he now and then let out a yawning and unnecessary "Amen". At home and at his affairs he so harassed his body that it brought about convulsions. He died suddenly, utterly unprepared, and though his funeral was splendid with fine horses nodding their sable plumes, the slow moving wheels (in life he would never have allowed such a dismal pace) kept time with the deep-toned bell.

Not every life shared in West Ham was prone to such excesses and untimely death as merchant Norris. There were those good people whose faults lay in unwise giving – who out of misplaced kindness spoiled their children. The Salmons, a genteel couple who came late to the responsibilities of parenthood, fed scantily and dressed meanly that their daughter Melissa might be 'clad in scarlet and feast on delicacies'. When, after a lingering consumptive illness brought on by her own indulgences, Melissa died, the doting parents now gave up all to their only other child who was seized into fashionable company in the city.

Notwithstanding pretty features which needed no artifice, she adorned and painted herself *a la mode* and threw herself into a giddy round of pleasure supported by the foolish generosity of her parents. Returning to West Ham for her dear father's burial, she was already so wasted that within a month she lay beside him.

I put these and other stories into a volume – *Reflections on Death* – illustrated with appropriate texts. Whenever an account was given of a death which in some way showed a departure from Christian pathways, I was careful to oppose it in the next pages of the book with examples of virtue and care. My intended purpose was always to do good.

A clergyman such as I, invited into the house where the blinds are already down or are shortly to be lowered, has a greater chance of carrying the gospel on wings of compassion to the people within. For me there was more advantage still – to gain my own heart's ease and to distract me from grief at my own parents' deaths by consideration of others' loss. I was improved by my life in West Ham's green pastures.

My carnal desires were subdued by spiritual works, the abandonments of my youth and its gaiety were if not crushed by melancholy, at least kept tightly cloistered in. I had ignored my father's advice so frequently that a less patient parent would have discharged me from his house and from his affections. Therefore, I felt some guilt at presenting *Reflections on Death* to the public, since both my parents were dead and I thought that these stories culled from my pastoral work would not benefit others to the same degree as they did me. Mr Wyatt had no such reservations and worked with me to improve the choice of texts in every chapter. He it also was who suggested dedication to The Earl of Bute, and he it was made sure that copies of my *Reflections* were given out at funerals, which became a custom so common that a second and third edition followed in quick succession.

I began again a most feverish habit of writing. Description of it puts to shame my leisurely literary efforts as a youth – and in my first years at West Ham. It was not unusual for me now to burn candles long after the household was shut quiet; and the scratching of my quill could be heard throughout the night. Ceaseless occupation made unnecessary the task of dressing for a new day.

Hetty, in the attic above, was alone in awaking on many dark winter mornings. On those days she quietly descended to the kitchen and with an equally soft tread returned carrying a bowl of soup or hot milk and honey. Her delicate form, and the glow of warm candlelight in her eyes put the strongest temptations upon me. Had she known it and still lingered by me; had she drawn her hair from her face as she leaned to set the bowl in front of me; had she looked for thanks, or allowed even a glance to settle upon me I doubt that even the most severe Christian disciplines and the cautions that I gave to myself and which filled my daily prayers could have prevented the escape of my bursting lust. Fortunately then for my strict conformity, Hetty never did more than bob a curtsy and say "Sir" in the most ordinary way – as if the room were full of haughty matrons and clergymen all beyond the age of concupiscence, who were there to censure our actions.

Letters also flew from my pen – some were published in *The Christian's Magazine* – where a wide audience would learn of my protagonists as well as of me. Mr John Wesley took what I regarded as the arrows of my intellect against his broad and gentle shield. I have shame in remembering my attacks on that good man although sometimes I sided with those Anglican Bishops upon whose patronage I might depend. I railed against the Methodists' reported claim to be themselves perfect Christians. It did not then concern me that they did not claim to be so – but it was their critics who said they were. Mr Wesley's replies were at pains to point this out and to argue that he and I were of a like mind – aiming to live Christian lives but having no claim to the achievement of such.

Quarrels about predestination took much space in the magazine. Arguments were extended that since we and all our fates are fixed unalterably as either good or evil, no purpose is to be gained by Christian efforts to change. So, despite the good he wished to do by discovering Christians in his congregations, Preacher George Whitfield – urged and supported by The Countess of Huntingdon – was satisfied when a man or a woman fell down in convulsions for that was believed to be a sign of grace and such were demonstrated to have been destined to be saved since the beginning of creation. Added to this, the fixed idea that all physical matter and moral principles in the world are vile Devil's work was poured into the boiling pots of emotion and religious fervour.

'It is so,' cried the Antinomians. 'Moral law is the

Devil's creation and as perfect Christians we must deny it.' There lay my shame as Antinomians permitted theft, murder, rape and every licentiousness to themselves, and the pages of *The Christian's Magazine* stirred up these sins from unsound minds. Neither Mr Wesley's nor any others' pen could pour balm on such as these. And there was further shame. I used the magazine to spread my name, to catch the eyes of the wealthy who disliked Mr Wesley but also would give generously to charitable causes that I espoused.

Shall a callow young man be pardoned? I did not then think to blame or forgive myself during those industrious crowded years. I was full of myself – no – I was full of the preoccupations of Christian endeavour and the means of expressing myself – or the God within me. Parish duties in West Ham and Plaistow, and similar cares in and around Garlickhythe and Hart Street in the City were a great part of my daily round. Up to five sermons preached every week were thoroughly prepared – even if that inspiration was on occasion drawn down from the great sermons preached by learned prelates of an earlier age. I read widely for these, searched and meticulously appended notes to every borrowed line – not so much in acknowledgement of those other sources, but to quicken my brain dulled from banging against the minds of people whose stores of wit and imagination, knowledge and perception were as poorly provided as the rations of a soldier at a long siege. I was, therefore, at great pains to make sermons easy for comprehension.

Unlike my dear father I weeded out Latin and Greek and Hebrew quotations, aphorisms and texts, for these, along with Mr Shakespear's and Mr Milton's best words, were better kept out of sermons and to be swapped with The Reverend Mr Wyatt or crowded into footnotes where I might indulge myself without hindrance – except when a complaining publisher wrung his hands at the cost of paper. I know that my sermons were well received, but I felt more than a puff of pride and then more than a stab of hurt when it was said that they would be as nothing if it were not for my "mellifluous voice". Alas for this. Alas!

At this time I delivered frequent sermons on subjects arising from scenes met in my parish work amongst the poor, so I came to be the first instigator of charities – for the relief of debtors and some of those self- same unfortunates who unrelieved from anxiety threw themselves into the Thames. A chance for their revivification was foremost in my mind.

I believe it was not only from the outpourings from my pen or my melodious voice that attention was attracted to me; nor was extravagance of dress the magnet, for now my only occasional flowery outbursts were hidden beneath a plain cassock; and my silver buckles had become tarnished by the seasons' mud. Word was passed around that I could deliver a sermon to order on almost any subject. There was common knowledge that for a clergyman I had an interesting past – gossip mongers and Mr Semple held that my present history had some colour about it too, and therefore I might be expected to bring luminosity even to a dark subject and make an acceptable sermon which would withstand the close scrutiny of unlettered prudes or libertines or scholars.

While at West Ham I preached and then published four volumes entitled *Miracles and Parables* together with sundry *Meditations, A Familiar Explanation* of *the Poetical Works of Milton, Dissertations Against Mr Rousseau and Other Unbelievers* and a new edition of Mr Locke's *Common Place Book to The Holy Bible* and other writings. I gave literary meat for scholars to chew to destruction or to digest. These scholars and the unlettered took pews to hear my sermons. How should it be I wondered, if future generations did not have churches to hear sermons, and no sermons to bite at us with arguments? What other way is there to put practical religious matters before the everyday courts of public opinion? Nor was it bad – although domiciled in West Ham and Plaistow – that I preached more often in London Town. Churches from Mary le Bow to St Martin's Ludgate, to St Anne's Black Friars and back to St George's Hanover Square and many more lent their pulpits to me.

Let it not be thought that the preacher himself is unaffected by his subjects. The two daughters and wife of John Ripley of Paternoster Row were took with the small-pox. In his sorrow I attended Mr Ripley, a prosperous butcher descended from Norfolk farmers. 'Why was not I taken with my womenfolk?' he cried repeatedly and I feared more for his sanity than his life. He carried his groans and weeping to his shop below. Meeting the butcher and a governor of the Small Pox Hospitals there ordering meat for his charges, I was prevailed upon to preach at St Andrews Church, Holborn on a Thursday two weeks hence to promote inoculation.

My benefactor Bishop Sam Squire, who had recently conferred upon me the Prebendary at Brecon, now added a small favour to me by giving me his sermon notes delivered on a similar occasion and on the same subject in 1760. Sam Squire had little in his sermon to excite the soul, but gave the mathematical mind full satisfaction. Following on from his introductory '. . . before the small-pox march disquietude, anxiety and tremor . . . its weapons are inflammations, putrefying sores and rottenness . . . and behind it follow languor, lameness, deformity and blindness,' Bishop Squire gave facts to prove his cases: 'more than a fourteenth of mankind die of the pox,' a disease that he declared arrived before the Arabians and Saracens settled themselves in Egypt. 'If you suffer the small-pox to seize you in the normal way of infection, it is no more than seven to one that you will not fall a wretched sacrifice to its virulence. If, on the other hand, the small-pox be given you by inoculation, it is at least three hundred to one you escape with your life.'

Though my preaching was thought to carry more persuasion than that of Bishop Squire's, when I said, 'inoculation can only give the disease itself, no other diseases get in and are companions to it' a gentleman at the back of the church bellowed his disbelief and two ladies on either side of him appeared to faint. (Such skilful dissemblers are the weaker sex, I do not know whether the women's attacks were feigned out of embarrassment at their companion's rudeness, or out of a genuine fear that inoculation would carry other dire diseases in with it and they did not trust my words. Dissembling and artifice are not easily discerned from within or without the pulpit.)

The text that I preached was from Proverbs Chapter 14, verse 28. *"In the multitude of people is the King's honour: but in the want of people is the destruction of the prince.'* It was not seen as too subtle a text for the congregation – nearly all had had their family reduced by the plagues of small-pox and they knew that the greatness of their country relied upon young and strong generations to follow. Sorrow and death are shared by kings and princes and their subjects. It is a patriotic duty to be inoculated, and as children are too young to choose their remedies, their parents must choose for them.

As if my sermon was not sufficiently stirring, the musicians at St Andrews struck up martial music by Mr Handel the moment I left the pulpit and if it were not a tribute to my preaching, my vanity had it so.

It is well, when the load of death hangs heavy on the mind, to contemplate life at its beginning. I was too often the mournful observer at the expiration of a new-born babe's too brief claim on the world's attentions and when I could do no more than signify the baptism in Christ with water mingled with the blood on the still warm forehead. I was with much less frequency invited to join families in prayerful thanks for a safe delivery.

In the meanest homes and the poorest lodgings, where

ordure splashed from the street against unvarnished doors - their cracks sealed with rags scarcely dirtier than the clothes worn within – many women in childbed had benefit from no one but the clergy and they had to offer little but words of comfort. And on those occasions when I was asked to preach before such as The President and Governors of the City Lying-in Hospital for Married Women, it was with regret that my words could not instantly transform the labours of all women, and give them each the looked for ease and comfort of a chosen few. The worthy Governors and patrons were to be praised for their charity towards those in childbed, but oh how little was their drop in the vast ocean of anguish suffered by that lovely and amiable sex.

I preached to men whose wives, and later their daughters, would lie in comfort at the Aldergate Hospital – women admitted from respectable homes – women who by The Rules must be married and free of any contagious distemper and be suspected of no lewdness or intemperance. These were the favoured ones of the fair sex. But beyond the walls of the church and down to the Clerkenwell Road and way beyond were countless numbers of women less cosseted than their sisters. Here poverty stretched its iron hand over suffering womankind. That same hand pushed its victims to crimes of necessity – to steal money or to earn it by the sale of their bodies. These brought shame upon their families, and they also suffered through the horror of their miseries when in childbed.

'You,' I said to my congregation, 'are not dull to the happiness of any of the weaker sex. You will not let those you love bear alone their distress and sorrow. You will give, for your womenfolk are mindful already of their good fortune compared with the lot of others. Give now thankfully to protect your wives and daughters, because to them we owe so much in our tender years, and in our riper old age we are also greatly indebted to them.'

THE HANGING OF WILLIAM DODD

The ringing sound of gold coin in the collecting dishes was music in the ears of the President and Governors – and to me, because I received by it flattering invitations from important people to preach again in their churches on this and other texts. Mary said that while I shook the purses of the well-to-do, I shook more so the hearts of every woman, those who had entered the church boldly and with pomp, or those who had crept in modestly, hiding their poverty and shame as they stood barefoot at the back.

The Worshipful Company of Apothecaries first invited me to preach before them in a year when the full richness of autumn was everywhere apparent. Each roadside, every park and field and tree, the banks of each stream, all gloried in the burning splendour of Nature. The surface of the red earth was clothed with flowers and herbs and vegetables: fruits incredible in their number and variety shone out from leafy canopies.

The houses themselves, to my imagination, were the small offspring of great mountains, with cool caverns and recesses darkened in the shade. It mattered not that my acquaintanceship with hills – nor any ground much above tree top height – depended entirely on paintings come out of Italy or of the mountainous parts of England. The whole realm of the animal kingdom was represented for me by the sheep and cattle in the pastures, by the birds flying or gathering in branches or on the ground, while serpents and lions, elephants and a whole myriad of other beasts were created in my mind from texts in the Bible.

As I came close to St Martin's Church at Ludgate my horse Bellows, who recognised his importance as a leader among beasts, pricked up his ears and broke into his sideways trot, to hurry me to the pulpit. I wished to preach while my mind was still inspired with the wonders of nature – by the miracles of insects about their labours, by scriptural accounts of the two-humped camel and that Leviathan whom God hath made to take his pastime in the sea. There was a Divinity that stirred within me.

The Apothecaries and the Physicians and Surgeons amongst them suspended their scepticism while they listened. Their spirits raised, I was emboldened to suggest points of medical interest, in particular the use of products derived from vegetables and their applications to health.

Approving smiles greeted my panegyric for the aloe gum, or perhaps the smiles were at my simplicity. For these men had greater knowledge than I of the use of aloes – in comforting weak stomachs and warming cold brains; as a laxative, as an anodyne and a splenetic; for giving relief in obstruction of the liver, and to speed delivery of women in travail; to soften hard tumours of the womb and guard against the gout. I listed other virtues – but not so many as to trespass into the fields of knowledge my congregation owned. I questioned – only to myself – if the medical men were more familiar with scriptural references to the aloe in its use to soak the linen of winding sheets at burial, or to perfume the linen on the harlot's bed. I added nothing new in speaking of the aloe, but more than one of the congregation leaned forward when I related the use of greens and herbs "which had a wonderful part to play in the speedy recovery of sailors from the scurvy" (knowledge come to me in a letter from an acquaintance of a very able person whose time had been for the greatest part spent at sea).

Having captured my audience I moved on with my preaching before interest might fade – following the precept that a lively mind even silently engaged in argument may be deliberately provoked without feeling insult to it, and so progress to new thoughts.

'It has been observed,' I said, 'that gentlemen in the profession of physic have been remarkable for their inattention to religion. As to how far this may be the case you are the best judges.' I continued and softened my harshness with liberal quotations from Ecclesiasticus –

"Honour a physician with the honour due unto him" – and other words to please them.

And, as I remember, I ended my sermon on this occasion with the proposition that it were well worth for them to study the diseases of the mind in some degree – as well as those of the body since their sympathy one with another is too notorious to be denied, and since all the drugs of the pharmacy are offered in vain without proper mental relief.

I told my horse Bellows, as we made our way home up Ludgate Hill that I had made good friends this day, and those friends had many friends, and I was glad. Bellows did not shake his head to deny it, nor deign to answer at all, nor would any horse when it had the sniff of grass in its nostrils.

The autumn sun shone on our backs as we set off for home.

CHAPTER 19
A MAGDALEN PROPOSED

A House for Penitent Prostitutes;
Introducing Jonas Hanway & The Dingley Brothers

A sermon if it is to be good, is an act of loving creation –
a formal text, from which the proposition is developed and
then, at the peroration, all coming to life. The lengthy parts
of a sermon may pass as in a dream – certainly dreaming
and sleeping congregations are not strangers to many
preachers – but when good people are truly awakened and
alive to the arguments and those arguments are restated
with passion, the thrusts are driven home and the gospel
and its message root firmly in that congregations' minds.

So it was that one of my perorations moved one
member of a congregation. It was on a Sunday in August
at St Olaves in the City. I wished I had not worn a waistcoat
however colourful beneath my cassock. I wished that I had
not powdered my face beforehand in the vestry that had no
mirror, for far from preventing the sweat from glistening
under my chin, it turned the creases there into shallow
canyons filled with sweaty white chalk from the rivulets
coursing across and down my cheeks. The sun beating in
from the great windows made the pulpit a greenhouse and
likely to cook and wither me within it.

The congregation on this Sunday was mostly of people
who lived in mean houses near the church and were
considered of small account in their community. These
people could not make their way to country cousins for the
hottest months, but gathered now as was their custom, at a
humble distance at the back of the church, where happily
for them it was dark and cooler. The pews in sunlight were
empty save for a soberly dressed man who followed every
part of my sermon – that day on miracles and parables –

fixing his eyes on me throughout. He leaned forward earnestly as I preached; I preached that beyond and outside the miracles we read of in the parables presented to us, greater miracles are possible in ourselves. I concluded:

'Let us therefore lay aside all other strife and strive only who shall love his neighbour most and so most approve himself to that God, who hath commanded us to love one another as He hath loved us.'

'Amen,' said the stranger who was the first to stand and wait for my descent from the pulpit. A diminished music party – one harpsichord, one violin, one flute – tentatively struck up a chord or two, then finding a tune they knew, served it up with enthusiasm like cooks who have found a surprising delicacy in their larder.

Meanwhile the unknown gentleman had persuaded the Church Warden to lead him to the vestry. There, as I was removing the clogged up powder from my face, the Warden introduced the man to me:

'Mr Jonas Hanway, Dr Dodd. He asked if he may speak with you privately a moment.'

I knew at once the name – indeed we had corresponded through the newspapers and occasionally by personal communication on matters of common interest – especially charities.

His reputation came before him. Now perhaps towards the end of his fourth decade, a legacy combined with profits from his business in the Russian trade had enabled him to spend the last ten years in retirement. Made ill by his work and by dangerous travels in Russia and over the Caspian Sea to Persia – and it is said by the disappointments of unrequited love – he lived with his widowed sister in the Strand. But if leisure and true retirement from business were the preferences of many who had worked as hard as he, for Mr Hanway leisure had an entirely different significance. It was apparent already from his many long tracts (which were dictated between four and six in the morning before the day's real work began) that as a business man he believed that the true wealth of the nation lay in the numbers of the labouring poor. They were to be given hope and work and relieved of poverty and sin – not with charity which removed the necessity to work but with work itself. Jonas Hanway, I knew, had more charity than John Locke whose philosophy allowed – indeed advised – that children should be trained to work from the age of three. Practicality and kindness were stamped on the face and bearing of Jonas Hanway.

He stood before me with his own invention: a tight rolled umbrella planted between his feet, and his hands resting on it. His face was worn but expressed the utmost benevolence and humanity. He remained motionless until his words were collected and ordered for delivery. I asked him what kind deeds did he contemplate now: was it more work towards the Foundling Hospital and pauper children, or providing through the Marine Society a new life for urchins, children who were in his words "bred to begging as if it were a trade"?

He did not answer but said after a while that he was most happy to hear me preach, that he admired my dedication even when the congregation was small. He said:

'I have been in a larger congregation when you preached before, and thought that the fine sermon that day was inspired only by the size and intelligence of your audience.'

I sought flattery and asked what and when and where did I preach?

He replied:

'The text was from Genesis and you preached it at the City Lying-in Hospital for Married Women. Genesis 3 v.16. Four years ago.'

Mr Hanway frowned in an effort to recall more detail:

'You charged the Governors then: "Do not let the weaker sex bear their sorrows and distress alone". And you concluded with an appeal for "that lovely and amiable sex to whom our tender years owe so much; to whom our riper age is so greatly indebted".

'I think,' said Hanway 'you will help. Our deep concern is for those of the "amiable sex" who have fallen. Prostitutes.'

He wrote down his address "24, The Strand" on a corner of the baptismal register, shook my hand and said:

'Tuesday next at 10 o'clock in the forenoon. The Dingley brothers, my colleagues in this, will be there and you and I.'

In the days intervening before our meeting, I wondered many times why and what I would be asked to do for harlots. Mr Hanway would know – for it was common knowledge amongst the titled and talkative and through their servants to the rest of the world – that I had married a harlot. (For such was my Mary described as soon as she was no longer the less vulgarly styled mistress to the Earl of Sandwich.) In whatever good man's company a woman might be, if she as an unmarried woman walked through Vauxhall Gardens or Ranelagh – or worse still The Marylebone Gardens – she would be considered a prostitute. It was not inconceivable to my mind that Mr Hanway wished to tap the barrel of knowledge I revealed in *The Sisters.* Or more practically, he assumed I would give names to fallen women and persuade them to receive the benefits that would be offered.

Speculation – no that is not the word I should use – *curiosity* is the word and it was raised to a high level; but it yielded no more information to me until on the appointed day I presented myself at No. 24, The Strand and was admitted by an ancient servant and taken up to the drawing room.

Here Jonas Hanway was standing with his old business partners (now partners in charitable works) – Charles and Robert Dingley – they sitting and sipping clear water from wine glasses. I had warning that there would be no tea taken, nor fancy cups to drink from. Mr Hanway in many things had decided views; as an example he had published a pamphlet: *An Essay on Tea* subtitled: *Considered as Pernicious to Health, Obstructing Industry and Impoverishing the Nation, with an Account of its growth and Great Consumption in these Kingdoms.*

This, with many other pamphlets, appeared on the breakfast tables of the Gentry. A companion to it was entitled *Pure and Genuine Bread, Comprehending the Heart of the Wheat . . .* Whereas tea was criticised by Mr Hanway as a stimulant which tended to excite those partaking and waste even more of the time of the idle rich, white bread was criminal in its intent. It used Alum to achieve its colour – and the Alum brought children to their deaths. Alum should therefore be destroyed. Fashionable readers of Mr Hanway's pamphlets were doomed to miserable breakfasts.

While Mr Hanway was summoning the old manservant to draw more water from the well, and while the Dingley brothers after brief introductions were again seated, sipping and observing me closely, I turned my attention to a cluster of six portraits of celebrated beauties, circled around a mirror reflecting the visitor's face. Upon the glass of that mirror in bold lettering was:

"Wert thou my daughter, fairest of the seven, Think on the progress of devouring Time,
And pay thy tribute to Humility".

I do not know how many ladies of title or beauty (or both) had been kept waiting before this sobering reflection of themselves. It was well known that Mr Hanway thought the aristocracy was more likely to be ugly than the rest of their fair sex, and more proud. Maybe his once unrequited love was due less to his long-time absence in foreign climes and more likely due to his capacity for moralising and be truthfully insulting at the same time. Such was unlikely to endear him to the
gentler sex.

I was forming the opinion that Mr Hanway's

beneficence was directed towards the lower ends of society, or at least away from noble females.

This class of aristocrat had been on several accounts held up to ridicule in the press. Hanway himself had put his pen to extra labour in making *Remarks on Lap-dogs,* which animals he said were faithful but also he said sycophants and though they bore no vile resemblance to the human species, were parasites. Fine ladies, therefore, in having an immoderate love of a brute animal, he said weaken their strength of feeling for and charity towards human creatures.

With such proscriptions against pug-dogs and their owners and the knowledge that Mr Hanway had inveighed on more than one occasion against the "proposed naturalisation of Jews", I wondered that this kindly man had ever embarked on a career of charitable works. Furthermore I questioned his ability to gain widespread support for his schemes which were presented didactically in long pamphlets.

These thoughts were dismissed from my mind when Mr Hanway began to expound his concern for harlots. He held his one palm open, as if it were a ledger, and pointed to it with the forefinger of his other hand to emphasise the figures and the facts to be recorded and considered:

'Fifty-thousand prostitutes in London alone,' he said. 'Children!

Children many less than thirteen years of age, some nine years old and festering with disease before they reach their tenth birthday. Mothers putting their daughters in those parts of London where, as prostitutes, they will thrive upon those who take their income from maritime employment . . .'

While making the most force of his arguments in my direction, Hanway turned towards the brothers Dingley from time to time and showed his palm-ledger for their inspection and approval. They nodded and said, 'Indeed, indeed, quite decidedly the figures prove it.' They chipped in with reminders about Irish milkmaids who were loath to continue heavy labouring with their churns and fell easy prey to fine gentlemen who offered a better life now and then later ruined them.

'Jonas,' they begged, 'forget not other women too – the thirty thousand seasonally employed in gardens yielding fruit and vegetables, which heavy burdens they carry twice a day to London markets. How many of these fail in their strength and honest tasks and decide pitifully to turn to an older and easier profession?'

Mr Hanway allowed a few more of these interventions and then addressing me directly said:

'All these are angels, just as much as the parson's daughter seduced by the Squire. But leave sentimentality to one side, there are practicalities to be dealt with when an angel has fallen.'

He closed his ledger and said rhetorically:

'What do we do? Mr Robert Dingley here,' he laid a hand on that worthy man's shoulder ,' has hit upon a plan . . .'

'And we have worked upon it and shaped it and wish to embark upon it straight way . . .' said Charles.

'It is a charity,' said Robert Dingley, 'A Magdalen. A house for penitent prostitutes.'

Charles followed on: 'An institution to help those unfortunates who have fallen into mental and physical wretchedness and are eager to repent.'

'But,' Hanway continued, 'in our minds and as we have drawn up the plans – which we will show you in a moment – a charity has to be both permanent and methodical. Gifts only, raised by the impetuous generosity of the rich, corrupt the character of the recipient so that they need not look for work and change their characters. The successful beggar remains a beggar. Why would he not? So our Magdalen House will bring our angel up from her fall to tearful penitence, and through fruitful and economical labour, recover her dignity and so achieve the angelic state again.'

By this time I saw something more of the angel in Mr Hanway himself and also in his partners the Dingley brothers, who now on their feet were eager to spread out papers showing the whole scheme in detail.

Robert said:

'Petitions will be obtained. Penitents presenting a proper petition completed and signed by a person of substance, will be examined by the Matron and the Physician and Surgeon. The duties and character of the Matron are to be clearly and easily stated. The demands to be placed on those who will have care for the physical state of the inhabitants were to be even more rigorously detailed.

'Physicians, Surgeons and Apothecaries need not,' Mr. Hanway said, 'seek to enlarge on their business. They will have full occupation for their application and the skills required. They will observe more humane and prudent conduct than is perhaps necessary in any other establishment. The surgeons particularly will not lack opportunities to exercise their skills with the knife.'

Charles Dingley took the next parchment and continued: 'The same rules shall apply for all Physicians, Surgeons and Apothecaries. They must all attend in their own persons and no pupil, apprentice or servant is at any time to be admitted into the wards.'

'The Chaplain,' said Hanway, 'will like these others make weekly reports to the Matron. He will attend all committees, read prayers morning and evening, take prayers and preach twice every Sunday: attend the sick and illiterate and instruct all in the principles of the protestant religion.'

Mr Hanway saw my face fall. I assumed that the purpose of my attendance that day was to advise me that I had been 'chosen' to be Chaplain. Hanway shook his head and held a finger to his lips to indicate silence. My concern then deepened, for if I were not to be asked to be Chaplain

– and I would not accept such a permanent position since beyond it there lay no preferment – then perhaps Mr Hanway and the brothers hoped for money from me. Similar applications to me were not infrequent, but only on a small scale. This scheme would demand considerable sums to support the Matron, the Chaplain, the Physicians and Surgeons and the Apothecary and all the retinue of officials.

I was not reassured when my charitable friends described how the penitents would work and be paid out of the profits of that work. The Magdalen was to be a manufactory of clothes and cloth making, of stocking knitting, bone lace, black lace, artificial flowers, children's toys, fine spun thread, woollen yarn, winding silk, embroidery, all branches of millinery; shoe making for women and children, mantuas, stays, coats, comb for wigs, woven hair for perukes, leather and silken flowers, garters, clothes for soldiers and sailors shops, carpets after the manner – all these tasks easily suited to their strengths and employing their several abilities and geniuses.

All three merchants rubbed their hands as the list lengthened. I did wonder for a moment if the scheme was to furnish the whole Russian Trade with all the items it needed from this one Magdalen; but I realised that those men had now retired from trade and stood to make no profit for themselves. They admitted to careful and constant and prayerful consideration in all things as they had written out in the Rules of Guidance: matters of retiring and rising – six in the morning to ten at night from Lady Day to Michaelmas; after Michaelmas seven o'clock in the morning to nine o'clock at night through to Lady Day again, thereby to save candles through much of the winter. Economies such as this were not harsh but sensible, as were rules of conduct towards the penitents.

Their true names were to be registered but they may use feigned names to conceal themselves should they wish.

Reproaches for past irregularities were forbidden and no discovery allowed of things which parties themselves do not choose to disclose. The Matron, always residing in the House, would follow the Committee's instructions to the letter and control everything from the diets at breakfast to locking the doors last thing at night.

When admitted, the penitents were to give in their own dresses to be cleaned and ticketed, ready for their eventual discharge. Meanwhile they were to be given plain and neat uniforms of a light grey colour.

Charles Dingley wished at this very moment to detail the stamping on the uniform buttons, and was searching for pen and paper to that end. His brother and Jonas, seeing perhaps that I was fatigued, dissuaded him.

I had been standing for an hour or more that afternoon and was weakening for want of refreshment. The earnest demeanour and enthusiasm of Mr Hanway and Charles and Robert Dingley allowed no room for consideration of my condition before that of the host of London prostitutes who were to benefit by The Magdalen. Rather than listen longer and by my compliance suggest that I might aid their scheme with financial backing – I made moves to suggest my immediate departure. At once the three halted in their accounts and the one hurrying to offer a chair and another pressing a further glass of water on me, the third said 'O, why are we so lacking in thought for poor Reverend Mr Dodd. He has listened to us with more patience than Job and still we have not told him our purpose for him.'

'Forgive us,' said Jonas Hanway. 'Let us come straight to the point at last. We do not and shall not ask you for money that will be regularly needed to support The Magdalen. We do not need recommendations as to suitable penitents and we have already found a Chaplain who, worthy divine though he is, is quite without ambition and will seek to go no further. He is also a man of an age that we might quite suppose will make him satisfied with the affections only of his wife and several children.

A MAGDALEN PROPOSED

We consider it no disqualification that as a preacher he is rather on the dull side, for in many cases the penitents will have proved already in their past lives that they are prey to persuasion by men with silver tongues. We have reformation as our object not further excitation of passions that yield poorly to control and are readily inflamed. It is not therefore as Chaplain we need you Reverend Doctor Dodd.'

I felt some easiness of mind for an instant, and then was alarmed again at having no idea of their intentions for me. Was I to make a public confession of my life in London a few years back? Was I to show from the pulpit perhaps that I had not always treated the fair sex with fairness? To show the perfidy of man? Even though none of this was the truth, might not their purposes be met if other men were led into confession by mine and so shocked into making recompense and turned that recompense into gold for the Magdalen?

It was Jonas Hanway's habit always to watch the face of whomsoever he addressed, to discover the effect of his speech.

'Be not anxious,' he said. 'We wish only to use your talents. We are business men, hard and practical in our dealings. Our efforts to persuade the noble and rich and our colleagues in the City to yield up money for the Magdalen would we fear fail. We do not have charm in the forefront of our minds nor on our tongues. Furthermore, I at least feel that I am too young and unmarried to escape ridicule if I am thought to be furthering the cause of harlots instead of occupying myself with the regular concerns of trade and commerce.

'But, but,' he continued, 'we know that you have touched the hearts of many from your pulpit. You can preach to rich and poor and I have it told that ladies swoon in the pews at the sound of your voice. Also you know well the sorry lot met by so many of the fair sex who have fallen, purchased for a few vile pence, and we believe that their virtuous sisters and brothers will empty their purses for the benefit of The Magdalen on your persuasion.'

I was by turns flattered and startled by this declaration of Jonas Hanway and the Dingley brothers' designs for me. My greater youth was seemingly now ignored and there was no truth in Hanway's denial of his own powerful tongue. That he had just now persuaded me to fall in with his scheme proved his tongue to be golden, and I told him so. For the first time that day he smiled. He and his companions beamed at my assent and shook my hand repeatedly.

It was settled there and then that the first Magdalen should open in a house hired in Prescott Street, Whitechapel. The Earl of Hertford had been approached and had consented to be President and all the officials as described were appointed.

The date was set for August 10th when I agreed that I was free that day to preach.

After Jonas Hanway's many tugs at the bell pull, the old servant appeared to show me down to the street where a boy held my horse with one hand. The other hand was held out for a vail until slapped by the old servant. 'You shall not ask for money for what it is your job to do. And you should never ask at any time for vails from gentlemen of the cloth.' The boy sulked dramatically, which drew a further reprimand.

I was elated and relieved now to know the purpose of my visit, and my vanity puffed up that I should be chosen to preach and to consort more frequently with people of breeding, with the rich, and in London – all of which advantages might fall to me as well as to The Magdalen.

Bellows my horse was steady enough at all times and today, because of the scorching sun, I was particular not to put him to more than a trot. The pricks of heat and dust as we came from The Strand and the further stings of flies and mosquitoes swarming across the marshlands prevented my nodding off to the lullaby rhythms of my jogging horse and the whisper of his scuffing hooves. Furthermore my head was crammed with texts for sermons. There would be great need for powerful sermons if I were to promote the Magdalen, and many more words needed to fill the coffers.

But before these thoughts I must think of me.

Samuel Squire and other clerics, who to all outward purpose consider nothing but the paths where ambition leads, have taught me that, unknown to their fellows, they spend much time in other contemplations. Should I not do likewise? Bellows' nodding head agreed. Then could I by throwing myself into a cause for prostitutes, however beneficent, advance my progression in the Church? Or would motives be attributed to me that would damage my prospects? What were my motives? I could not imagine that the patrons of bishoprics would consider me innocent and saintly – for even the bishops themselves were not. Had not Jonas Hanway told me that one of these bishops (known to us all but his deeds not so widely spread) had procured for himself at least one young woman after she had fallen into the hands of a schemer. She had suffered a not much worse fate by being introduced to his palace. For when the bishop was worn with her, she was dismissed to fall back into that society where, out of necessity, virtue sank out of sight. Ambition would not be favoured by a firm association with harlots. Then why was I delighted with the thoughts of such association as the Magdalen would provide?

I thought on some lines of St Augustine that said:

"Lord, I have difficulty, and I find my own self hard to comprehend. I have become for myself a soil which is a cause of difficulty and much sweat . . ."

I dug into my soil and wondered what virtue was there in me to appear to care for the harlot even while lusting with my mind's eye under her skirts. Does my concern for Christian affection take second place to the satisfaction and stimulation of my carnal desires? Neither Bellow's head nor my heated conscience gave the lie to this. Yet – for I will ever seek mitigation and try to find some *pro* to the *contra* of myself – by caring for prostitutes should I rise in my own esteem and give more abundantly of myself in the pulpit. If this were not all the truth about me – and I did not then dare to test all the utter depths of myself – it would suffice for today. I was impatient to finish these thoughts because other thoughts arising from my own confessions were jostling to be put in place for my first sermon and to shape the pattern for others.

Though it would be improper from the pulpit to attribute to the men of the congregation the same dishonourable motives discovered in me, I should not be blind to their lusts of the flesh raised to high proportions through the wanderings of their eyes. In a sermon which would inevitably apostrophise the penitents, I should also be mindful of the need to engage the critical consciences of the men, and bring them away from *"the bought smiles of harlots' loveless, joyless, casual fruition."*

When we reached the tree lined lanes of West Ham, Bellows was rejuvenated by the shading coolness and at the sight of home he at last broke into the angle of his quick trot.

I had fixed by this time upon the text for my opening sermon . . .

"He that is without sin among you, let him first cast a stone at her."

CHAPTER 20
THE MAGDALEN OPENS

Flourishes; Criticism; Strengthening of my belief;
My sermons bring money to The Magdalen House.

A newly painted sign "The Magdalen" was fixed to the gate of the house hired for the penitents in Prescott Street until larger and more suitable premises could be found. This road was a backwater with ground to spare between the houses and long gardens before them.

Thursday, the 10th, was no busier than any other August morning.

Irregular showers, more sudden than lengthy, discouraged residents from loitering about their outside tasks, and only a few people gathered in the street when the carriages of the Earl of Hertford and his party arrived for the opening ceremony.

These same people who had written to the London papers decrying a "house of shame" in the neighbourhood, called out to the Earl and shook their fists and urged him to take himself and his "lewd doxies" away from their street. The Earl merely doffed his hat as he descended and all the officials of the Magdalen did likewise as they arrived. The opening ceremony in front of the house was briefly performed with a few words from Jonas Hanway as an introduction to The President, who then spoke with even fewer words to adjure the young ladies rescued from distress to be grateful and beholden to the worthy people who had founded the Magdalen for them. The young ladies – only eight in number – were suitably subdued, as was likely since they were barely out of childhood, the eldest fourteen and the youngest nine years of age. There were four times as many officials and invited onlookers overshadowing the penitents, and they surrounded the little subjects as we moved off for a service at the Charlotte Street Chapel in Bloomsbury. In such a fashion the small neat figures in their grey-brown dresses and flat straw hats wound round with blue riband, were protected from the stares of the protesters as we walked. These latter, seeing the objects of their anger were scarcely an enemy to fear and that in any event were guarded by more threatening bodies – particularly the Matron who was an awesome woman – these protesters meekly joined at the end of the column and entered the church last.

Music by Thomas Arne, composed first for The Vauxhall Gardens, was this day solemnified by a band of fiddlers. We were led by the Chaplain in prayers without him inflicting any damaging dullness on us and then the whole congregation sang a hymn – *Awake my soul and with the sun* – and to touch the hearts of everyone the penitents sang the Twenty-third Psalm, which they had committed to memory and well rehearsed. As they had been commanded, they lifted their heads to sing and we had ample opportunity at last to see how young and pretty those penitents were. There were no signs yet of ravishing diseases in them – giving one to believe that the Matron and the Physicians had chosen wisely. Fifty petitions in all, including these eight angels, had been presented to the Committee, but the first admitted were the youngest and most fit and least likely to be with child.

One or two of the penitents had let tears fall when the Earl of Hertford spoke to them and I was sensible that it would be to the advantage of all if I saved the larger fire-power of my sermon for subsequent occasions.

The Commemoration Service thus ended quietly with not too many tears nor too much loud trumpeting from me. The final hymn I have quite forgot on account that my head in particular and the whole church at large was bursting with the thunderous voice of the Matron bringing plaster off the chancel walls.

My sermon met with approval and was pronounced by the public press to be a manly, a rational and pathetic address. The preface written to it and the sermon itself registered many of the messages occurring again and again in all the subsequent years of preaching for The Magdalen.

The Magdalen flourished. Mr Jonas Hanway and the Dingley Brothers believed that this was a result of my constant efforts to part the citizens of London from their money. They had in part chosen me for my sympathetic nature towards women and my style in the pulpit, though I believe they shuddered in their pews at some of my touching flights of rhetoric as when I preached of:

'Women prostituted to the vilest purposes, by the foulest lust; see them languishing, decaying, dying before their beauties are in bloom, to see these beauties wholly wiped out and defaced by nauseating diseases . . . and yet of late so fair, and now so filthy and disgusting that their own most happy lovers behold them with horror. . .

'What mind asked on this reflection will not be filled with gloomy sadness, and generous distress, and must lament their fate, but would

rejoice to have preserved, or to have rescued them from it?'

The sad objects of my address regularly had amongst their number at least a few who would faint with shame while others wept.

And so the Sunday services immediately became a fashionable sensation and an entertainment through the weekly theatrical performances from choir and pulpit. And men in the congregations emptied their purses.

It was thus the Magdalen grew, watered with the penitents' tears. If Hanway and the Dingleys fidgeted at my wordy excesses, they did not complain. Nor did they endorse such as Walpole whose quills dipped in brilliant colours conveyed a lofty view of The Magdalen and yet cast criticism on me. Scholars, not perhaps half as learned as I, gave it out that I was a "voice and nothing more", and tapped their noses and said the same again – in Latin – that I was *"vox et praeterea nihil",* as if their use of Latin to speak their minds lent greater veracity and dignity to their pronouncements.

In the early days there were indeed difficulties in persuading some people of the virtues of The Magdalen. As I picked my way through the snagging thorns of criticism, I gently laid the briars aside and took each barb in turn. As there will ever be, there were those who standing apart from regular worshippers regarded the enterprise with light mirth – saying it was a scheme as foolish as one "to wash the Ethiopians white" – and so in their opinions placing themselves on a far superior plane to that of prostitutes. I proffered them the thought that they had only a superficial understanding of the religion of Christ; that their mirth was as indecent as weak when the salvation of fellow creatures is concerned; and that the life of a common prostitute is as contrary to the nature and condition of the female sex as darkness is to light.

With minds like acrobats and as easily tilting in an opposite direction, the critics argued that having the charity at hand was an encouragement to sin because the rescue from it was at hand.

'Does a bricklayer,' I refuted the scoffers, 'deliberately or with indifferent calculation carelessly fall from his ladder because a hospital is nearby to treat his injuries?'

They leapt again in another direction seeking to accuse me of "Methodism". No sound theological argument sustained the charge. Itcould not. The torpor and avarice of the Church of England, against which John Wesley and his followers were fighting, was a battle in which Jonas Hanway and many others joined. Were we to be tainted with Methodism because our scheme was methodistical – an enterprise practically designed and promoted and sustained? I answered that it was absurd to think it sufficient to decry a good man or a good work by branding it "Methodist". In such a particular venture as The Magdalen I declared it would well become us all to be such Methodists, and denied for my part any raving "Enthusiasm" in the design.

Even those most given to carping at fine intentions were brought to see some advantages in the economy of a charity that paid its way with needlework and such like. The doubters from the city finally argued that The Magdalen would improve the chances of matrimony for the penitents and therefore the regular provision of children – children having a tincture of virtue about them – to raise the population. For a population dedicated then to work (and philosopher Locke was not alone in advocating the training of children to work from three years of age) would bring up a wealthy nation in its train. The penitents from our Magdalen would play their part: if recovered they would make good marriages, have children and all be useful members of society not only at home in England but also in the colonies whose need was as great or perhaps even greater than ours. Only the stupidest of men did not realise that the population fell because of abominable lust. For lust leads to the very prevalent promiscuous commerce of the sexes and all the diseases descended upon it to the prejudice of honourable matrimony and the procreation of healthy children.

The Magdalen flourished still further. By the end of the first year there were already one hundred women – of whom fifty or more were under fifteen years of age and many below thirteen. Within seven years nearly seven hundred penitents had been received and just under half of these recommitted to and received by their families or placed in service with reputable families and traders. Only two dozen had proven to be lunatics. The Dingleys and Jonas Hanway were distressed that a hundred prostitutes had been dismissed because of a want of temper or other

THE HANGING OF WILLIAM DODD

irregularities. Some were dismissed at their own request – and we know not if they returned to the paths that led to their admission. A handful with incurable fits were admitted to St Luke's Hospital for care.

The expense of all this was raised in a great part by the Sunday Services and my sermons. Collections amounted not infrequently to thirteen or fourteen hundred pounds. This is not to boast, but to remind me that although I could raise funds for a good cause, I could not raise it for me – though I must allow that within a few years I was paid an *ex gratia* sum of one hundred pounds per annum. This perhaps did little more than encourage me in my somewhat reckless extravagance beyond the pulpit. Consciences were bought clean by the men in the congregation without my need to accuse them of promiscuous commerce. I repeated frequently from St Matthew *". . . for I am not come to call the righteous, but sinners to repentance."* Yet, regarding themselves as righteous or having the opportunity to be righteous, when the offertory plate came to them, many men were ostentatiously generous.

The women observed their men and drew what conclusions they saw fit. At a service attended by Prince Edward and therefore with all the best people crowded into the Bedford Street chapel, a Warden heard the Duchess of Northumberland remark to her companion as the "quality" left their reserved pews,

'Lord Uxbridge is markedly generous. He has left enough on the plate to clad all the Angels here and set up each with a golden harp as well.'

'Not,' said Lady Joan Byford, who accompanied her, 'not as much by all accounts as he has lavished on the young women he has first used and then forced, discarded, into the ranks of fallen angels.'

At this point I was in the train behind the Prince, marvelling at myself because my flowing purple gown and fine lace dripping at the wrists and neck were all richer and more admirable than his. Also, to my satisfaction he was not so striking a figure, now descended from the large armchair with its cushions of blue damask and the black and gold prie-dieu and footstool put for him before the altar.

Even though I was wrapt in myself, my eyes were caught by the intense blue eyes of a penitent. She, standing in the pews reserved for such as she, was touching my shoulder with her straw hat as I passed, and her curtsey for the Prince lingered to include me. As Lady Byford's clear voice carried ahead of her the penitent straightened and said as if to her neighbour:

'The Earl's gift was then more than two sovereigns and a florin?'

I heard and saw but in that instant felt the unease of recognition without recollection. Time to time over the next years she was present amongst the penitents' choir, but never took occasion to speak to me and only rarely let her eyes meet mine. I did not mention her to Mary and have not properly remembered her until now when I look back to my early years in London. And perhaps before?

Neither penitents nor congregations are submitted to my private judgement for I do not judge, I describe. But then and now I do make one remark more, and that is on the excellence of the Christian religion which brought the Magdalen into being: it affords abundant consolation for the returning sinner, yet it gives not the least countenance conceivable to sin itself.

CHAPTER 21

AT LE CHATEAU DE VOIRONS

March 1778
Mary Perfidious?
And M de Blanc?

Today is the 29th of this month – The feast of St Gregory
– which date has popped into my head quite by chance. It
has, I think, no relevance. But there it is – an odd
remembrance surfacing as if deliberately to distract a
troubled mind; yet itself causing irritation by raising
another unanswered question – why? Indeed, why this
morning when I am indisposed and mightily put out by a
bewildering mess of papers on my desk? And where is
Mary? She would say that I am peevish again. There is
never any answer to my prayers for a voice. My arm still
hangs useless at my side and suffers its own atrophy. And
the more I think of the litter on my writing desk the more
my neck aches.

Mary helps with my toilet – a limited ablution until the
warmer weather comes when I shall bathe. This morning
Mary was impatient watching my backward progress
downstairs – the trickiest manoeuvre of the day because the
wretched balustrade is on the opposite side to my good
hand, and my temper is not helped either by Mary
pretending to read my sour face through my wig and saying
as she does every single day that it will be easier on the
way up. Obvious observation. No consolation.

Today in place of breakfast she thrust a bowl of tea at
me and some cheese – a cheese so foul that church mice
might spit it out – and bread which would also do service,
if it had not already done so, as a baton for the militia.

By the time I had relieved myself of yesterday's

congestion of the bowel and bladder – presently to my delight functioning as easily as those same parts in a farmyard bull and not greatly paining me – and I had taken a turn outside, Mary had left. Cocking an ear at the bottom of the stairs and at every door leading off the hall, it was apparent to me that the chateau was empty.

Lying at the summit of the papers and letters randomly heaped and spilling over my desk was a morning note. On one side it said simply "jambon". As this same note had been used three times successively this week to indicate "ham for supper", I surmised that I would finally have the ham-bone itself to hold in my hand to gnaw. Mary would not have to cut meat for me tonight.

On the other side of the note freshly inked and smudged was "*Avec M le Blanc*". (Mary's knowledge of French is becoming satisfactory for communications to and from Cook, but sadly limited in the use of verbs, or any part of grammar that might aid in the construction of a full sentence.) I wondered angrily in what way was Mary "with" M le Blanc and where and why and for how long?

Such thoughts brought le Blanc partly into my memory but only with a vague recollection of my kindness to him on some occasion. Even though in my mind I was reassured of his respect for me, I began to rifle through the top-most papers as if further answers might be there, and then I tunnelled into the hillside. I retrieved a variety of documents which at once distracted me from thoughts of Mary and le Blanc.

Some of the documents were printed and others written by different hands – including mine. A published *Sermon on Hanging* – against it and other punishments as disproportionate to the crimes – came in the same fistful of withdrawals as my notes relating to the establishment of an humane S*ociety for the Resuscitation of Persons Apparently Drowned*. Together with these was another of my schemes – *The Loan of Money without Interest to Industrious Tradesmen.*

By this time my mind was quite off Mary and her unforgivable desertion, and stayed so when I found a newspaper cutting recording the success of *The Society for the Relief and Discharge of Persons Imprisoned for Small Debts*, written five years after my sermon to inaugurate it. The report gave 3,241 as the number of prisoners released. Feeling a glow that I should have started such a benefaction I looked for the sermon itself. It was missing but I remember well enough with what passion I spoke for the numbers of honest citizens at that time who through ill health or fateful accident – fire, flood or tempest – had fallen into debt and spent the remainders of their shortened and now fruitless lives in the prisons of The Fleet or The Marshalsea, until disease and hunger carried them off.

It was too tiresome to gather, smooth and fold such a number of sheets of paper with one hand, and so I separated those I wished to read further and in a last resurgent and petulant gesture swept all to the floor. Two heavier items fell directly at my feet. One, a horse's nose-band. It seemed to indicate an eccentricity in whoever used it to tie a sack which now lay empty and neglected on the window seat. The other item, an envelope, proved the ownership of the first. Sir Philip Thickness's large and energetic script formed the address to Mr William Farrier, Chateau de Voirons, and within this was another letter written to him by Mary Farrier some months ago. This latter I had not seen and no copy had to my knowledge been casketted. I read it first:

Chateau de Voirons October 15th 1782

Dear Sir Philip,

I do beg you to forgive me for disturbing you once more. I should not bring my cares to you except that I have no other person to be doctor for my William, nor to be my confessor neither. Apart from M le Blanc being ever solicitous, I have no one here who can give even a single word of sensible advice. I do not know what more I can do for the husband that the fates gave to me and for whom I have been grateful for the most part.

You will have learned from Lady Ann when she returned to you after her last visit here that William is still without speech, and he still limps and has a useless right arm. It may be partly in his imagination – no, I am sure that these injuries are real and are of great consequence to him – for truly the pain in his neck and the effect of it on his temper are real. If I may speak boldly, as I have no one else to listen to me, I do not trouble myself greatly about the mess he makes of his clothes – dribble from his mouth falling upon his shirt and all sorts of human soil staining his breeches – but these disgusting insults are compounded in many ways.

More than once he has attempted the rudest violation of my person while composing his face into what he may suppose is a picture of tender regard, but what in truth, and at the best, is a smile of the most fatuous sort. If I recoil at such bestial attacks, his temper, bad at any time, has no bounds, and then he sulks and writes a pompous bit of a sermon in his "history".

What perhaps is remarkable in me is that none of this would matter a tittle if it were not for William's secrecy. Could he speak I might prise everything out of him. Sometimes I have the silly thought that William deliberately holds from himself the power of speech. Then my temper rises like a caged wild-cat. I am not speechless, but I make what exchanges must be made between us in messages on scraps of paper that he calls my "morning notes". His replies are as short as mine or not at all. Furthermore although every piece of writing is put into the casket he has now forbad me entry to it, taken my key and made himself entirely the master of it. It does not soothe me at all that he has written "Confessions' at the top of some pages as yet innocent of any other writing. I am not persuaded by his note that said "confessions" is nothing

284

more than a word to test his quill because he dare not write his name too frequently or loosely upon a page. I think he has in mind revelations so horrid that they cannot be allowed to see the light of day, and certainly not come before my eyes. What can I do?

Please give my affectionate regards to Lady Ann whom I am sure delivered our sincere greetings to you both and the warmest invitation to come again (at Christmas?) to make a concert with us. At the very least I beg you to write some kind of comfort and advice for me. I am sorely pressed.

I am honoured to remain,

Your sincere friend,

Mary Farrier

So often Mary's morning notes were all I had from her. Those squeaking fledglings left on my desk gave no measure of her feelings and asked for no full reply. But here was a full blown epistle loaded with contempt and criticism and wailing; a vulgar jumble of wild and distorted descriptions gathered from chance and isolated circumstances pertaining to some time since.

I was of a mind to dash down my own answer at that very moment and to thrust it under her maggoty eyes as soon as she returned. It was only the eagerness to learn what her advisor The Great Thicknesse said in his letter before I crumpled it that delayed me. It was not Christian forbearance had me rest my quill in the inkpot – the lone survivor from the desolation of my desk. Here is what The Great Thicknesse said:

At Mrs Gravener's in Share Gate Street, Dover. 9th & 10th November, '82.

Dear Madame Farrier,

You were writing a letter directed to me in person therefore

I shall reply likewise. I shall barely give you thanks for it
– a most complaining thing not befitting the wife of such a
great man who has fallen on hard times. I will not share
sorrow with you over commonplace events of the wedded
state which must be so, unless we are surrounded by an
army of servants. I *will* give you advice however.

If you would wish to ease the bodily and mental
burdens dear

M Farrier suffers, give opium. I have proffered this advice
before – when the good man's mind was not in as much
peril as it is now by all appearances. Why did you withhold
the opium and did not give it grain for grain as I advised?
It will keep your husband on a steady footing while what
he now calls "confessions" come out of him as surely they
must do to loosen his tongue. Of a certain, M Farrier must
keep some of his secrets to himself for they may be
exceedingly nasty and would do harm to you if told. I
should have expressed these opinions to you before this but
could not know how long M Farrier would be about his
history.

I brought your letter with me from Bath. Lady Ann and
I were at Dover six days ago, intending to be with you by
now for celebrations at Christmas. Our small retinue
included only Jocko – for the Whippets, remaining in Bath,
had proved long ago to be bad travellers – as indeed has
Jocko in these latest events. We were delayed for two days
at Mrs Gravener's – as sometimes before when we waited
for a favourable tide

– and then two days more held up for want of a sober
captain, the crew too fearful to sail without him who is
unhappily for us also the owner. Yesterday we embarked
and lay in harbour while the seas rose and a storm raged
around us. Lady Ann and Jocko were violently ill – the one
holding the other by the heels and they both leaning
perilously over the bulwarks to be sick. Lady Ann appealed
tearfully to the Captain for him to put out to sea at once

where we all might die immediately rather than to be rocked slowly without mercy until we died a lingering death in harbour.

As dire as any of this was the breaking of three of Lady Ann's musical glasses, and two strings from my fiddle. A wheel was also lost from the chaise which had been badly shackled to the deck. This might have been easily replaced in Boulogne, but discounting the *mal-de-mer* of Jocko and Lady Ann, which are only temporary bars to our progress, we might search for weeks in France before finding musical glasses to suit, even if Boulogne quickly yielded a new fiddle string for me.

Lady Ann is most emphatic about our immediate return to Bath. I must allow this because she says she will not again face the high-seas and every peril for me, until some time resting beside the placid waters of the River Avon has restored her health. Therefore, this letter and yours which I had intended to answer in person when we came – are put in a painted sack made four or five years ago from a canvas rejected by Mr Gainsborough – a neighbour at the time. Nestling inside this portrait-in- a-landskip are numerous papers M Farrier may be glad of. He will not notice – since my printing machine is of such excellent quality – that a few of the sermons put to the press by me are faithful but facsimiles only of the originals. The ship will sail without us but with the sack and all it contains, since none of these has quite the sensibilities of Jocko and my wife and will withstand whatever the seas have to offer.

My felicitations to Mr William and let not my admonitions to you lie too heavily on your mind. But do not forget them.

With sincere and permanent regard,
Philip Thicknesse

I have been sitting here for an hour now, my anger boiling worse than the waters of Thicknesse's tempest. I have seized my pen a dozen times to reply to my tormentors, only to stab the quill deeply back into the well until ink flowed beneath my fingers and stained the feather flights. Anger at Mary remained – for speaking ill of me and for her desertion. (I have not eaten all day apart from a green apple and a cup of warm milk found on a raid into the kitchens.) Anger at Thicknesse was at first on account of his rude rebukes to my wife. Not until I had read both letters again did my boiling cool. Sir Philip, after all, understands me and gives to Mary at least a high opinion of me – "a great man" and "a good man".

So I held my hand, let ink and pen settle in the well, plucked papers from the floor and, as long as light held, studied closely those lines which contributed favourably to any description of me. I will not have opium. Nor do I think I need it. Sleep falls quickly and comfortably on me, however I am disposed, and even now my head will rest over my useless arm laid on purpose as a pillow on the desk.

A gentle cough followed by three or four more brought me out of one dream to another dream in which the doors to the hall were flung back wide and I should think that every candle in the chateau had been pressed into service and lit and fixed on its bracket or held forward in the hands of the servants. M le Blanc himself stood in a gallant posture at the door pointing to the foot of the stairs where first appeared the silk shod feet and then the petticoats and dress and bodice, neck and face of – Mary – smiling and glowing more with happiness than with powdered and painted artifice as she twirled into the room and kissed the pale cheek of M le Blanc with her full crimson lips. Before my heart could sink at the instant imagined evidence of her desertion and the reason for it, she was upon my knee and kissing me with a fervour that denied all deceit and discomfort. She said beneath the servants' applause:

'I love you, The Reverend Dr William Dodd, DD, I love you.'

I shall tomorrow begin again the history of me that I understand a little better than the present order of events. How can the fair sex change so rapidly? It is a fact, an accepted mystery I suppose – and on this occasion just described, Mary's full account was contained in one small morning note:

'M le Blanc had business at Voirons and took me with him. I was left with a milliner and was to act deaf and dumb while she fitted me the dress I chose. Cook and other servants went off to market as usual,

Is not my gown the very best? Is not M le Blanc the most kind and generous?
The ham bone will be thrown out.
We shall have mouton for supper.
Mary'
So that is how matters lie.

I think of St Gregory again – how in his portraits a dove sits on his shoulder – the spirit which guides his writing. What bird should sit on Mary's shoulder? Or on the unsteady and restless shoulder of Sir Philip?
Or mine?

I shall take a falcon. It will direct my pen to hunt out truths where they hide like vermin in the long grass of my life.

CHAPTER 22
WRITING; LADY HERTFORD;THICKNESSE

Warden Semple; Captain Thicknesse; The promise of Bath

The twelfth year of my clerical life was marked by an indifferent summer. Well-watered crops grew promisingly at first but then as the rains continued they succumbed under leaden skies to mildew and rot. Travellers by any means – foot, horse or carriage – became navigators by necessity, the most successful finding safe ground in the shallows of the flood waters, and a few of the least provident, out at night, drowning when their horses took across swollen rivers where no road or bridge could be found.

There was every inducement to stay snug in the Curate's House at Plaistow, rarely visiting the metropolis. And had Bellows, faithful animal, still been my transport, I think I should have allowed my ambition to be dampened and stayed at home. However, that able horse who had listened to more sermons from the saddle, spent more time tied and shuffling his hooves outside churches and homesteads and had more rain drip from his flanks and mane while I argued with printers than I dare say any horse in the world was retired from service the year before. The spring had gone from his step in whichever direction he went, and age showed in the grey of his coat and the grey rings in his eyes. When I had taken off his saddle for the last time and released him into the Reverend Mr Wyatt's vicarage glebe, Bellow's snort and toss of head were evidence of his pleasure and my wise decision to use the chaise and horses recently given to me. My Vicar was ailing now and his intellect receding and he did not leave the Vicarage. The conveyance provided gave some measure of protection from the rain – at least the leaks were constant and could be allowed to drip and sing into a tin bowl and be emptied when the tune changed.

Such mundane matters tipped the balance from inertia to activity, and I was encouraged by the prospect of protection from the elements to make almost daily journeys into town to prosecute my schemes. One of these on which my mind was set – a *Commentary on The Bible* – occasioned many journeys up to town and was made more laborious for me there by Mr Newbery, the printer and publisher of *The Christian's Magazine*. For years this august journal took writing from me for its monthly issues, and then to supplement my income and to save Mr Newbery's sweat, I became its editor. Mr Newbury lived in the city and above the shop and would not move out of it to more gracious premises. He was parsimonious in the extreme, keeping a close eye on my expenses: six shillings a year allowed for entertaining authors (and happily also their wives!) to tea. After a time, even this was deemed too extravagant – and the same sum was subtracted from the meagre advance of twenty-six pounds per quarter year paid to me as editor.

In response, I took advantage of the magazine to publish and to advertise my own literary efforts. Sermons and poems appeared in the magazine, and best of all the projected *Commentary on The Bible* was printed in it and launched upon the public a month at a time. It did a favour to Mr Newbery by relieving him of the anxiety of a promise to publish the three projected volumes all together when they were written. I was made regularly aware of Newbery's timorous nature as he rarely began or ended a discussion without reminding me of "the horrid risks dependent on the public opinions which determine profits".

He did so strongly wish for benefactors to be found who would support his schemes with blind faith and open purses. With such impossible ambitions, Newbery scarcely had the grace to thank me for putting his *Little Goody Two Shoes* in *The Christian's Magazine* though none of his other books for children achieved a profit for him; the such ungrateful author.

It might be that Newbery regarded me as a hired hack, but others respected my writing and showed no surprise when a Lambeth Doctorate was conferred upon me – notified by a glowing tribute I wrote for me in *The Christian's Magazine* wherein also I referred to the projected *'Commentary'* and to my previous *'Meditations'* – all to gild the lily of my literary reputation.

These brought almost daily requests to preach in London. I refused very few invitations but had great difficulty in finding empty hours, let alone idle days in a nearly ceaseless round and dared not, nor did wish to let my mind slip from the Magdalen Charity. I had also a dream of having my own chapel to preach in, which dream was encouraged by my appointment as a Royal Chaplain – to King George.

My old benefactor Dr Samuel Squire, not satisfied with his gift of a Prebender's Stall at Brecon, had arranged this advancement for me at the Court before he died. (I never went to Brecon but remember that I prayed daily, prayers that gave thanks for the emolument received, and asked His blessing on every soul in that distant diocese.)

To support The Magdalen and for it to flourish continually, patrons in polite society were frequently to be visited and courted. Amongst many of these, and nearest to my heart, was Lady Hertford. Her beauty was of the soul but of such magnitude that her eyes and softening smile lit up a face that in repose could show nothing but a skin coarsened by pox marks. Not so her hands. Their dove-like whiteness tinged with rose, moved in expressions as gentle and as soothingly modulated as the cadences of her voice.

It was my belief that her husband did not love her despite any outward show of his. His generosity however – he was President of the Magdalen

— was widely praised and merely tittle-tattle that it owed much to his wife's handsome dowry. A stern and superior look was an aid to his advance in worldly affairs, but to my knowledge drew few glances of the gentler sex towards him, and those of Lady Hertford were rarely returned. Her consolation was that the legal arrangements attendant upon their marriage deprived her of less than half her considerable fortune.

She dispersed large sums for me to hand to the Trustees of the Magdalen, but never did she give solely to the Magdalen. As she gave to the charity, with shining eyes my Lady Hertford gave presents to me. Her excuse perhaps would be to thank me for a slim volume of Christian prose that I pressed upon her – with an ode to her of my own composition – or "a trifle given as a small present to compliment you on your sermon today".

When in her elegant drawing room the footmen and Lady Hertford's companion had followed the teacups out, she would often times take my hand in hers, prise the fingers slowly open, and then fold them again one at a time – as though playing solemn notes upon a keyboard – until my fingers were entirely closed around a gift. In this manner and with my eyes held warmly by hers, I received many gifts – which, although given with other donations for the Magdalen, were clearly marked as being for me alone.

The good Lord in His mercy brought great joy to me, and through me thus to The Magdalen penitents and other recipients of practical charity. However, there was always a cloud hanging over my head. When I contemplated my own old age my brow furrowed. Without a secure living – with full title to it, I could then no longer turn sermons into guineas; and would fall upon the parish. Such gloom became more profound when in quick succession The Reverend and Mrs Wyatt died.

It was in the wet dawn of the first day of January this year that Mrs Wyatt fell – struck dead – outside the back door of the Vicarage. She had not moved more than a step across the yard to the brick privy and lay amongst the pottery shards and discharged contents of her husband's chamberpot. Her pride and humility had prevented her rousing either of the maids and they had not risen from their beds until an hour or more later, when they were woken by the broken crying of Mr Wyatt. That brought them down to the yard to find him in a wet nightshirt standing in a fall of rain and looking, apart from the movements of his mouth, motionless upon the body of his wife. The maids later conspired to confirm that Mr Wyatt was soaked more from rain than his own urine.

But the cold he caught was the same cold from either cause and I dare say the death he died the following week the same death too.

All Saints Church was crowded for the funeral. I preached a sermon little changed from the address I gave at Samuel Squires' memorial but since this was my own congregation I began in the pulpit and then still preaching, descended to the chancel steps as it were to embrace the people . . .

I spoke of the greatness and the kindness of the man. How God knows better than us – how that the deeds of that cleric, and all our deeds, might be insignificant in the eyes of the world but would have resounding effects in unknown ways upon future generations. At my words I felt a stillness in the congregation, their emotions lifted and suspended and shared, until I closed with:

'The words of my mouth and the meditations of our hearts and the gifts of that life now taken from us to your Kingdom, be always in Thy sight and ours, O Lord our strength and our redeemer. Amen.'

Outside the church I caught up with Mary, who had left as

soon as the rain appeared to ease.

'You will surely be appointed to the benefice?'

'It is to be hoped. I had not thought otherwise.'

'It must be so. The parish is strongly in your favour.'

'Today may be witness to that but I shall write immediately to the Earl of Hertford – the Patron – before others may aspire to the same claim.'

'And when you are the Vicar of West Ham shall we stay here in comfort, in that large Vicarage, until we follow the Wyatts to our graves?'

'Oh, so sad the prospect you describe. There is more to be given and gained than a quiet incumbency. But still, yes, we will stay, keep house here but have curates to serve the parish.'

Mary made no response to that but walked more slowly than before, and since the rain held off, led us down one lane and up to another to point out things of remark in houses, gardens, and even a curious tree and a fallen wall – all she was at pains to say objects of interest in their own right – but at the same time Mary declared herself surprised at the coincidence of names of "dear people – friends of mine and yours" associated with everything we saw and how she wished never to be apart from them. I forced myself into an attitude of interested agreement but pointed to dark clouds gathering again, and with no great subtlety or wit suggested how a bedchamber was a better place to be on a wet afternoon.

In the days after the funeral Warden Semple began to call attention to himself. He was seen in all parts of the village weaving in and out amongst the parish folk's houses like an artful girl tripping around a maypole.

Until this time I had an almost infinite lack of curiosity about Semple – about what he did, how he amused himself, or whom he loved. It was more than sufficient knowledge for me that I was told that he "had means" and that these means were enlarged by the wealth of a long- nosed maiden aunt who had come to join his household of one. She it was whom Semple ushered into his pew before a service and she who directed glances down her nose at everyone as they entered – as though sniffing out their characters and circumstances. I assumed that she took a dislike to me yet I never saw her nose directed at me, and her eyes like Semple's never met mine but stared at a point above and beyond my right shoulder wherever I might be.

I do not know by what strange physics Miss Semple's effects were made on her nephew, and I did not care to enquire; but since her arrival and the funeral of Mr Wyatt, Semple was set upon a course in the parish, (and I wondered if elsewhere too?), designed to put me in a poor light.

Semple's fellow Wardens, brothers, were of generous natures and low mentality – a combination which allowed free rein to Semple's schemes. He, thinking that he might be able to offer to the patron of the living opinions as if arising from the parish, set about sowing the seeds, or planting his own fully grown crop of opinions about me where they would grow further.

The housemaid Hetty in her days off, released from her duties at the Curate's House, took gossip in from other households like a poor washerwoman taking in dirty laundry. In this way, Mary "learned" that I was too often away from West Ham; that I should not have descended from the pulpit at the funeral of the "very good Christian Mr Wyatt"; that I had been seen fumbling the skirts of a woman in town, but worse still two people had seen me lifting the petticoats of the young widow of farmer Tetley – who had been gored to death by his own bull – as she took chicken into the grain barn during the last harvest. This could not be denied or confirmed, the rumours said, because Mrs Tetley herself died soon after "of shock poor woman", they said, leaving little doubt as to which sad matter contributed most to that shock and death.

Hetty saved the dirtiest piece of laundry 'til last, even

though it was the first, all others being invention following upon it. She built up a climax in her narrative so that Mary would not cut her off but must wait to hear her out:

'Warden Arthur Semple has told villagers in confidence that from the street outside this very house, he saw me, Hetty Milsom, kneeling to kindle fire in the parlour grate and the Reverend Dr Dodd standing behind me with his breeches loosened – which in the Warden's tale was clearly making him ready for "a disgraceful connection".'

When she had listened so far, Mary put a hand over Hetty's mouth and said that if Mr Dodd had done so much it would be his breeches that were kindled and on fire. She added that such impossible stories show how foolish it is to listen to rumour. And then they both laughed at the thought of the reverend breeches being ignited by passion and Mary could not stop a little spurt of urine falling upon the floor and they laughed again and said that was just the thing to quench the flames.

Semple had in fact witnessed only what might be without too great a pun called the closing scene. Hetty was at the grate when I entered the room. Her skirts fresh cleaned and starched had been lifted as she knelt and stayed part raised above the smooth white of her thighs and the dark valley between. Then silently I beseeched my God to save me from temptation: I lowered Hetty's skirt until the hem lay decently across her heels. I did so, stood and turned, and loosened my breeches to disengage the stiffened member from its painful restraints in that tightened fabric.

Hetty saw nothing, but guessed a little. Semple passed by during the last few seconds of the scene only and can have viewed little but imagined a great deal. Mary, over the next months instituted a cross examination of me, asking questions as I was about to put food into my mouth, or was leaving the house, or had closed my eyes in sleep, so avoiding accounts which she feared might be unpleasant, and at the same time giving me an excuse not to answer.

Warden Semple it is to be presumed continued to gather and invent scandal about me but had no fear of asking an indulgence of me. At the church door after evensong – in the company of Mistress Longnose and one or two others whose rheumaticky limbs made them slow to leave – the Warden asked if he "might be so bold as to crave a seat in your – I mean The Vicar's – conveyance, if you are travelling to town in the morning?" It was common knowledge that my Monday habit was to visit the prisons of The Fleet and Newgate or the Marshalsea – or as on this day The King's Bench prison. It would have been churlish to deny Semple, who pleaded that his own horse was sick of a belly of wet grass and the skies were too heavy with rain to permit "a journey on foot which at other times would be better to improve a healthy constitution than a whole armoury of apothecaries' remedies". Therefore, I acquiesced with a good grace.

Monday morning found Warden Semple at my side in the chaise. He
obtained my agreement that I would let him down at the top of Ludgate Street. Then he started asking sly questions about The Magdalen and my part in it. Did I choose all the fallen women myself? When were they considered "beyond redemption"? What happened to them then?
Seemingly on a different tack Semple dropped his voice and looking at me earnestly and with conspiratorial intimacy suggested that I should "deny the other establishment in Bromley" as strenuously as he, Warden Semple, denied it on my behalf. For the rumours, he said, after all were no more than half-made. As I raised my eyebrows in question, a torrential downpour occupied the Warden in positioning the tin bowl in his lap to catch the leak. He spoke loudly above the ring and splash of water: 'A house in Bromley . . . promoted by you . . . young gentlewomen . . . wishing to make connections in high

society . . . introduced to titled gentlemen of means . . . But never such gentlemen as bad as such bucks and rakes were said to be . . . I am sure.'

We pulled up at the top of Ludgate Street with a jerk that emptied the bowl into Semple's lap.

'Thank you,' he said, abandoning any tones of sincerity as he stepped down. 'My journey was to take your part since the Earl of Hertford has asked his agent here to seek my advice as to the wishes of West Ham and Plaistow's good people with regard to qualities desired in their new parson.'

Semple wrung out the cloth at his crotch and reached to have his hand shaken by me saying, 'My fellow Wardens are of a like mind with me.'

My hands remained gripped on the reins. A sharp nod disturbed one curl from my wig, but did not make Semple's eyes move from their fixity beyond my shoulder. This rumour of a pleasure house in Bromley surfaced again and again, but it was again Semple's entire invention and to refute it pointless. I drove off to The King's Bench prison.

There may be only one door into a prison, but many different ways to find that sad entrance.

I came this day having seen a notice (at Mr. Davis's, Booksellers, of Sackville Street) to the effect that a subscription was being raised for a Lieutenant Nathanial Bunting lately of His Majesty's Navy and presently residing at The King's Bench and likely to expire there unless he were relieved. I learned more when I found him in the poorest attic room of that place, closing his window on the savoury smells of food rising from the apartment below, which were likely to taunt him to death.

Lieutenant Bunting had risen from humble beginnings through the favour of Admiral Boscawen, who marked him out as an intelligent and active seaman worthy of promotion. The same qualities had been less apparent when Bunting was loitering with a full pay packet about the Royal Exchange. He saw there a fresh painted sign being hung outside a house and just then came out onto the street to admire it, the shapely figure and handsome face of a weeded widow. The sign bore large gold letters which said "Marine Assurance" and declared in smaller letters that the insurance was safely to be left in the widow's hands. On the instant she invited the Lieutenant in to drink tea and after the second cup he invited her to become his wife. This hasty proposition was impelled by both the lure of her attractions and the prospect of a shore berth with prospects of financial security. The widow also, it was said, had been readier to show "her own good looks than her late husband's books", but an ankle and a knee had been displayed to advantage before the eyes of the sailor just home from the sea.

Alas, within two weeks Lieutenant Nathaniel Bunting was removed to The King's Bench Prison as the person solely responsible for his new wife's debts – and, to rub salt into Bunting's wounds, the debt included an additional two pounds and thirteen shillings for the gold painted sign that first drew him into the widow's trap.

But none of these miseries played presently on the mariner's mind so much as the immediate prospect of starvation. Bunting had nothing to pay for food, and what was worse his nose and palate were provoked beyond endurance by the smells of beef broth and roast fowl and pork floating through the casement from the floor below. Bunting said that the cause of his agony was created by a soldier and gentleman by the name of Thicknesse, Captain Philip Thicknesse, who was imprisoned below.

Although in gaol, this man was nevertheless generous to a degree and through his friendship with Lady Boscawen (the late Admiral's widow) was instrumental in starting the subscription at Mr Davis's Bookseller to the benefit of Lieutenant Bunting.

I listened to the sailor's story, appalled that small weaknesses of the flesh had so often such dire consequences in a person not strengthened by sound faith and a restraining morality. Then although I had not admonished Bunting, I felt keenly my own hypocrisy and sought to make amends. I promised him that he would have daily supplies of food and drink – at my expense – and gave him two guineas for his immediate needs. I bade him farewell.

In the hope that I might find a way also to stop the tormenting smells of cooking rising to the attic from Captain Thicknesses' rooms below, I went in search of him. He was easily found. Over the great bellows of laughter and occasional sounds of breaking wind and snatches of song came the loudest and most martial sounds of Thicknesse himself. He was entertaining his fellow prisoners and the Tipstaffs in his rooms – in what he called his "Town House in St George's Fields".

I was begged to join in the revelry. The whole company knew who I was and hailed me as "The Great Preacher", "The Harlot's Friend", "The Ministering Angel to Drowners and Debtors".

Captain Thicknesse, in case any should deny his right to be amongst his fellow prisoners, read out the charges that brought him to be in the Kings Bench prison:

'Wilful and premeditated perjury at a trial of a Captain Lynch;

Printing libellous papers at the time of an election;

Making appear ridiculous one of his Majesty's subjects.'

Thicknesse mocked the charges and read them out again, changing "perjury" to "honesty", "libelous" to "factual" and adding "how truly ridiculous indeed was one or more of his Majesty's subjects".

I had no choice but to stay until the exhausted company could depart and I might have a quiet word with Captain Thicknesse. Then I thanked him for his intervention on the part of Bunting, and I had only to mention the lieutenant's current torture from the savoury odours emanating from the room in which we were talking for Thicknesse to send up a message at once to insist that Bunting should come below and dine with him every day.

I praised the Captain's generosity and he said in turn that he was grateful for my visit and touched by my concern for so many people. For himself Thicknesse said he did not want anything unless it were a friend who would love him through every adversity, for he denied that he had any present friends – having lost them through quarrelling to which he was inordinately liable and having different and emphatic opinions about everything. Neither did he quibble or temper his justifiable opinions or his anger because some other person was wrong and stupid and unlikely to heed good sense. Thicknesse admitted he did not mince his words, which he agreed with himself might rather have been spoken quietly, and to his advantage on occasion.

Captain Thicknesse avoided choleric outbursts while I stayed with him, and he thanked me. He said that not only was I a fine preacher – he had heard me at St Paul's only last year – but by reputation a good man "who listened without temper and was at the service of every claimant for assistance and pity." He begged that whoever else he quarrelled with, I would never allow him to quarrel with me, that he should always "have one friend in the world amongst so many who are just companions for the moment."

He bit the knuckle of his forefinger and searched his mind to think of something he might offer me in gratitude for the expected friendship. Some gift? A name that would advance my career? Suddenly he hit upon an idea:

'Go to Bath,' he said. 'That is the place to go for a man who would have his star rise in the firmament. You shall carry introductions that I will give you to men of influence who know further men of influence.'

Within minutes he had broken two quill pens in his hurry to write lines to The Earl of Chesterfield, the man of letters, and to Thomas Gainsborough:

'Not that he himself is a man of influence I agree, but he knows many who are and he is an artist of the first rank. I vow he will leave Bath for London before long to do portraits for even greater numbers of the famous.'

'I cannot,' I said picking the superfluous lumps of wax spread around the seals when he passed the envelopes to me, 'I cannot leave my work here'.

'Nor should you be away for more than a month or two from Bath. But in that time, I warrant you will have secured your future. Many of high society are gathered there in close proximity, mixing and vying with each other to be the first to promote someone or something, to set or to follow the smartest fashion.' Captain Thicknesse then said in an aside as though it was of equal consequence:

'My first wife and my second wife also but recently dead, were both discovered in Bath. And should I marry again, doubtless that fortunate woman too would be found in Bath.'

He had the look in his eye which indicated to me that the third Mrs Thicknesse was already identified and would succumb to his advances unless she were very fast in retreat.

Captain Philip Thickness's advice to go to Bath was so strongly given and the recommendations so earnest and honest, that instead of merely toying with the idea for a second and rejecting it, it was immediately stuck firmly in my head. Thicknesse said:

'I would come with you but for my confinement here, and for the fines put upon me which are without reason.' He sighed: 'my sentence is three months long and I await a messenger from Bath with a purse of one hundred pounds to pay my fine, and sums of five hundred pounds from each of two friends (if I still have any such) and one thousand pounds of my own must also be found. These are all to be securities for my keeping the peace for seven years.'

I commiserated with the poor man in such a plight and he was touched by my concern for him.

Mary was not against Bath. Nor was Lady Hertford when I visited her a few weeks later. To the contrary, she came up with a plan to aid me in my decision. The Earl was detained in London for several more weeks but Lady Hertford intended to go to Bath and would "welcome the company of The Reverend Dr William Dodd and his wife Mary in one of the Earl's carriages to Bath – even if their return had to be by stage coach." As for my clerical duties and engagements, the Earl had expressed himself happy to lose the services of his own Chaplain for a while and for him to preach in West Ham or elsewhere in my stead. It was settled. I made no further petitions with regard to the incumbency of West Ham and though I was departing for a short time only and not beyond our English shores, I hurried around town to say farewells to those who would not receive letters from me while I was away.

Gascoigne and Bulkley joined me for coffee at Child's off Ludgate.

Barbara gave me tea in her parlour while the eldest children remained in the shop – prising the younger children and babies from under the feet of Porter who was spitting on his hands and polishing the latest furniture acquired. This scene of domesticity and family enterprise summed up for me what was best and most important about the Porters. I felt that however long the interval they were left unvisited they would not change substantially. Barbara had half a dozen children to receive her wisdom and maternal care and Porter was as proud of these as he was of his finest furniture. He only showed regret that he could not straighten the rickety limbs of the eldest boy but he said that he could do that if the lad kept still long enough to have clamps applied.

Newbery had already plenty of writing from me to keep his presses busy and *The Christian's Magazine* supplied for two months.

The brother Wardens at West Ham expressed

themselves content to have the Earl's Chaplain at All Saints. Semple – addressing a jackdaw perched some distance behind me – made a comment about a lesser number of services, but I was too urgent to leave his company and took no time to interpret his looks, or to find out why he seemed so ready to welcome the Earl's Chaplain.

Such arrangements before my departure gave me no concern. I convinced myself that all was right with the world, that nothing would change while I was absent – nor for any season afterwards as far as I could see.

Mary caught the sense of excitement although I suggested she stay behind in West Ham where doctors she knew were in attendance, but she would have none of it. She said she was well and Hetty, she said, was quite capable of "closing up" the Curates' House and then living at her mother's home until our return from Bath.

CHAPTER 23

BATH; THE EARL OF CHESTERFIELD

Thicknesse given a character; A commission from The Earl of Chesterfield; Sermons and Pleasures; The disappointment of West Ham

I have good reason to look back closely at those long months in Bath although I paid little attention to a remark Mary made on our return. She said that I had stepped out in a new character, and that only she was unaltered. Yet later it was clear to me that the opposite applied. I was not minded to quarrel at that time, nor to look deeply into my thinking or the moulding of my character. I dismissed her remark with a glib quotation, "*For there is nothing either good or bad but thinking makes it so*". I was certain that her downcast spirits gave the reason for her criticism of me, therefore when we were private, I suggested a familiar remedy for her ills knowing that more domestic arguments are settled between sheets than between lawyers or by any self-appointed Daniels come to judgement.

However short the time to be in Bath, here began the summit of my happiness. It was as soon as the skies cleared above the chalk white road out of Marlborough. There was a last quick drench of rain at Box, and at Batheaston Lady Hertford had us pull up in the courtyard of the King William Inn for the coachman and two footmen to dry their livery coats in the kitchen. Then they washed the mud from the carriage doors to allow the Earl of Hertford's crest to show in its full colours.

A post-boy came upon us here, asking to take our names into Bath so that the customary peal of bells might be rung to greet us. Lady Hertford had withdrawn into a nearby coppice for her natural relief before entering the town. Mary was stretching her legs in a short dance amongst the daisies to relieve cramp and I had clambered onto a nearby knoll to take a view of the town. The post-boy sought the nearest footman for the names of the passengers, and barely giving time to hear the answers galloped off back to Bath to earn his penny.

Shortly we came into the town and stopped in Pierrepont Street where the Earl of Hertford's mansion stood next door to an even larger house belonging to The Earl of Chesterfield. This latter boasted a ballroom that could swallow at least two other houses in the street and was said to need none of the fine plaster and panelling lavished on its inner walls because all were covered with tapestries and canvases by old masters, hanging floor to ceiling.

The post-boy's message was taken into a certain Dowager Lady Frances Blakemore who had few possessions – and neither ballrooms nor works of art – but was a considerable collector of information, scandal and rumour from all parts of the town. It was on her instruction that the bells were rung and for whom and for how long. She had no easy way of checking the veracity of the post-boy's message nor interpreting his garbled account as it came to her ear further garbled by her maid. So the maid was sent down to ask directly. She understood that Lady Hertford was in the coach, without the Earl, but accompanied by a Doctor Dood who it must be assumed was a medical man of some importance. The deduction was therefore that Lady Hertford was suffering from an equally important illness and was come to Bath perhaps to spend her last few hopeless days on earth in the healing air and easing waters of the town. The bells therefore could not be rung until an appropriate and sympathetic peal was chosen.

I handed Lady Hertford down and she and her maid went straight to their house. As I handed Mary down she was urgently addressed by the Dowager's maid:

'Lady Frances would have you present her compliments to Lady Hertford and offer her regrets on whatever indisposition has put Lady Hertford into the care of London doctors and brought to Bath.' She spoke with a very slight and condescending sneer copied I thought directly from the Dowager.

'Why, no such thing,' said Mary trying to put an aristocratic polish on her Northumberland vowels. 'This fine gentleman here is no less than The Very Reverend Dr William Dodd – the great divine and famous preacher.' Mary curtsied towards me and continued. 'As for the Lady Hertford – both body and soul are in good order – she has no attacks of illness requiring a physician and no heathen tendencies that might raise the necessity either for a methodical clergyman at her side. The Reverend Dr William Dodd – a Doctor of Laws – if you please as well as Divinity – has come to Bath for pleasure . . . but he might preach if asked.'

By this time Mary's haughtiness was as lofty as any spire in Bath. She curtsied again in my direction and looked straight into the eyes of the Dowager's maid:

'I am Mrs Mary Dodd, and I have the honour to be his wife.'

Now that Lady Hertford was known to be in good health, and that I was a famous preacher not a physician, the abbey bells were very soon rung with chimes of great cheerfulness and Lady Frances Blakemore made up for deficiencies in the post-boy's message by trumpeting my arrival to everyone she met and by claiming that I was the greatest catch of the season and caught in her net.

Since the damage was then remedied it was hardly necessary for her to deprive the post-boy of a halfpenny from his wages, or to instruct her maid to box his ears more than once as a reminder to apply those organs of audition more diligently to their function in the future. Therefore, when I saw the lad the following day as I took the air in my new finery, I charged him to tell no one lest he get another boxing and gave him a penny. He was surprised by my generosity but more surprised as he failed to recognise that I was the Dr Dood he had announced the previous day. It is marvellous what a change can be rendered in a man by good cloth and a fresh wig. The boy ran off, the coin gripped in his palm and looking over his shoulder at me. There is no doubt I did cut a splendid figure. My purple cloak was held open to reveal the flashing of buckles and a froth of lace which complimented a waistcoat of truly multinational beauty – cream silk, embroidered with roses, thistles, shamrock and Prince of Wales plumes and scattered flowers. How my tailor in Drury Lane had exalted in the patriotism of that waistcoat and how well it fitted with the latest Italian fashion of the outer clothing.

Startled and distracted, it was no wonder the post-boy did not recognise me! I barely recognised myself!

By the end of the second week in Bath – two soirées and a ball having already taken place – word went round that named me "The Macaroni Parson". This title was given not in envy I believe nor to mock, but in genuine admiration. Lady Hertford said she had heard praise of me as a clergyman already well thought of in the pulpit who now brought colour and liveliness to a calling not noted for those qualities. She also had made certain that I received an invitation to the Earl of Chesterfield's Evening of Dance.

Invitations to The Earl of Chesterfield's entertainments were reckoned by connoisseurs of the Bath scene to be the most prized. On this occasion, however, Mary complained of a headache which she said – against the odds of medical advice – was more likely to be relieved by a quiet glass or two of wine. I therefore presented myself in the company of Lady Hertford. No further introduction to the Earl of Chesterfield was needed, so I tore up Captain Thicknesses' letter which Lady Hertford said would not advance my case. Thicknesse, she said, was too low in society to give a reference to a person above him in the ranks, and would himself be unlikely ever to receive an invitation from the Earl – but Lady Hertford told me that his sons had. Captain Philip Thicknesse fathered two sons by his second wife, now as the first, deceased. George, the elder, as soon as he became of age, had taken his mother's name and so did his young brother Philip. In this way, they both had inherited considerable estates and George the title "Baron Audley" with a seat in the House of Lords. Such enviable advantages to his sons gave rise to the most quarrelsome features in their father's nature. On the occasion, he had immediately returned to Bath from Landguard Fort at the mouth of Harwich harbour – where he had purchased the Lieutenant Governorship. The first purpose of Captain Thicknesse's return was to lay siege at the family home of Miss Ann Ford whom he had decided to make his third wife. Not unnaturally, that lady's father made difficulties for the Captain and he in turn to vent his spleen rounded on his own sons. He denounced them loudly in public and vigorously and at length in print. They cannot have been much wounded because they were already on a Grand Tour to Italy and the horrid sounds made by their father were dimmed by the distance. Returning now to Bath – their father

by this time being safely detained at The Kings Bench prison on other charges – George and the young Philip were immediately accepted into the best company because of the title and the good name Audley. The best company at that time in Bath was at the Earl of Chesterfield's Evening of Dance. Shortly after arrival that evening I made my introduction to George and Philip. For an instant I thought I had come up against a mirror, for the length and cut of their coats were identical to mine. And their waistcoats a reflection of mine – but not so graceful and true to nature – so I had the advantage of them.

Although it may have been an annoyance to the brothers when I remarked upon their imitation of me – and, worse still, mentioned their father's name – they had none of their father's quick temper. They were, on the contrary, full of friendliness and amusing in their descriptions of their father's eccentric ideas. These were widely spoken of and some of them gained a following. One, of biblical derivation coming from the courtiers of King David, praised the properties of a virgin's breath, which when taken, it was said, warned off death. As King David was cherished by Abishag, so, said Thicknesse, can we be saved by taking deep lungs of air from unpolluted maidens. Thicknesse was also said to say that he envied the well-known Bath physician who took lodgings near a female establishment so that he might never be far away from the breath of innocent young women.

George and Philip claimed that my company was preferable to the dance and made no effort themselves to point a toe – or to seek a virgin in the quadrille to inhale her breath. I danced and was grateful for the Joliffe family of dancing masters (tapping their toes in Cambridge since 1326) who had taught me elegance in movement and all the niceties of posture. Also now my own silver tongue was just as likely to break out in high flown poetry on the dance floor as in Christian proscriptions from the pulpit.

By these means if I did not every time catch the eye of a beautiful woman, I did catch the eye of the Earl of Chesterfield. His look was of such intensity it drew out understanding from whomsoever he looked upon and made them ignorant of his short stature and slight figure.

Now of unreliable health, and an age that made him pay respect to his joints, he danced but little – but in those rare steps upon the floor Chesterfield outshone all others half his age. He did not look down on his feet – which knew perfectly their proper place – but looked out to see the performance of other men. And so watched me. Soon I saw him return to a knot of noble ladies whose dresses blended so well with the upholstery they sat upon one might mistake them for needlework cushions themselves. Standing amongst these, but notable for her youth and bearing, was Lady Hertford and The Earl with his cupped ear close to her mouth. After a few more moments, detaching himself from Lady Hertford, The Earl placed himself directly in front of me and said:

'Will you agree to be tutor to my little boy Philip Stanhope?'

The Earl saw my pleasure and took it rightly as my assent to the task and withal told me of all he expected.

'I know from your late friend and mine, the dear Bishop Samuel Squire – God rest his soul – how well you are versed in the classics and the Gospels. He spoke too of your brilliance in mathematics, and your works for charity which are very well known.

'Now the matter is settled, if there is any want in your life of proper connections I can and will supply them for you. You shall have other tutors to help school my godson and I shall write regularly to my little boy just as I do to my natural son. But I cannot give my little boy practical instruction in deportment and dance. I am hobbling towards the grave myself, and am less good in lively company. You shall be in charge of all that, and introduce Philip also to important people in polite society, and show him how to hold himself.'

Earl gave favourable mention to *The Beauties of Shakespear* and paid flattering tributes to my *Commentary on The Bible*.

'You have,' he said, 'talents in all those departments in which I would have you instruct young Stanhope. You are a physical man as well as one of head and heart, and my little boy should learn as I did that life must not ignore pleasure and gaiety.'

The Earl, to prove it, gave himself a bumper glass of claret saying, 'despite the gout.' Seeing my small glass empty he put a very little claret into that too.

'You will want for premises I suppose? Lady Hertford tells me you have only a mean house in West Ham?'

I thought to ask the Earl to put in a good word for me to the Earl of Hertford about the incumbency at West Ham too. Then I thought not, since the Earl of Chesterfield would wish me to give more attention to his godson than to the people of West Ham. Despite his parsimony with the claret – which I think he deemed of too fine a vintage to be poured for any but his equals – he made the promise of generous arrangements about fees and payment of the rental on a fine house in Pall Mall.

'Mr Plessey my agent will settle all that,' he said. 'He is familiar with it as it stands barely six doors from my town house.'

Our business was concluded, and the Earl made himself satisfied that I would take the ten year-old Philip with me and Mary when we eventually returned to London. He said he felt himself invigorated by the claret and meant to give the parquet some more light impressions of his dancing feet.

I observed that in her own way The Dowager Lady Frances excelled at the dance. Seldom taking the floor, she moved elegantly around the borders of it making a contribution to general conversations before luring the object of her immediate ambition to one side. So the Rector of Bath – who had the benefit of numerous other parishes – came into her orbit:

'Your labours are extensive at this season?'

'They are Lady Frances, kind of you to enquire.'

'So many parishes and so many thanks to give for so many tithes.' 'Quite so. I cannot, therefore, confine myself entirely to the Abbey, of course.'

'Indeed.'

'Indeed.' The Rector paused and looked at his timepiece as if at that very moment he must depart to tend his flock and shoulder other burdens heaped upon him. But he could not detach himself from the Dowager until she had finished:

'Would you allow the Reverend Dr Dodd your pulpit if it should be asked of you? On an occasion?'

'Oh, most readily; as often as he might wish.'

The Rector was delighted that the Dowager's approach had been to offer relief to him and not to solicit gifts of money for some charity. He was most comfortable outside the pulpit amongst a society that did not feel embarrassed by eating and drinking to excess. He might have left preaching always to curates who were sufficiently underfed and therefore light enough to ascend the pulpit steps without arriving too breathless to preach. But he knew that any parson who follows that course entirely will as a consequence receive far fewer invitations to dine at the tables of the rich. In Bath as in London the aristocracy do not underestimate the importance of a clergyman who owes obligations to them. He becomes a species of butler to their households, but allowed to sit at their tables and occasionally and briefly to put the cutlery of conversation into a moral and religious setting and to pass the port quickly back up the table. A further duty imposed upon the clergyman is to preach the sermon that is wished for. Failure in this respect could lead to whole plates full of meat being removed from under the poor cleric's nose as soon as laid before him and his glass standing empty all evening.

The Rector of Bath granted me the freedom of his pulpit at whatever services I named. He would ask my forgiveness he said, if he took advantage to absent himself to take up other pastoral cares while I preached. I did not presume to ask what these other cares might be for it was guaranteed that he would be away securing the good will of distant patrons whose tables were not so very heavily laden nor with such various foods, but could be relied upon to send an occasional roasting pig or a full-horned stag to the rectory kitchens in Bath.

The question that exercised me most at this time was what text to choose for my next sermon. I was much taken by the invigorating breath of Abishag the Virgin and searched the first book of Kings, chapters one and two to find a text that might be put to my purpose. Alas, there was nothing suitable even if a verse or two were hung upon an elevated discourse such as I might preach at The Magdalen. Bath, I thought, would not give its ears gladly to an harangue about fallen women – even in their recovery – or be grateful if the congregations were exhorted to show themselves sensible of the exquisite blessings already vouchsafed to them. So I fell back on a verse from Samuel I:

"Moreover as for me, God forbid that I should sin against the Lord in ceasing to pray for you: but I will teach you the good and right way.

In a quieter oration at a small chapel new built in Bath, I tested this text before a congregation with a less lofty opinion of itself and it received it well – so well that they made me preside there for the rest of my time in Bath and also again if ever I should return.

Mr Gainsborough came especially to this service following, he said, ,a long absence from religious observance of a regular nature. Afterwards he spoke of that and of other things:

'Your letter from Captain Thicknesse spoke of you in glowing terms.'

'It was most kind of him. I presume he spoke of my preaching; for he can know little of me apart from that.'

'That was certainly the account he gave – that you preached from your heart but with your head directing it. And your voice, he said, would turn heathen clay into Christian rock.'

'Such flattery is more than generous, but . . .'

'It is quite sincere. I only choose to quote Captain Thicknesse because he, at leisure, had found the words to praise you that escape me now when I am reeling still from the power of your sermon.'

I thanked Mr Gainsborough and inquired more of Thicknesse, who seemed to have discovered the artist and brought him to Bath.

Thicknesse had said that here Mr Gainsborough would have a rosier time painting portraits of the nobility than painting the fat cattle and the Suffolk landscapes in which they graze. Mr Gainsborough, having made full acknowledgement of Thicknesse's help, returned again to my sermon:

'It has made me take a liking not only to your preaching but also to this chapel. I shall attend both at every opportunity and bring my wife with me.'

Encouraged by such compliments, I preached much the same sermon – but with more power – at the Abbey Church. Those who had attended at St Margaret's Chapel were as enthusiastic after this second sermon as before and more praising of me now and mightily respectful in their commendations. I took this not to be a sign of new powers in me, but of an increased confidence in the congregation – that I was a moral man as upright in honour and sensibility as I was in posture. It must be that the repetition of a text not only gave them the comfort that resides in familiarity, but strengthened belief in my preaching. And, in this case, I believe it also added to my reputation.

I received more admiration from the Dowager Lady Frances. At a musical affair three evenings later, she waved at me imperiously to follow her onto a balcony where The Earl of Chesterfield with a very young creature – whose towering head-dress did not take men's eyes from her more splendid breasts – scuttled away with her. The Dowager said that I was a finer man than the Earl for all his wealth and title and so brought my sermon to her mind.

'"Moreover as for me . . ."' she quoted '"I will teach you the good and the right way".'

I said I was not asserting such authority for myself; but she restrained me, holding up a hand that had a hole in the tip of the gloved forefinger. '*You* do know "the good and the right way", however. Of that I am certain. Quite certain and I would not otherwise ask of you the intimate service I intend to ask. Sit by me.'

We had been standing together, I leaning on the balustrade and both of us looking down upon idlers in the street. A few of these turned their faces up to look at us and to listen to the music coming from within.

Lady Frances noticed the frown and puzzlement on my face and took it to be concern that we should be overheard. We took seats nearby.

'Oh it is not that serious a matter, but I do need your help.'

'Could not your hus . . .' I bit my tongue that I could be so forgetful of her widow's weeds, and angry with myself for entertaining even for an instant the thought that such a woman wished for an "intimate" service from me.

'He would, of course, were he alive.' She waited while the look of disgust faded from my face, and I hoped she would realise that the disgust was mine for me and had nothing to do with the imagining of an "intimate service" performed for her.

'I have,' she said, 'a niece. In fact, I have seven nieces. All of the same family – sisters. Three are too young to cause me anxiety and the eldest is a quiet girl – serious and biddable and has been so for all her nineteen years. The second child, Cristobel, is a wild young woman to whom all the rest look up, yet she has caused more anxiety to her father and mother than all the half-dozen others put together.'

I fear a frown had appeared on my face again, and Lady Frances, seeing it, thought to put speed into her request for help.

'The four older sisters came yesterday, as I had promised to give respite to their parents. Cristobel is full of a plan conceived in the harvest fields at Moreton-Cruise where lies her father's estate. Her "plan" – if it can be called such – is for mixed bathing.'

'Mixed?' I said. 'Mixed with whom?'

'The sexes. As there are no brothers, Cristobel has invited Captain Thicknesse's sons and several other young men amongst their friends to take them all on an excursion to the river to bathe. A suitable part of our River Avon . . .'

'Ah! Not the warm baths at the Pump Room here in Bath?'

'No. I would be aghast if there was such a proposal. Too many frail constitutions would suffer at the shocking sight of naked youth.'

I shook my head.

'You will be guardian for me over those young women?'

'No. Oh yes,' I responded quickly, 'I shook my head at the awful thought of nakedness.' I was ashamed of my hypocrisy.

'At least you will be spared anything but your commanding presence.

With your eyes upon them they will retain all the modesty they owe themselves.'

The Dowager appeared relieved to have passed her burden to me and engaged me now in an earnest discussion about the music and the musicians and how these days every concert began and ended with Handel and how a poor string player was more common than a poor one upon wind instruments.

The Earl of Chesterfield returned in the company this time of a lady of advanced years and though once clearly of striking beauty she now gained attention by her vivacity; her head was crowned with nothing more eminent than a narrow banded tiara of emeralds, but her eyes were lit as though by sapphires and all manner of precious jewels.

The quiet waters of the Avon were soon troubled. The party chose to gather below the first stone bridge upstream. Here the river ran slow and wide and deep between the drooping lacework of willow trees, before tumbling over the weir. Amongst the branches of these, Cristobel and her companions made screens of their outer clothing and slipped giggling into the water. The men were bent behind the parapet of the bridge supposedly preparing themselves for the bathe. Despite shrill cries for them to come out, no one appeared and the girls splashed back under the willows' shade. I, in my capacity as bathing-master, was sat fully clothed on the parapet. Behind me the men now stripped to the waist were cowering in their trousers and bare feet. Cristobel pushed Maria her elder sister forward, to beg me to bathe.

'If you will Mr Dodd so will we,' called the cowards on the bridge.

Maria had entered the stream again and gestured towards me, her hand dripping diamonds of water. I stood on the parapet and with elegant show removed all but my pantaloons. To gasps behind me and squeaks from beneath the willows I jumped. The splash and wave rose up to Maria's chin as she waded towards me where I stood chest deep in the shadowed water below the bridge. Then all jumped in – falling from the bridge and the banks and the willow tree roots and shouting and laughing at the shock of cold water and at their own gaiety and madness.

As the first merriment faded, Cristobel by her deliberate calculation (and his) drew close to George Touchet, Baron Audley, as though to seek refuge in the thick hairs of his chest. She affected to look down into the water.

'A fish attacking me,' she said. 'Oh! Oh! Is it only I sought out for attention by trout or salmon? Are there other predators in the pool?'

Her younger sisters, each having already taken laboured steps through the water to reach her chosen man, were struck by the same idea and peered into the water beneath them.

'A pike, a vicious pike and monstrous large . . .'

'The biggest perch ever seen: t'were for an instant still, I'd sit astride it . . .'

'Oh sisters, be not alarmed for me. I have a small and wriggly thing – the meanest eel that ever dared approach a lady of refinement.'

At this they all sank deeper in the water, laughing until their choking and spluttering ended their frivolity. Maria took no part in her sisters' game but stayed with me under the arch of the bridge. Her head back and lips parted she offered no resistance to my kisses, and when I raised her to me the water took her shift down from her breasts 'til the garment was only a linen skirt floating at her waist. Our flesh touched gently. The silence and the dark alerted no one to our union. Not then. Not ever. The arches of the bridge were our confessional.

My shameful betrayal of The Dowager's trust stays with me always, even though lightened by the romance of memory.

The season was well advanced in Bath. This year there was no Samuel Johnson holding court at The Pelican in Walcot Street, and other equal giants of the intellect and some dazzling conversationalists and wits were absent – Horace Walpole and Oliver Goldsmith had returned to London. So had Dr Falconer, who had such extraordinary recollections of all he had read that if a question arose as to where a certain passage of Greek was to be found, he could give the chapter and the page in the quarto edition. A similar skill had been attributed to me, but moreover – though I did not boast of it – I could give the line as well.

My company in Bath was less erudite – fashionable

names – the Linleys, de Giardini, the Beaumonts and others were in evidence at every evening event, but supplied little originality to morning conversations over coffee in the Assembly Rooms. They brought some tittle-tattle from London and took away as much. I formed the opinion that those who came from town for a vacation in Bath let their brains take a vacation too; the power of original thought being jolted out of them by the journey and the recitation only of what other people said, or they had read sometime before, being allowed release now into the general chatter of conversation.

The Dowager Lady Frances, duty done, had sent her nieces home to take their fortunes with "country bumpkins" and she herself looked for a new name to bruit about and claim as her own. Rumour – or rather spite – had it that she hoped Garrick would arrive and be claimed by her. It did not happen, but already his reputation far exceeded any need for help from the Dowager and her mind was far away from the matter of mixed bathing, so I did not suffer on that account. The subject was raised of course – but solely in idle discussion about mixed bathing in the Roman Baths, the antiquity of which might lend virtue to it. One gossiper questioned how that any man could look with indifference on lovely women in loose attire when their beauty was heightened by the glowing warmth of the bath. Another, with a greater air of sobriety, sniffing at the first man's lasciviousness, quoted a clerical opinion that: "the gender which has been so miscalled to be named "the fair sex" is the danger in this case; for the profligacy of females has been a strong mark of the approaching dissolution of Kingdoms". He went on to cite examples in the fall of the Roman Empire, and in his narration he described more lasciviousness than his opponent in the argument and earned the disdain of every woman in earshot.

Although Miss Ann Ford had already departed – being summoned, willingly, it was related – to Captain Philip Thicknesse at The King's Bench prison, her great admirer Mr Gainsborough was often present at the Assembly Rooms. He sang her praises as a beauty and as a musician and surprisingly, he said as his most apt pupil in fan-painting. All in all, not to have clapped eyes on Miss Ford was perhaps the only severe regret from my sojourn in Bath.

Her presence would have been a balm to an ear growing accustomed to endless talk of health and intimate medical matters. I understood that Thicknesse himself had contributed to the public awareness of some aspects of health by his seeing "twenty and seven stones in one day". Judging by the talk at the Assembly, his was an insignificant number.

The recent sad case of the Reverend Mr Smith of Bath was frequently told, with the number of gall stones found after death when he was opened up increased each day – even when the same person was telling the story. When I left Bath the figure had risen to two thousand and nine hundred in his gall bladder not to mention those "roving stones that were already making their way by a swifter route to the outer world".

Bath physicians had never suspected stones as a cause of the Reverend Mr Smith's disorder any more than Mr Smith himself but those few people who spoke in support of the quack and self-styled Dr Thicknesse said that he suspected Mr Smith's condition all along. Two reliable physicians, Dr Charlton and Dr Mogsey threw up their hands in horror at an account which gave so little credit to their profession; and they threw their hands up even further at the quack remedies given for a variety of complaints. They talked quite freely about 'Mr Gainsborough's disorder' – when he was not in company with them – merely tapping their noses and lowering their eyes while muttering about the inadvisable connections men will make when their wives are 'not given to much humouring of their husbands.' The quack remedy in this case, they said, was that very man's sister's prescription – which he stuck by – of 'six glasses of good old port every evening'. The doctors' expostulations were all the more loud since it was suspected that their applications of the Bark and Salim Draughts had done no good at all but the sisters' six glasses of good old port had made the other remedy palatable and the disorder tolerable while divine agencies provided the cure.

Mary, after all, was quite contented in Bath. Our rooms occupied the whole of the third floor in the Earl of Hertford's mansion, and since the household servants were on the floor above, Mary had company to suit her late in the day, while walking with Lady Hertford and her friends filled daylight hours. Conversation need not stretch to great heights if it is between women as they look in through the frontage of milliners' shops. If discourse between Mary and ladies of society had been conducted by letter, she would have had a great advantage since her father had insisted she wrote in a good hand and she could express herself elegantly on paper. But for Mary to hold a wineglass three- quarters full for an hour, with the little finger cocked just so, and to talk animatedly if required about nothing all evening, was entirely beyond her, particularly if her dress was not – and it could not be – as modish and elaborate as theirs. Given Mary a serious subject and an earnest listener who was not preoccupied with the slippage of a beauty spot or who did not intersperse French words in every sentence – she would hold her own. Since there were few of these serious occasions it was comfortable for her to pass the evenings with "below stairs" upstairs while I trod the dance floors in search of gaiety, which pleasure was a contrast to the heavy load of preaching which descended on me from all quarters. It was apparent that every pulpit in Bath and the surrounding countryside was in need of a rest from its regular incumbent or curate.

Some even developed maladies that required retreat to bed on the very occasion that I was known to be free to visit their churches.

I was not tiring of Bath, but had promised the Earl of Chesterfield to take young Philip Stanhope with me up to London as soon as possible.

Therefore, I had booked on the following Monday's stage. This, I hoped, would allow two more clear days in Bath to bring influence to bear on Hertford to give me the living at West Ham. Predestination or, by the fates' conspiracy, or merely through the clicking of the world's machinery which God observed, The Earl of Hertford on his way to Bath in his best carriage lost a wheel on Hounslow Heath, the axle broke and thrust its broken shaft and both springs through the floor boards. There was no injury to the Earl who was travelling alone, and he at first was inclined merely to curse his coachman. Matters looked bad, however, as he was ejected from the carriage and landed under the rear end of the more alarmed of his two horses. Surveying the damage to his crested carriage, he cursed whoever had neglected the stretch of toll road that caused his grief. He made a mental note to complain whenever he could and to demand some compensation for the wreckage he viewed beyond the horse's tail. Worse was to come – I had all this subsequently from Lady Hertford herself – the coach was irreparable. The Earl was forced to take the stage to Bath.

It was on the Saturday night he arrived at Batheaston – where the stage-coach did not stop and did not even pause for the post-boy to take names into Bath for a ringing of bells to announce them and the great Earl of Hertford. Meanwhile, Lady Hertford was at the same masked ball as

I and half the population of Bath. Therefore Hertford was unheralded and unwelcomed when he finally arrived at his own door to be greeted by a whining footman who had drawn the short straw to stay in on a Saturday night.

Had he been so before, the Earl was not now inclined to charity on the Sunday morning and when he heard from Lady Hertford – who thought it was a happy thing for a poor parson that I had been rung into Bath – he became as frigid as one of the ice-mountains of which mariners speak.

'I shall give the West Ham benefice to my chaplain,' he said to her. 'The man has been accepted by the good people there,' and added *sotto voce,* 'he shall not be near enough to bore me again.'

I was crestfallen beyond belief. Mary, my good, my loyal wife was spitting angry when I told her. She said: 'This same man who has been given your living was the curate who at St George's, Hanover Square – when I at least and perhaps you too were contemplating our marriage . . .' Mary looked at me inviting my assurance, '. . . who preached on the Vegetable Creation and pressed down on us with so many miserable proscriptions and exhortations that we left the church, with others, and had you been of less Godly mind I think we might have left religion all together. So dull and pompous is the man, you must have angered the Earl beyond reason to have given that old Scottish curate your rightful station.'

Mary could not be held back and her voice carried above and below stairs, where Lady Hertford hearing it took the first opportunity to take me privily on one side to express her sadness at the unhappy end to my hopes for advancement and security. But more than that, when the Earl had left the house – presumably to lower the temperature in the rest of Bath – Lady Hertford came to our rooms and pressed upon me a great ring with a diamond stone as large as one of my knuckles, and for Mary a lottery ticket already won for £1,000. She had she said intended part of these for The Magdalen, and it should not run short now, but for me and Mary, these were but trifles that she hoped might begin to help to heal the great hurt she felt her husband had brought upon us.

Lady Hertford and Mary were at any time given to great sensibility and now they fell into each other's arms letting their tears stain each others' cheeks and fall upon each heaving bosom like rain on a parched landscape.

CHAPTER 24

RETURN TO LONDON

*The School House in Pall Mall; Chesterfield, Sturdy
and other pupils; The Magdalen; My Chapel;
Sermon:"Thou shall not kill";
Ladies in waiting.*

In London again, I determined never to return to Plaistow and West Ham, for I would not share a parish nor even a pulpit with the Scotsman – a man whose sermons and indeed daily conversation were considered greater soporifics than opium, and gave nothing of benefit.

Mary wrote a sad and tender letter to each of her many poor charges.

She explained that my duties as preacher and writer and now schoolmaster kept me close to the centre of the metropolis and my pupils. She wrote that, notwithstanding, I would work always for the indigent, for debtors, and for those who had failed in business; and that I would be resolute still for the destitute of all classes and particularly – as they knew – for those female children who were daily forced to lead unnatural lives and to surrender their bodies at a price.

Some wrote back letters and others caused letters to be written and put their marks beneath. All expressed their gratitude for my and Mary's good offices over the last many years, and conveyed their wishes for our future. That future was undoubtedly to be seen as rosy, however much the present was occupied by small irritations.

The School House in Pall Mall was a large and echoing building, scantily furnished and craving the attention of duster and broom.

327

Therefore, Mary wrote to Hetty at her mother's house asking her to come quickly to serve our domestic needs. Hetty sent a message back via the carrier – now Porter's boy quite fully grown – who was bringing our personal effects from the Curate's House. Perhaps the rough cobbled roads down from Holborn shook the niceties out of Hetty's message, but the remaining kernel of it was that neither Hetty nor her mother nor her grandmother before her ever travelled when their courses were on, indeed were even reluctant to leave the house under those circumstances. It was, therefore, several weeks before Hetty's calendar allowed her to travel, by which time Mary had engaged two serving girls, the one exceedingly pretty and the other exceedingly plain. She could not have the plain one – a girl unlikely she surmised to distract me – without the pretty one who would. They were sisters and not to be parted. Had Mary been a "lady of quality" with the customary heartlessness of such persons, she is likely to have sent them both away and found another serving girl less fortunately endowed. But Mary had the greatest sensibility for those of her own sex and admired the bond between these two as she had felt the strong bond with her own sister who early through flights of vanity had fallen into the abyss of prostitution.

The School House was not, therefore, perfectly organised when the Earl of Chesterfield called. He had returned from Bath and was stopping at his house in The Mall for a few days before going to his country estate at Blackheath. The note that prefaced his visit gave his reason as wanting a report on his godson, my pupil Philip Stanhope.

With that easy informality which comes naturally to the very rich and powerful when they move amongst their social inferiors, the Earl did not wait on a reply to his note, but walked into the School House unannounced. Mary was on her own and declared to me later how enchanted she was with his Lordship's manners. He immediately removed any doubts she might have about her appearance by remarking immediately what The Earl of Sandwich said of Dr Dodd: '"How well he picked and with what good taste he had made his choice. It has been said that he has an eye for the most beautiful women in London", and I must now believe the old rascal is reported correctly.' Mary let her silence and her softening eyes admit the compliment however much without tact it might have been.

'And Dr Dodd clearly is in a high class of connoisseurs,' he added.

The subject shifted smoothly to his godson, and The Earl told Mary about him as though she were an old and trusted friend. First he explained why he called his godson Sturdy – and how the whole world may do the same.

'It is not just because of his size, though indeed all other Stanhopes are but one size above a dwarf.' The facts were emphasised by Chesterfield lifting himself to sit on the long table running down the schoolroom and swinging his legs as he talked.

'My natural son is also Philip Stanhope, and like me in all physical respects and ailments too. Philip, my godson who is only a child will have little likeness to my son, but we distinguish him further by the name, Sturdy.'

The Earl put no obligation on Mary to be a mother to Sturdy because he had no mother of his own – she had died in childbirth – and his father Arthur, a fourth cousin, would no doubt marry again. It was a family habit, he said, and as an example spoke of his younger brother William Stanhope, now in his fifties:

'He is, against my advice, looking closely to a young woman to be his third wife. This intended iteration of nuptials, as Lady Wishfort calls it in *The Way of the World,* is an unhealthy practice unless there is a weakness in the line of inheritance to be corrected. We have no such weakness in the Chesterfields. My natural son Philip will inherit and after him– or before if he succumbs as I expect him to from one of his rheumatic conditions – my godson Sturdy will carry on the title as Fifth Earl of Chesterfield. It will not be pleasant to see who shall go fastest to heaven, but I doubt that decision will lie with anyone but God.'

As a way of closing one paragraph of his conversation, The Earl asked if he might see Sturdy's room – that being next to ours and connected by a panelled doorway. The Earl expressed himself well pleased by an arrangement which was comfortable for Sturdy and gave him a sense of safety and affection close to hand while he slept.

The Earl mentioned his ambitions for Sturdy, indicating that his father Arthur Stanhope was already losing interest in, or losing the battle for Sturdy's education, and promised that he himself would keep an eye on all aspects of his godson's welfare, would visit him, write to him, and advise the excellent Dr Dodd on points that he the Earl wished to be most explicitly expanded; "suggested" – he used the word as a command – the literature Sturdy should be led to read, and the places to go and the society to mix with. Moreover, women were not to be neglected, he said, as their company was necessary for a gentleman to learn manners. The Earl made it clear that his godson was one day to be a Secretary of State at least.

By Mary's account, the Earl was the most earnest and dedicated father she had ever encountered, and yet he was but a distant uncle. Now without his own ambitions, and rarely consulted by the Prime Minister and never by the third King George, his interests were more heavily weighted towards his new gardens at Blackheath. Here his pineapples, Muscat grapes and Mesopotamian melons grew by Divine and his own attentions, 'And how I have enjoyed reading all Dr Dodd's sermons on The Vegetable Creation . . . how his wisdom reflects mine,' he said.

A portion of the Earl's time, he confirmed, was devoted to visit to Bath "for only there could one escape pills and purgatives; one had to go there to be cured of cures." But his natural son and now young Sturdy were the great passion of his declining years.

'While I live,' he told Mary, 'I shall grudge no trouble nor expense for his education.'

Chesterfield stepped out with an elegant bow with "his foot turned – just so". His eyes were full upon Mary's, she said, with an intensity of looking that told of admiration. I remarked that I understood from what she had related to me that admiration was flowing equally in both directions.

The Earl was named as "The recluse of Blackheath" by some. It can only be that the name-callers were excluded from invitations to Blackheath, or did not move in those exalted circles where he was entertained and where he would seek out knowledgeable and intelligent people for conversation. Even though Chesterfield, as the years went by, was seen more frequently with an ear trumpet in his hands, he still talked continuously with vehemence and sense – even if that were partly so that he might avoid the embarrassment of listening and begging pardon and raising his trumpet towards the mouth he perceived to be spilling words.

Over the years of my tutorship to Sturdy I did on occasion wish that the Earl was a recluse in either Pall Mall or Blackheath or Bath, for his character was to dominate. His reclusion alone, however, would have been insufficient unless he had also lost the power to write. Letters to me were frequent and direct, and bore words of instruction put into a request:

'Sturdy to be read daily from The Metamorphoses . . . his father wishes him to go to school in Paris but I have said he must get better Latin first . . .' (It is likely that the same intention was delivered to Arthur Stanhope too, because Sturdy did not go to school in Paris.) Letters to Sturdy contained praise and criticism when they were due and each bore evidence of the old man's overpowering affection. 'I am told that you are the best boy in England. This makes me love and admire you. You must not be inattentive or rude.'

Sturdy was required to write back to his godfather and, if he were able to report progress in his studies, a present came from Bath or Blackheath in the next post. With the present perhaps a promise that it would be doubled if he "got forty verses of Ovid by heart" or wrote an essay to set out "who is the worst of the two, Avarice or Profusion", or some such moral proscription.

Sturdy, having two masters, was alone likely to keep him to the grindstone. But the heap of learning upon him was greater than that provided by me and the letters from Chesterfield.

In taking the house in Pall Mall, I had promised the Earl that Sturdy would have the best teachers obtainable: M Rustan for French and history, Mr Davidson for mathematics, Signor Ghirardi for dancing and, to keep within the bounds of economy, me to teach classics and the scriptures and a little of Locke and Descartes too and all else necessary for a young man to move socially. The intention had been to have four pupils in all, and I was disappointed that these were not forthcoming.

Perhaps the hundred pounds a year was too great a sum to ask, for few men were as enlightened as Chesterfield who reckoned that rank and fortune were not necessary ingredients for happiness – "which must be internal" – but the broadest and deepest learning was. As four teachers for one pupil was in my view enough extravagance, for convenience and economy I took a smaller but more handsome house in Great Russell Street. Though my patron regretted that the frequency of his visits to the school would be curtailed now it was no longer next door to him, the house in Great Russell Street found favour in other ways because it opened "back onto Hampstead and Highgate where there was very wholesome air." The position also pleased the English uncle of a German boy whose family were at the court of Dresden.

This was Henry Ernst, a year older than Sturdy and also

fair-haired and tall and with a complexion as clear as that of a fine lady. They were joined at school by Walter Gason, a slight young man whose dark eyes were so suffused with mystery that he was always cast in the woman's part for any drama the boys produced. Henry Ernst would not be a woman because he said that he was too tall and hairy – and destined therefore to be an Esau to Sturdy's Jacob. Philip Stanhope claimed his nobility made it impossible to act in any way unsuitable for anyone who was to be a Statesman. Another reason came in letters from the Earl. He had, when he called upon Arthur Stanhope in Nottingham, been impressed by the knowledge and cleverness shown by his daughter – Sturdy's sister Margaret – despite her having none of her brother's educational advantages. Sturdy was warned in a letter that mentioned me as "the most learned clergyman in England", that if he allowed his sister to excel him, he must change clothes with her "for ignorance is only pardonable in petticoats."

Sturdy replied with a line of Hebrew, which sent his godfather into an ecstasy of praise. He wrote from Blackheath that I must reward Sturdy with a trip to Ranelagh, but set him a further task to write his next two letters one in Greek and the other in Latin. Furthermore, he was adjured to "steal more German from Henry." Henry obligingly gave Sturdy and Walter as much German as they liked, for he was of a generous disposition and asked only that his fellow pupils would be silent when he played on the harpsichord.

This instrument had however a short life in the schoolroom. On one of Lord Chesterfield's now rare interruptions at Great Russell Street, he caused it to be moved to a back room, summoning his coachman, the two maids and Hetty to aid in its transport. They were beyond earshot when the Earl addressed Sturdy while Henry hung his head and I attempted to put on three expressions at once – stern agreement with the Earl, magisterial understanding, and for Henry a comforting look of conspiratorial reassurance.

'Music is a necessary accompaniment to the dance,' the Earl looked around to see if Antonio Ghirardi was in the vicinity, 'music is a necessary accompaniment only, it gives no further benefits.'

I moved to protest on all our parts, for music for any but the stone deaf was pleasure and ornament in all circumstance, "*If music be the food of love play on*" came to my lips but died in the withering heat of Chesterfield's words:

'You promised your godfather, me your best friend, Sturdy, never to turn piper or fiddler. Nothing degrades a gentleman more than performing on any instrument whatever. The Duke of Devonshire has fallen so low . . .'

'Surely not the Duke,' said Sturdy, who had only weeks before accepted an invitation to dine at the Duke's table.

'Yes, fallen so low in taste that now he spends most of his evenings with that scum Bach and your Mr Ghirardi – the one whom occasionally even sings at The Haymarket and at other times joins with the German in dragging noises out of the guts of dead cats stretched tight over pieces of hollowed wood.'

'How then can it be that music is named one of the liberal arts?' I asked.

The Earl did not pause for an answer but concluded by saying, 'I would rather be accepted as the best barber in England than the best fiddler.'

Ernst was not seriously affected by the outburst even though by this time he understood every word spoken to him and as he got up to his uncle's carriage to be taken home before nightfall, he shrugged and said to the coachman, 'Strange are ze vays ov ze Inklishmen Lords,'

It will ever be recognised that the pupil is formed in part by the master, but less readily remarked that the master himself is changed in some degree by those youths he would teach. The master must bend to the circumstance of his charges. If they should have a thirst for geography, he will search in libraries to find and himself learn the subject; if they would be actors he will bring down dramas from the shelves and join in with them in the new worlds thus created. For my pupils there was another powerful agency impressing itself through them on me – that was the Earl of Chesterfield. He told Sturdy that I was "the pure and precise Dr Dodd and that for him the sun both rose and set in me." The repetition of such sentiments in letter or in conversation lent force to the Earl's proscriptions on us. Music was but one *bête noire* in the Earl's stock of horrid animals. Others: "Never wear over-fine clothes" and "give nobly to indigent merit and do not refuse your charity even to those whose only merit is their misery" – provided the Earl with expandable texts for his outbursts. As to the first of these, I had not sensed, so long ago it seems, that a remark about my dress – "it is a foolish thing, yet it is foolish not to be dressed" – was a criticism.

Therefore now, when about my parishes I took for the first time to wearing a flowing cloak in purple that hid my lavish waistcoats; and I put more modest buckles upon my shoes. However, my nosegay and the diamond ring and lace cambric kerchief were not left in the closet, but continued to add feeling and even passion to the movements of my hands.

With regard to instruction upon charity, my own example was, I thought, sufficient, but the young, possibly Earl-to-be, willingly took up the idea of giving. From as early an age as twelve he was to boast that he "kept a woman". She was in reality a beggar woman who lived a street away and he gave her three pence a week as a charity which he recorded in his book of receipts and disbursements. On inspecting these accounts The Earl remarked, for Sturdy to hear, that he "hoped he would never keep a woman more expensive than she."

So every aspect of Sturdy's life was reviewed by the Earl.

A present of game sent to Sturdy by his father, led to a discourse on rustic sports – in which he was never to kill or even partake – though he should eat as much game as he might please. 'The illiberal rustic sports which characterise English country gentlemen,' the Earl said, 'show those gentlemen to be the most unlicked in the world, unless sometimes licked by their hounds.' After which advice, Sturdy wrote a formal letter of thanks to his father, who would have been in actuality better pleased by a

compliment on his skill at shooting or a question about his breeding of pheasants.

The Earl returned to Blackheath or to the Pump Room in Bath after his sermons on such occasions and was well satisfied with his advice, and content to battle with his friends at Whist, or to be mildly purged by his doctors.

As advancing years took their greater toll on the Earl, he made more frequent visits to Bath. To disguise his real need for reassurances about his health he said to his acquaintances: 'One knows the company there.' But to his friends he confided, 'My wretched health is so very variable,' and he spoke with sorrow to say to them, 'death seen near to hand is a very serious consideration.'

The Earl's letters from Bath were full of admonitions to Sturdy which never failed to reflect on me too, but when those passages grew longer and the lines about his health grew shorter I was able to judge his illnesses and his convalescence accurately. If he wrote, 'I suffer now only fainting, giddiness, vapours and poisons in my stomach but have left off now dwelling on the great abstractions,' it would be certain that such cheering lines put health matters out of mind and were followed by lengthy paragraphs of advice sprinkled with hundreds of *bon mots* which were impossible for him unless he was in fairly good health.

Signor Ghirardi left in the winter 1770. His farewell to his pupil was dry-eyed. Sturdy made semblances of sorrow on the one part, and gratitude on the other, but he could not even on this last occasion bring himself to address the dancing master as Signor. Again – as always did the Earl – Sturdy used the title Mister and put a slighting tone upon it.

For although the Earl would praise the Romans of antiquity – Horace and Cicero standing most favourably in his opinion – Italian men born in his lifetime were reckoned of no account. The Earl inveighed at Signor Ghirardi and at all Italians and at Italy itself, "that sink of atheism and of the most degrading and scandalous vices . . . that seat of sodomy and bad manners, traitors and vagabonds . . . " Signor Ghirardi was too proud a man to endure these insults eternally in silence. With a bow and his feet placed so and measuring his words with similar nicety he said:

'I thank you for any compliments you have in the past bestowed upon me, who am an Italian. I am sure those compliments are worth double – given as they are now – in the face of your contempt. I will in return tell how much I admire your fierce defence of all the bad habits your godson displays: how he slouches and walks, as Mrs Dodd observes, like a Macaw, and tilts his hat upon his head like one of your English bandits; how he guzzles beer with more noise and relish than any ale-house sot; how he mimics those who would correct him – with all an actor's skill; as if the Great Garrick might have taught him as his Mr Barges taught Hamlet's players in *The Meeting of the Company.* You mark it sir? So I make my departure.'

The Earl's face showed that he recalled the lines too well. Heard at the Haymarket every night in the previous weeks, they were learned by every theatre-going gallant and recited many times nightly at their dinner tables:

"Distort yourselves – now rage, now start, now pause –

Beat breast, roll eyes, stretch nose, up brows, down joints,
Then shout, stride, start, goggle, bounce and bawl,
And when you are out of breath, pant, drag and drawl."

It is no doubt that Sturdy had delivered these lines to his godfather at Blackheath the day before, but put neither of themselves as subjects of the verse. The Earl was silent and left more quietly than was his wont. I was put down for a conspirator with Signor Ghirardi.

A few weeks following this ruffling of the even contour of our lives, the Earl's letters began to come regularly from Bath. Carried on the night coach, they were delivered early in the morning since in those days the mail from Bath was as quick as from Blackheath. He wrote:

'The course of my dreadful illness is worse. I have no relief of the rheumatism, yet however good the air when I was at Blackheath, if I had stayed there even my garden would not have dispelled the aches and dire pains of my condition, and opening wide my nostrils to sniff at my hyacinth, gillyflowers, violets, snowdrops and polyanthus would not have raised me from this morbid despair.'

The Earl's next letter from Bath spoke of a serious and sad matter and 'a foolish one at that, for your father, Sturdy, has taken a young wife – Frances Broade of Derby – a lady of no great quality but with an outstanding fair complexion. Even so early in the marriage, Cousin Arthur's fifty two years would do little to add spring to the step of his twenty seven year old bride.' He regretted that others than Arthur would be paying court to her. To soften the blow for Sturdy I assume, the Earl wrapped his letter round a packet containing two volumes of Voltaire.

Subsequent letters from Bath mentioned nothing of Arthur or his doings but bewailed the Earl's own health again and his recourse at last to other medical opinions. The first decreed a three month diet of milk with rice, sago, barley and mullet – "when it arrived fresh enough to eat." His own doctor, in whom he had "put the most outstanding confidence" was himself indisposed and another medical man summoned to the Earl insisted on a diet of mares' milk and turnips. The Earl believed that this was because it would be the best profit for the physician who knew exactly where to obtain the fresh mare's milk and a regular supply of the turnips as he owned several of the first and grew the turnips himself. Furthermore, he gave out that his diet was not to be abandoned inside six months, by which time the season for turnips likely would be over and mares in foal again. Intimations in the Earl's letters were that this second physician was only respected because he had cured the Earl's legs two summers before when these were vastly swollen and with moisture seeping out of the skin. Pickling in hot brine for three weeks as prescribed did effect an improvement as the Earl's shiny swollen weeping legs changed slowly to dry wrinkled pins slim enough to put into stockings again.

Sturdy wrote The Earl a letter of commiseration in Latin and in return received a volume of divine poems by Edmund Waller – which the Earl had had rebound – and two manuscript poems *Go Lovely Rose* and *On a Lady's Girdle* with the command to have them off by heart – which might impress the ladies if one was not too open about the poems' actual authorship.

Sturdy suggested to me that the Earl of Chesterfield's worsening health forcing his return to Bath was occasioned by the "impudence of Signor Ghirardi". Sturdy was deliberately not appraised of the more serious matter – the deteriorating health of the older Philip Stanhope, which in my view was of greater disturbance to the Earl than the insults of an Italian dancing master. In any event, Chesterfield was now a very rare visitor but an even more frequent letter writer.

The absence of a regular dancing master was a hindrance to the growth of the school, and remained so until a young clergyman up from Margate was pointed in the direction of Great Russell Street. His name, Weedon Butler, was familiar to me as a protégé of Bishop Samuel Squire. His knowledge of the classics and his fervent desire to teach Latin and Greek cheered me considerably, and I was not too disappointed about his inability to teach dancing as I was left with this lighter burden of bringing my pupils to an understanding of posture and movement and taking young Philip Stanhope into polite society and to the churches where I preached. What is more, the Reverend Weedon Butler was enthusiastic to continue his biblical studies, which in the first case had drawn him from being articled to a solicitor to enter the Church. He worked with great rapidity on my *Commentary on the Bible,* making sure that the printers received their copies well written out and in good time. I saw him as I was only a few short years before that – cheerful in rising before dawn – at a time of day unknown to Sturdy – and with a love of good conversation and fine performances at the theatre. He became my right hand, joining fully in all that was to be done and releasing me to preach more widely and more often than before.

The Magdalen grew apace. From eight young penitents at the start now over a hundred swelled the choir alone. The promised new chapel for the Magdalen opened in Goodman's Fields with acclaim in the newspapers and amongst ordinary citizens. The growing congregation seemed to represent the whole of London. Smartly dressed men and women from black families. Living often I guessed in communities around St James Square, the City and along the Hampstead Road, they were as devout and earnest as any. I knew only by sight and reputation Ignatius Sancho the kindly black grocer who corresponded with Sterne and was said to be a friend of Garrick. Perhaps a number of the worshippers were at the church to see their fellows who were black servants to high born ladies and their gentlemen.

Half the court was there and peers or their wives without number – Lord Beauchamp, Lord Huntingdon, Lady Mary Coke, Lady Carlisle and, torn between leering at them or at the penitents themselves, the Earl of Sandwich. (His appearance put Mary to flight and she never came again to the Magdalen's Chapel in case he should be there.) The choir sang in parts with such exquisiteness that the larger part of the congregation was wet-eyed well before the sermon and the collecting plates rattled generously at the end.

Court Ladies bore messages back to Queen Charlotte, and she let me know how sad she was at being unable to attend this first service at Goodman's Fields. At the same time she intimated that she would not be prevented from hearing me preach on another occasion. That I was one of the King's Chaplains and could be summoned to preach at any time in the Chapel seems to have escaped Queen Charlotte's attention at this time. Two of her Ladies-in-Waiting, however, were hardly able to speak their admiration at my sermon for the necessity to dab their eyes free of tears, and to press fingers to their lips to stop their trembling.

Such praise was enough to urge me on with a scheme longed for – My Own Chapel.

For this, with Mary's lottery money from Lady Hertford, the land was purchased and the builders engaged. Friends in the city pointed me towards a draughtsman who had drawn up buildings for them – a Masonic connection which might prove helpful – and ensured a simple but regular design that fitted well into the area hard up against the King's new palace. Several large old plane trees were left standing at the West End of this my Charlotte's Chapel– a reminder for me of the churchyard at West Ham, and a fitting place for horses to be tied and their carriages and grooms to wait. I remembered – but only to myself aloud – how much I missed the quiet, honest and careful life of West Ham.

In my Chapel four boxes at the front were saved for the Queen and her Household. Rising, not too powerfully, in front of them was a carved oak pulpit – lit for evening services by glass candelabra, and for sermon notes was a brass lectern holding a crimson pillow with golden bells hanging by tassels from it, and to the side an hour glass.

The Ladies-in-Waiting had more than fulfilled their promises. On the day the Charlotte Chapel opened, I preached in the morning before the King and Queen and the Dukes of Cumberland and Gloucester at the Chapel Royal, St James's Palace.

At two o'clock I preached at the opening service at my own chapel. And in the evening a farewell sermon at St Olave's.

I could no longer preach with any regularity at smaller churches, and reluctantly gave up my lectureships there. It is true the very poorest members of this church felt I had deserted them but my attendance was necessary at the Charlotte Chapel. Pews were regularly taken by Lords Athole and Kingston, Earls of Marchmount, Aylesbury and Romney as well as the regular merchants and shop keepers and their wives, and the Royal Box pews also were seldom empty.

The Queen had not seen it politic perhaps to join the crowds gaping at the penitents at Goodman's Fields, but here at the chapel I named for her, her presence was frequent and her attention earnest. I used no difficult language for her nor did I, however, tread softly on her conscience.

Sturdy marked these services more than those in other places. That was, I fear, because I had made him a Warden at the Magdalen Chapel – and his processing there with other dignitaries with their ornate wands of office – black and silver entwined – took his mind entirely from the sermon to rest on his own importance. He picked out a penitent in the choir perhaps to build an imagination onto her, and fixing his eyes on her lips, neither saw nor heard from mine.

Ever mindful of education in the broadest sense for all my pupils, I brought Sturdy, Ernst and Gason to Pimlico with great regularity.

THE HANGING OF WILLIAM DODD

Before them and before Queen Charlotte I preached on texts that spoke to the heart of Christianity and to the hearts and minds of my congregation. Critics were ever in the press – although they only rarely stepped into the chapel itself – yet they made much of my pulpit manner, my nosegay and my diamond ring that drew all eyes as my hand came to my mouth and followed my words as I gestured towards everyone even in the furthest recesses of the chapel.

Once on a winter's afternoon when the whole of London was enclosed in deep lead grey clouds enveloping sky and earth, I preached to the text *Thou shall not kill.* In the box pew two rows back, Sturdy's eyes opened widely: The Queen nestled in her furs and opened her eyes more widely still.

Thou shall not kill. This, the sixth and the shortest of the commandments, steps into and out of the catechism with barely an eyebrow raised. I warrant that in any congregation if there were to be debated all Ten Commandments, the least time would be spent on this, for each person would say, "I have not killed nor would I – therefore it is not necessary to warn me against following a path I would not tread."

> By rational argument I attempted to lead their thinking in other ways.

I asked had they thought, had they given thought to the duellist for example – an unfortunate murderer perhaps but with his hand stained with the blood of his dearest friend, and destroyed by precipitous wrath.

> Had they thought, had they given thought to the crime of suicide?

Pride and resentment commonly giving way to the desperate resolution of the gloomy suicide who, too haughty to support injuries, too resentful to forgive or to implore forgiveness, flies into a horrible future to end that life which God had been pleased to give.

'For man,' I said, 'is made in the image of God and life is to be held and treated as sacred. The voluntary destruction of life should admit no pardon:

'The purification and rectitude of our intentions is the only sure and substantial basis of virtue.

'Correction and example are the only proper objects of punishment and these cannot be obtained by the death of the sufferer . . .

'Guard with the strictest caution against trivial crimes – hundreds of those on the statute books that carry the most severe penalty – of death, those crimes which we may consider the least, but the consequences of which are truly formidable – death.

'Thou shall not kill . . .

'There are small crimes that do no injury to society. They do not require to be capitally punished. How many people are in this way hurried into eternity in the very bloom and flower of life? The ends of government might be better answered by saving them – for every method to promote and increase the population must be desirable – saving their lives that they may be rendered useful to the community.

'Public executions are not of the least avail – common people flock to them as a spectacle but while they are there crimes are committed against them that are more serious than the crime being punished on the scaffold – pick-pocketing is but one example and that in itself leading to death. 'The good ends of punishment were better attained by perpetual servitude and labour. For it is not the intensity of pain which has the greatest effect on the mind, it is the continuance of it.

'This is the voice of humanity, and Christian charity and benevolence. . . *Thou shall not kill.*'

I paused for a long time. The congregation was still and silent. Seeing the Queen as rapt as all others, I let my eyes fall on her direct and I praised the King: how much glory he had and how much even more would come upon him by serving Justice – which cannot fail to secure universal affection.

This sermon on the text *Thou shall not kill* became known as "The Hanging Sermon" and had great popularity, particularly when preached amongst the less fortunate and common people of London. I had no great ambitions for it as an instrument of change because the lawmakers and the senior divines of the church saw little beyond their blinkers. But I hoped that the Queen might persuade the King to an even deeper liberality of mind with regard to executions.

Beyond this Hanging Sermon but still of suicide: I wonder now how many times instead of blaming the victim of the crime we might have more care to understand; for the mind's working is still a mystery.

And death by warfare? Are we impudent to suppose that God is on both sides? Or neither? And will we find alternatives to war?

While I preached, Lady Hertford – boxed with Sturdy, Henry Ernst and Walter Gason – held her eyes upon me wherever I looked. She transmitted through that look eternities of meaning, as if the lines of her vision would bridge the gap between us. She not far short of royal, only a notch below the Queen, and I the servant of all the common crowd – a mere voice for popular opinion. But she could – would she – carry my voice to places I could not go? It was sometimes said that this sermon was the bitter focus of my life: the sermon to spare me from any penalty that I might in future deserve or not deserve; but I did not understand such and spoke only ever from the heart and mind, for my preaching was never about me but about the hope of this world being a better and more godly place.

There was on that day and many other days another pair of eyes in the chapel, as though watching me from beneath her bonnet. I had seen those eyes before but could not put a time, a place, an event or anything to remind me of their history. Had their owner passed through the Magdalen? It were useless to ask the name, for a new name was given to each penitent as she entered that place and, like as not, a different name again when she left. Now I had not seen those eyes at Goodman's Fields in recent times, but only at The Charlotte Chapel, and there many times; and every time as I would approach to speak to her as she mingled with the leaving congregation, her eyes and she would disappear like honey melting in warm mead – gone but leaving sweetness in her wake. Small reminiscences from my youth could not combine a picture full enough to tell a story.

Mary had taken – as a habit – to attending another church , usually St George's, Hanover Square. Here she would not come face to face with the Earl of Sandwich who affected to prefer the choir of Magdalen's – or Lady Hertford to whom she knew she felt obligation, but did not wish to be forever thanking her for it. At the same time, Mary said that her husband "appeared to preach for Lady Hertford and had more time for her than for me." Ah! the jealousy of the fair sex, how little I deserve their undivided attentions!

I confess that apart from my natural inclination to be drawn towards the fair sex, there was a more serious purpose in cultivating particularly the company of the Ladies-in-Waiting and other women with influence upon the Queen. My intention, or at least my hope, was that the Queen might be borne upon to trust me as tutor to Prince William. It was not at first apparent to me, however, that several of the Ladies in question had their own desires. "Desires" is not too strong a word. Lady Dorothea Tucker and Lady Sophia Doyle were two most splendidly amorous women and their voluptuousness was matched by their daring. Whereas the other ladies who gathered with us in my rooms at St James' Palace indulged fully in the "bible-talk" as we called our conversation, and then left – Lady

Tucker and Lady Doyle stayed until twilight. They would not allow the one to leave without the other as if they were sworn friends not to be parted. Intimacies began on their parts with such small gestures as a pat upon my hand and a rebuke as if to a naughty schoolboy at some pleasantry I had made. As they sat they would laugh uproariously at the slightest witticism, closing their eyes and throwing their heads back – the better to show their shapely necks, milk white breasts or slyly to reveal a knee and thigh beyond it.

I would not before imagine how bold they might be, but was wrong to assume that the female of the species is never a stranger to lust. Nor how determined to satisfy that craving. Within a little time both Dorothea and Sophia, as they insisted they should be called – realised that neither one could have me to herself and therefore they had better act as friends together however hard the pretence. Since there is greater pleasure and safety in numbers, I was as obliging as I could be to the whims of both. Polite kisses led to more sincere contacts of our lips and that to their caresses as soft as the hands of a child. One could no more easily arrest a waterfall than stop our passions growing. And it was no more than a gentleman could do but help to satisfy and so cool those ardent ladies' embraces. Never did one of them hit upon a delightful sensation than the other strove to better it, and it were ungallant of me not to thank them bodily in the manner they most sought – remembering that they brought news of how they had "spoken to Her Majesty about the Prince's education, and how Dr Dodd was upon this earth for very little other purpose than to teach." And I thought to give satisfaction to these handsome women. Their appreciation and their purposes at the end of our bible-talk were clearly indicated.

From acting absent-mindedly and having forgot what they did the week before, Dorothea and Sophia each time brought in from the chapel another two pairs of kneeling cushions 'for our comfort'. When we three were alone and charged up to a fervour that was not entirely religious, then

the plentiful supply of royal hassocks beneath us gave a
comfortable descent into lasciviousness as the sun set over
St James'.

CHAPTER 25

AT LE CHATEAU DE VOIRONS

Letters and life and food

January 2nd 1783

My Dearest Wife,
I will write to you while you have gone for an airing in the garden.

Mary it is very strange to declare anything in a letter to the person I see all day and to put what would be a jumble of unconnected conversation into writing, and to answer your questions and enter into arguments. I have not yet become accustomed to my loss of speech; to be unable to reply quickly to your concerns – or tell of mine – are the hardest things to bear in my involuntary silence. I would rather be deaf as well as dumb than hear other voices and not be able to make response with mine.

You have said many times and now again this morning how it is as awkward and distressing for you as me that I am speechless. I believe that to be so, but I cannot feel it as closely as I do my own misfortune.

Words on paper lack much force. My strength with words has been when they are spoken – when my tongue has been a ready servant. The finest sermons – judging by other's opinions to be the finest – rendered on paper are emptied of half their meaning. Only the greatest poet can with his ink alone make you a listener, make you hear the sounds of his poetry. And I judge that the cleverest poets do themselves injustice by reading their verses aloud. All their art must be in giving shape and volume and colour through the written word. It is why I freely admit that the poems I once composed and you criticised, were bad in essence and

349

example, and not worthy of the purposes I had in writing them:

"He saw me toiling for the scanty mead
Of hireling parson, humble and unknown –"

Do you remember that – addressed to the Lord Chancellor in gratitude for a gift of money? I burn with shame at these and later lines which meant to tell how thankful were my young pupils for his largesse:

"Full hard beset the little race to feed,
Who waited for their bread from me alone
He saw; he pitied! Pitied and relieved!
Lisp, lisp, my little ones, his name how lives
To glad the wretched with his golden rays."

There is no real poetry in that, and now I join with those who mocked my feeble verses. Have I atoned for that? I think, I hope I have by putting Shakespear into a small volume wherein even the idle reader may find gems for his consideration. I make no apology for agreeing with those who say it is essential to have Shakespear in the pocket at all times. It is my ready source to call up Shakespear to do my thinking or my writing when I cannot do so for myself, or if I make poor use of language.

I do wander a little from the path: you will forgive me for that when I do so to lead into remarks on your "speech" this morning. You were not angry at first when you brought a cassock mocked up from old riding cloak of M le Blanc and put that on my shoulders and also the Geneva tabs – made from my own writing paper – and hung them about my neck:

'There,' you said, 'now you are my boy, my parson. That is how I like you.'

It was no wonder that I looked at you quizzically and tried to indicate by mime what character you should wish me to be in; and you let me know with a full voice – which might have brought Durham miners out of their burrows – that you did not approve of my behaving like a lecherous buck at Court. That action with the Ladies-in-Waiting at St James' was indeed inexcusable. You gave it away then that you had been reading all the casket papers you were earlier banned from, but said you did not steal the key, but read over my shoulder when I nodded to sleep.

I will explain the business in my rooms at court. I cannot forgive my bad behaviour any better than I can forgive my bad poetry. Both are condemned by my quill – would it be I could condemn them out of my own mouth! I offer as explanation, which is an apology but not excuse; it has ever been my practice to reward a slight exercise of virtue on my part with a large portion of pleasure. Thus if I had worked to relieve penury or suffering in the parishes, or offered a good sermon and necessary devotions, I thought myself entitled to a temporary and slight relaxation of the strict morality that bound the rest of my life; nothing vicious you understand and not breaking up the whole ten of Moses' tablets – but only an easing of the tight bonds of a clerical life.

Your anger at me then was justified, but it is not now. You must not denounce me for telling my history. It is what I have to do. There is no hope for me otherwise. Nothing else can loose my tongue. Accept me as I am – for it is all that I am. I could not now, nor could ever be a Reverend John Wesley, whom you admire so much. Even though I can sit a horse comfortably and ride enough to meet daily needs, I would not have the seat to ride as Mr Wesley four and a half thousand miles a year! Perhaps he endured it as an irritant – to counter the soreness of his throat after a tenth of that number of sermons delivered in each twelve months!

You were in a fine temper this morning my dear wife. When you came back from a visit to the kitchens you discovered me on my feet waving my left hand and arm in the manner of a miming actor but whereas his lips are motionless, mine, you say, were silent but mouthing words or kisses or the shapes of laughter while slobber gathered on my chin as will the mouth of a slavering hound held back from food – your description, not mine. I thought it unnecessarily unkind. You know how my disability itself distresses me and how when after long hours at my desk my neck hurts worse than being set on fire and under the rack and all at once, I gain some relief by being the actor not the author. Limited as I am to my one arm and with my lips not entirely obedient to my command, I do no doubt make a poor show as an actor, but the great Garrick could do no better in such circumstances as mine.

You laughed and said that were I in this manner re-enacting here a scene but lately written – with the Ladies-in-Waiting – you had nothing to fear. My reputation as a Lothario would not be raised by such performances. You declared emphatically that you would rather be courted by the hound itself than by my imitation of it.

Your knowledge shows that you have read "over my shoulder" as you say for a long while. I did not know I slumbered so and yet still held a pen in my hand and wrote a fair script while the snores drowned the scratching of the quill. 'B-----!' I say to you or another rough Northumbrian expletive, the use of which doubles your vocabulary of rude words.

Let us not quarrel further. Would you be kind enough to return to the kitchens and there take command of M le Blanc's cook who is much in need of advice.

This from Your Husband, who Eschews Humility, Avoids Obedience and Yet Surrenders His Heart Utterly to You.
Your sometimes faithful,
Wm Farrier

There were further responses from Mrs Mary Farrier which I have no duty to record. It is with the greatest sadness – above all the others that I have lamented – that on this and all occasions since my affliction, she has had the last word.

I have said that Cook is in need of advice. It is harsh of me, for left on her own choice in the kitchen she boils a ham and bastes a mutton joint with the best cooks in France. And it is through the overwhelming kindness of her heart that on learning of our disappointment that Sir Philip and Lady Ann Thicknesse were not to enliven our company at Christmas, the good Cook said she would prepare an English dinner for us. She knew, she said, exactly the food we English eat – had not Sir Thicknesse himself told her when he chastised her about the copper cooking pots?

Therefore, on Christmas Eve, Cook ushered Mary out of the kitchen and with a wink and a nod made her understand that all was to be left in her artful hands. Alas, Mary did not recollect the word for turkey until she had passed some way from the kitchens to the hall. Then remembering at last, she called out "*Dindon*" but Cook thought it was the clock that struck and carried on hauling up a calf's head from the salt-bin to form the centre piece of her meal. We do not know from where the idea came to Cook that a calf's head would do as Mock Turtle – but it was perhaps after all the least obnoxious of the dishes she presented.

No other Christmas dinner – as I remember – by its foulness so depressed all jollity until the New Year, as this one did. It started well enough if you were so minded to take potage first. M le Blanc did and we followed suit – Mary covertly but needlessly tucking a napkin into my already coloured and well-nourished shirt. Cook stood in the doorway clapping her hands silently in delight as we passed the steaming hot soup into our bowls, and she gave an unseen but approving smile as M le Blanc helped us and made particularly certain that we had each the eye of a sheep to bob about amongst lumps of turnip, carrot, boiled potato and sprigs of parsley. Each of the three of us stranded the sheep's eye on the edge of our plate to leer at the flotsam remaining, but that was after Cook had gone to fetch another dish.

A large pike was next. This was never a fish which even

its brother fish would describe as tasty – and its foul breath was only partly distracted from us by a green apple stuck between its jaws. A rank and steamy odour rose from its grey flesh and it was with obvious relief that M le Blanc passed it across to Mary who just as quickly passed it to me. I was rescued by M le Blanc again who said "*un peu plus tard*" and put the pike behind the Mock Turtle for companionship.

Sheer hunger made me eat – for the repast advertised for five o'clock was not finally assembled till nearer eight – and I shall never complain about the quantity of food, nor its variety, nor its very Englishness. The table, as one says, was groaning with the weight put upon it. And other groans filled the room – not appearing to come from any one of us – but from our neighbour next – as if we were all gastriloquists.

Transmogrified Pigeon in Pastry served – if you wished it with bottled peas – was accompanied on nearby servers by an assortment of pig's trotters and piglet's ears in Rhenish wine heated in the jelly. Our exclamations of delight were for the Cook's benefit and hoped to indicate at once, before any other dishes appeared upon the table, that we were now sated. An understandable but unfortunate lapse in judgement so to encourage Cook. With a smile of beatific proportion she stepped back to the kitchens and sending her son and husband before her with more candles, set upon the table where the calf's head and pike had been, a sugary concoction that rose almost to the level of our mouths. On the walls of this edifice – which bore a passing resemblance to The Chateau de Voirons itself but partly ruined – frosted purple plums glistened as though to defy us to resist the tasting.

By this time M le Blanc's smile was so fixed that no further food could pass between his lips, and Mary made a fuss as if I was about to have one of my "turns" and so brought about our salvation – I acting the invalid – Mary my nurse, and M le Blanc as ever the quiet and courteous host who led us like lambs away from the slaughter.

New Years Day.
I was at a loss to know why M le Blanc should allow such liberties to his cook, and not to chastise her for this "Christmas dinner" which proved all but fatal to us, and from which we are still suffering now. Was
M le Blanc so in the thrall of his cook that she might escape with her impudence? I asked Mary: was his philosophy entirely liberal – to the point of *laissez faire* – since I supposed her to have a closer knowledge of our host following her journey in his company to the milliners. I scribbled the thought about M le Blanc's philosophy on the back of a morning note of hers which asked on the other side, 'will you not be quite content with "plain" mutton or ham as the only offerings from the kitchen now?' Mary sat beside me at my desk and replied:

'We women – we of the fair sex as you will style us – do not extend our thoughts into deep philosophy; that is a thing for men. We engage ourselves in more practical matters. I do not know what doctrines guide M le Blanc. He is a very good man, but he will not jump to a decision. He is slow. He is a hound who lags behind. He allows events to occur and other people to move and he takes whichever directions they wish. I wish it were not so. He has never made an unwanted gesture towards me even if I have with slight sauciness provoked him. Our recent trip to the milliner was at my suggestion. M le Blanc fell in with it because he is a very kind man, and that's the long and the short of it and there is no philosophy at all.' She put my useless hand up to my eyes:

'Look,' she said and then raising it to my forehead, 'think less, in case you should wear out your great brain.'

'What of Sir Philip Thicknesse?' I scribbled.

'A very different man – and you should know him well. See the letter from Lady Ann that I spoke about before.'

I put my good hand to Mary's eyes and pointed to the

letter and then to her lips. She smiled in the way that had won me outside the theatre so many years ago.

'Yes, I will read it to you. But I cannot speak with the voice of Lady Ann nor shall I mime it – though you seem to be at present much taken with that art.'

Bath
November 11th 1783

To My Dear Mary,
Sir Philip has said we may not come to you at Voirons as intended this year at Christmas. I am very put out about this. It is not mine nor any concern of his about us braving the sea crossing – I am quite recovered from that and it is almost forgot. Being held up in Bath is entirely due to the business Sir Philip says he has to conduct here. I shall give you some taste of it so that you shall know how glad I would be to be away from here however high the seas between us. Furthermore, it may entertain you to hear a little of my exasperating husband. You may think at the end of the account that your more sedate life with William – with all his dreadful suffering – is to be preferred to mine with my mad-cap squire.
For he will not settle down to a single thing for a moment, but jumps up without warning and is gone from one venture to another in a flash.

I imagined this year that his preoccupation with garden matters would entertain him for two or three months at least. He has dashed off an article "*Trees and Shrubs which thrive near the Sea*" and I believe bullied the Magazine *Rusticus* into publishing it. In his mind – and indeed truly I do not believe that journal lost all its subscribers because of it – Sir Philip (he does prefer me to title him thus even in the marital chamber) on the strength of that one article persuaded himself and then the editor of the *St James' Chronicle* that he should write his own gossip page above the name "A Wanderer".

There is no doubt that here in Bath – or wherever he goes – that he has the ear for idle chat and scandal. To my shame he may be seen in the Promenade and Pump Room, the Coffee Houses and circulating Libraries and the theatre with notebook in his hand jotting down tit-bits to dress up for the public to read in *The Chronicle*.

Do not think he is not a serious man. In April *A Treatise on the Art of Deciphering and of Writing in Cypher with an Harmonic Alphabet* came off the press – at his own expense. No harm in that of course, although it was incomprehensible to those few who attempted to read it. The harm did not come from the dedication either – for it was to The Right Honourable Lord Viscount Bateman – who is one of the few men who do not deny publicly that Sir Philip is a friend. The harm came when Lord Bateman, flattered more than his dim wits could express, said of the book, "Some parts seem not clear to me". That might not have been the trigger that caused the explosion inside my dear, dear husband's head. He had driven over to stay the night at his friend's house. At dinner, Lord Bateman gave out no praise to Sir Philip and very little thanks, offered no champagne and brought the worst port to the table. Sir Philip rose angrily from the table, left early in the morning before breakfast and wrote a letter of complaint to his friend almost as long as the book which sparked the quarrel. Even though the Viscount does not read a great deal and therefore may not have done much more than open the seal of the letter to him, I fear that it will be some time before the embers of the quarrel have cooled sufficient to allow continuance of the friendship.

Lord Bateman is a peaceful man, even placid, and although – Lord knows how – a member of the Privy Council, he is most happy in his capacity as Master of the Buck Hounds and conversing with his four footed friends rather than the two.

My dear, dear husband does need friends but it seems

hardly possible he will gain many to keep. He took up in June with the Reverend Henry Bate, Editor of *The Morning Herald* and fell out with him almost at once. The matter was not about anything I can remember but it was not wise of Sir Philip to cross him as he can put about very strong opinions in *The Herald*. These are enough to ruin anyone in Society. Sir Philip says now that he "abhors all other News Paper writers," and says how exceedingly ill he took Bates' behaviour, and his language and his description of Sir Philip as "an hoary offender" and "a blackmailer who buys letters and sells them back to the writers". I have urged him not to go to the courts with this libellous charge but to lie down under it this once for the sake of economy and peace of mind.

Sir Philip has this very day embarked upon a scheme to aid all sufferers of gallstones, and is assembling them at the Assembly Rooms to give advice as to treatment and prevention. I am certain he will raise a few quarrels with the medical men in Bath, but there is nothing I can do, alas.

All this turmoil is interspersed with endless gossip in Bath. Rauzzini, the castrated singer, has we understand been paid ten thousand pounds by a young married Lady – not of age and with two children – to go off with her.

So you see dear Mary, Bath is a miniature of the world at large. But you knew all this before. As for me, I am performing some concerts here and preparing for a Paris Season next year – I hope.

Give my most affectionate regards to yourself and to your dear husband.

Ann Thicknesse

P.S. Sir Philip says to "command your husband to apply himself diligently" to his history or he will not be released from his trouble. He expects to know the result of William's endeavours with the pen "before the year is out". A.T.

Mary's reading of her friend's letter contained some mime in the accompaniment and a little gentle imitation of Lady Ann's movements of her hands and eyes.

I do not feel cheered by Lady Ann's catalogue of Sir Philip's enthusiasms – nor do I think that her lot with him as bad as Mary's lot with me. The reason is plain to see in my undergarments. My departure from the Christmas dinner table was not only a drama rigged to get us away from Cook's murderous fare, the call for me to make stool was imperious and urgent. Worse, what followed was a reminder of the grievous disorder which I thought had gone from me at last. It was not. Finally, unrelenting passage of a watery squirt brought with it my parts down into my garments. Mary who became a saint at such times cared for me and my clothing with a resignation which did nothing to lessen my shame. In short, I and Mary were of the opinion that our case was worse than that which Lady Ann and Sir Philip could imagine, and we were not consoled.

Since this misery is upon me – though lessening by the day – I look with pleasure into my history's progression. There are some bright threads to entertain and distract me from present unhappiness and I will hope eventually to extend the weave of the coloured tapestry of my life and so to recreate myself.

CHAPTER 26
PLEAS FOR PATRONAGE

Sturdy grows; Lady Hertford; House at Ealing;
Gascoigne;
The Free Masons; Bulkley and the Theatre; Chaplaincy;
Pleasure Gardens; The Bon Ton & Others

In 1769 or 1770 or thereabouts I found a tattered copy of
A Free Inquiry into the Nature and Origin of Evil. It had
created great excitement when it was first published in
1757, Dr Johnson and others contributing lacerating and
witty criticisms proportionate to their own passion and
intelligence. I was less critical then than now, and
cherished the sincerity and honest thinking of Soames
Jenkyn, the author. I had this small volume bound in
vellum together with some of his poems which were
without covers but less handled and abused – and marked
mostly by thoughtful coffee stains proving previous
ownership.

A few lines from *The Free Inquiry* have stuck
comfortably and memorably like a litany in my mind:
"Happiness is the only real thing of value in existence.
Neither riches, nor power, nor wisdom, nor learning, nor
strength, nor beauty, nor virtue, nor religion, nor even life
itself are of any importance but as they contribute to the
production of happiness." This was not a philosophy to be
hawked around freely amongst the clergy, and particularly
not to be offered to patrons of fat livings. Most of these had
not read Aristotle and Plato let alone Berkeley or Locke,
and would not be tolerant towards a far lesser philosopher.
For me religion – or at least Christianity – was not a
miserable thing – an excuse to wear a sober exterior and to
frown upon jollity. Although it would be ill advised to take

Jenkyn's lines as a text for a sermon, otherwise they contained thoughts which warmed my nightly prayers in that cold and solitary time when I considered whatever mountain of pleasure had been ascended during the day, and where there was at the summit of each an ice-capped peak of anxiety for the future – the desire, indeed the desperate stark necessity, for preferment. I prayed for that.

West Ham had provided a barely satisfactory living, but all retreat there was cut off from me. There were to be no more gentle days in that pleasant place where all was familiar, all was constant, and in which my Mary changed as little as the elm trees standing sentinel in the green parklands, giving shade and shelter throughout the seasons, and where my homecoming was ever as glad as that of some young Adam returning to his Garden of Eden. If there were to be any fateful days darkening my life I thought the seeds of them cannot have been grown there, for if the world made me wretched – *si miserum fortuna simonem* – as the poet says, West Ham provided healing without cost, a balm beyond price.

To The Archbishop of Canterbury, The Duke of Newcastle and The Earl of Northington my letters of appeal asking for the favour of their patronage had been sent at the earliest opportunities, often with verses of praise for their virtues. I wanted to become a Bishop and to have the power of conferring a place instead of going about begging one. The salt of bitter failure had been rubbed in with the denials coming from those patrons. Enough to say that:

"I regret there is no living, and no Bishop's See that I may grant to you yet." Too often to that would be added with some sharp point of criticism such as, "I am uncertain as to your position with regard to Methodism," or "We are told that your vanity of dress exceeds in luxuriance the clothing of an Eastern prince," or "It has been said that although you are awash with sympathy particularly for women of the lesser classes, you have little concern for the nobility and the ranks of high society."

I replied to these rebuffs in letters of modest and humble expression to turn away anger or disdain and to leave open a door for future application. Ink so spent, like mud from a beaten cur's tail dragging its stain across the floorboards, was distasteful to me – but I could not allow my name to be ignored and lost amongst the legions of downtrodden clergy who prayed as much or more for their own advancement as for the souls of their congregations.

I therefore became a supplicant again to The Earl of Chesterfield that he might have a word in The King's ear to seek an advantage for me. The Earl certainly already knew and I think admired me, but even so my letter to him spent more words extolling his morality and wisdom than in reminding him of my qualifications and worth and justification to wear the lawn sleeves of a bishop about my wrists.

He replied quickly and shortly from Bath saying that he would do what he could whenever it might be possible.

It remained for me to establish myself firmly – to be as *solide* as The Earl presented me to be; to look in the eyes of the world that it would be no great transition from reputable and successful preacher, Royal Chaplain, clerical instrument in the foundation and financing of various Christian charities, writer, teacher, and capable associate of men of influence – to a See in our great Church of England.

Walter Gason and Henry Ernst were shortly to leave on their Grand Tours for a final polish to their education. Weedon Butler tended to their scholarly needs and they in turn helped to teach a few smaller boys who came to my small school. Philip Stanhope, my good pupil Sturdy, remained almost as a companion to me. His godfather wished me to take him into all the pleasure and gaiety that London society could supply. 'Round off his education,' he said. 'No corner should be left unrubbed.'

Furthermore, he expounded that this was the final purpose of a private education – another boon for those whose fathers did not bundle them off to public schools when they were barely seven or eight to be out of sight and not seen for more than a day or two from one year end to the next. At Winchester, Eton, Harrow and St Pauls, he said, the sons of the rich became too easily ruffians and blackguards, learning arrogance in their independence and fierceness from the habits of defending themselves from older bullies. Then they became the bullies. The Earl insisted that Sturdy would learn much by the private education that I provided in the schoolroom and in society at large. For every £20 of classics he had from me he would have now £20 of experience. This would equip him for his Grand Tour – likely to be only a short while ahead.

Before this, Sturdy learned a little of life by being present at his godfather's mansion when the Earl was absented for a few hours and the young man alone. By his story – utterly believable since he was timid and ignorant in amatory matters – he was pursued by a serving maid who took some liberties with him that he said later he ill understood yet stirred him somewhat. None of this would have been of consequence for in many rich households the circumstances described above are exactly the way the "young master" is brought out of innocence and the girl in the case dismissed as a liar or a whore or both. Sturdy, either out of ignorance or in an attempt to follow his godfather's precepts of kindness to serving classes, said nothing about this matter at the time.

Two months later, however, there was unfortunately another meeting at Chesterfield's house with the same person approaching Sturdy again, but on this occasion – by indications even Sturdy understood – that he could take the fullest advantage of her now since she already carried his child and the Earl would bring his wrath to bear on Sturdy if he was made acquainted with the matter.

Sturdy confided in me asking that since he had spent no

money on gambling the £500 lodged with me and approved by his godfather for that purpose might be used to buy the young woman off. Sturdy said that he could not prove he was not responsible, there was an infant to be considered and the Earl will take it ill if he heard that he had descended to a vulgarity with a servant in his house. Despite I made it clear to Sturdy that there were always those who sought to make the rich and innocent pay for their own indiscretions, he wished the whole business hushed up whatever the cost. He gave the £500 to me and I carried out his wishes except to give only £100 to the wench and her fellow servant to go back to their own Kent village, and put the rest into the Magdalen.

I still had a little of Mary's lottery money and augmented that and subsequently replaced the expensive life it supported by taking out annuities – a thousand pounds here, two thousand there – which were not too burdensome to repay over a long term. These gave me a freedom not given even by the relatively handsome returns I expected annually from my own Charlotte Chapel and sermons, school mastering, writing, the Royal Chaplaincy and occasional gifts. And too, my adored Lady Hertford would never see me lost for – what she assured me – were "quite trifling sums", which increased as her health declined. For by the month and then by the week more pink roses flourished on her pallid, pock marked cheeks; her eyes grew brighter and softer in their response while a dry cough took words from her mouth and left more speech to the expressions of her giving hands.

How fortunate I was in her friendship.

I was then sufficiently breeched to enter with Sturdy into the froth of high society, always dressed freshly and in the best fashion and I better dressed than he. I instructed a Mr Twist of Bishopsgate to build me a splendid carriage and to find for me some handsome horses, and a coachman to keep them all well ordered. The Earl, I knew, would be impressed by these accoutrements as evidence of my devotion to his godson, and reassured that we would be entering at the front doors of the best houses, not scrambling in at the back as though I had aspirations but no entitlement.

My town house in Great Russell Street was convenient to my charitable morning work in the city and not too far distant from the stately houses further west where *the ton* lived and took their entertainment. The Great Russell Street house, however, was too small for me to entertain. A company of up to ten persons would be comfortable there, but should I wish to make a dozen, Mary and I had to be pressed into our seats at either end with no room for the hired footmen to pass behind, and Sturdy had to be sent off to the Theatre without making up the baker's dozen.

The answer was to take a house at Ealing. It had to be large enough to be styled a mansion but not lost in so many extended acres that its dimensions could not be appreciated by passing carriages. It was also nearby to the quality, who also had houses there. Spanish chestnut trees bordered the turnpike up from London and lent an air of dignity to the area. Hospitality was possible on a grand scale and the kitchens adequate. Whether keen for company and gustatory delights, or to retreat from importunate callers at Great Russell Street, "Jubilate", as I called the mansion at Ealing, was a solace and a credit to me.

Mary sought the help – and advice and generosity of Porter – to choose from his stock striking pieces of furniture. These were placed artfully to their best advantage. He threw in a pair of good blue turkey carpets and for the hallway several large paintings – the canvasses of which had suffered as much as the torn sails of the men-of-war in the battles depicted. Porter spat on his hands a great deal as he described how he had made repairs and cunningly restored paint where it was wanted. Mary was not above giving flattery when she felt that encouragement was needed, and Porter was so pleased by her gratitude he came back twice – all the way up from Frith Street – with religious paintings for the dining-room. With the candles judiciously disposed, these too were most acceptable.

Mary was all excitement again and put into deep thought about the curtains. After much knitting of her brows, which my kissing could not undo, and consulting me as to expense – knowing that I would be easy about that – she settled with my advice for silk damask in crimson, blue and green with a gilt border. The investment was worthwhile the mercer assured her because the curtains would wear as well as the longest of any of Dr Dodd's sermons – which impudence caused much merriment and threw us all, Porter as well, into gales of laughter which eased the pain of my parting with twenty pounds outright.

Hetty was brought up from town to gaze at all the splendours but begged to be allowed to continue at Great Russell Street even if there were creditors banging on the door.

Hetty's good sense pleased me, for Mary could not be in two places at once – the ordering of domestic affairs in town required regular attention. Here the young men's education was paramount. The labours of Weedon Butler – the best amanuensis a cleric writer ever had – asked for nothing else but the support of my library and my guidance. Therefore his necessity and my pleasure encouraged the expansion of my city of books.

I did always intend my small extravagances to be small indeed and was surprised in the buying of books how the costs of education can penalise the man of learning. To provide my pupils with every branch of knowledge, I purchased generally the needed books in the most modest bindings. If it were possible I held up buying a book until it had done the rounds of a lending circle and then I had it rebound – only if necessary – in ordinary calf. Sometimes Mary received at the door offerings from a pinched bookseller called Priest with dropsy and no tails to his coat who knocked timidly on the first occasion and with increasing bravery thereafter. He brought – at very reasonable price, at the most 3/- – books such as Potter's *Antiquities* in two volumes and *Holmes on the English Constitution*. These were never planned additions to the library and cost more in rebinding than their original worth. Additionally, and a point for conversation at dinner, Mary never failed to give Mr Priest a cup of tea and a plate of beef by the kitchen fire. The sadness of the indigent always affected her more than the sorrows of the rich.

There were, of course, circumstances when I must have the most up- to-date and perfect references – especially for a sermon. When I looked at the bookseller's tally for me I reminded myself for the hundredth time that my income came from preaching and writing – the only talents I possess, and niggardly printers scored against me twice in the cost of books bought to read and the costs of printing my own books and sermons. The largeness of my extravagance is echoed in Sam Johnson's observation that "a man will turn over half a library to make one book." However, one economy I had made was in the appointment of the excellent Reverend Mr Weedon Butler. He came to me with the very best references and at the very lowest cost – nothing – apart from small presents and tickets for the theatre as often as he wished. In his quiet and gentlemanly way he made me understand that he was entirely privileged to work on *The Commen*tary and to teach my pupils; and by his manner indicated that I need not enquire as to his financial circumstances and that his ultimate happiness was to be surrounded by a fine library – the city of books growing daily around him.

Gascoigne wrote me an affecting letter at this time. It was supposedly an apology – or explanation – for not informing me of his wedding:

'You might be startled,' he wrote, 'not that I was so tardy

in my informing you, but in the fact of my being married at all, since a wedding was not what you ever expected of me.'

He continued:

'Bulkley my lifelong friend and will always be, has taken my nuptials very strangely. He was not invited to attend the ceremony which – although marriages in church are more common now – was held at the house of my bride's father. It was not a secret but a quiet and private affair entirely because Honoria's father considered it to be too much of a trial for a bride to face the gaze of the curious public.

'You meanwhile, dear Dodd, you are a pretty close friend, but as neither you nor Bulkley are known to Honoria you will not have been dismayed I hope by the absence of an invitation.

'The fact remains that Bulkley has gone off in a strange mood and is seen now most frequently dressed with unusual abandon and frequenting theatres and standing at the doors by which actresses and actors come and go; but has no intention, as far as I can see, to be looking for a wife,'

As though to give full account of all that had happened to justify his personal feelings, Gascoigne wrote that Honoria was not a beauty, and he was not in raptures over her air, her thin figure, or her voice . . . but . . . the moment he set eyes on her he knew he should never wish to marry any other woman.

Such unaccountable chemistry occurring in a man past middle years must be another of the mysteries of life that will not be unlocked for us until it is so by the good Lord when we rise from our graves.

Some time after receiving Gascoigne's letter, I chanced to come upon him in Threadneedle Street. We both entered The Baltic Coffee House, where he spied some city traders discussing their business. It was surprising to me that he should know such people when he, as a lawyer, was far removed from the interest of buyers of fur and timber and stout bottomed ships. Between long sips of very strong coffee, and with many cautious looks to either side, accompanied by phrases such as *"cum rara fide"* and *"sub silentio"* which indicated that he was about to breach some confidentiality, he said – his lower lip hanging below the saucer:

'Those men, whom you see have recognised me here, are also Freemasons. Fellow Freemasons. I am surprised you are not one of us.'

Gascoigne then, under cover of more legal Latin and his coffee cup, named names who might agree with him to recommend me for the Brotherhood, if I should believe it something I wished for. If not, never speak of it again.

It was something I wished for, but had not been approached, and had on occasion wondered at the discretion and secrecy of so many men about the city. As time went on I began to recognise and acknowledge their membership by signs. Several of the Church Wardens at St Vedast where I occasionally preached; men in the congregation at St Olaves, which was even more thickly populated with the Brotherhood – and the Rector himself – all declared the fact by a few words and a handshake. There was no certainty in my mind about Chesterfield until I was initiated into my Lodge at The Mason's Tavern in Great Queen Street. Then I learned that the Fourth Earl had been installed in 1721 immediately preceding the Grand Feast when the Duke of Montague was installed as its Grand Master. The Earl of Chesterfield was known thereafter to be a regular attender at his own Lodge, and was also present at an occasional lodge – granted dispensation by The Grand Lodge of England at The Hague where he was Ambassador. To my regret, none of his Masonic ties were communicated by the Earl to Sturdy, or to me and I never spoke of Free Masonry to either. I suspect that Chesterfield made a number of enemies in Masonry and wished the enmity to be confined there and not break out loose amongst friends and other companies or upon Sturdy. This was not, I think, a sound judgement, for the strength and assistance in affairs that might be shared between like individuals bound by the rules of The Craft is greater I believe than the benefits to be gained from membership of any other congregation.

Any disadvantage caused by enemies of Chesterfield might have been overthrown by more intimate society with fellow Free Masons. The Earl always met with influential friends especially in his early years, with close attendance at The Horn Lodge. There Pope, painter Ramsey and fleetingly Montesquieu, and Sam Johnson were men to stand up for their friends. Sam Johnson, even though reputed not to love Chesterfield because he once kept him hours in an ante-room awaiting an audience to solicit a subscription to his Dictionary, still spoke well of the Earl, saying that his manner was "exquisitely elegant"; but even this acquaintanceship was not brought to the notice of his godson Sturdy.

For my part, I quickly obtained a great respect for the Order of Freemasonry, and also made many friends. In London I grew a small reputation as an historian of the craft and was rapidly made the First Grand Chaplain – in the very first lodge – The Moderns Grand Lodge. Such importance was recognised by the Fraternity when I wore the Chaplain's Badge – a Book on a Triangle Surmounting a Glory.

The Masonic experience into which Gascoigne so felicitously introduced me reinforced my belief that man is a being formed for society, and deriving from thence his highest happiness and glory. To all my pleasures was now added this, and it mattered not that I could not wear membership upon my sleeve, or boast of it in any company – the inner man was better for it and I had a new confidence with new friends.

I spent a little of that very little time I was not occupied in other things walking in St James' Park. Even on December days I halted my carriage and descended to walk amongst the throng of nobility – who were there like me for the constitutional exercise and to be seen. For if one is not seen, one does not receive invitations and one misses many of the opportunities that society offers. Moreover, although it may not have occurred to all of those promenading, many a soul – however high ranking – sought another congenial soul to whom they might unburden their anxieties. So it was Lord Melford was brought under my kind persuasion to mend a quarrel with his eldest son who was distributing the family silver as fast as his gambling bets accrued. I advised a regular allowance and a less stern proscription on the son's gambling to allow him to take his own advice about how much to put upon a horse. I hope those proposals fermenting in Melford's mind after our conversations in the Park brought about the happier state of affairs and the smile on Melford's face when we were again adjacent in St James' Park.

It was one of these occasions when, tiring of exercise and when I had met no one further to whom or from whom I could give or wished to receive advice, I made my way to Betty's famous fruit shop in St James' Street. I called to Josh my coachman to follow a distance behind me, but not so far as to break the connection between me and my stately carriage, and I picked my way between the Society beauties tripping with their abigails out of their sedans, to watch them enter Betty's most fashionable lounge.

There went Bulkley in company with a young man with golden locks and a pair of breeches as richly scarlet as mine, and was about the same business as I – admiring the beauties and their frivolity.

Bulkley introduced this nephew to me and as we were equally gallant as any other buck and dandy there – except that Bulkley looked faded and haggard – we entered to take tea and to converse. The nephew, Archie, was more forthcoming than Bulkley who after the first enthusiasm at our meeting subsided into a sort of sulk and disapproval of everything about him. Archie attempted to raise his spirits a little by mentioning the last play they had seen but as his uncle was not desirous of communicating with us, he took it upon himself to give me a full picture of the present state and life of Bulkley. He skirted over Gascoigne's wedding and brought the conversation round almost at once for me to enquire why was I not surprised that Archie's Uncle should have a plaster on his forehead and one eye that was darker than the other and had evidence of a little old blood at the elbow of his coat?

Gascoigne had hinted at it, but Archie gave it out as a bold certainty that Bulkley had become quite violently a patron and self-styled critic of The Drama. 'He had the habit now of mouthing Shakespearean quips – some culled from a book titled *The Beauties of Shakespear*' (here Archie paused to let his cleverness seep glowingly into me) 'and my Uncle studies his own expressions in mirrors and nods wisely when Mr Garrick's name is mentioned.'

Bulkley did not raise his voice or even his unhappy head in dissent at this and gave but a wry smile when his nephew also reported that over Bulkley's bed was a large print showing Mr Garrick and Mrs Pritchard as Macbeth and Lady Macbeth.

I asked how any of this could possibly explain the injuries my old friend had suffered.

'Oh, a separate case entirely,' said Archie. 'At a burlesque on the story of Dido – well spoken of in the *Evening Advertiser* and *The General Evening Post* – Mr Bulkley decided it was a stale dish and peppered with obscenity. Therefore, at this moment Mrs Jane Jewell – a woman with elaborate charms – entered as Venus and my Uncle Bulkley (incensed, I think, by the nonsense he beheld) let out a great derisory cry which shocked Mrs Jewell and the whole company. The audience, not to be left out of this drama within a drama, surrounded your friend, my Uncle, and drove him out of the theatre. One amongst the crowd that beleaguered him – I had already escaped to sit in some noble's carriage to observe the scene – this vicious playgoer fetched my dear Uncle a blow upon his head with a billboard that was nearby and then planted his fist into his eye.'

Archie drew breath for a while and looked into his Uncle's face to seek approval or disapproval of the narrative of which he was so enjoying in the telling. It is possible that the darkened eye of Bulkley could not give sufficient hint of disapproval of the story so Archie continued:

'The damage done to my Uncle's features which undoubtedly will recover in time, was as nothing compared to the cost to replace his new tricorne beaver – it will be five guineas for that. Nothing however will replace the lost blood and the apothecary's fee, which rose higher as Bulkely struggled and denied the need to be bled. Even though the bill shot up another two pounds we all agreed it was a small amount to pay to have a great quantity of anger and stupidity let out of my dear Uncle.'

I sipped a little more tea while listening to the history of Bulkley the stage-struck drama critic, and then left the party to prepare for an evening's revels; and to caution Sturdy to take the theatre in small doses and never to provide from the stage-side anything more interesting than moderate applause for the actual plays themselves.

'Be warned by Bulkley's example,' I said to him.

On the day after Christmas that year, Bulkley came again into our horizons. Gason and Ernst had left to return to their families for the season and were making preparations for their Grand Tour. I, together with Mary, Weedon Butler and Sturdy, was determined to make festivities at Jubilate. The servants were sent off – Hetty remained in Great Russell Street – and Mary, with unaccustomed glee, took command of the kitchens. Punch

373

was made and a good claret in several bottles selected – all declared to be from the Margate vintry that supplied the great Pepys in his time and Royalty since; and the Reverend Mr Weedon Butler was particularly proud that wine from his own town was chosen for the Dodd cellar. Sturdy was given a striped apron to keep his velvet breeches from stain and commanded to be servant to Mary. Before long he brought in a great roast goose which must clearly by its size have begun its journey on the spit much earlier in the day. Lest its flavour became too commonplace with the eating, several plates of other meat were put beside it. Merriment continued. Weedon could hardly be restrained from bringing his mandolin to the table right away, but restrained he was, not so much by our insistence as by our eyes all being fixed on the mouth-watering sight of a plum pudding of such weight that the Hon Philip Stanhope's knees buckled as he carried it in, while the great fat plums sticking out of it glowed in the candlelight. Mary took applause and curtseyed and bowed enough to represent a whole household of servants, and the Reverend Weedon Butler finally was released from his scraped-clean plate to sit on the back of his dining chair – Porter would not have approved and Mary did not much either – to strum and sing tunes and words that made a good sound but were instantly unmemorable for me. (I do confess it is a lack in me, that although I remember with ease every tune I may dance to and the pointing and notes of all music for matins and evensong, and many hymns – words and music – and much of Thomas Arne's *Artaxerxes* which has been played at The Magdalen services and at the Locke Hospital, yet all other tuneful sounds pass out of my mind as quick as the price of gold brocade).

In much company at similar tables to mine at Jubilate, that evening would have continued with the consumption of many more bottles of wine until the gentlemen rolled under the table and the womenfolk retired to bed. Not for us such dissipation – for none of us was born to the habit of drinking to oblivion. But because someone might call for other entertainment, I had arranged for Josh, the coachman, to leave the horses harnessed to the carriage. And it was therefore a glorious surprise to Sturdy, Weedon and Mary when I burst back into the dining room and laid open my plan. I had taken a box at Drury Lane to see a performance of Mr Garrick's new piece *A Christmas Tale* – a fairy tale to set the whole town talking.

We set off straight away, rattling down to town at a full twelve miles an hour. A sharp frost bound the road ruts and puddles each to the same hard iron, and the horses sent their steaming breath back over their shoulders almost to hide Josh and his smart livery in the enveloping cloud.

The theatre was crowded and an assortment of different behaviours to be observed – from white and black servants in the gallery, from the gentry and their ladies in the stalls, and from the loungers sitting on the stage's edge. The box next to us was empty as we arrived, enabling us to play the guessing game of "Who comes there?" Mary thought it could be The Prince of Wales and was quite put out that Sturdy should pooh-pooh such an idea and favoured a courtesan towards whom his fancy had leaned in idle moments; Weedon Butler in his most solemn tones said his wager – if he could sin so far as to make a wager – was on John Wesley himself with Lady Huntingdon. All derision was heaped laughingly upon him for this but quietened when I said that his suggestion was not improbable. For Lady Huntingdon was Mr Wesley's apostle and he had preached on Christmas Day in Bishopsgate. I knew this for a fact because, after I had taken a service and preached at Charlotte Chapel and started upon my walk home – as a penance for fleshpots the night before – I lingered for a while at the edge of the crowd that gathered round Wesley. Lady Huntingdon's carriage was nearby.

This was not the occasion, however, to give my companions any further account of man or sermon, and all bent their eyes towards the curtains backing the neighbouring box. An instant before business began on the stage, my Lady Hertford entered with the Earl behind her looming over her shoulder. All our wagers were lost – without sorrow – and we exchanged our mute greetings across the space between the boxes. My dear Lady Hertford how frail she looked – even to excite the care of the Earl seen now in a new light as the solicitous husband. He had only stiff and cold regard for me but exuded warmth for her. I hoped that she divined my tenderness and Mary's high regard even though our eyes had perforce to slide their meanings across the chasm between us while the Earl was paying attention to the stage.

Garrick had brought a new man to the theatre to paint the scenery and set all the stage effects – Philip de Loutherbourg – new come to London. The whole performance was of a high standard of course – nothing that Mr Garrick put his hand to was ever less than that – but the stage setting was of a magnificence and magic quite apart. To astonished eyes a summer landscape was gently turned to autumn and then to winter's hard outlines but softened with the whitest drifts of snow. All this done, I was told, by nothing more mysterious than careful lighting in the wings, and filtering bright candle light reflected from tin shields through silken screens of various colours. Not mysterious perhaps, but

Mr Loutherbourg a genius, and our applause enough to have drawn him onto the stage had Mr Garrick let him come.

As we left – without Archie who most likely had already taken refuge in case his uncle was in a controversy again – Bulkley was at the centre of a knot of people surrounding Loutherbourg. I pushed through and shook the artist's hand and Bulkley's but I did not stay. I was anxious to see my party on their way back to Ealing, and once they were deposited in the soft leather of my carriage, I left Drury Lane to walk back to Great Russell Street.

THE HANGING OF WILLIAM DODD

On the way with little detour, I called in at The Turk's Head in Gerrard Street where even at this late hour I might find a member of The Literary Club. I wished to sow a few seeds on this ground where great writers and artists and others of an all-round intellectual power exchanged ideas in sparkling discourse.

What offerings I had already made to the world of letters – *The Beauties of Shakespear* – numerous sermons and the first volume of my *Commentary on The Bible* – to mention only a few of my published labours – I hoped would recommend me to the exalted company of The Literary Club. It included amongst others Johnson, Garrick, Dr Nugent, Dr Goldsmith and William Jones. This latter, before he was turned thirty, had established his reputation as a scholar in all matters Persian. Histories and a Persian Dictionary were to his credit – thrown off between appearances as a Barrister at the Middle Temple. It was he alone I found later at The Mitre – engaged in conversation with the landlord. I introduced myself but without making I thought too great an impression on him. The glaze in his eye suggested that he had not had recourse to *The Beauties* or *The Commentary* nor heard me preach.

Mr Jones expressed more interest in my friendship with Gascoigne whom he knew casually by his passage to and from chambers in the Middle Temple, and thought that Gascoigne had some knowledge of the law surrounding bankruptcy – a source of income for Jones himself. Our conversation at first was slight but the two very good bottles of claret that I ordered at his suggestion loosened him – and took all the gold coin in my purse. We parted with the warmth given to us by the claret and Mr Jones made a promise to remember my name – when I reminded him of it – should it arise in conversation at The Literary Club. This was enough to raise my hopes that admission would not be denied me if a few others knew of my work. I returned not disheartened to Great Russell Street – to my library – for quite awake and stimulated by thoughts of companionship with men of letters, I wished to read and muse 'til dawn to fit myself thoroughly to join the exalted company at The Literary Club.

Whatever progress I had made, I knew by this time that I had not sufficiently advanced upon the hill of success. To have made friends – or at least acquaintances – who might change the course of my life was to be counted in my favour. The carriage, the house at Ealing were good and in particular my library showed some varnish of refinement, but I had not attained the solid comforts of life. Only entering easily and frequently into a high society which recognised my talents I thought might bring the sweet incense of approbation upon me.

Sturdy, an ungainly youth but with his head as stuffed full of learning as I could make it, accepted his godfather's advice that "pleasure is now the principal remaining part of your education." For my part to be in elegant drawing rooms in the afternoons and dining and dancing in the evenings were no bad preparation for my sermons the following day. In fact, I preached at various churches on this text from Matthew Chapter 6, v. 16. "*Moreover when ye fast, be not as the hypocrites of a sad countenance. . . but anoint thine head and wash thy face that thou appear not unto men to fast . . .*" This teaching carried for me the truth that holiness is not proved only by the demonstration of self-inflicted misery. My detractors said that I was "given to a life of indulgence which was greatly removed from discipline and neglects my reputation." These sorry souls, wishing others to be as severely miserable as themselves, denied that there could ever be innocent pleasure in congress with fellow mortals in joyful activity. I excused myself further that I took only a little claret during a year; that I never gambled either at table or race-course and would take my share in the small talk of the ladies standing by with all imaginable affability. None of this prevented me from speaking against *the ton* habit of

378

whispering and sniggering when a reputation was being grossly and falsely described.

A few hours of ascent to be amongst *the ton* were shared many times with artisans and their wives and all walks of life spending their guineas at Vauxhall.

Now overtaking the Vauxhall Gardens as a pleasure park was Ranelagh at Chelsea. The tiered boxes in the amphitheatre of the Rotunda contained Princes and Merchants looking down on the orchestra or on an organ playing throughout the night. The whole of London in crowds of eight hundred a day promenaded in the Rotunda and gossiped and took their tables below the three decked colonnade – olive green and gilded and lit by a rainbow across the ceiling at intervals which never failed to excite the throng below. "From supper with wine and music to breakfast with bacon and ale" the proprietor advertised, and did not need to mention the gossip which alone drew many of Society's luminaries to Ranelagh.

The bursting life of London at leisure could never have enough of gossiping. It elevated its hostesses to the most commanding positions by virtue of the strength and originality of their circulating rumours. Miss Chudleigh, a lady of middle years, and voluptuous and very rich (for a lady has to be striking in some way and have a deep purse to be a credible leader in Society) was reckoned to give the best parties in London. The Earl of Sandwich had not escaped Miss Chudleigh's attention. He had been particularly successful in a lecherous response to her and for a while dropped out of her circle while rude stories were being related about him. It was said that, as a Secretary of State, Sandwich was "ruining the navy" by neglecting it "scandalously." In his private life – which strangely he appeared to live almost entirely in public – he had given up hunting dairy maids to bring them to his bed since that sport had become stale. Now he was reputed to be half mad. Dressed in fully starched surplice he delivered blasphemous travesties of religious services to a church filled with squalling cats.

It was joked that The Earl walked too crookedly "on both sides of the road at the same time" to be able to return quickly to Miss Chudleigh's circle. Even so this "despicable insect", as one correspondent described him in a letter to her country cousin, somehow found a means of entering a rumour into the Chudleigh lists even when she was in the room to hear it. According to The Earl of Sandwich, Miss Chudleigh had just returned from a visit to Berlin. At the time it was said "officially" that she was the mistress of The Duke of Kingston but he was left behind in England while she flirted with the King of Prussia. In his "quite tolerant sight" she had "emptied two bottles of wine, staggered as she danced and all but fallen on the floor". The King of Prussia was said to remark to a courtier – but it is believed the words attributed to him came actually from an acquaintance of The Duke of Kingston who said that the King of Prussia said: "I can put up with Miss Chudleigh's large bovine eyes, sensual mouth and bulky nose, but I cannot abide the ridiculous nests of pearls she wears constantly in her hair." Whether the flirting and drunkeness of Miss Chudleigh were true and she hoped that by separation from the Duke of Kingston to increase his fondness for her, I do not know. If it was her plan it failed. Of course, the whole story could well have been an invention of The Earl of Sandwich who was quite easily capable of such a creation.

Society was littered with the Bucks and Bloods of London who divided their time between gaming houses and bagnios and had always upon their lips the curse "Damn you" and called everything they disliked "damned things". As Chesterfield cautioned in a letter to Sturdy, 'These puppies are in a fair way of damning themselves.' They rarely come into polite drawing rooms unless they are in their mothers' houses. Sons who had the most notable and expensive education – at Winchester, Eton, Harrow or elsewhere – were less equipped for polite or moral society, than those who, like Sturdy, had personal attention and direction from a tutor devoted to them. Sturdy witnessed and was surprised by the coarseness of Roger, the son and heir of The Duke of Lincoln – a Buck by deed and reputation. He gained entry to Miss Chudleigh's house and there spoke of his younger sister with a vulgarity that shocked even the worldly-wise Miss Chudleigh.

'Our line of inheritance must continue,' he said, as he belched among the tea cups at one of Miss Chudleigh's quiet afternoons, 'since my sister has taken herself a man – a domestic tyrant, middle aged, paunchy, bloated by vice and drink' – here Roger Lincoln took up an uncorked bottle of Madeira from its lodging in his jacket pocket and held it to his lips – 'and since this husband is not capable of mounting his own carriage steps let alone my sister, she should make her own arrangements to have a child when she goes next abroad.' He took a swig from the bottle and as if composing his face to look intelligent said, 'If she will not employ somebody to get her with child, by God I will over to her in Italy and do it myself.'

To forestall any moves by the company to remove him from the drawing room, he took himself off, leaving his bottle emptied of Madeira balanced precariously in a teacup on the arm of a chair. I assured Sturdy that such disagreeable libertines are not common in drawing rooms but form unwelcome examples of the worst kind of aristocrat wherever they appear.

The span of Sturdy's attention was not always very considerable. He would listen to gossip of an ordinary kind, but slink away when any medical man held forth. Were they ever in the future to seek his patronage, they had to mind his squeamish nature. Two medical opinions he held, both of them in direct descent from his godfather: one was to have his teeth well kept by the best operator – the

Earl's own black and empty gums bore tribute to his failure in this direction. The second advice I never knew the testing of in the Earl or the godson: it was claimed to be the best way of driving away the effects of over-indulgence in wine – "one sovereign remedy for all gentlemen of dissipation is rhubarb: it makes them brave next morning!" As a personal observation, rhubarb at any time put a brave attitude into only one part of my anatomy and left the headache entirely untouched. By his silence on the subject Sturdy indicated a different view.

Mrs Cornelys' dinners and elegant entertainments attracted Casanova, when rarely he was in London, and medical men in a regular stream. This was because she had the knack of listening closely to them and forming an opinion about them and their practices and passing on her view to the many young ladies at her affairs. They were by the inevitability of their attractions likely soon to require the service of a doctor wise and experienced in female conditions. In this way, accoucheurs and surgeons and men-midwives who obtained invitations to Mrs Cornelys' events advanced in their professions by her favours. It is said that William Hunter and John Knyveton the man-midwife benefited by Mrs Cornelys' standing amongst her peers. They held the women enthralled when the gentlemen present took the opportunity to refresh and to relieve themselves.

Sturdy was always absent when blood or death were mentioned despite I advised him to steel himself and yet view compassionately the hard facts of life. He had no argument. At Mrs Cornelys' Ball in Soho Square he took out a lady for a minuet and entreated the same person to accompany him also onto the floor for Roger de Coverley – a dance which he normally made excuse for – rather than he listen further to an *accoucheur* seeking a wider reputation. This man recounted his management of a lady – known to the present company – who consulted him about a severe headache in the temporal region three weeks after he had delivered her of a fine boy. The surgeon regarded her headache as a sinister matter, administered an emetic, drew two back teeth and took a pint of blood from her jugular. Despite this desperate remedy, the lady when relieved of her headache 'fell into a melancholy,' he said, 'and died that morning,'

There were others than Sturdy who did not wish to hear this narrative twice, but there were more who thanked and applauded the operator.

A mere clergyman such as I seeking patronage and advancement and to get the nod from important personages, or their wives, had serious competition at the balls and in the salons of the rich. Nor could I do what a Dr Day did to attract attention. He had his footman in various disguises come into a theatre every night of the week and call for Dr Day to come at once to see ". . . a lady in an urgent way immediately . . ." or ". . . a gentleman with stones who must have relief . . ." or ". . . a child with a critical fever" or . . . but there was no end to his abilities – or his imagination. It was said, but I cannot vouch for it, that Bulkley was at a theatre when Dr Day's man did his stuff. As he was a very similar man, if not exactly the same man who delivered an urgent call for Dr Day at another theatre the night before, Bulkley was enraged. But Bulkley was also angry about the play. It might have been of no significance had the play been good and the audience quiet and rapt in close attention. Such was not the case. It was Mr Foote's new entertainment – *The Primitive Puppet Show* at The Haymarket – a skit on the modern drama. In the report I heard from Thicknesse who was also there, the play was widely advertised before the first night and had a great mob fighting for admission at the door. The backless benches were crammed with play- goers from all walks of life and a footman endeavouring to keep a seat for his mistress was knocked senseless and thrown out of doors.

But when the curtains parted and the piece had proved both obscene and dull, the audience were so enraged, they broke up the benches and threw them at the actors and tore down the panelling and curtains. Booing and cat- calling, fighting and rioting, women shrieking and fainting, and a round dozen of fights taking place on the stage and off. Bulkley, even though recognised for his previous interventions at this very theatre, did not have the sense to remain apart. He was butted in the stomach by a stout sea captain, and had all the wind knocked out of him: his wig lost and his cane broken. Thicknesse at a later date assured me that the floor was knee deep in smashed wood fragments and hats and fabric torn from gentlemen's cloaks. When I told this story to Sturdy he barely raised a smile. It may be that he was fatigued with the dance, or perhaps I had taxed him too much about Locke's view of pleasure-seeking when we had returned late to Ealing the night before. In any event his wan smile was accompanied by some few words culled from The Earl's latest letter to him: 'I would have you seek the taste of refinement, the culture and intellectual accomplishments of a gentleman of society, and follow no other example.' So I marked down the Earl as a correct example and Sturdy as a prig on this occasion.

Even if I was unable to match the extravagant tales of medical men, I found a way into a small corner of Mrs Cornelys' heart. As I intended her to, she overheard me admiring her panels of china wallpaper painted by hand in brilliant colours with flowers and birds. The young city-living ladies of fashion to whom I addressed my remarks were curious to know from where Mrs Cornelys obtained her wallpaper, and being told, I learned later she made sure that a handsome gift came from the seller to her for her recommendation. But I believe it was above all the natural charm and vivacity of that lady which secured her that and many other benefits in society.

Lady Northumberland's dinners and balls were more

splendid and expensive than those I have recalled of Miss Chudleigh and Mrs Comleys, but she was too varied in her mood to be universally liked. Added to this, the rumours and scandals dispensed between the gluttonous mouthfuls of beef and pork and mutton and game and fish at her table were frequently of a cruel kind. Whilst being a devoted admirer of senior figures in the Church and of The King and all The Royal Household, her intimate circle were usually fed with a juicy morsel of tittle-tat before the company sat down. A tale begun thus at one end of the long tables in Lady Northumberland's Hall, was outgrown by the time it reached below the salt. So a story that began:

"A daughter of The Dean of ------, aged 23, has married a man twenty years older than she, who has a title but no expectations and whose only claim to the public's interest is that he is extraordinarily handsome; but Society is not pleased." This became in the retelling:

"The Archbishop of Canterbury – as is well known – has a natural daughter whom he has always failed to acknowledge or support. She, to spite him, has married the most abandoned rake of his time. He is more than seventy years old. Society is outraged at one of "us" in his late Autumn marrying a person of little quality in her early Spring. The fifty years of difference in their ages alone is shocking." My dear pupil Sturdy agreed.

Consistency in public affection was not always apparent. The Prince was always supported by the ladies because he was a rake, but laughter greeted the occasional story against The King – which was more likely a re-woven myth than fact. Lady Dorset bore out the truth of the popular belief that the more beautiful a woman is, the more stupid. She was said to have said to The King that the thing she "most longed for is to see a coronation". Perhaps because he was at that time suffering from a malady which his physicians advised could be fatal at any time, the

King was most unkind to Lady Dorset. However, he

gained no sympathy at my table for his remarks against her. Particularly that was so when he said – so said the hangers-on at Court:

'We do not have confidence in the wisdom of ladies who dress their hair three or four storeys high. And though we believe each storey is inhabited it is only inhabited by fleas, for I observe a great deal of scratching but no signs of intelligent life.'

Stories of The Royal Family furnished endless scurrilous gossip for the coffee houses and always will, but always seem to start in the smartest company. As a counterbalance to this I took Sturdy to The House of Lords. His godfather warned him that he should start early in affairs of State because such matters needed the resilience of a young man. However, he should learn from the great speakers because they set a mark for lesser mortals to aim at. The Earl cited Chatham who was said to be so debilitated by this time that he would have to speak horizontal if at all. Having heard the great Chatham speak, Sturdy (and on this occasion I concurred) agreed with his godfather that he would go to hear him again even if he were seventy-five and deaf and horizontal: for the most agreeable things ever heard in life were from persons in that position.

In these now precious moments when Sturdy and I could engage in conversation in the library, we found a new understanding. We took turns to take books from the shelves and read – skimming through passages in my case, plodding for Sturdy – and then exchanged the volumes and made our commentaries. Several books have passed out of memory, but not Nicholas Barbon's *Discourse on Trade.* Barbon's many interests – in the sale of property, as a physician, Member of Parliament and most famously a writer on money – gripped my imagination and held Sturdy's for more than the usual few given moments.

"*The wants of the mind are infinite,*' wrote Barbon in 1698. "*Man naturally aspires and as his mind is elevated,*

*his senses grow more refined, more capable of delight, his
desires are enlarged and his wants increase with his
wishes . . ."*

I applied this sentiment closely to myself, but Sturdy
took other passages to his heart which set a greater value
on money "and the returns that might be expected from it".
Seeing that we were, if not at odds, at least of unlike minds,
we changed the books and the subjects of our small
debates.

At about this time, when summer heat drove everyone who
could afford it out of town, Sturdy headed for Bath where
he could spare his ailing godfather the necessity of writing
letters. I, encouraged by flattering remarks to me from Mrs
Cornelys, sought a fashionable artist to paint my picture to
hang in the library. Lady Dorset inserted a contribution to
my talk with Mrs Cornelys to say, 'My grandmother was
done by Sir Peter Lely and her father I understand by
Raphael.' She would not have it that centuries do not pass
so quickly, but it were unkind to shake her beliefs. I
thought to silence her by kissing her hand and saying:

'Madame, your beauty is not marred by time and it is no
wonder that years mean so little to one who has such
permanent attractions.'

Mrs Comelys hid a smile behind her hand and Lady
Dorset punished my smooth speech by responding with a
shrieking giggle that brought cockroaches in alarm from
the woodwork. She then moved into different company and
I was left with my adviser on portrait painters.

'You will do well Dr Dodd,' she said, 'to seek out an
artist who at least understands religion – for that is your
trade so to speak. Now, I think your man is Mr John
Russell. I imagine, if I may speak boldly that you will not
wish to afford sir Joshua Reynolds whose price for a half
length has doubled since he was knighted. In any event, he
gets character and uses a great amount of paint but does not
put "atmosphere" on to the canvas. However, there is a risk

with Mr Russell. He is an honest man and recently converted to Methodism. This does not show up in his portraits for he is very cheerful though earnest and paints or crayons with much use of colour and poses his subjects how they would see themselves most happily placed. The Ladies are invariably well satisfied but his portrayal of children is not regarded so favourably, and I wonder if he can do a handsome gentleman with absolute satisfaction.'

Mrs Cornelys went on to say that Mr Russell's failure with children was on a false basis. Mr Walpole, who is a better judge of an artist – but of that only – said that the painter was competent, but had had some ugly children before his easel when their mothers' wished, perhaps even believed, them to be beautiful.

I was not to be discouraged, said my advisor, because Mr Russell would delineate my true character and intelligence, so that I had only to have a care not to be converted to Methodism for Mr Russell talked all the time he painted, praising Methodism and trying strongly for the sitter's conversion. Thinking again she said: 'After all, he will not make any great efforts to convert you who have heard the Methodists' trumpets and have blended their souls into your own preaching.'

Therefore, with not a jot of change to my religious beliefs I sat through that summer for Mr Russell. I found him a kind man, an enthusiast for Methodism, and oil, and crayons and portraits of beautiful women of quality – and I was led to believe that he admired me too. Had I asked him to paint me in the clothes of a Greek God or an Ancient Scholar he would have obliged me with no further charge, but he paid me the compliment of me being "a natural subject, needing no disguise as a greater thinker, since I was already that."

John Russell hung my portrait in his studio in John Street off the Oxford Road for months before he returned it to me. It was because, he said, the picture excited the interest and admiration of other people who wished to be done in oils, and he was reluctant to be parted from it. I was glad of his flattery and his marking down the price for me.

Sturdy was impressed at my portrait and begged his godfather to allow Russell to paint him in theatrical apparel. So it was done. Sturdy, full length in doublet and pantaloons, looked wise in profile and at the same time melancholy as befitted the character of Jaques whom he impersonated in the painting. Chesterfield took Sturdy's portrait away to hang it near to him in his house in Bath.

My portrait was taken – and paid for – by Mr Hicks, a governor of Magdalen House, to hang in the boardroom there. I was not ungrateful for this sign of approbation, particularly since shortly afterwards Thicknesse pointed me in the way of Thomas Gainsborough, his protégé, come to try his fortune in London. Here was a painting fit to hang in my library, and the hours sitting for Mr Gainsborough allowed us to renew a friendship so happily made in Bath. Mary sent Mrs Gainsborough a dress which softened her towards our friendship too – a needed gesture since the great artist's wife lived for economy and profit and regretted her husband's discount to me, and time spent in pleasurable conversation instead of at his easel.

Sturdy was gone on his Grand Tour – every part of its calendar and destinations fixed inevitably by the Earl. This frail, declining man seemingly would command all until and beyond his last breath.

The "season" was over, and only the pleasure gardens kept up their nightly frivolity. Mary claimed to be exhausted though she took little part in balls and routs and feasts. Nor was there truth in rumours that she stayed "at home with a bottle of claret for company" while I was out on the town.

I think I was never jaded; I did not tire of life however long the hours given to pleasure or preaching. Visits to humble households in the grey light of morning were also welcome to me. All these and the high hopes of preferment elevated my spirits daily – and my prayers were all of gratitude. For Mary's sake then I devised a different sort of pleasure away from the clamour and smells of London which effects could not always be subdued by the sound of my voice and the fragrant nose-gay which rarely left my hand. I hit upon the small town of Margate for visits

– for pleasure only.

CHAPTER 27

MARGATE; CHESTERFIELD'S FUNERAL

The Earl of Chesterfield

The name Margate does not have the ring of Ranelagh only because it is not a name sounded on the aristocratic lips of *the ton,* yet Kent in *Caesar's Commentaries* is described:

> *"the civilest place of all this isle; sweet is the country because full*
>
> *of riches: the people liberal, valiant, active, wealthy."*

Margate came into my awareness – as the best notions often do – from several directions all at once. Weedon Butler suggested to me that if the din and clangour of London palled, Margate – the place of his birth – was a quiet place and furthermore a place where the whiff of sea would be a safe restorative. Trying to avoid insult to me by his manner, Weedon said that the air was bracing, "and known to rouse sluggish men of advanced or middle years so it may do much more for us". I nodded and forbore to enter into discussion to discover whether his thirty-three years or my forty-six would be counted as "middle years".

Suggesting a journey to Margate to my Masonic brethren as a place for jaunts brought instant agreement. One pointed out that friends in trade who lived in Kent but came up regularly to London were not strangers to the health-giving properties of Margate. They admitted they even took their young wives – or at least the bravest of them, to Mr Barber's new invention of a bathing machine in Margate.

If these were not recommendations enough, further words in favour of Margate came from a recent neighbour. Born at Margate but now at Ealing, the beautiful Mrs

Lascelles (Anne Catley before her marriage) had established reputations both as a singer and as a courtesan. Said to be scandalously rich – but Lady Bountiful to the poor in Ealing – she was a constant topic of conversation, all the world debating whether her income was greater from earnings as a songstress or from her other more private and individual performances. As Lady Catley, she returned to Margate towards the end of each of her many pregnancies and took up lodging again in the humble cottage of her mother and coachman father to await delivery of her latest child. She declared that if her voice had quality it owed everything to the sweetness of the air of Margate, and insisted that her infants be at the same place to draw in their first vital breaths.

On many a bright Monday morning, my party would set off eagerly for the green pastures of Kent and the golden sands of Margate with Josh driving the glad horses at a spanking trot. The first occasion of these was as all others later – I rejoicing at deserved release from clerical duties and the fatigue of sermons prepared and delivered and from the vexations of poor parishioners and high society. When the landscape of Kent came into view all ordinary anxieties were pushed to the back of my mind; for the flat fields of turnips and shallow streams recalled my childhood at Bourne, and the simple cottages and crowded gardens there soaking up sunshine. The idyll was by nature made.

Soon our jovial companions were all at ease; Margaret – who offered up "Peg" as a shorter name – was married to Edward who disliked any shortening of his, and earned disfavour with Peg by admiring every woman in the party but her and attempting to repair his reputation so damaged in her eyes by extravagant admiration of her artistry with pencil and colouring box. She, in turn, punished Edward and us all – in the mildest way – by holding up the whole company – while she set up her easel at the mouth of every cave and inlet between the cliffs along all the coastline from Margate to Brighton; which drawings she regularly abandoned in my carriage. On our return, Weedon treated these with great regard, cataloguing and preserving them in a great folder in the library.

Corinda was a beauty who gave the manner of being unaware of the effects of her attractions on the men around her. Nor did her husband Rowley acknowledge his wife's beauty and innocence.

Mary engaged Weedon closely in conversation but her eyes fell more often on Rowley and his shapely legs and so did the eyes of many of the ladies and Rowley's own eyes too.

I was indebted to Weedon for occupying Mary's attention and his return with Josh to London on the Tuesdays did, therefore, a little mar my freedom. He made excuse that firstly, although he could sit a horse as well as any man, the un-bred nags provided for us in Margate put him into unreasonable discomfort. 'It is my long legs,' he said with tact, but I estimated he had a greater desire to be amongst his books and the pupils in his charge. There was also a deal of flirting in our company and none readily to hand for him, which made his disapproval soon unmasked.

I made my task to keep the whole company jovial, reassuring them that although the roads to Margate were not up to the standard of toll roads into Bath, they had an advantage not encountered there – that of freedom from highwaymen – that fearsome ruination of the traveller's ease.

But to be the master of ceremonies on our jaunts was not without responsibilities. If a lady's horse tripped so that she took a tumble, it was demanded that I rub her bruises and then produce a verse or two to mark the occasion. I have no need to remind myself now of all the horrid poetry I composed but note that it caused some merriment at least. I do, however, have a duty to examine my behaviour and to think again about the evenings' entertainments – or those evenings at the Town Hall where I arranged for us to be in at the dance and at the tables for cards. Corinda on one occasion remarked on my absence from the party – in truth it was the fish I had eaten forcing my absence – but she demanded a poem when I returned. I gave her:

> *"Who now' said she, 'shall through the rooms advance*
> *Guide the gay band, and lead the sprightly dance?*
> *Who now the graceful miscreant direct . . .?*
> *Or who the tables in the card room fill,*
> *For sober whist, brisk loo, or blithe quadrille?"*

These lines were quite poor enough, but were given privately to her, until she gave them to the company at large. Even more to my shame, but emphatically intended for Corinda alone, were the lines:

> *"I pressed her lips, her eyes now lustre gained;*
> *Her cheeks a fresher tint of crimson stained . . ."*

Mary had no sight of the action that inspired this nor the verses, and rightly would have condemned both if brought to her attention, but the poem was meat and drink to Corinda.

While in Margate we stayed at The George, an Inn so well spoken of by Mrs Lascelles. It brought no complaints on its landlord's head for the cleanliness and comfort of its rooms but could not avoid evil comment about the food offered to his guests. The landlord claimed to have the best brandy in Kent – however far we might search. This, it was said, because he had a secret passage underground direct to the smugglers' caves and the best French brandy was brought in direct. His reputation was built upon this, but if his fish came in by the same route it was a sad mistake. For even Rowley, who was a tolerant man more given to smiling than to complain, said the brandy was good and proper but that the landlord "should be punished by death" for the fish he brought to the table. It is not unreasonable then that I cast all blame for my deeds and my poetry on the fish, which, if it did not arrive with a stink, soon gained it by the cooking. There was a certainty about this. The cook was heard to say that he had learnt his art from a French smuggler and he said that any poisonous taste could be hidden with garlic. I do maintain that the poisonous tastes were not hidden in any way, and certainly not hidden by the garlic but poisoned by it again. And truly I believe it poisoned me.

But why think of the noxious effects of food maltreated when all other pleasures of Margate were there to rekindle delights. Not since Bath had I so much warmth brought so often to my parts at the sight of Venus in abandonment. That a simple carpenter such as was Thomas Barber with his bathing machine, could give such excitement to man is remarkable.

When Dorinda, tiring of our exploration of partly hidden caves, consented to dip her lovely form under the canvas umbrella fixed to Barber's machine, I knew that Venus had descended from Mount Olympus to grace mortals with her lithe limbs and breasts as soft as doves kissing the incoming waves.

> *"Beneath the canvas, with enraptured eyes,*
> *Apollo saw fair woman from the waves arise."*

Not only were these glorious sights accommodated to my view in plenty, but also those natural and common sights of pleasant Margate. Scenes of Nature, sensible and tender, bid me not leave Margate now without my soul being melted by the soft blue sea; by the sky turning to the pink of sunset; and the shadows cast onto the small hill fortresses and churches. So then I resolved that until The Great Master summons me to leave his terrestrial peace and harmony, I shall offer a prayer to Nature that I lie regularly in comfortable peace at Margate and let no corrosive thoughts spoil my enchantment in her arms. Oh would it be true!

The last jaunt from London, an affair of nearly five weeks duration to Margate and along the coast beyond to Brighton – our modern name for Brighthelmstone – filled me with gratitude for the pleasures we obtained.

Every cove and secret inlet, every cavern and smugglers' haunt bore our cheerful inspection. The sea, when the sun was high, held our naked but innocent bodies in the warm troughs of its waves. And that same sea in the cool of mornings and evenings, let its growling inward tide make murmuring retreat across the sands, while all our conversation, all our laughter, rose above it.

More than mere junketings were these weeks of escape from the great city. Thanks to God our eternal Creator for this refuge from ambition; this idyll in the bosom of nature; this solace to senses battered by the bitter sorrows of mankind.

Return from Margate found Josh come down from London as appointed and waiting impatiently to depart. He had us up at dawn seemingly as affected by the poetry of the place as we were, adjuring us to "Come! Watch the sun climb red out of the eastern sea and high into a blue sky".

The carriage wheels hummed over dirt and stone as if they too were alive and content. I let my mind float back to other journeys, other carriage wheels making their music on the roads. From Bourne to Ely, to Cambridge and to London, from London to Bath and back – but what songs the wheels sang then could not surpass the cheerful rhythm that brought us back to London now. Even Mary, who was ever one ready to acknowledge clouds on our horizons, was at this time cheerful – certain of a happy journey's end.

So it was until the last mile.

We had taken a circuit into Mayfair where our companions and Mary wished to view the new houses springing up in the fashionable area south of Shepherd's

Market.

At the end of Audley Street the road was blocked by a collection of carriages with black plumed horses. Undertakers slow and solemn mingling with the crowd issued cards bearing skulls and skeletons. The end of a coffin could be seen preceding a mass of men in mourning cloaks into the Grosvenor Chapel. I made Josh halt my carriage in a side street and stepped down to ask for whose parted soul I should pray this day. A bystander handed me a card which told in large print that the Undertakers were Gooby & Gooby and in small print amongst the pictured ossary "The Earl of Chesterfield". And beneath it, *"Surgam"* –"I will arise".

I sent Mary and our companions on their way and entered the chapel by the north door to stand in a side aisle to pay my respects. A number of principal mourners, who were not so stricken by grief that they could not lift their eyes to assay the crowd and who was in it, saw me and marked my place and dress and turned to direct their neighbours' glances at me. Until then, shocked at the sudden knowledge of my patron's death, I had not thought how much my dress might surprise the mourners so proper in their attire. A worthy citizen simply garbed in dark clothes and with a mourning band on his arm, observed my discomfort and with a gaze which indicated intelligence and nobility of mind, leaned towards me and said:

'That you should come into the funeral so sudden and in such attire must make it apparent even to the meanest mind that you are sincere. More sincere perhaps than those who have dressed up their sadness in black to give it the similitude of reality.'

I shook his hand as we left and asked his name.

'You do not know me,' he said, 'but I have many times heard you preach and know that you are not, as they say, a Macaroni at heart but a good man who gives that heart and your voice to good works.'

I was deeply touched and pressed his hand again as we

parted on the Chapel's north steps.

CHAPTER 28
HOPE; SIMONY AND MOCKERY

Chesterfield's support no more;
Hope for the benefice of St George

My heart, I thought, could not sink lower. I left the precincts of the Grosvenor Chapel and its burial ground, pausing only for a minute at the fringe of the mourning crowd to see The Fourth Earl's committal and to hear said those words rendering a finality to life ". . . *earth to earth, ashes to ashes, dust to dust in the hope of Resurrection to eternal life . . ."* and then strode off to Great Russell Street and let no one see my tears. For should I not confess, those tears though bitter salted for The Earl, were also for the loss that I must have to bear: my loss of his patronage to suffer, his guiding hand on my dear pupil Sturdy – who, although in foreign parts would nevertheless feel the absence of his godfather's letters with their wisdom, affection and supporting knowledge in all the affairs of the world. The source of these was now all dust.

My door opened not onto a hopeful resurrection of my fortunes but to a mountain of bills, demands, reminders of annuities due and all the piled paper of a life lived on uncertain credit. I stirred the heap absentmindedly like a man looking for a good whole cherry in a bowl of rotten fruit and there it was, a letter in the dead man's hand – shaky, but no doubt in the Earl's writing – and the crested seal confirmed it was so. The letter dated six days before, said in its first line that I was to forgive the writer for his brevity:

'. . . I believe it is the last letter that I shall write and I am very sorry that it contains no good news. I do not wish to dwell upon my frailty which is terminal – but will come straight to the matter which has troubled me greatly, viz: that my efforts have failed to find a bishop's mitre for you. I have no voice at Court now; Northumberland, who has the power of patronage over many Benefices and Sees, never looks towards me these days for worthy supplicants. So I am at a loss to aid you and I am grieved that it is so.

Shall you try for the Rectory at St George's Hanover Square? It is worth casting about for. I cannot write more. I give you my last felicitations and beg you to pray for me sometimes.

Your friend 'til death, Chesterfield'

Mary was deeply distressed at the Earl's death and at the news contained in this last letter, and bade me inquire more about the vacancy at St Georges'. I said it was of little use for me to do so. The living was in the gift of the Lord Chancellor – Lord Apsley – and he almost certainly had a man ready to take it up. I knew well about the Parish – one of the richest in the land. The church – dedicated only fifty years before – had fine houses around it where lived numbers of Dukes, Marquises, Earls, Viscounts, and Lords and the residences of The Bishops of both Durham and Salisbury. The higher clergy were indeed no exception in these cases of amassed wealth; they were truly as once described by Chesterfield in a letter to me as "those formidable gentlemen of business", and they were not ashamed to show their riches to the world.

I learned that the fortunate Reverend Dr Moss – now for a few fattening years the Rector of St George's – had been given even richer rewards with the Bishopric of Bath and Wells. Wealth beyond avarice in this See would dwarf the income at St George's, where the stipend was a mere £1,500 a year but had a handsome rectory and many perquisites.

Mary had a glint of envy in her eye when I told her of these benefits, but I reminded her firmly that I had no shoe-horn to ease me into the benefice as I had never sought favours from The Lord Chancellor nor fawned to Lord Apsley before he was in that exalted office. Of Lady Apsley I had a nodding and smiling knowledge which was no use to me, though she was a kind of innocent unpretentious woman whose feet trod the dance floor with prettier movements than many of her haughty friends.

Although a future as Rector at Hanover Square, with my other income, would render me solvent and comfortable, I saw no prospect of gaining that living. I shut it from my mind, and looked to my affairs to make economies. I let half shares in both my chapels – The Bedford and The Charlotte Chapel in Pimlico, and increased endeavours by proceeding to raise income all round. I did not let up at The Charlotte and hoped still for the King's presence there. At the Bedford Chapel where the Magdalens most frequently assembled, I set myself also to deliver regular sermons. This was not just to raise income for me and the Charity, but to reassure the Governors at The Magdalen. Some of these had remarked unfavourably on my absences in Margate, and they needed to know and believe that I was still a clergyman dedicated to good works.

It was barely two weeks after my return from Margate that I received a most surprising summons to present myself before Lord Apsley at his office. When I arrived there my astonishment was all the greater. I had entertained after all on this occasion some slim hope of recognition of my worth – and even though highly improbable – the gift of St George's.

Alas, to the contrary, the Lord Chancellor was not exuding charity but was in a fine rage. Towering above me while I sat – his invitation to sit was the first and last courtesy I received from him – I could see little more than his great hooked nose and his wide mouth like the spout on a gargoyle. He raged:

'You will not credit it – yes, you will credit it because you know – in fact you instigated it – the letter I have received. Received from my wife The Lady Apsley – which shocked her enough to pass it straight to
me . . ."

The surprise on my face convinced him that I was about to burst into speech, so he continued louder and more vehemently than before and put his great knobbly hand over my mouth:

'. . . Do not deny it. The letter . . . you do not need to know its contents because you know them. And you know that this is simony. Simony,' he repeated more loudly still, 'not simple-simony-met-the-pie- man simony,' he said, 'cardinal sinful simony as in buying or selling church preferment.' He drew up to make himself another six inches taller to emphasise his dignity and superiority and mercifully by that spared me a few seconds away from the shower of his spittle.

'We, I, engaged a thief taker to find this letter's source – but you know all that – how a clerk in the chambers – or dirty fox-hole more like it – of a solicitor called Gascoigne – penned the letter in proper language
. . . improper language to this purpose by heaven and all that's decent . . . and he admitted he wrote it for Mrs Dodd, Mrs Mary Dodd! That is your wife, I suppose?' Lord Apsley sneered – as far as a man can sneer when his mouth is working as hard and furious as the town square pump, all motion and splashing ejections.

Now he put his fingers to his bulging purple lips to close and dry them. In the few seconds allowed to see the letter I saw in it that Lady Apsley was asked to use her influence over the granting of the benefice of St George's to "a certain person to be named later". In return for this kind office she would receive £3,000 in cash and an annuity of £500 per annum for the rest of her life.

The Lord Chancellor again continued:

'It is monstrous. The most monstrous, obvious, devious, nasty, sinful simony I have ever heard of.'

I held my silence. If I confessed to the act and it were truly Mary's, it would damn her in Apsley's mind, unless I were to accept all guilt for myself. I kept my tongue in its proper place. This angered Lord Apsley even more and he became inarticulate with anger, which made me believe that he had already made an appointment to St George's, but on far less favourable terms to him than £3,000 now and £500 per annum after.

I was dismissed.

My turn now to be angry – angry a small part because the chance I thought I had of preferment was gone for ever; and angry in a greater part because of Apsley's hypocrisy. He knew that the very foundations of our Church were built on bribery and corruption, and the State itself and all its Offices were bought and sold to the highest bidder – to the one who did the most oily fawning, and did it without demonstration so as not to excite the interest of outsiders.

When I reached home my anger was abated by Mary's tears.

'How could I know,' she said,'that my secret would be exposed. You know . . .' I interjected to say it was a wonder to me how many people knew I knew and did not know, when I knew nothing of these transactions on my behalf. Mary continued:

'I took advice from Lady Hertford who counselled me to be anonymous in my letter and to appeal to the sympathies of a woman – Lady Apsley.'

'And this money – £3,000 in hard cash?'

'It was Lady Hertford too. She said it was the very least she could do for a man, a preacher, a clergyman in his prime who had received no reward from his richer peers. She thinks so highly of you. It was Lady Hertford who suggested Gascoigne and his clerk so that everything should "be tidy and legal". Alas it has all fallen about our ears!'

Mary then sobbed for a long time, and all my comfort, all my embraces were of no avail.

Matters became worse in succeeding days, I supposed through Lord Apsley's anger leaking to the clubs and in the corridors of Parliament. Newspaper men began to concoct their own version of "the story". *Tete a tete* columns bulged with explanations of simony – "the Uncrowned King of clerical vice" they said – and they reported and accounted for my part by my simple-mindedness and cupidity, and my cowardliness in letting my wife and "another lady of title and means who has fallen under The Macaroni Parsons' spell" – take all the blame.

Gascoigne came stiffly to Great Russell Street, wringing his hands slowly and reluctantly. He came to express his sorrow at my predicament and to beseech my forgiveness for his part in the design.

'We were attempting an overwhelming kindness,' he said 'but the entire scheme has gone foul upon us. This was in a great measure due to the strict unfairness of the legal system he said and explained to Mary perhaps what he might have explained to me before his clerk put pen to paper.

'By *femme couvert* in law,' he said, 'a wife is assumed to act only under the authority of her husband. Therefore you, my dear friend Dodd, take blame for an act in which you had no part, and in which you would have directed differently if at all.'

A week later I received an unprecedented visit from Lord Hertford. He knew nothing of the implication of Lady Hertford, nor ever would. That perfect Lady never broke a trust, and was never without friends to plead a cause for her. Lord Hertford had barely entered the library when he said, 'I come as Lord Chamberlain first – it is to say The

King has commanded me to strike you off the register of Royal Chaplains.'

I was too dry-mouthed and weak at this to give any response.

'The King,' Lord Hertford continued, 'has given public voice to his opinion that there is little else as evil in the Church of England as place- buying. It lowers religion to a level below the market place he says.'

I am not the first victim of the double dealing in morality, but I felt it so.

'We shall expect you to preach still at the Magdalen, but I will ask Mr Hicks who is so resolutely your friend and protector, to take down the portrait of you in the board room. We do not need a framed example in oils of the perpetrator of such gross simony.'

This last mean and petty action had little power to hurt me more. I held my peace.

By this time Mary and I were almost prisoners at Great Russell Street. And the newspapers directed the ignorant to come and gaze "at the Macaroni's house", and if I passed out to walk I was sure of some sniggering group of idlers dawdling by my gate, and the most impudent chalked up rudenesses on my door.

Bulkley came at the beginning of the third week of my "disgrace". He was subdued, having been taken to task by his partners at the Bank and bound over to be modest in his costume and polite in his behaviour in the theatre. He had, however, continued with his visits to The Haymarket and Drury Lane and any theatre where a performance took his fancy. So it was *The Cozeners* at The Haymarket that Bulkley came to report.

'*The* Cozeners, Mr Samuel Foote's latest farce, purports to ridicule "popular" cheats and swindlers,' said Bulkley. A scene had been added in mockery of me and Mary – naming us "Dr Simony and Mrs Mary Simony". How I was portrayed might have brought a smile to my face if I were not so deadened by my misery.

'There is Doctor Simony upon the stage,' said Bulkley
. . . 'a bouquet in one hand and a diamond ring in the other
– and in a white wig "tight curled as a cauliflower" – not
your "Draggled brown curls like a Newfoundland
spaniel",' he quoted. '"And how he sings," says Mrs
Simony, "and writes hymns too – see this one – Promise
to pay the bearer £3,000 for just one small favour".'

Bulkley did the parts well but that only added to my
discomfort, as did his telling that this sketch in the whole
evening's performance was the most laughed at by the
audience. He himself had great trouble in keeping his anger
quiet and said:

'I wished to tell the stupid curs that they know nothing
of The Good Dr Dodd and should be ashamed to laugh at
Mr Foote's jibes.'

I thanked my old friend and laid counsel with myself to
do what was best.

However much it might be said by discerning people
that Foote's work was a vulgar piece of roguery unworthy
of public notice, it had attracted the attention of a number
of undesirable people. Now scarcely an hour passed but the
idle and curious – drawn by the beating of newspaper men
and creditors' fists on my door – presumed it was their
proper duty also to call for Dr and Mrs Simony. They
raised great shouts that could be heard in Hampstead.
Others climbed the railings to rattle the windows as if to
loose their sashes from the frames.

Sieged in my own house, I sent Mary and the servants
away and found other employment for the newest maids.
Josh left with Hetty by the back basement door to return to
their own homes. Mary took her departure similarly and
made her way to the Porter's establishment in Covent
Garden. Weedon, my dear and faithful amanuensis, was
reluctant to leave his books, but consented to go when I
thrust a bundle of old sermon notes into his hand and
begged him to work them up into whole sermons for
publication in a single volume.

The clangour did fatigue me – not as much as it did Mary who had her own unhappiness to bear as well – but I had some firm schemes fermenting in my brain. With the money that might have been spent on an annuity to purchase the St George's living, I dreamed of having made a very fine edition of *The Beauties of Shakespear* engraved and illustrated by the most skilled craftsmen. This could only be obtained in Paris. The plan conceived, its execution was immediate. I propped the boldest wig – a ginger thing I could not wear outside the house – above the back of a chair in the library so that by those pressing their noses against the window panes I would be thought deep in study – and donning my dullest clothing which had not been much used over the last two years – I left by the back door, and skulked along back streets to Lincoln's Inn.

Gascoigne, against a promissory note, gave me sufficient money to reach France and to live there modestly for a month or two. The transaction was made while Gascoigne's junior was in the room, so stifling Gascoigne's urge to moralise. In the silence, he allowed a smile to his lips and a handshake that carried more meaning than was visible. I took the Clerk's paper and a quill to write to the fifth Earl of Chesterfield in Geneva, sealed it with my signet ring – the diamond ring was safely I hoped with Mary – and left for France. In four days I was comfortably lodged at *Le Coq d'Or* within the shadow of Notre Dame and conducting my business with printers and engravers and awaiting a reply from Sturdy, the young Earl.

CHAPTER 29
TO FRANCE

*In Paris; awaiting Sturdy the 5th Earl; two rogues and a
friend;
M Le Blanc; Sturdy recovers; Sturdy generous – I love
the man as well as I did the boy; more of Paris and great
names; news from England; the journey home from piety
to lust in Bromley*

It was two more weeks before reply came from Geneva to
Le Coq d'Or. I had expected an invitation to Sturdy's
house in Geneva and hoped for a bank draft to cover the
expense of travel there. Sturdy wrote that there were
pressing matters needing his presence in regard to his
godfather's estate which was now passed entirely down to
him, and he was therefore on the point of departure from
Geneva and hoped "to be at *Le Coq d'Or* within six days if
this miserable cold and rain does not delay progress on the
roads".

He enclosed a very generous banker's draft.

While I awaited my patron's arrival, I set to work with
the printers and engravers to obtain their estimates of costs
and the promise of publication of *the Beauties* of
Shakespear in the following spring. I had wished to hold
up my business until I could take Sturdy with me to the
printers, and to let him see the beautiful engravings so far
commissioned in the hope that he might further loosen his
purse strings and contribute generously to the costs – as
well as pay the mounting bill at *Le Coq d'Or* where his
rooms were held for him. I was ever at this time conscious
of the rarity of ready cash and my mounting needs.

Yet as always was my habit to seek silver linings in
whatever clouds hung above me and this cheering process

was much aided by a new suit of clothes. Since I was no longer hiding from the curious and the hostile as in London, I thought I might go about brightly and openly and take enjoyment wherever it was to be found.

Firstly, I purchased striped breeches and a jacket to match them in colours that were all the rage in Paris that season. I allowed my own hair to grow and hid the more sparse crown under a cockaded hat fully plumed with feathers of every colour. Such dress was not made to be hidden in some dark corner of a hostelry. I went about on the town and being quickly noticed as an Englishman who was presumed to be well provided with money, I was quickly accepted into the company of two Englishmen – who though denying their character as bucks and rakes fulfilled all the promise of their kind.

The first of these, squat, fat and hairless and oozing with the manners of a fop, hailed me as I crossed the Plas de Notre Dame, announcing himself as Rupert – "a happy exile from Bath". We had barely made our introductions when he was on tip-toe searching the crowd and soon with a wave and a shout brought his friend to our side; his features were hidden by the shade of an enormous hat which clearly had in the making stripped many ostriches of their plumage and given the dye-master a full week's work.

'Laurence,' said Rupert, 'William Dodd to make your acquaintance.'

Laurence bowed deeply, sweeping the ostriches away in a long low flight.

'To make acquaintance *again*,' said Laurence, removing his glove to wave the last feather away. This revealed his fingers upon the back of which thick black hairs jostled for room.

'Marsden! You here?'

The shock of my exclamation was happily lost in Rupert's chattering – for he not so much invited me but described the arrangement he had decided upon: to go with him and Marsden to Sablon's Fields for the season's races

– which every year emptied the Paris gaming rooms.

I was agreeable and hired a chaise and went with them. Soon I discovered that the pair were not bucks in the ordinary mould but hard and skilful gamblers and yet, between deadly intent at the tables, their roistering and song and cheerful talk was much to my liking though I could not raise a high regard for the man who had so ill-used young women in earlier years.

Rain fell out of the sky and stopped all races for two days; but with that resourceful habit shown by Englishmen in distress, the bucks insinuated us into the hospitality of The Marquis de Sablon et Chardin, one of whose country mansions lay in an estate less than a mile from Sablon's now watery fields. The Marquis himself was away and his son Gerard as *maitre d'hotel* more than ready to set up Roulette and large gaming tables. He did so for Faro and Baccarat, and put Bezique on smaller tables for those of quieter dispositions. So we let the disappointments of constant rain and many horses being absent for the races, evaporate in a riot of gambling. As is my custom, I did not bet, as I am averse to spending guineas if there is nothing to show for it. Therefore I acted as a second *maitre d'hotel* commissioning the best wines and causing them to be freely dispensed.

In the midst of this, a M le Blanc was introduced to the assembly. He was said to be a cousin of our host Gerard, the only son of the late Marquis de Fontainbleau – at which information I detected no glimmers of interest between Rupert and Laurence, though I realised M le Blanc must be for them a "mark" of serious significance. There were no signs however that M le Blanc was of a reckless nature: he had a reserve which showed in an impassive face, unlined, unfurrowed by time or passion.

His direct gaze met whoever spoke to him and therefore it seemed strange for such a man to enter immediately into the play with bold stakes calmly offered. He displaced others at the tables by the wild enormity of his stakes. But Laurence and Rupert kept their places.

Over the first four hours or so M le Blanc gained or lost equal amounts to either Laurence or Rupert. As the dice fell or the wheel turned, fate was even handed with those three and others present. And so it was when by mutual consent they turned to Faro – happy to take turns to be banker and sink back into their *fauteulles* – at least the two bucks appeared content to recline a while, but M le Blanc leaned forward as if urging play on. His face remained a mask – or nearly so – just a shadow of disappointment showing in his eyes when he gained around £2000 more from Rupert than he had lost to both him and Laurence in the hand before. If the shadow crossing M le Blanc's features was noticed by the bucks, the cards fell equally as before for another hour.

Such play lost my interest for a while though it puzzled a corner of my mind. I drew young Gerard aside and asked him more about M le Blanc. That there was some mystery about him seemed certain whereas Rupert and Laurence were open books – even though with deeply stained pages between their covers.

'M le Blanc,' said Gerard 'is grieving. He gambles to forget.'

'What?'

'A death. His young wife died within a year of marriage. Though why such short acquaintance should result in such unparalleled sorrow I cannot understand. But I do not know him well. He is my father's nephew – to whom, although he had never met, he felt he owed some obligation when he learnt of Madame le Blanc's death.'

'Will you make excuse for him to leave the cards for a moment or two and persuade him to see me in the hallway?'

'Sir I will. We must eat, and that shall be my excuse. But please do not detain him longer than you must or the

company will become tired and disperse and we shall have
no more jollity tonight.'

'As to your first request Monsieur, I cannot promise. I
shall not know how long to be with him, but hope it is but
a little time. As to your second fear, this company I assure
you Monsieur will not grow tired for want of interest.
There is more in this business than is told by clubs or
diamonds, spades or even hearts indeed. We shall see.'

We bowed and I waited, tapping my bright yellow heels
on the black and white squared marble floor. In the twelve
gilt mirrors on the walls I admired the brocade of my
waistcoat and jacket and as my eyes rested on the lace
pushing out at my collar I felt suddenly the unsuitability of
my apparel for the task I had set myself. At the very least
– if I were not wearing a full cassock – a sober suit and
Geneva bands were the proper requirements.

In the time it might have taken to make a meal and eat
it, M le Blanc came through to the hall. I had looked for a
chapel which had been an advantage to me, but found only
a small side room within it coats and riding boots and
benches at the sides. There was neither curiosity nor
surprise shown on M le Blanc's features as he entered and
sat upright on a bench. I shook his hand and sat opposite.

'Monsieur,' I began. 'You do not know me beyond my
name, and you do not know why I have asked to see you
privately.'

There was no response expected or given so I continued
while the young man's eyes looked at the door by which
we had entered.

'In my calling – which is in this present clothing well
hidden – my pleasure is to ease the burden on shoulders
afflicted by the woes of the world, and in the name of God
give help.'

M le Blanc's eyes turned to me for a time and then
moved back to the doorway.

'Yes,' I said, 'What I have said has the sound of high

falutin' pomposit . . . "

'Falutin'?'

'Yes. High flying. Pompous. Exaggerated speech. Not a word used by   grammarians who are more careful with their language.'

M le Blanc burst into tears. He cupped his face in his hands and in the next instant drew the tears down his face with his fingers to wipe them on his knees. He stood and bowed a slight bow and stepped out.

I onto my knees and prayed.

When I returned to the gaming room M le Blanc was impassive as before. A notary had been called. He was drawing up a document that passed the whole property previously in the title of his wife to M le Blanc – but now to be signed into the hands of one of the bucks.

With even more urgency than before M le Blanc took his hand at cards and signalled to the notary his intention to sign over his lands and chateau – field by field and room by room against the increasing bold but never failing wagers of Laurence and Rupert. They showed dramatic astonishment that Fate should be so often giving favour to them and affected not to see the shrug of M le Blanc's shoulders.

I walked up to the table where sat the Frenchman and the English bucks, now both to my mind fully exposed as sharpers. My look begged M le Blanc to step away from the table a moment. He held his hand up in refusal of me and in so doing delivered every card's value to the sight of the others. To their visible anger I spoke:

'M le Blanc you owe me an apology. I demand that you step outside with me this instant on your honour as a gentleman.'

He stood and followed me as if in the whole realm of manners there was no other response he might give. We went again into the outer room, and closed the door behind us. I drew a sign of the cross large in the air against the wall and surprising him with the quickness of the

413

movement pulled us both to our knees.

'May our God preserve us. May He in the greatness of His mercy deliver us from evil. May we not shed that evil onto others but let judgement on them be given by that same God who observes all and in the final reckoning receives us all into his Kingdom. Amen.'

'Amen.'

We stayed side by side on our knees. Prayers fell from my lips offering comfort to him. As his "Amens" grew more heartfelt, the words I used and the expression given to them rose in feeling and in power.

Language from the Gospels, in simple prayers at first, mounted quietly into a sermon where I pleaded as though with God – but in reality for M le Blanc – to let every sorrow lie on the shoulders of Christ our Saviour for mortals are but specks on the face of the world whose greatest trouble is the smallest thing to our Creator.

M le Blanc remained upright on his knees, his hands loosely joined in prayer and his lips parted only for "Amens". I turned towards him but his eyes were closed. No muscles quivered nor was there any trembling of any feature. Through those closed lids tears appeared on his cheeks.

"Our Father which art in heaven, hallowed be thy Name,
Thy kingdom come, Thy will be done, in earth as it is in
heaven.

Give us this day our daily bread; and forgive us our
trespasses

As we forgive them that trespass against us

And lead us not into temptation, but deliver us from evil.

For Thine is the kingdom, the power and the glory,

For ever and ever,

Amen'

By the last line the floodgates of M le Blancs' grief were opened. He sat on the rough bench beside me and bent forward to let his tears fall direct upon his knees where they dissolved in the dust taken from the floor.

I remained silent. And was so for a long time. 'Most Reverend Doctor Dodd, I thank you.'
Another silence.

'I owe you an apology and explanation. I think you have saved my life. No, I do not think – it is certain.'

M le Blanc retained the reserve which I took to be his natural manner, but told me what had brought him to the idea of his own ruin and death. His dear wife – Marianne – had an illness. Her doctors told her that it was of a venereal nature and would be severe for her although with little effect on one with a less delicate constitution.

They hinted and nodded to her and to her husband that she was to blame for her illness. It was clear to the doctors that in their eyes and in the eyes of all people of sound morality she had sinned unpardonably before her marriage. M le Blanc knew that he had indulged some indiscretions before he knew Marianne, as might be expected of a wealthy young man of good appearance, but he also knew that Marianne had had no sexual congress with any other man before him – or since.

Here upon in M le Blanc's story he referred to my "high falutin'" speech and his questioning the meaning of it:

'When the doctors told me of Marianne's complaint it was my, what you call, "high falutin'" and exaggerated pompous and dramatic speeches to her that brought her through inanition to her death. In the doctors' presence I rejected her. Even, even though I loved her I sent her back to her parents' house to die. And as I understood it later, those previously tender guardians of her welfare took the same view as I – why else would I send her away?

'I gave her little comfort. No, I gave her none.'

M le Blanc held us both in silence again for minutes as his chest heaved and his face took up creases it had never known before. After a long while he broke into speech:

'That is why,' he said, 'after all my money was gone at the tables, I wished to give away all that Marianne had brought me at our wedding, to reject it as finally as I had rejected her.'

My thoughts that such wealth might have been better bestowed upon a worthy charity, I kept to myself. It is true that in giving all away at the gaming tables would be seen by others as a fault in M le Blanc, who prior to this was thought to be without fault. The suffering he wished further to inflict upon himself was to gamble away everything he had until destitute and broken in spirit he might wither and fade, succumb to any passing ague and die like a beggar at the roadside in that year's first frost.

'Oh dear, dear man,' I said folding my arms around him, "only by living can you do good. Nothing can be rectified without a head and heart and arms and legs to stand upon. Put them and your soul into whatever service to man the fates that you rely upon may decree.

'High falutin',' he said and wept.

Since the Notary and Gerard had taken it upon themselves to cry quit on further gambling, Rupert and Laurence had reluctantly departed. I and M le Blanc also made our farewells. I took him in my hired chaise the two day's journey to Voirons – and despite his protests for me to stay – left him on the steps of his entrance door. There he was welcomed by a servant and a woman I presumed to be the servant's wife – the cook – who both were as tender and familiar and showed as much pleasure at their master's return as the Old Testament father did towards his prodigal son.

I returned immediately to Paris, refusing the pressing hospitality offered to me, accepting only M le Blanc's invitation to call upon him at any time: 'My house, my heart, my life itself are yours,' he said embracing me. And this time, to stem tears springing to his eyes, I laughed: 'High falutin' sentiments, M le Blanc,' and he smiled and wrung my hand and let his mask again for a moment fall quite away.

The new Earl of Chesterfield was not arrived at *Le Coq d'Or* and he did not come for another many days in which time I wrote to Mary telling her a little of the matter with M le Blanc, saying only that I had been of some assistance to a good man in need of a friend; and I sought news from London.

    With the knowledge that an English Earl would soon be able to settle my account and start up a new one for himself, the proprietor of *Le Coq d'Or* agreed to my continuance at his inn – despite my unpaid bills – of which he reminded me several times a day, but I was to take up residence in an attic room more suitable to a person of limited means or none at all. Since all my money had been given to M le Blanc, I prayed as fervently and with as much anxiety as *le patron* that Sturdy would come soon. I had some boastful satisfaction in my rescue of the good M le Blanc, but the penance I was now paying in a monastic existence in Paris was hard to bear. In a foreign city – or indeed any city at all – life without company is not a life at all. It might have been good for my soul, but I shall not dwell upon it as that thought now is as disagreeable as the circumstances were then.

Sturdy, The Fifth Earl of Chesterfield arrived at the end of the second week of my martyrdom. He did not enter in triumph but borne in the strong arms of his footmen. Sturdy was horrid pale, with the shining eyes of a man in a fever, racked with coughing, and taking no heed of anything nor anyone about him and he appeared to be on the point of death. His retinue – the two footmen and the coachman and a black servant to carry baggage – had been desperate to know what to do. They said that they and The Earl placed all confidence in me and had pressed on in their journey at all costs. Little faith, they said was to be put in French doctors and 'If I am to die,' the Earl had said, 'there is no one better than the good Reverend Doctor Dodd to conduct my funeral.'

Not only my charity and love for the boy, but also the urgency of payment of sundry debts weighed on my mind. I put it to *le patron* that if the Earl died in Le Coq *d'Or,* his reputation and his profit would suffer without possibility of recompense. Therefore, I ordered the best adjoining rooms for the Earl and me. The retinue took up residence in the attics. The most reputable medical man – but only one – was brought urgently from the English quarter and I kept a free hand to have the best and prettiest maids at my disposal to nurse the Earl.

It was all done and with the least experiment and with no clever nostrums exhibited by the doctor before the Earl made his recovery.

Whereas on each of the first three days, *le patron* had talked sideways with one hand over his mouth and asked whether or not a priest should be called, on the fourth day he asked if he might be allowed to enter the bedchamber and give compliments and a welcome to the Earl. To grant this request was a necessity, for I think *le patron* believed that we had been nurses to a corpse and would all fly in the night, leaving him with a cold body, and a large bill for its burial.

Not only was le patron mightily relieved at Sturdy's recovery, so was Sturdy himself. His gratitude to me was more than he could express in words. He listened attentively to my troubles, added up on his stubby white fingers the thousands of pounds I was in debt, and balanced the amount with gifts of money to settle nearly all I owed currently to tradesmen in England and in France. Though this was money generously given, it could not be sufficient and I did not ask for the amounts necessary to cancel any outstanding annuities. As if understanding my reticence to enumerate every part of my prodigality, Sturdy said:

'You must, of course, want for regular income especially now that you have lost the Royal Chaplaincy. I shall give you the benefices of Winge and Hockcliffe and

Chalgrove. All of these have lain empty – without a curate
– since my godfather's terminal decline. You should take
up the parishes – they do not lie too impossibly far from
London. Winge and Hockcliffe being close to Luton – and
the other, Chalgrove, nearer to Henley – have been a long
while without clerical attention. If you should care to give
them a sermon now and again that will satisfy them I think.
In fact, when your circumstances are not any longer
constrained – why then perhaps you might think to employ
a curate.'

Sturdy's strength grew. Soon, on the excuse of waiting
for a letter from Mary to tell how matters sounded about
me in London, we took to the pleasures that Paris allowed
– indeed encouraged. No gambling certainly – but the old
Earl had given Sturdy countless letters of introduction –
each wrapped up in a cautionary letter of biography about
the subject of the introduction and we paid visits to
numbers of important people in Paris.

So at the British Embassy I was brought into conversation
with Mr Benjamin Franklin who was passing through Paris
from the Low Countries before returning briefly to
America. Mr Franklin's method of discourse was mainly
interrogatory – conducted by clever questions dropped
innocently into others' speeches. By this means their
opinions were changed or at the very least re-shaded, and
it was apparent Mr Franklin's head was a vast storehouse
of knowledge as well as of wisdom. He flattered me by his
close acquaintance with *The Beauties of Shakespear* which
he said he had seen in the hands of a Mr Hawkesworth of
Bromley. It was easier to draw this latter name back into
my memory when I recalled his compilation of
Parliamentary debates in *The Gentleman's* Magazine and a
dim recollection of his school – *The National Female
Seminary* also in Bromley – a school upon which Semple,
Warden at West Ham, thinking it was a scheme of mine,
had cast scandalous aspersions. Mr Franklin begged me to

give his greetings to Mr & Mrs Hawkesworth at the first opportunity I might have, and I readily agreed believing that such a trifling obligation would have no consequences for me. How wrong I was.

In other ways, the Earl and I were able to pass time in a pleasing manner often in the company of interesting Parisian women – much more libertine and yet better organised in affairs of the heart than their English counterparts. I shall not search my memory too hard to recall details of these pleasure-laden weeks in Paris. Suffice to say that they extended the young Earl's knowledge considerably, but I did not allow them to extend mine at all as I was rehearsing a modest and moral way of life that I felt should be incumbent upon me when I returned to England.

Soon enough, an answering letter came from Mary telling me that there were no new alarms for my safety as the newspapers were fully occupied with other excitements. The first of these, she wrote, concerned Miss Chudleigh on whose "voluptuous body" I had once remarked. This lady was embroiled in a legal tangle – a mix up of marriage certificates and no marriage certificates which proved or did not prove that she was or was not a bigamist. There were respectable witnesses in the shape of two titled husbands who both claimed Miss Chudleigh as their wife, one of whom wished to divorce her and the other did not but was so ungentlemanly as to die while the court under Judge Mansfield was sitting. Miss Chudleigh's dilemma caught the imagination of the more scurrilous papers and of Mr Foote the dramatist.

The second excitement was about a Mrs Rudd – wrongly described by Mary as another of my acquaintances – who was beautiful and artful. She had persuaded twin brothers – The Perreaux – to do fraudulent dealings on her behalf, and they were charged with forgery. Mrs Rudd had taken her scheme so far as to marry one of the brothers, but that did not persuade her to honesty nor the Judge to leniency. That learned old man – so Mary declared – was besotted with Mrs Rudd and when she had appeared in Court for the umpteenth time in a new dress, he sent the Perreaux brothers to the gallows, and acquitted her – according to Mary – because "her neck was far too pretty for the noose".

The third distraction in England was the American war which created painful divisions – some claiming that the Americans were enemies of the King, while others had more of a common mind with those of our colonial cousins who had cried "no taxation without representation" and had hurled tea into Boston harbour.

Bearing all these matters in mind, Mary was confident that there would be no trouble for me in London unless it was of my own making and she begged me to return.

Our ship blew us out of Boulogne harbour and towards Dover, impelled by ferocious winds that carried torn black clouds travelling even faster than we. Sturdy's face took on the green colour of his own domestic pastures before he had gained the safety of his cabin, but I boastful, about my mariner's legs, took to striding across the deck to encourage passengers cowering against the bulwarks. When we were in sight of England, I put on my clerical black suiting and framed my mind for the excess of religion and piety that was henceforth to form my new character. Intemperate sallies of high spirits were banished from me and I, gravely treading the decks again, our passengers believed that I was come to offer last rites before we all descended to a watery grave. They could not be otherwise assured, some taking hold of my frock coat and begging me to pray with them. The most fearful and desperate of these were the quickest to recover with land under their feet and made off into Dover without a backward glance, nor a religious thought. The Earl too regained a more human colour and an optimistic view of life, and hurried us to make a few leagues before nightfall.

TO FRANCE

At noon next day we arrived in Bromley, and presented our cards at Mr John Hawkesworth's house at *The National Female Seminary*. We were greeted with a warmth that charmed us by Mr Hawkesworth himself, his wife – pale and ailing with thin, wasted and twisted hands – and their cousin, a Miss Hawkesworth, a young woman with a serious look but who smiled and laughed readily. She introduced us to her pupils – about a half dozen young ladies – who came chattering to the steps. In their train, servants to the household appeared to take our baggage in. Sturdy immediately declared that he had stopped only to put me down and had to go quickly on to Blackheath where there was much to occupy him of a serious nature. He did I think put rather more stress on the importance of his affairs than was strictly necessary, but he had been in some measure disconcerted by the way that most attention had been paid to me.

Miss Hawkesworth, in particular, seemed enraptured to have "The very famous The Reverend Dr Dodd call upon our little school", and she and the maidens positively cooed when I opened my mouth to wish them "good morning" as though that were a sermon in itself. I realised, of course, that I did have some small distinction whereas poor Sturdy was just another Earl of whom there were numerous in their fine houses in Bromley and its surroundings. The troupe of pretty women would have hauled me away to their schoolroom immediately if Miss Hawkesworth had not insisted that I be allowed refreshment first. Sturdy doffed his hat and drove off rebuking his coachman as if he had delayed their progress.

The glow that came upon me so mightily then, endured until late in the evening and I was flattered to such an extent that my reasoning was smothered in excited emotions. In such a state I was even more vulnerable to the blandishments of Miss Hawkesworth, whose seriousness overlaid the brilliance of her smile and let only her eyes shine radiantly.

'You were, I suppose,' she said, 'born to be a clergyman. You have that perfect disposition so necessary to a man in that calling – amiable and mild of manner, devoted to study, to virtue and to friendship . . .'

'Well, as to friendship,' I gently interrupted her, 'that may truly be accounted part of my character, but as far as the other compliments you heap upon me, I cannot answer – nor should I readily believe anyone other than you if they had put so many flowery compliments in my garden and claimed that I grew them.'

'Then perhaps I might ask a very – a very monstrous favour of you?'

I hesitated a moment in case I should be asked a thing that was impossible but then I said, 'I can refuse you nothing.'

'This evening, would you take a service and preach for us in our chapel, for all my pupils to hear and be improved? We can never go to your Charlotte Chapel or to St Paul's Cathedral, or to the Bedford Chapel but we hear how you bind your congregations there with spells of godliness. Our loss of such religion makes us full of envy – which is a very unreligious state in which to be.'

Miss Hawksworth was not laughing at me even if her eyes were smiling, but how could I resist her request. How great is the temptation when a man has fallen – I say "fallen" not "risen" into the estimation and favours of a beautiful woman, to fall utterly into her command; to acquiesce with any whim. To the glow I had earlier felt now was added an almost state of trance.

Oh! Oh! How Miss Hawkesworth thanked me with her smile and took me by the hand to light candles in the chapel, to choose a hymn and psalm and usher up the youngest pupil to play the spinette (the organ was heavily built and a man's work only to work its pedals) and all the others to rehearse parts to every tune. Mr John Hawkesworth agreed to put his bass voice with mine to match the angel trebles, and his dear crippled wife said she would have the servants prepare supper for everyone at the finish.

And so it was that the smallest but the most excited congregation lifted its voice to the roof in the Hawkesworth's tiny chapel and sank more humbly to its knees for prayers than any congregation in any church in my acquaintance. They sat in admiration – no, in religious awe – when I began to preach. I took no formal text, but spoke of the virtues of maidenhood – of the obligations all of us have to friends, dear friends (and here I do confess I looked earnestly and tenderly upon Miss Hawkesworth) and families – mothers, fathers, brothers, sisters – and within this whole company the ever-presiding presence of Our Lord Jesus Christ. Amen.

When I gave the Blessing and my congregation left for sustenance of a worldly kind, the chapel stayed filled with an atmosphere of piety, of strength in Christ, in hope, in love, in the beauty of our lives. And as the door shut with solid sound upon the last retreating foot, Miss Hawkesworth came to my rescue in the pulpit where the guttering candle wick had descended so far into the stick that I had burned my finger in attempting its extinguishment. In the tight confines of the pulpit as we turned her warm body pressed against mine, and I – for which I can never forgive myself – I pressed against her. By what magnetism I do not know, by what lustful intent her raised dress admitted my member beneath it I do not know; I thought I read in her eyes that she loved me or wished to love the act that she contemplated and I with ravishing effect spoke the words:

'I love you. I love you. I love you.'

Do I not know that irregular love is wrong? Have I not laboured throughout my years to rescue the fallen from the foul depravations of men such as I? Did I not know as I took Miss Hawkesworth to me that it was the vilest deed of my sullied life? I shudder to recollect. I am utterly contemptible. I am wretched sunk into despair. As if I had not stupidity enough and to spare and evil and selfishness and indulgence and denial of the very Christ I follow. Oh. Oh. Alas – *nihil est ab omni parte beaticum* – there is no perfect happiness here – nothing human can be perfect – *nisi Dominus frustra* – unless the Lord be with me all efforts are in vain.

With a hurried note to Mr Hawkesworth I left without breakfast early in the morning. The glow which was put upon me when I arrived at the Seminary less than a day ago was entirely gone. Instead the pain which this affair gave me shocked me to the most severe degree and filled me with the greatest sense of shame on account of my weaknesses. I was in a deep melancholy, full of the blackest ideas and brooding over my faults and sunk into despair. I took a post-chaise for London that a thousand times I wished was the road to Hell – that I might burn away my sin in everlasting fire.

CHAPTER 30
AT LE CHATEAU DE VOIRONS 1791

Mary's love

I have left off writing for many months now. My poor left hand, unaccustomed to the labour once so enjoyed by its companion and now for a long time idle, creeps over the pages – making worse progress than before. This the shuddering production of a man who has found himself wanting and unsatisfactory and absurd. I wonder why I was not struck dumb those years ago when I took excuse to undo a woman whose sweet folly had made a lively impression on me, and whose only sin was an intense and sudden affection set free.

My sadness is so deep, a melancholy that cannot be given expression by wearing black garments and praying throughout the day, nor by allowing "the fruitful river of the eye" to run, or by hanging my head low upon my chest.

Mary has seen this and urges me with morning notes to be of good cheer – as if such advice betters my tormented soul. I cannot reply – even if I could speak – but I look upon her with feeling and love, and hope that it is not a vain hope that she will return my love.

This morning with the supreme effort it needed, I unshackled my body from the prison of my mind and stepped out of my room, out of the chateau and out of the shadows it cast upon the spring landscape outside. Mary and our host stood looking at his beloved tulips in the stone planters. Mary and M le Blanc were lost in their own conversation. I joined them and tried to suck out their thoughts in exchange for mine. Mary gently squeezed my arm:

'By next year's tulip flowering at least . . .' I raised my able eyebrow to question what event might be expected

426

then.

'. . . you will surely have told your history then? And your voice returned?' I put my accommodating eyebrow to further business.

'. . . You cannot hide it from me. Your sadness now indicates, does it not, that your history is approaching the fateful day?'

Neither eyebrow, nor eyes, nor face could give answer – they could not tell Mary that if my tongue was not loosened by now I had little hope of it ever being so; or tell what or who could exorcise the malignant spirit that binds up my tongue? Or, if I am my own physician, what new remedy employ or what one already tried be applied again?

Hope for a favourable reply shone in Mary's eyes and I was not the one to deny and dampen that. I would not shake my head; I took my hand from Mary's to touch my neck as though that were a signal she might interpret if she wished, that I agreed that the fateful day was approaching.

Mary turned to M le Blanc and he smiled back to confirm her opinion.

He was not frequently given to opinions of his own about others – not because of any dullness of mind – but because he was most often wrapped up in thoughts of his own. This morning his tulips brought him to observations outside his head and we all looked kindly upon each other, and he confessed to us that he was troubled by the rumbles of revolution brought from Paris.

Mary has written to Sir Philip Thicknesse in great excitement saying that he must return to Voirons soon because "if there is to be a resolution of Mr Farrier's greatest difficulty you surely must be witness to it since you are the first architect of the new built man to be."

I have not shown emphatic agreement with Mary's forecast – nor denial either. It is no great hardship to have Sir Philip in our company if it be flavoured also by the presence of Lady Ann, and it makes me sufficiently encouraged to return to my desk sooner and in a more agreeable frame of mind to put my quill to servitude. I had remembered to ask Mary to make a firm invitation to Lady Ann – and to secure the consent of M le Blanc to that invitation – but as my spirits having been elevated to within some short distance only below Mary's I have completely forgot to ask her to copy her letter to the casket. Perhaps I am also distracted by Mary copying out a verse I had written for her – on the back of her latest morning note – and which she has enclosed in the letter to Thicknesse.

It says that M Farrier is fortunate in his wife:
"That like a jewel has hung twenty years
About her neck, yet never lost her lustre;
Of her that loves him, with all that excellence,
That angels love good men."

Mary has talked again with M le Blanc seeking reassurance that all the expenses he incurs on our behalf are easily accommodated: which assurances have been given lightly and gladly since the sale of some land in his ownership has brought a good price. He and his household will be comfortable, *"tres confortable"* for as long as may be foreseen he says. To prove that money is no object to him, M le Blanc has shown Mary into his inner sanctum to view a new large and extravagant microscope sent for to Paris, and delivered earlier today – and which to his pleasant surprise has cost but a fraction of its worth.

I have sat down more lightly at my desk this afternoon than I rose from it this morning, and am casting my mind back to the spring of 1776.

CHAPTER 31
MARY'S ILLNESS AND RECUPERATION

Willoughby; Chalgrove and Wing; Hockcliffe and
Writing The History of Freemasons; to London;
Highway robbery and hanging;
Dining with equals; News of Miss Hawkesworth

Throughout the Spring of '76 Mary would not be cheered. Although she had quite forgiven my long desertion of her while I was in France and I had not troubled her with the facts with regard to Miss Hawkesworth, Mary had taken ill. There was no defining her disorder, which therefore necessitated recourse to numerous physicians, and as I had noticed in Bath – that haven and heaven for hypochondriacal indulgencies – the doctors' fees and the costs of their remedies rise in direct proportion to the mysteriousness of the distemper. I am entirely convinced that Anderson's Pills and Hodge's Analeptic Pills – the fashionable remedies that year – have been more destructive to His Majesty's subjects than pestilence or the havocs of war. Even so I did not for one moment begrudge Mary the expense incurred, for generosity was a part of my new character – a generosity that made me press sovereigns into beggars' hands, to settle bills with poor tradesmen on the instant and even though I must borrow to replace my loss, to give with very little ostentation to any appealing charity. However, in the dead of night when I was alone – for Mary said she should not wake me with her ailments and had taken herself to another bedchamber – I felt and dreamt of the neediness of beggars and a whole crowd of spectres who sighed over my poverty. I told myself that I had come at last to be of an age that can hold back from the enticements of young women – Miss Hawkesworth was to be the last of an angelic throng – only

429

to find my mind excessively occupied with my own pecuniary distress.

Mary's departure to another bed did not protect her from knowledge of what angry creditors had done and might do again. These had called on hired villains who had broken into the mansion at Ealing, lifted out what was of value and destroyed everything else that might be rendered useless by other means than fire. I thanked God that they did not carry out incendiary attacks for, unable to answer to the landlord for the whole value of the house if it had been burned down, I would as a consequence have been imprisoned in the Kings Bench immediately.

The same wretches who ruined Jubilite caused as great an expense at Great Russell Street. Windows and their shutters, the porch, lead guttering and down spouts, the rails at the front and the garden wall behind were demolished by the creditor's hirelings – assisted, I heard, by various newspaper men who added to the destruction to improve their accounts of it. At first, I thought it to be entirely my good fortune that a neighbour – a younger son of Lord Willoughby whose wife's endowment was provided out of the Indian Trade – in the spirit of doing for others as he would do for himself set builders to make good the damage to my property. He had spared me no expense by engaging a builder frequently employed by the fashionable and the very rich. In addition to ornaments dictated by fashion, the builder had extravagant ideas of his own – the brickwork was cleaned and the old mortar lines raked out and new put in; woodwork was renewed or repainted, fancy glazing put in above the front door and the door itself lavishly "improved" by fabulous brasswork. To protect all this new elegance of the house, new and higher railings at the front and a fortress high wall at the back had been erected.

I might at not much greater expense have rebuilt St Paul's.

Mr Willoughby presented the receipted bill, with the

most generous smile and said that I might have as many days as there were days in the month to settle with him. I could not be churlish in the matter even when I noticed recent improvements to his house which now bore the same characteristics and appearance as mine. Indeed the entire street was raised to a greater impression of wealth and attracted a great number of admiring traffic – sufficient to encourage more than one crossing sweeper to ply their trade here and whose pitiful tales of distress drew a sovereign from my purse every time I appeared.

While Mary made some slight recovery, she still could not dismiss her physicians and I, as I had promised myself, devoted all my energies to preaching. At the Magdalen and at The Charlotte chapels, at St Paul's and the city churches the congregations drawn to me were as large as ever – but there were far fewer of the aristocracy who seemed seldom able to sustain a fashion for more than a year or two – yet I could not feel that my sermons failed. Even those which had been worked up for me by Weedon Butler carried the same effect. Sermons extolling the widow's mite, or expressing sympathy for the rich man's difficulty in entering heaven, were equally as well received as those in imitation of the thundering expostulations of St Peter ". . . *when we walked in lasciviousness, lusts, excess of wine, revellings, banquetings and abominable idolatries . . ."* Purple cassock and diamond ring recruited again with a nosegay at the ready let the congregation know that nothing was held back in my preaching, but with larger numbers of poor people in the church the collection plates, alas, were lighter.

Therefore my income lessened but my following in the City grew so large that Brother Free Masons recommended me to their fellows that I be made The First Grand Chaplain – and I was therefore asked to give the Oration at The Dedication of Free Mason's Hall. This was in the May of 1776 and there were many men at the ceremony who were already caught in my acquaintance as members of the churches where ordinarily my sermons were heard. Thus my words were as welcome as the friendship existing between us all and reinforced the bonds now tied twice over in the houses of our God. "Benevolence" was the message I put out, that all pervading, all-performing virtue which in one short and easy word, expresses *"Thou shalt love thy neighbour as thyself"* and comprises all duty, and so consummates the round of moral perfection.

I took my fellow Free Masons prisoners of my texts, whether taken from Holy Scriptures or from the greatest philosophers whose thoughts were so akin to be indistinguishable from the spirit of Free Masonry ". . . in its wide bosom embracing at once the whole circle of Science, and Arts and Morals." I could not but remark that in whatever else man may dispute and disagree, yet they are all unanimous to respect and to support the institution which annihilates all parties; conciliates all private opinions and renders those who by their Almighty Father were made of one blood to be also of one heart and mind. I concluded, 'Brethren be bound firmly together by that indisputable tie, by the love of Your God and the love of Your Kind.'

The Feast that followed was more splendid than any other I have ever known and I was one of those few of my Brethren conducted to the table-head by Gold Stick in Waiting to a thumping rhythm of applause that made the silver jump like marching troops of soldiers with the waving candle flames their banners.

I feared that being so excessive on the virtues of Free Masonry I had, in the Bard's words, attempted *"to gild refined gold, to paint the lily, to throw a perfume on the violet"* but Brother Gascoigne and a dozen others came up from their end of the table to shake my hand, several quoting back to me parts of my oration and smiling with all the good will and kindness that marked them out as members of the Brethren. More than one expressed the

wish – each as if it were his own idea – that I would write
up the History of Free Masonry. Of course, I agreed that it
was a splendid idea and as they had spoken of it so it would
be.

Return to Great Russell Street brought an end to the elation
that followed my Oration. Mary, vomiting from her
remedies – or the Madeira she earnestly hoped would make
them palatable – had marked every step of the staircase to
her room. I vowed upon the instant to give her more regular
assurance of my affection and for convalescence to take
her with me for a month or two visiting the parishes
recently gifted to me by Sturdy. I hoped that in one of these
at least I might also find the peace required for
contemplation and set about the task of writing and
arranging the perfect "History of Free Masonry" to make
volumes which in themselves would command a perfect
price.

Within two days we were bound for Chalgrove where
Mary began the recuperation of her health. A narrow lane
winding up from Cuxham to Chalgrove kept travellers in
some doubt that there was a village to be found at all – until
suddenly the road widened onto a green and through a
shading of dark yew trees the church of St Mary opened
into a view. A brook, with cottages on its bank, completed
the rural scene, and filled me with sentimental memories
of Bourne, my childhood home.

The Vicarage, miraculously prepared for us, was only
a step from the church where in its solid oak pulpit looking
down upon wide and sunlit
aisles, I preached on two Sundays. For the first sermon I
took as my text *"Are not five sparrows sold for two
farthings and not one of them is forgotten before God"* – a
spontaneous but quiet sermon gleaned not from Weedon
Butler's notes but inspired from the incidence of these
common birds found in the church's eaves and gathered by

433

the stream amongst the ducks. My congregation was not much more numerous as the sparrows of the text, but I did not press the comparison too hard and the following Sunday the Church was bursting full. Then I did not preach of sparrows but from St Matthew: ". . . *that whosoever looketh on a woman to lust after her hath committed adultery with her already in his heart"*, which sermon was as well received by the worthy ladies of Chalgrove as it had been at The Charlotte Chapel in Pimlico and at The Magdalen. The women let their eyes look severely at their men folk who would have rather heard homilies on sparrows again or any other text but this.

After two weeks Josh carried us to Wing and returned straight to London to leave the carriage and horses with Mr Porter. At Wing, congregations did not wait for a second sermon to find their reasons for attendance: by ten o'clock they all but filled All Saints church in time for matins at eleven. I preached: *"Let thy soul love a good servant, and defraud him not of liberty"*. It was, I judged, an appropriate sermon since there were many servants in the back pews – sent on ahead by the gentry and titled persons who were very numerous in the great houses in the countryside surrounding Wing. My text on the second Sunday was on *"The Vegetable Creation".* At my final Sunday in this parish the text was again from Matthew: ". . . *whoever looketh on a woman to lust . . .'* – but this excited so much coughing from a pew at the back it was a full minute before I could begin again.

There were regrets expressed by parishioners that I should leave them and their churches after so short a stay, but I gave my firm promise to the good people of Chalgrove and Wing that I would return before the next summer drew to a close.

At Hockcliffe, two leagues from Wing – a distance easily covered in a morning on the back of a slow horse – any intention I had for a swift return to London was dissipated

in the melting friendliness of the parishioners. They were
directed – by a Mr Gilpin who lived in the mansion
opposite St Nicholas' Church – to make the rectory
habitable for a prince. Meanwhile, he entertained Mary and
me in his house and at his table and in his library. Here I
began what I decided would be my greatest work, it being
both secular and religious and entitled *Free Masonry or a
General History of Civilisation.* In it, the rise and progress
of Arts, Sciences, Laws and Religion would be detailed
along with account of the lives of sages and philosophers,
eminent men and Masons.

There was little enough in Mr Gilpin's library that was
not connected with life in the country; but once the huge
area of his desk top was cleared of riding crops and dust,
and supplied with many good Hockcliffe geese-pluckings
of quills, and ink wells filled, my wrist began to ache as I
started the pleasurable task of filling quires of paper with
genius. Each day a letter was despatched to The Reverend
Weedon Butler containing my requests for needed volumes
and references to be found in my library. So great was my
industry that between the ushering in of the last green
leaves of spring and their first golden falling from the trees,
the manuscript for Volume 1 of my *History of Free
Masonry* was written.

I had not neglected the parish or the church, nor did I
preach old sermons but gave of myself and present
thoughts as I would to a congregation of bishops – but in
language modified to be understood by country people
whose simplicity by and large was as great as the
disinterest and knowing-all-ness of the senior clergymen
of my acquaintance. I therefore preached several times on
the thaumaturgy of St Nicholas – the Patron Saint of
Hockcliffe's church – for his "miracles" touched and
excited wonder in everyone. Stories retold – exampling the
three bags of gold discovered and given to poor virgins,
which gift gave rise, I told them, to the golden balls of the
pawn shops in every town – made excuse for me over the

course of several weeks for the preaching of Christian charity and morality. If I did lose the comprehension of my audience on occasion – as I fear I did in three or four sermons disguised but closely linked to the virtues of Free Masonry – Warden Spellar said, speaking for the congregation, 'Your words may pass over our heads Dr Dodd, but your voice enters every ear and works there miracles as great as did our Patron Saint, and if we sit gape-mouthed you must know that it is due to our rapt attention and never Sir, from unstifled yawns,'

Whereas when we left London, Mary was slow and heavy by day and suffering the gloomy terrors by night, the balmy air of Bedfordshire wrought miracles in her worthy of the works of St Nicholas. Indeed it should be believed that he did such works as the agent of Our Lord. But Mary, in her common sense, ascribed her new found youth and bloom entirely to my prescribing for her brisk capers in the garden and drinking a small pail of water each day.

The rectory at Hockliffe was ready. Mary had been shown in secretly and on her own to approve and delight in its appointments. The villagers rehearsed a small ceremony to welcome us, but to everyone's dismay I had already determined that we should return to London on the very day proposed for the ceremony. Had we stayed I might have hoped for further adulation from the congregation, but more importantly I wished my manuscript to be in the printer's hands at once. Mary's hints and vague allusions to the benefits of a longer stay in Bedfordshire turned within hours to tearful pleading for an eternity at Hockcliffe. That our indecision might not be the victor and weaken ourselves corporally or in our purposes – for *mens sana in corpore sano* – we left for London on the day I had appointed.

The day was not auspicious. Good weather and a dry road brought us quickly to Baldock but as we came up a rise four or five miles beyond it one of the horses fell down dead in the harness. The consequent delay sending back for a fresh horse made us late at Barnet and later still obtaining a post-chaise to take us on to Tottenham. We were fearful of attack in such parts with night falling, and therefore we concealed our valuables under the floor boards and kept a little money only in our purses. This was a sensible precaution which was fully justified – for as we came up to Tottenham Turnpike three men came out from amongst the brick kilns and one went up immediately to the boy who drove the post chaise and pointing a pistol at his head, ordered him to stand or he would blow his brains out. I heard the words distinctly, yet the moment the words were delivered, a pistol was fired into the chaise and went through the fore-glass and almost instantly after the pistol was fired one of the men opened the door and demanded our money.

I desired the man to be civil as Mary and another lady in the chaise were much intimidated – as indeed were we all. We gave them all we had in our purses and they went off carrying away what they had taken.

The lad who drove the chaise was frightened near out of his wits, and was glad for the first time in his life that he had no money to be stolen and his life with it. We in turn had no stomach for argument with the highwaymen who would take no greater risks with their own lives if they shot us all dead

Mary was much frightened by all this and demanded action of me saying that all the benefit to her health gained in the balmy air of Hockcliffe was undone unless I took firm and manful measures to defend us. I therefore ordered the lad, who had set off at a gallop with us as soon as the highwaymen were gone, to drive straight down to Bow Street where we were able to describe at once all that we had seen and beg the Magistrate (blind Sir John Fielding – half-brother of Henry with whom I was acquainted through his novels) to set his Bow Street

Runners to find the highwaymen.

There was little doubt from our description that our persecutor with the pistol was a young highwayman called William Griffiths and, in fact, he was soon apprehended and taken into custody by the best of Sir John Fielding's thief takers, John Denmore. Griffiths was examined in front of Mary and me by Sir John and before Christmas sent to trial at the Old Bailey.

Mary was most hard at the trial, and though I made efforts to have Griffiths set free, all that I said to put shades of uncertainty into my description of the thief, was decried by Mary's firm assurance that Griffiths was the highwayman, and he who had fired at her and he who had stolen her money. Mary was in the witness box before me, eloquent and determined in her account – even detailing the little green purse that I had made up containing two guineas and some silver, and a note of exchange for £10. She also described in detail the way Griffiths tore open the purse and ripped the cloth into shreds:

'He tore up the note,' Mary said, 'and let it blow into the twilight.

She had no doubts. She was very sure of the man and the drama in the chaise when she had cowered against me all the way until we arrived at Bow Street.

When I was in the witness box it was I who had cowered. Twice or thrice I was questioned if I knew that Griffiths was the man and I denied it but less certainly each time and then said that I was on the opposite side of the chaise and could not be quite sure in my recollection.

In his turn, Griffiths said that he was a poor lad and had no witnesses.

The jury had him guilty and condemned him to death. If money might have bought off his sentence I would gladly have incurred the debt, the greatest debt, to save his life for there was a deep sense of shame in me. Even though others charged me with hypocrisy I enclosed a copy of my "hanging sermon" when I wrote to influential persons asking them to petition the King for mercy. Mansfield the Lord Chief Justice proved his heart as adamantine as fellow lawyers said it was, and a few days after Christmas Griffiths was hanged with four others – one a forger and none of them a murderer.

Mary restrained me from attendance at Tyburn.

At this time our spirits were sunk quite low and not to be raised by the habit we took then of dining in taverns with strangers or with no company at all. I grew impatient for good food and wine and convivial souls to dine with me at my own table. To hire cooks and staff to serve us was not difficult and I reasoned that Hetty and the plain and pretty sisters were better occupied in polishing silver for an occasion than in idle gossip below stairs. We therefore resolved to hold dinners at Great Russell Street and if the first should be successful make a business out of further feasts. Guests were chosen for their gay society which might be improved even more by the mellowing effects of good wine and plentiful food to put them under a pleasant obligation – if it were in their power – to fan the flickering flame of my ambitions by bringing advancement to me.

There were upwards of a dozen invited for dinner on the Friday 31st of January '77 and all accepted apart from John Wilkes, Member of Parliament, and the Fifth Earl of Chesterfield – the former being pressed with parliamentary affairs and the latter my pupil Sturdy giving no reason.

The guests shook snow off their boots and sat down to eat while the light chatter and laughter of the ladies brought out mirth from the most serious of the men.

Dr Shipley, the Bishop of St Asaph, sat on my right hand. Opposite to him was his own daughter – Anna Maria – the wife of William Jones who was next to her. He was by this invitation extended a further opportunity to mention my name at The Literary Club and so was Bishop St Asaph, who was also a member of that company of learned and literary men. I might have pretended to greater fame than he as a man of letters, since Dr Shipley had written very little of consequence. He was, however, most capable – almost as capable as my dear mentor Samuel Squires at securing preferment. This gave me some hope that I might be offered a prebendary stall, or a fat living in a country rectory. If St Asaph did not suggest any such thing, I hoped that his friend and colleague in lawn sleeves, John Hinchcliffe, Bishop of Peterborough might do so. He was only a short distance down the table.

To arrange the places for such formidable company and expect conversation to be tilted in the ways I wished was a far-fetched plan. The higher clergy are, as a breed, gifted with the power of speech and have a wide range of interests but religious matters were on this occasion avoided and William Jones held forth – claiming the whole company's attention – with recitations of poetry he had translated from Asiatic languages. To end a polished performance he gave us, from memory, lines from his translation into French from *The Life of Nadir Shah*.

Gascoigne, who at my suggestion had begun conspiratorially and in poor Latin to hint to William Jones at the possibility of his becoming a Free Mason, lost the opportunity when he led in with a question of law which Jones dispatched with speed and authority and opened two more of his own subjects – fencing and dancing – and left poor Gascoigne looking speechless across the plates of pineapples and oranges at his wife Honoria. She, despite Gascoigne's claim that she was not a beauty, had graceful deportment and a gentle manner that put me in mind of my Lady Hertford and distracted me this evening from the disappointments so far sustained.

Mr John Willoughby – my courteous neighbour with a marked interest in the restoration of my property and the refinement of his own – talked to his wife and Mary of the war in the Americas, a topic quickly taken from him by the Bishops who had like opinions which they were prepared to air for all our benefits. Too late I realised the folly in having the Bishops at my table for they would noise it about that I was also of their opinion and against the King's policy towards the American Colonies. Although I had lost my position as Chaplain in Ordinary to the King, I still kept embers of hope alive that I might again receive some royal favour, and had avoided reference in my sermons to the American Colonies, and never mentioned their great protagonist Benjamin Franklin at any time. When the women withdrew, argument became more heated amongst us, the Bishops arguing for conciliation and Jones and Willoughby calling for the Americans to change their system – and Gascoigne and the rest of the table feebly echoing both.

Well past midnight, Josh sent in word by a hired footman that the snow was falling hard and would be axle deep within an hour. Those who had their own carriages or would go on foot left at once and Josh waited to deliver others to their doorways, however many journeys it would require. Willoughby, as he went, thanked me for the evening's entertainment and like the master of the house pressing a gift modestly into a servant's hand, gave me "a bill quite forgotten before but wanting settlement now". Surprised, I thanked him and dropped the piece of paper onto a table in the hall.

Mr William Jones was the last to leave the table to attend on Josh's return. He was flushed with claret – some of the half dozen bottles I bought of the very same vintage he had called for at The Turk's Head. Applause for his linguistic brilliance also warmed Mr Jones and he was not afraid to be open with me.

'You are in my opinion a good religious man – you have Greek and Latin better than most and Hebrew does not puzzle you. And I do not belittle your writing. But . . .'

'Say no more I pray you. I can see you have not been able to make a case for me at The Literary Club. It is a sadness, but I shall survive it.'

'There is another matter,' he said, drawing me out of earshot, 'entirely different but perhaps more sad. Miss Hawkesworth who, as you know, managed her uncle's prosperous school at Bromley, has sent all her young ladies back to their families and gone to America in the company of Mr Franklin and his friends.'

'But why?'

'She has a child – a mere baby – with a deep mystery about who the father is – yet she has taken a name supposed to be that of a husband – Brodeau.' Jones repeated the name, pronouncing it fully and perfectly with all the title: 'Madam Anna Brodeau.'

Mrs Jones appeared wrapped almost to the point of invisibility against the cold and she and he stepped into my carriage and were driven away.

CHAPTER 32

MARY MOCKED

Letter to Madam Brodeau; Raising a loan; a Visit to Sturdy;
Bills; Books as a consolation; Self pity;
The Bond signed; Bankers & Lawyers; Lady Hertford dead;
Arrest; The Guild House Courtroom

I made straight towards the library to digest in privacy Mr Jones' news of Miss Hawkesworth. There was much to consider, but before I could do so Mary entered with frowns and other lines of irritation drawing the prettiness from her features, and seeing that my pulpit face was less rigid than it had been all evening, she was encouraged to come close to me seeking affection.

'The high and haughty Mrs Jones,' she said, 'took little time or care to reduce me to a small size.'

'How so?'

'"Where",' Mary mimicked Mrs Jones, '"Where dear Mrs Dodd, did you learn your clever accents? They cannot be from London Society – although we are sure when you move amongst *the ton* your speaking will be all the rage. We are so quick to catch a new language from wherever it may arise." And then Mrs Jones was joined by Mrs Willoughby and the whole company of ladies in the drawing room attempted to say "Durham" in the way I do. I was mortified. I am still.'

Mary let tears glisten in her eyes and said:

'Do you love me, William?'

In response I had in mind to give that reassurance to Mary that I always believed to be best, but Hetty, fussing with a lighted candle and a dish of iced cold water "for your

443

headache Mrs Dodd", put my consolation of Mary beyond a possibility. In truth also my mind was too occupied with the problem of Miss Hawkesworth – now Madame Brodeau – to allow me easy indulgence in pleasures of the flesh. I therefore bowed to the women and showed Mary that my eyes were as wet as hers and pressed her hand in mine.

And when she was quite engulfed by the dark at the top of the stairs I turned to the library and into my study. Here Hetty had put coals on the fire and fresh candles in the sconces. In such comfort, while my heart was inclined to generosity and kindness towards others as well as to myself, I composed a letter to Anna Brodeau.

The intention of it was to be practical – to offer help – but only by many scratchings out and rewritings could I be sure that false sentiment was ruled out and similarly that I had avoided any suggestions of impropriety on the part of Miss Hawkesworth, but took all culpability upon myself – having been driven to a moment of utter madness by her virtue, her beauty and her captivating intelligence. The note for £500 that I withdrew from my desk I enclosed with an explanatory note:

'For a lady of refinement who may be in some distress consequent upon the foolish and deeply regretted actions of me, a clergyman who had only this day realised the effects of his impulsive action and wished Madam Brodeau and any in her care – infants or pupils – to receive some pecuniary advantages.'

I do now wonder if my guilt at a young woman's downfall was in fact only my conceit that my overpowering person should have persuaded her to sin. Certainly I did wrong, but could it be certain that I was the father – for the first time in my inglorious life? Should I not to have written to her but merely given her a note for £50 just as a gift without detailing the reasons and insisting my guilt? But it was done and money could never atone for a crime. My expiation would always be in the torment of my mind.

My letter ended after the usual repetitions that are customary between acquaintances and with a footnote mentioning the current political troubles in the Americas and how that if circumstances might ever take me to those shores, I would be certain to call upon her if she had been good enough to lodge her address with Mr Benjamin Franklin. 'For I would be,' I said, 'as determined to help you as to give my services to the State.'

The letter and the note in it were sealed with the flame of a guttering candle and my burnt fingers again smarted and I recollected from that again the business in a pulpit. I scribbled a covering letter to Mr Franklin firstly asking him to convey the enclosed letter, if possible, 'to a worthy young woman who in an unfortunate hour went to America, and to whose fortune and situation there I am a stranger,' and secondly assuring Mr Franklin of my willingness to help in the grand struggle in which he was engaged.

I have heard no further from Miss Hawkesworth or Mr Franklin. Again it was perhaps my conceit that I should have heard from either.

By this time the snow no longer kissed the window panes with melting petals and I took to my bed to permit the soothing power of *Lethe* put shape on as yet a formless plan in my head – to rescue from disaster Mary and me and all our responsibilities once and for all.

Very few though they were, the hours of sleep fortified me and shaped my plan entirely. I consigned the package for Mr Franklin to the post and took my way through the snow to Fenchurch Street to see a Mr Lewis Robertson – a broker recommended by his fellow Free Mason, Gascoigne. He agreed, for a good discount to himself, to obtain a loan quietly and in confidence for me but with me acting as it were for the Earl of Chesterfield, who, I explained to Robertson, needed a large sum – £4,200 – urgently and did not wish to appear in the transaction, nor his friends nor his household to know about it, and that secrecy was so important in the Earl's mind that whatever the terms set out by Robertson they were to be agreeable to him.

Robertson, in his part, had knowledge of Chesterfield's youth and the honour of his family name and considered the lender would be of the same opinion.

The bond when signed would be for £8,400 since by law once half the stipulated sum had been paid, the bond was no longer binding. The terms were stiff, but I did not blanch when Robertson said that the lender could be paid £700 a year in quarterly payments of £175 with the yearly interest on £700 added to the last quarterly payment for the remainder of the Earl's life – or until the sum of £4,200 was repaid in cash.

Robertson's own commission was for £200 of which £100 was to be paid immediately on the morrow when I would hand him the signed document and receive £4,200 from the bankers whom he hoped would grant the loan.

With other duties in the city – concerned with The Magdalen – and some time spent with friends at The Crown & Rolls coffee house in Chancery Lane, it was late evening when I set out in the carriage to call on Sturdy to have his signature. Snow was dripping off the eaves and rain washed all into the gutters and drenched the crossing sweepers. Their brushes made them an income from the snow but had no answer to stemming the flooding watercourses. As ever, I had coins for them and had no doubt that my old pupil The Earl would be in proportion as generous with me I mused as my carriage took me to him.

I believed him ever conscious of the duty owed to me for giving him the greatest personal attention in his education and for introducing him to polite and gay society at an early age before the uncouth languor and awkwardness of youth set in. I had made certain that before the pimples on his cheeks were covered by burgeoning manly hair he could turn a knee and point a toe with the finest courtiers in town. It was said amongst that most elegant company to which I had introduced him that I had brought him to perfection as a gentleman of the first quality and those unsung, unnoticed, and almost secret arts without which a man cannot move between the different ranks of Society, were all taught to him by me. He learned to be at ease with prince or pauper and an intimate understanding with me had grown up through all the little things done for him. I had paid off the wench who charged him as a fifteen year old boy with fatherhood – when he had no more courage in the amatory way than to blush and turn away when a brisk gale or a dog's nose lifted a woman's skirts.

I believed in Sturdy's kindness towards me too, for on the occasion just recalled when my settlement of £100 to the wench left £400 of the £500 he offered, he insisted that I take it for myself and then was doubly happy when I gave it to The Magdalen. Sturdy repeatedly acknowledged that he learned more of life and of the arts and literature by listening to me, than from all the books I pressed upon him, and any sermon of mine he said taught him more of the necessity of Christian charity than all the letters of his worthy and estimable godfather the Fourth Earl of Chesterfield.

Despite the impoliteness of the hour when Josh brought me to the door of Sturdy's imposing mansion, the servants welcomed me and made me at ease in the hall, my outer garments taken away to be shaken and dried – a chair drawn up to the fire – and the opinion voiced that the Earl himself would soon be down directly to welcome the good Reverend Dr Dodd. The same servants sent for Josh to be sure that he too was temporarily housed in the dry.

None of this was a surprise to me for I had ever been at pains to show Sturdy how to treat servants with the same courtesy as their masters and mistresses, and never to pry out littleness and faults in them, and to recognise that their livery was no more to be looked down upon than the ermine of dukes or purple of bishops or the coarse black cloth of curates. The surprise was then that The Earl did not come down himself or ask me to come up but left a servant to tell me that he would not see me.

Perhaps Sturdy had heard of my straightened circumstances and perhaps he feared I was come a-begging. Perhaps he was fatigued or truly ill or – unlikely thought – closeted privately with a pretty woman.

The most senior manservant brought the decision down. He was a dignified man and was distressed to give such news and took an extended liberty in saying that 'His Lordship will not see you, Sir. I beg to offer indisposition as the reason. For this whole household and many similar know, if I may say so Reverend Doctor, how many hearts and heads are turned to better things by your preaching and how much good you do for people more important and others much less important than us.'

The manservant's humility and warmth touched me and more so when he signalled to the other servants as they returned my hat and gloves and cloak that they were not to hold out their hands for the customary vail. I would gladly have given the men my last sovereign just for the courtesy these servants had shown me.

Suddenly now I was without hope. I had thought it an easy task to persuade my pupil to take the loan in his name and almost as easy for me to repay it when once I had cleared off every other outstanding debt. But I had fallen at the first obstacle in my course. Prayers were on my lips but brought no answers. I sent Josh and the carriage home without me and began to walk back to Great Russell Street.

Some dirty snow was piled at gutter ends and caught in crevices like worm-riddled bread, while an evil sleet-bearing wind had started up and drove beneath hat and collar before dissolving there and in a brown sludge underfoot. Had I a lantern to light my way and to catch the eyes of thieves I might have been that very night robbed and despatched to eternity – and in that hour I would have welcomed such a quick entry to the next world. Yet Lady Fortune was beneath such simplicity and my distress stayed deep within me unrelieved. I walked on without sense of direction and thinking and having no understanding of my pupil's rejection.

Somewhere distant, in safer streets than those I took, a night watchman called the first hour of the day, a day charged with desolation and putting on me a leaden burden that could barely be supported as at last I dragged my feet up the steps and into the house.

In the hallway, now lit by one chamber stick, there was no one to greet me. I dropped my heavy rain-soaked cloak on to the table where still more bills turned to pulp as I dripped over them. Wigmaker, hay carrier, seamstress, wine merchant, wheelwright, printer, grocer and a dozen others made their claims. The coal merchant had brought his account with the coal, his black thumb-print hanging like a cloud above the total sum. I gathered them all up, and took them and laid the bills and the unsigned document for the loan alongside more bills already collected on my desk and I passed back through the paneled door into the library seeking distraction in the company of books.

Oh Dodd, how wrong you were to suppose that any words between the bindings of your books would comfort you when your mismanaged life has ruined so much of your circumstances. How in error you were to hope for ease, for rescue, while your soul was disturbed and your brain infested and like brimstone boiling.

The first shelf on the right bore a few volumes with letters poking from their covers. Weedon Butler had gathered together these various communications and placed them – as a reminder to me – into the books their

449

authors' had written. The first friend down was William Woty with *The Blossoms of Helicon* – which contained verses I had contributed freely to. This dear man's letter began with familiarities gladly accepted by me – a Grub Street colleague and a fellow devotee of the dining table – and then continued:

'Word has come to me that you are about to prepare and publish a splendid new edition of your *Beauties of Shakespear* illustrated with engravings brought in from France! I congratulate you mightily and hope that I may certify that this is not the only evidence of your present wealth, but is also a prognosticator for your future. In contrast, dear friend, my state is quite perilous and beyond any extravagance.

Publishers are greedy for my work, but when they have it are reluctant to deliver me a just reward.

My expectations in other directions have also very sadly failed. The dear lady who has been at the centre of my growing and entire affections for this last year or more has most grievously departed this life – and her fortune gone with her.'

The letter continued with expressions of guarded optimism and emphasised the temporary nature of Woty's finances before concluding with a request for 'whatever you could manage in the way of a loan on the most reasonable terms you would consider for a friend.'

I took sadly to heart that I had not replied to this letter dated a month since and thought why Woty had not, like me, raised annuities.

I left a letter from John Wesley and the copy of the reply both poking above his volume of thoughts *On Original Sin*, and did not touch Jonah Hanway's *Reflections* with its letter browning with age in its visible part. Neither these books nor their authors could cheer me now.

On the far wall hung a full length portrait of me with a bejewelled finger resting lightly on the two volumes of my

Commentary on The Bible. With an unusual economy, I had employed a journey-man artist for this portrait, which had cost little more than canvas and frame, and until this night, only the sternest critics would have remarked that the books were painted with more care than the face. Few guineas had been spent on the entire portrait, and my face only cost a few pence; and now I realised how pallid it was and how wanting in features; and how empty the eyes were directed without expression on to my books. (I wondered if I died by my own self murder if this painting and the painting in the board room of The Magdalen which Mr. Russell made of me and the very fine portrait of me by Mr Gainsborough which Weedon admired excessively and which Mary insisted hang in the hallway – would all three be turned to face the wall, or would they be taken down and removed entirely?) From the full length portrait my unwrinkled face and the shining gilt and leather volumes of *The Commentry* looked down on the two volumes themselves propped on the centre of the great library table, and I approached them and stroked the bindings – monuments to my vanity and extravagance which I could not excuse now despite my humble acknowledgment that the work was largely a collection of other men's learning.

At the table were the study places of Weedon Butler at one end and his charges, my current pupils, Karl and Nathanial and James. Karl, needing help to translate from his native German before entering into the Greek and Roman languages, had his place at Weedon Butler's left hand. The other boys shared a table-end littered with their rough workings. 'Latin is no more difficile,' wrote one, 'than for a blackbird is to whistle', and in a different hand, 'W.B. is known to spout the Greek as easily as pigs do squeak.' I sensed the hurt so easily given by boys to their teacher and hoped that the boys' Latin and Greek translations fell as easily into the vernacular as did their bad verse.

Books floor to ceiling: I looked to them for reasons for

MARY MOCKED

my soul's despair, or for its easement . . ."*By his books ye shall know the man*". I searched in my memory for the quotation's source and could not find it. I left the words sounding in my head.

Shelf on shelf, book after book, with wavering letters the titles surrendered in the candlelight to this wretched cleric's mournful, self- critical eye. There, close by my study door, all the more readily to be taken into the manufactory of my preaching, sermons fat and thin; one hundred and fifty volumes, some tight packed and upright on their shelf and others leaning like marching pilgrims and tilting in the wind. Atterbury, Bull, Burnett, Burns (the good Weedon had ordered by author alphabetically), Clarke, Cleaver, Coneybeare (clever men whose words had entered more ears from my mouth than ever from their own), Dodd, my own six volumes, (those I called my "borrowings" before, but now I called them "theft"), Evans, Forster, Fothergill, Harvey, Hicke, Horneck, Horton and Hume, (Hume's *Suicide and Immortality* still in the printer's binding), Littleton, Markland, Ridley and Seed (no subject left unpreached against), Sherlock, Sharman, Smallridge, Shape and South (aspirations mixed with condemnations), Talbot, Wakes and Young (the nature of life and the God within it explained). May God forgive me for quarrying without shame at mines also worked more assiduously by others: I remembered The Reverend Dr Griffith's Cambridge confession: "I lard my sermons with the fat of other men's learning." And so had I.

I stretched my chamber stick up to higher shelves where those few books undisturbed for years were regular and neat in their postures.

Harris and five others *On Elocution* – these had enabled me, a young proud parson, to put a high polish on stolen words and wet the surfaces of dry sentiments. I had stood then in youth before my own giltwood mirror in the vestry at All Saints, West Ham and formed my lips into the best shapes for searing climaxes and apostrophes that would move the congregation to tears. I was able then in those careless days to pose and compose myself and to tune my voice while my imagination was taken up with visions of admiring women, their eyes rapt upon me, while sublime thoughts necessary for sermons also jostled for a place in my fevered mind.

But shame and disgust with me took all imagination now. Yet still the products of my vanity stared back at me from the covers of books extravagantly bound at unaffordable expense. Foremost of these my own books – *The Beauties of Shakespear*, *Reflections on Death*, and *The Hymns of Callimachus* stood face-about and with studied negligence displayed themselves like Macaronies at a ball. I, Dodd, reached out fingers to trace the books' tooled leather, to caress deep incisements and feel the firm embossments, and then withdrew my hand in rebuke for my earlier indulgences and moved to other shelves: *Ajax* and his author Sophocles claimed their place in the candlelight, another reminder of self-murder – suicide forced by jealousy and vanity – a wasted sacrifice but withall a dressing of nobility on it.

Head reeling, candle flickering I ran past other books of which their miscellany was in no greater confusion than mine and I spoke their names: 'Wraxall's *Tours, History of Poetry*, Paschal's *Thoughts*, Philips' *On Language*, *Account of Denmark*, Potter's *Antiquities*, Woodward's *Natural History*, Fresney's *Art of Painting*, Rousseau's *On Education*, *Roman History*, Francis's *Horace*, Porter's *Observations on the Turks*, Owen's *Dictionary of Arts and Sciences*, Thorley's *On Bees*, Raffle's *Cookery*, Haylin's *Cosmography*.'

These all just at eye level, I did not stoop to read below, or rise by ladder steps to visit upper shelves. I approached the door of the study and saw Milton's works and groaned for my mother's memory.

Dryden's *Dramatic Works* in six volumes gave way to

Beaumont and Fletcher's ten volumes of the same. Steel's Plays, Cibber's Plays, Killegran's Plays. *An Account of America* (slipped in here with Russell's *Characters of Young Women)*, Capel's *Shakespear* in ten volumes, Voltaire and Farmer on *The Writings of Shakespear, Shakespear's Tragedies*; *King Lear* by Farmer, Griffith's *Morality of Shakespear's Dramas* and Johnson's *Shakespear* in Eight Volumes – published thirteen years after my own anthology *The Beauties of Shakespear*.

I would say Dodd you were mad then – were beside yourself with much learning making you mad. You noted this library with a flicker of pride and then regretted it. Mad – or fallen among the dull, the proud, and the wicked mad. The Gods are just and of our pleasant vices makes instruments to scourge us. How gently I put the candle on the table and dropped to my knees and then cried aloud and sudden:

'*Whom God would destroy He first sends mad – Quam Jupiter vult perdere dementat prius.*'

Then I wept and threw back my head and spoke disjointed but as if in prayer:

'Of comfort no man speak: let's talk of graves, of worms and epitaphs. It is the very error of the moon . . .' And rambled then and rambled more and wept again.

What made me continue so anguished, cleric? Did I know what I was about to do and was made mad and guilty both – the one to excuse the other? Did I not in that moment have the ear of God? Why was I sunk down to make the smallest snivelling figure that could be made? No pride, no dignity, tears not in single droplets but running in torrents down my cheeks, hands slack white together in my lap, and I shrunk in my own littleness, all spirit spent. I rose from my knees and straight to the study; tested a new quill on the coal-merchant's bill; took the bond, signed . . .

THE HANGING OF WILLIAM DODD

Chesterfield

. . . put sand on and blew it away.

I fell asleep at my desk.

Lewis Robertson the broker called at 10 o'clock in the morning and we went together to Sir Charles Raymond's Bank with the executed bond. Here Fletcher and Peach, merchants and partners in the bank and their lawyer Manley were ready with the money, but Peach quibbled that Robertson had not witnessed The Earl of Chesterfield's signature. He demanded him to sign now before releasing the money. Robertson hesitated and Fletcher said that therefore a new bond must be drawn up and taken to the Earl for signature and witnessed. I asked them on the Earl's behalf not to do such a thing – for I said as far as he was concerned the matter was of the greatest delicacy and he would not see any new faces or discuss it any further. Still Robertson hesitated despite learning that if he did not sign his £200 would fly out of the window.

I put pen to paper to write a covering letter with a new bond to Chesterfield. As the bank's messenger put out his hand for these I said, 'If this is sent the whole business will be overturned. The Earl will take such offence that we shall never hear from him again on the subject.'

Robertson signed and the money was handed over. I gave him half his commission and hurried back to Great Russell Street.

A news-crier on the way gave out that Lady Hertford was dead.

On the morning of Friday 7th February I rose earlier than was my wont, driven from my bed by an adder's nest of thoughts of my guilt, and of shame and I prayed for a long while in silence. When I had dressed – since it was my

intention to walk in the park before noon – I put on a sober
coat of deep blue over my brightest waistcoat and had
Hetty – as always – clean my blue shoes and shine their
buckles – for it was my sentiment to make this and all
subsequent days ordinary and commonplace – days
wherein I would by industry and proper observances
become a far better man than I had previously been, and
settle again to those tasks which I had always before-times
applied with virtue and completeness in their
performances. I prayed that I may never again be wrenched
from straight and narrow paths in the management of my
affairs by debt or extravagance, by rude lusts or ill-judged
behaviours of any kind.

Within the library, Weedon Butler played his
customary and peaceful part while the pen-sucking, brow-
puckering pupils – Nathaniel, Karl and James broke open
Latin verses and distributed the translated ruins of them
into English prose. Cheerful fires burned in the grates of
library and study so giving me excuse – restless as I was –
to go from one to the other poking and piling on more coals
as the devil stokes his furnaces. I composed in my head a
letter to The Earl of Hertford, and began the lines for my
next sermon – a eulogy of my dear Lady Hertford – to be
preached at The Magdalen Church on Sunday two days
hence. The very thought of this, my dear friend in her life,
brought quiet to the agitated mind and now at her death a
heavy stillness to the heart. I grieved with Hertford and
wrote to him that his wife would be lamented by all who
knew her, and that she, even after a lingering illness borne
without a murmur, continued to be a bright example of
fortitude and truly Christian resignation shining on all the
company wherever she went. I had this letter despatched to
the post boy together with one to confirm my presence that
evening at a dinner in Pall Mall where Chevalier Ruspini –
a man made rich by fashionable quackery – was
entertaining Casanova and Mrs Cornelys. It would not do
to fall out with Society merely because I was set on a new,

more righteous path. I did however with a new found
caution wonder how Casanova was greeted by *the ton* – for
it was said by some who knew Venice that he was well
versed and immersed in the immoralities of that city.
Perhaps hiding in the "immoralities" would protect
Casanova in his business as a spy to the Inquisitors of
State? The mere mention of spying heightened no doubt
the romantic interest already enveloping him.

Satisfied with so much achieved and fixed before noon,
I called for Josh to fetch the carriage round and while I
waited exchanged a civil word with Weedon and patted the
boys' heads. I addressed them:

Dodd: "'Omnia bona bonis" – what means that?' Karl:
'All things are good with good men.'

I congratulated Karl loudly to carry above the groans
and jeers of Nathaniel and James who said that Karl
cheated and had learned the phrase already.

Above the noise came the rattling of carriages drawing up
outside'. Anxious to begin my promenade, I seized my
cloak and threw open the door to reveal on the steps not
Josh but Manly and a constable and behind their coach
another from which descended Corry – whom I knew to be
The Earl of Chesterfield's solicitor – and Lewis Robertson
(the broker) and another constable. Manley (the merchant
bankers' lawyer) had hardly crossed the threshold when he
said,

'I regret the occasion, but it is on a charge of forgery
against you.'

An exclamation died in my throat, stopped by the same
shock that stunned my brain. I said nothing. A prayer
jumbled in my head . . . O
God . . . O help . . . Forgive . . .

'It was an urgent necessity,' I trembled hurrying to
speak while I opened the door to admit the rest of the party.
Josh, who had joined them, stood just inside the door
passing his whip nervously from hand to hand.

'But it was an urgent necessity,' I said again. 'I am hard pressed to pay some tradesmen's bills.'

'Robertson,' said Manley, indicating the broker standing close to his constable 'is on the same charge of forgery as you and lays it all upon you.'

I do not know why, perhaps seeking time to give better answer, or perhaps to gain an advantage in the presence of my imposing bookshelves and the scholars and their master, I ushered the crowd – Manley, Corry, Robertson and the two constables – into the library and stood before them as firm as my sagging knees allowed. Weedon Butler sat in a trance. Mary came and waited beyond the open door, listening.

'What could have induced you Dr Dodd to do such an act?' Manley looked at each of the men around him as I answered again:

'Urgent necessity. I will return all the money within three months. I have the means and I certainly meant no injury to Lord Chesterfield.' Robertson pulled away from his constable and pleaded:

'Dr Dodd I desire, please, please do declare my innocence before all present.'

'I do. I do. Most certainly I do.'

'Do you have any of the money to restore now?' Manley's voice took on a kindly coaxing tone:

'We have witnesses to certify all you say.'

'Yes, I have. In the study.'

I stepped towards it. The second constable looked to stop me but Manley said that he would go with me, which he did, holding in his hand the forged bond showing sums due.

I could not in detail total all the bills paid out of the £4,200 received – but remembered with alarm that £500 of it had yesterday settled an account long overdue. I drew up a bank draft on St James' Banking Company where, marvellously, there was sufficient in my account to bring the sum required up to £3,500. A further £600 was raised on furniture and books and other possessions in the house. Manley assured me that Robertson had already given a draught for £100 for his commission so far received. Manley then left the study, leaving the bond on my desk.

The bond on my desk! Should I not burn that? Would not that remove all evidence of my guilt? Or would it both prove and compound my guilt?

Manley re-entered my study while I hesitated and took the bond out with him.

I and all the gathering appeared to sigh a little and allow smiles to make appearances on their faces – except for the constables who were sullen, telling Manley and Corry that I and Robertson could not be set free of them until morning when the draughts written by us had been proved. An arrangement was made for all to meet at the York Coffee House on the morrow, and everyone left except for the constable who was put over me. He, a Mr Prosser, was made comfortable in the hall and fussed over by Hetty with a kindness she later said she regretted.

At the very crack of dawn, signalled again by the arrival of a coach, Mr Prosser broke into my chamber – and would have done so even if I had been in flagrante – demanding that I dress and come to the Guildhall immediately; no ceremony beforehand and no breakfast though Hetty had seen to his nourishment abundantly well. Mrs Dodd was to follow on after if she were inclined though it would be a long day, if he were any judge, and I must hurry now but – and also if he was any judge – after today I would have no need or chance to hurry. Prosser then pushed me into the coach like stuffing put into a chicken. This forced the occupants, Robertson and his constable into closer proximity which was intolerably increased when Prosser himself levered his great tree trunk legs and backside through the door. His body stank. He held up the great meat- plate of a hand that a few minutes ago had made onion and sage of me – I presumed this hand was to silence us or the carriage wheels while he spoke – not at all

necessary for us – dead men are no quieter than I and
Robertson at that moment. My terror was immense and
even in the half-dark the pallor of Robertson's face showed
under what horrid uncertainty he suffered.

'Mr Manley,' Prosser said, 'Mr Manly went yesterday
straight to the Lord Mayor's house and laid an information
of forgery against *you* and *you.'*
He stabbed with his finger near deep enough to pin us to
the seats . . . 'He done this for Mr Fletcher and Mr Peach
who 'as the most to lose from this villainy. You might not
be aware of it now but will do soon enough – you both will
be charged with a capital felony. The Lord Mayor Sir
Halifax signed the warrant of arrest and he's a better friend
of the gentlemen Mr Fletcher and Mr Peach than the old
Lord Mayor before him – that Mayor Wilkes – and any
such-like who side with Americky and not with The King.
So you'll be done for.'

Robertson's constable, who as far as I knew was dumb,
eased a knee free from Prosser's knees and nudged them
again and shook his head slowly through sufficient degrees
and back, to catch his eye and silence him.

At the Guildhall the Courtroom was already crowded. A
few faces were recognisable to me as members of the
nearby churches where I preached, but most were the idlers
and the curious who spilled out of the taverns as soon as
word came to them that there was business at the Guildhall
– exciting enough if to do with a clergyman and an Earl –
and that they might have news to impart widely before *The
Morning Post* and *The London Chronicle* had spread their
ink. The earliest comers – mostly vagrants and prostitutes
– had taken seats reserved for the public, and all the rest
stood – unless they were able to displace persons who kept
too loose a hold on their seats.

I stood gripping the rail in front of me, rigid with fear
and my tongue as dry as a burned crust.

I looked and failed to catch and plead to the eye of The

Earl of Chesterfield as he came in with his solicitor Corry by his side.

These and Fletcher and Peach and Manley sat opposite each other and much below Sir Thomas Halifax, the Mayor.

This official waited for silence and then opened with a harangue which took from him all possible measure of impartiality. He puffed out his cheeks and then his words toppled loudly over each other:

'Take heed, take – forgery – most dangerous crime – casts the vilest shadow – on the honour of every merchant, banker, and any of the countless good men who support . . . this great nation . . . commerce . . . nation . . . King . . . and it is the duty of . . .'

I begged Mr Prosser to intercede in some manner – to ask if proceedings might be held in private, but he looked at me as if I were already judged a criminal and had no rights.

'. . . the absolute imperative of everyone who can . . . to prosecute perpetrators of forgery and . . .' (had no one whispered to him the idea of a private hearing?) . . . 'and it must be done in public, in public, because forgery is, of all crimes, a public matter.'

Halifax's storm and foam abated and he turned quietly to Corry who was in discussion with Sturdy (O, my dear pupil!) as to whether as a peer of his rank he should give testimony on his oath or on his honour.

The Earl stood and held the court in silence for nearly a minute.

Finally he spoke and said:

'I insist that there should never be any appearance of irregularity and I will be sworn like everyone else on oath.'

He then gave his evidence as to the forgery of his signature and added (O, my dear, dear pupil!) that he saw no need for a prosecution.

Fletcher – of Fletcher and Pearce merchant bankers, partners in Sir Charles Raymond's Bank – followed the

Earl and said he too did not wish to prosecute.

He gave his evidence.

I was asked to stand and give my evidence though it was abundant clear to the crowd that no one had offered me a chair since I entered the court two hours before and now leaned weakly on the rail. What words I spoke may not have been audible and when my straining efforts to be level and calm in speech failed in a choke and I sobbed against my will, there were slight and similar sounds in the public gallery and on the floor of the court. I whispered that I had no intention to defraud, had already returned the money of which I had only temporary need; that I loved the Lord Chesterfield and that he would not forget my kindness to him and would wish to show clemency to me.

'Nobody wishes to prosecute me,' I said finally as loud as I could. 'Pray Lord Mayor dismiss me and Mr Robertson the broker who is entirely innocent.'

Sir Thomas Halifax had only puffed out his cheeks again in silent expostulation while I gave evidence, but now, releasing all the bottled-up affronts that he felt, he addressed the court: 'that any leniency seriously misguided . . . harm to the country . . . to the laws and therefore to society,' and then he glowered at Fletcher:

'Mr Fletcher, I wonder you should decline to prosecute – I should not hesitate a moment if I was in your case . . . the expenses will be trifling.'

This set up an argument at once between Manley for Fletcher and his Bank and Corry for Chesterfield as to who should pay for the case against me.

The matter was decided only when both parties agreed that neither should bear alone the cost – or the inhumanity – of the prosecution of a clergyman. At which point, Sturdy and Fletcher were bound over to prosecute.

I and Lewis Robertson were formally charged with forgery and bundled out of the court to the Wood Street Compter – the foulest debtor's prison in London – where I

fell thoughtless on to my cell's stone floor and remembered
nothing more.

CHAPTER 33

THE TRIAL

In The Compter; Gascoigne; John Wesley; The Old Bailey

I lay less than twenty-four hours in the filthy dungeon at the Wood Street Compter. Soon friends were alerted to the dreadful predicament I was in and which was likely, they thought, to cause my death. They paid the keeper to allow me to take residence in a large, new-built cell.

Porter brought beds for Mary and me and on his way passed directly by Great Russell Street where Hetty gave him a reading lamp and a cupboard and a set of damask curtains. These covered the cart to hide the desk which Barbara and he had given me before a happier journey to West Ham so many years ago.

Porter unloaded and arranged the furniture precisely before explaining that my sister, who had never supposed any right to my company when I was of some importance in London, could not now bear to see me suffering but would send food and drink and any small things that I might desire as long as I required them. Porter then spat and wept into his hands and wiped them and said that as soon as, and if, I was sent to Newgate to await trial he would transport everything to me there and any other comforts my other friends could not guarantee.

Brother Richard, now Rector of Cowley in Middlesex, wrote a long and tender letter proffering his prayers on a daily basis and sent a purse of £2 – which money being a tithe of more than two weeks of his yearly income, should have moved me to pity. Yet to my shame, like a child who cannot tell the worth of anything, but takes, I accepted Richard's gift and stored it about my person, I was not now living in a real world. I moved, I spoke, I lifted the Bible as though to read it; I smoothed my waistcoat and breeches;

464

adjusted my wig to sit perfectly; made sure that my hands were washed before eating; took a mouthful of food and left the table to pace the floor; addressed Mary or admitted some visitor who had paid the gaoler a few pence to be allowed to gape at me and who hoped that I would speak a few lines of Latin or quote from the Bible and smile and nod like an idiot in Bedlam. All these actions were credited to me; but there was no reasoning or truth behind them.

On the second day, Mary was reclining straight upon her bed, while Weedon Butler, good man, prayed with me and then indexed for me the actions to be taken and the people to be brought in to help. He asked my opinion about everything he suggested and then promised, without making me reply, that he would do faithfully what was agreed, even if I had not visibly nodded to him. I was starting about the chamber placing and replacing every object in it and barely knew what Weedon said.

Mary comforted me from her bed, made me stand still by it and took me in her arms and said times enough until she believed it:

'We shall shortly have doors opened to us which will never close,'

But Mary's strength ebbed daily. She stayed in her bed and let Weedon Butler call a physician who was very grave and sent out for a restorative that was "beneficial when the heart is pierced or broken" and said that I should do more than pray and pace the room but should administer the potion regularly on alternate hours and send for more when it was gone. Later I repeated his words to Mary. She said:

'And I shall never leave you. And I shall never leave you,' and quite forgot her medicine.

Weedon sent the first time for John Wesley, knowing that he was more akin to me in spirit than any living bishop or dignitary of the Church and while he was rejected by them he would not despise me in my distress. If he would come – whether or not he remembered our brief correspondence so many years ago – Weedon hoped that he would pray with me. Would Bishop Squires were still alive also to visit me and offer some counsel and a sound preferment on my release.

Gascoigne, an early caller, assured me that I should not wait long before being set at liberty. He would not bring me newspapers to let me read opinions for myself – for the newspapers were generally not favourable to me. They sought cruel justice even for a clergyman who was wronged by his accusers. For forgery, the newspapers said, was a felony deserving the death penalty which had been so rightly ordained by statute in 1729 – the very year of Dodd the malefactor's birth they said as if that made the penalty entirely just and suitable for me.

'Why do they say wronged by my accusers?' I asked Gascoigne.

'*Ipso facto et ipso jure,* by the facts and by the law itself. You returned the money. They kept the bond – the instrument by which they intend to send you to the gal . . .'

I could not let him say the word he was about to utter and I gave out a great shout of anger and I raged and hurled myself against the wall and beat my fists on the cold stones and the iron clad door until Mary called out to me:

'Be calm for we shortly shall have doors opened to us which will never close.'

'Quite so. Quite so,' said Gascoigne. 'Manley and Fletcher and Peach are driven to serve their own ends by fawning to Sir Charles Raymond, but they have no case in law for their prosecution. They have no evidence and no amount of their influence should persuade the

witness . . .'

'What witness?' I shouted. 'The Earl.'

'No. No. I cannot believe so. I will not believe the Earl, my pupil, my Sturdy. He will not give evidence against me.'

'Yes. It is rumoured so. To secure your conviction, the banker has guaranteed any future borrowing Chesterfield

466

may require – because you are a forger – which crime he says puts Sir Charles' reputation in particular, and the probity of all financial businesses in general, at the gravest peril. You should not frighten yourself nor weep on this account. Will you consent to Mr Howarth to conduct your defence? He is a very clever lawyer who secured convictions against Daniel Perreau and Mrs Rudd and he will have beside him two others to argue with him – Cowper also in the Perreau Case when he defended Mrs Rudd – and

Buller who is known to discover niceties in law that other counsels will never find.'

Gascoigne said much more and he talked legal Latin and made soothing predictions which only threw me further into Stygian depths of despair before raising me to Olympian high pinnacles of rage. I understood him as little as I understood myself and was tossed by my emotions until Gascoigne left and I, weeping and exhausted, fell upon my bed and slept.

Gascoigne came back with Howarth on the following day – late in the evening I think it was – unless this leaden February day was already dark at noon. They stood together to examine their papers, and then looked through the barred windows at the rooms where Lewis Robertson was confined.

'There is your answer,' said Howarth to me, 'Robertson.'

'Why? How so?'

'He is on the same charge as you, therefore cannot give evidence against you – *lex terrae,*' Gascoigne added, 'the law of the land.'

Mary was cheered by the news. Opening the curtains around her bed and framing her face in the folds she asked if it were really true that we could be found not guilty.

'Not we,' I said. 'You were never found wrong in this or in anything. I bear all the guilt.'

467

'It is all the same,' she said, 'because we are indivisible dear husband.'

Mary would have left her hiding to throw her arms about me had not modesty forbidden and therefore only one bare arm and hand were stretched out towards me. She touched my hand and I in a senseless gesture returned hers rejected to the bed. I said nothing and Howarth paused before speaking to me slowly like a father,

'You will be glad Dr Dodd. Although today a newspaper – leading others to be in your favour at last – has named you "The Unfortunate

Dr Dodd", your fortunes perhaps are in reverse. The trial is fixed for Saturday 22nd February and the rule is that the prisoner should be at Newgate six days before his appearance at The Old Bailey. Lord Halifax has insisted that rule is to be always followed exactly. He is now dismayed that Wardens and other respected members of your churches have joined in league with us and made him yield and allow you further time in the Compter – up to the eve of the trial. And we believe – not to our disadvantage – Robertson has been granted the same indulgence. As if he could be seen more clearly across the way, Howarth pointed to Robertson's figure outlined at his window:

'He might be seen to be rejoicing too.'

I did not express full torrents of pleasure at Howarth's news but supposed if he thought it good I must be satisfied, though I felt nothing in my heart. Howarth patted my shoulder while Gascoigne, good friend, shook my hand as if to press into that unresponsive member his own expressions of confidence in a happy outcome.

Had I been master, from my rooms at the Wood Street Compter, I would have thinned the crowds who assembled there every day and given appointed hours for each to visit. However, the keepers did keep back the tide of gapers who appeared when Mr John Wesley, after repeated requests from Weedon Butler, finally came to the Compter. His presence filled the room and left crowds outside. Howarth and Gascoigne – this day joined by Buller – looked as though they wished to stay but when after courteous enquiries as to everyone's physical health Mr Wesley dropped to his knees, I and Mary – who had snatched my cloak from a peg – followed suit, and the lawyers rustled papers and left. Mr Wesley led us in brief prayers and then listened while I confessed every sorrow and (almost) every sin and begged the Almighty for forgiveness saying, 'It is not as I will but as Thou wilt O Lord.'

'Amen,' said Mr Wesley. 'I do not doubt God will bring good out of evil.'

He took it that Mary was as frightened as I, and talked in quiet voice for a long while and listened with equal gravity when we spoke. The keeper, bringing in lighted candles, joined in The Lord's Prayer and asked a blessing of Mr Wesley as he left.

Howarth and Buller, who had spent this time in the keeper's room – where there was a better fire than in mine and no praying – came back with Gascoigne, who was in distress and repeating continually:

'Robertson is gone. Robertson is gone. He is to give evidence against us. Manley has obtained his release and taken him before the Grand Jury. It is certain that with Robertson as a witness they will decide there is sufficient evidence for a trial. By this one evil act by Manley, Robertson is no longer a prisoner – and is free to "prove" that all guilt lies upon our friend.'

Howarth and Buller made efforts to explain to me how stood the law on this point and what was Manley's crime. Robertson could not have been legally released from the Compter since prisoners to stand trial at
The Old Bailey must be in Newgate six days before. Only then an authority for release from Newgate could apply in law. Manley, knowing that the prosecution against me would fail without evidence from Robertson, had secured

the order for his release by confusing or tricking the Clerk of Arraigns at The Old Bailey into signing a warrant for Robertson's release, believing that he was already in Newgate.

'We ourselves should have done this before Manley,' said Gascoigne, 'and so secured the release of Dr Dodd for the Grand Jury would have found our case more sound than his.'

Howarth and Buller shook their heads and said that to do so was just as much a criminal offence as forgery and added:

'The trial will decide this before all else, but if The Grand Jury has ignored the illegality of Robertson's release, we hold out no great prospect of our success at The Bailey – but we still shall endeavour to change opinions.'

I was tossed into an even deeper pit of impotence and despair. Neither the legal reasoning of Howarth and Buller nor the reassuring Latin of Gascoigne, nor the comfort of Mr Wesley's "God will bring good out of evil", could lift me out of despondency. Throughout this night, Thursday 20th of February, I slept not at all, knowing that on the morrow I was to be taken to Newgate ready to stand trial next day on the Saturday, 22nd of February. Mary, who was the echo of all my sentiment, wept and smiled and held my hand tightly and silently as if she could keep my hand even when I was separated from her.

More than my conscience and deep regrets kept me from sleep and although my cell had only a little less space than earlier at the Compter, it had not Mary, and my loneliness was intense. She at a nearby lodging house, I did not doubt, was as sleepless as I, for a wakening wind blew across the whole city taking smoke and soot from the chimney pots and dashing it with rain through every window crack and into every lung. In my cell the wind shrieked through bars and shutters and, blowing in the grate, quarrelled with its fellow wind in the chimney to make noises like a piped organ and to throw white ashes in the air.

Six o'clock sounded with the warder striking the bolts back on my door to hasten me through for a prison breakfast. The warders had been told to take me early to The Bailey before crowds appeared – but we were too late.

"Oh, we have had crowds before,' said one warder. 'Mrs Rudd drew nearly as many – but that was on a Friday. Your fame Dr Dodd and the good fortune of a Saturday for your trial has brought many more.'

If I had thought that the spectators at the Guildhall a fortnight before were the greatest number to be gathered together on my account, I was quickly obliged to change my opinion. Every approach to the Old Bailey was shoulder to shoulder with people of every description, all dirty, battered by wind and sleet and all determined to enter the building and take a seat. Ruffians dressed as officials of the court took money from those who had it and pushed others back into the street. My guardians, with the cunning of experience, made me offer money to the official ruffian guarding our private entrance. Pushing behind us were law students in their coloured gowns and hoods and with their wigs and clothing awry and stained and wet from the elements. They argued with the door keepers saying that it was the regular and legal custom – and only recently confirmed again – that gave up a whole gallery free to students of the law. Some – rich and disloyal to their companions – paid two guineas and were admitted and seated in the body of the court. The rest left in packs, searched out other doors, broke them open, appeared triumphant in their gallery, took the official who had attempted to block them on the stairs and heaved him back down the very same steps, collecting the "immoral coin" that fell from his pockets – "justifiably" they said and by "legal confiscation". Other students enquired of each other for precedents and failing to find answers said that "the guardian was a robber and would commit further crimes beyond this one and when he crept back needing a lawyer

– then it may well be one of us who will be able to regard today's money as a down payment on a future charge."

More discussion of this sort amongst the law students was overtaken as the trial began.

I was called and stood to say that the indictment was an evidence improperly obtained – Robertson as well as I should be prosecuted – and if not, I should not plead. Then, while I remained standing, there began a disputation between the lawyers: Howarth, Buller and Cowper for my defence and two whose names I did not catch supporting Mansfield (he not related to the Lord Chief Justice Mansfield whose courts were the House of Lords and The King's Court of Privy Councillors). These men for the prosecution troubled their wigs with a great deal of scratching while they searched for nice points of law, and were slow and deliberate in their speeches and looked frequently to the gallery of students to solicit admiration for their cleverness. There was little admiration forthcoming, however, because late risers from the schools of law were still breaking into the court and climbing noisily to the gallery. There was compelling reason for me to try to follow the lawyers' quibbles but I could not. Their talk was incomprehensible, was tedious, was tortuous, was an exhibition only of themselves, and it became a necessity for me to look elsewhere about the courts to feel the reality of my situation. The Reverend Weedon Butler, dear amanuensis, with fresh-starched Geneva-tabs at his neck, came to my side and pointed out other – he supposed comforting figures – in the crush. Gascoigne was edging himself near to the opposing tables of lawyers to hear them better. He had Bulkley in tow. I whispered:

'Was he not to be barred from attendance as Gascoigne had intimated?'

'He could not be barred from such a performance in such a theatre,' Weedon said. 'Gascoigne has relented but extracted a promise that Bulkley will stay at his side throughout the day and be of perfect conduct.'

Thrusting themselves with importance upon the scene, The Fifth Earl of Chesterfield and his retinue of lawyers settled at their table and not a single pair of their legal eyes spared a glance at me now or during the whole day long. But other eyes beneath a bonnet and shrinking against a column as though to hide, were those of the woman I had seen many times at The Charlotte Chapel in Pimlico – and where else before? The Magdalen? St James Park? Or even years before that – an unplaceable memory of deep saphire eyes. Weedon brought my attention back to the centre of the court; Counsel for the prosecution – Mansfield – was attempting to shorten the lawyer's arguments:

'There is no argument,' he said. 'A true bill has been found to make the case against the prisoner.

He would have continued, directing himself to Judge Baron Perryn Gould on the Bench, but his colleagues at the opposing tables did not wish matters to end so soon.

Buller spoke: 'No permission was granted for Robertson to appear before the Grand Jury, and since that body meets in secret, we do not know what was said. For legal purposes, therefore, Robertson has never been before a Grand Jury, and cannot give evidence.'

To and fro counsels debated for another hour or more when the Judge, speaking for his fellow Judges, offered the prosecution a postponement of the trial while they prepared a new indictment – in which case they would bear the cost of both this and the postponed trial; or he said the trial could continue today and have the question about Robertson's evidence settled by the twelve Assize Judges at a further date. Mansfield did not hesitate. He was sure of his point, his clients did not wish to waste money or time, and he was certain that there was no possibility that if I were found guilty today, those twelve Judges would find Robertson's evidence inadmissible and acquit me. Therefore, he begged to insist that the trial continue and finish today.

Suddenly, Bulkley jumped up from his seat and

shouted that: 'Mansfield is wrong in law and reason, and Manley is guilty with Fletcher and Peach, and Sir Charles Raymond – proved by their attempt to throw all blame on The Reverend Dr William Dodd to disguise their own illegal rates of interest upon a loan which had anyway been repaid.'

Gascoigne dragged Bulkley back onto his seat and put an arm round him, as a restraint, rather than what he hoped would appear to Bulkley as a sign of affection and congratulation on a speech well spoken.

The Judge thumped for order, called for the indictment to be read and the trial to proceed.

I was sagging over the rail, having been standing now for three hours, and when Weedon asked that I may sit and leave was granted, I blessed him silently and held my knees against their trembling. Weedon passed me pencil and paper stiffly folded for any notes I wished to make.Mansfield opened for the prosecution by begging the jury to consider only matters brought to their attention in this court – they were to dismiss anything the newspapers had said about me, since *they* were inclined to re-tell every piece of gossip favourable to me. (I wondered if he would have so instructed the jury had the newspapers been heavily against me.) He then, like a Garrick bringing on his actors, called Lord Chesterfield to the stand. When the consequent loud murmuring and a spattering of applause had died, this young man whom I loved and to whose education and welfare I had devoted years of my crowded life, said straight and out loud that the signature *"Chesterfield"* on the bond was not his, repeated it was not his and looked boldly round the court to have his rectitude and truthfulness admired. Although he had nothing further to say, he still was reluctant to leave the stand and stood swelling his chest until Manley, being called up by Mansfield, gently elbowed him off. Manley's account was largely of what I had said before I was arrested but he gave no supporting facts nor did Mansfield bring any witnesses to support him. Had witnesses been hard to find? Or unwilling to appear against me? Or had they all asked for too much money to be witnesses? Did the fat constable who had guarded me come with too high a price for Fletcher, Peach and Sir Charles Raymond? Surely not.

At this point and for an instant I thought to plead "not guilty". But that would be an absurdity. I knew I was guilty. My knees, which had ceased trembling for a moment, started up again and the flicker of rising hope went down to the abyss once more.

Robertson was called to give evidence and he put all blame categorically on me – he who was put on the same charge as me turned by trickery to give against me; Manley nodded his head and smiled.

Mr Howarth rose for a final attempt to secure my release:

'There is a matter about a blot. The word "seven" in the bond was blotted and illegible. This was not mentioned in the indictment which was therefore imperfect. Dr Dodd has been accused of an offence which differs to some degree from the offence now made against him.

Therefore in law this indictment should be rejected and the case dismissed.'

The scholar lawyers began arguing amongst themselves while the prosecuting lawyers remained impassive.

I was called to offer my defence.

Mr Howarth had warned me to be nothing but what I am – to put up no pretence of greater knowledge than the Jurymen – and much less knowledge than any lawyer – and to use my powers of oratory, if any were left in me, with humility. This congregation was similar to congregations anywhere, but the pulpit was not mine and the court room not my church and it was a forbidding place; my address would not end with my blessing or a sacrament: it would end with twelve critical opinions agreed to advise the judge, Baron Perryn Gould, to pronounce my innocence or guilt.

THE TRIAL

Silently, I rose to my feet and prayed to myself, 'May the words of my mouth and the meditation of my heart be now and always acceptable in Thy sight, O Lord, my strength and my Redeemer.'

I fixed my eyes on Sturdy and for the first time in this court and for the last time in both our lives I drew his eyes to mine as I said in a loud clear voice:

'I do not deny that I forged the bond, but I have repaid it.' Slowly, I turned before the judge and the court officials:

'My Lord, I humbly apprehend, although I am no lawyer, that the moral vileness and obnoxious nature of the crime of forgery in the eyes of the law, religion and reason lies in the intention to defraud. The act itself under which I am charged says forgery with an intention to defraud. I believe this has not been proved upon me and I made full amends on the instant that I did wrong, so that no injury real or intended has been done to any man on earth. Do not these circumstances demand clemency?

'In this court, before you Judge and Jury, I have been received with fairness, but it has not been so outside where I have been treated with cruelty and even oppressively prosecuted at first despite the firmest agreement, and finally after the most soothing assurances from Mr Manley when Robertson was admitted as a witness against me.

'I am so sunk by the infamy about me and loaded with distress that I cannot think life a matter of value to me anymore and death to be preferable and a blessing for me.'

It was without any theatrical attempts to work myself into tears – words came out of my guilt, my grief, my confusion and I wrung my hands fiercely to hurt them more than the hurt in my mind. A few women – some I thought by their grey habits to be from The Magdalen – began to sob, and the spectacle of their tears and mine moved men in the jury to wipe their eyes. Weedon stood up to comfort me and said,

'Oh dear Doctor Dodd, dry your eyes. See how much

476

affected we all are.' I gathered myself together again and said to the jury:

'But there are reasons why I ought to stay alive – my wife – who has been an exemplar of fidelity and conjugal attachment for twenty seven years – needs me. There are creditors – honest men – who will lose by my death. I have never had the intention to defraud, and hope for mercy for them and me . . .'

The scholar lawyers began arguing amongst themselves, while the prosecuting lawyers remained impassive.

Judge Baron Perryn moved to his summing up. My eyes rested bleakly and as if without sight as he addressed the jury with a sneer about my speech:

'You may give due weight to Dr Dodd's words,' he said, 'but they amount to little more than sentiment and tears. You will listen to his plea that he had no intent to defraud – yet every crime has a criminal intent unless it can be proved there is none. The prisoner gives no evidence but only his solemn assurances that he did not intend to defraud . . .'

For an interval I heard only snatches of what the Judge said, for I was preoccupied with the heavy sense of my failure before the court.

'. . . If you believe it was not the word "seven" beneath the blot, but some other word – you must acquit . . . Remember, Dr Dodd has not made complete restitution of the money despite his fine and pathetic word . . . he has, however, confessed to the forgery and there are witnesses to confirm it . . .You must now decide the facts.'

The jury hurried out as if to complete an unpleasant business quickly, and they returned after only a short time, slowly, some sobbing openly, the rest damp-eyed. The foreman choked as he said:

'Guilty,'

Into the silence that followed the lone rough voice of a

man cried out 'Hurrah' and he clapped his hands and instantly received the angry, roaring and hissing abuse of everyone around him and the glares of al the scholar lawyers in the adjoining gallery. The foreman said, clear above the crowd's noise:

'The jury humbly recommends the prisoner to His Majesty's mercy and will this night present a petition to that effect.'

I repeated to Weedon what I had said in my defence, as though he could change the Judge's mind even so late and after the guilty verdict had been given:

'But there are reasons why I ought to stay alive – my wife – who has been an exemplar of fidelity and conjugal attachment...."

The scholar lawyers began arguing again amongst themselves, while the prosecuting lawyers remained impassive.

Judge Baron Perryn dismissed us all.

It was past four o'clock when officials, bringing in lighted candles, were waived away by the judge, he as anxious as the jury to be gone. Weedon was joined by Gascoigne and Bulkley and the three of them lifted me from where I had sunk back. They and the accompanying gaolers returned me to Newgate.

Ballad singers offering their one-penny sheets stood outside the doors of the Old Bailey, and on the street corners they sang my past history and my sorrowful prospects for the future. Mary, who had spent the day in her lodging, heard that the trial was ended and awaited me in my room.

She knew the verdict without telling and temporarily strengthened by my weakness – for I was nigh collapsed – arranged the room and fetched food and drink and my father's prayer book. Gascoigne explained to me that the

Twelve Judges had to decide the legality of my case – in particular Robertson's admission to give evidence – and would not sit until they came back from their Assizes two months from now.

Gascoigne left, saying that I would not be transferred to the condemned cell until the Judges' decision was made. He thought two months or more remained before I would know the verdict.

CHAPTER 34

A CROWDED CHAPTER

In Newgate; Before the end at Tyburn;
Many good people do not desire my death

Now that my memory has at least partly returned it is
crowded with incidents, prayer and the rising and falling of
hope – all of which makes past suffering trivial in
comparison.

It was not God or the Fates that had conspired to bring
me to this place, but I myself who had conspired against
myself while God looked on. So in my prayers I searched
to find the means of rescue from my mind and my
impoverished soul – and to know perhaps what distraction
might occupy and even restore my faculties:

"The lunatic, the lover and the poet
Are of imagination all compact;
One sees more devils than hell can hold:
This is the madman . . . as imagination bodies forth
The form of things unknown, the poet's pen
Turns them to shapes and gives to airy nothing
A local habitation and name,"

Whereas even in my most vainglorious moments, I
could not pretend to dip my pen into the same inkpot as the
Bard and bring forth verse as great as his, I decided that
with care and earnest application to the task I could better
the ballads I had heard in the streets and might bring out in
epic form the kernels of both my happy and my sorrowing
life so far.

These thoughts were suitable to a Sunday – the first day
of my confinement as a convicted felon – and as Mary
arranged the linen carried over from Great Russell Street
and her lodgings, I read aloud my first *Thoughts in Prison*

– so far for her ears only.

No congregation lent me better ears, and Mary urged me to write regularly and recite to her as often as I could. My voice, she said, was the only music she wished to hear and bid me read on – to recall the peaceful fields and woods of West Ham and Sundays there to which:

"We owe at once the memory of thy works . . . We owe
divine religion, and to those . . .
The decent comeliness of social life."

It was the second Sunday at Newgate when Bulkley and Gascoigne joined Weedon Butler in my room. The latter had been with me for an hour or more and had remained almost invisible while I declaimed my verses to Mary – he only indicating his presence by the nodding approval of his head. Bulkley, when he came, was inclined to applaud me but each time he began to do so, lost the moment and the line admired and so let his hands fall to his sides again. Gascoigne fidgeted and continually rustled the newspapers he had brought to such an extent that I, thinking that he disapproved of me or my verses, was on the point of stopping.

At that moment Captain Thicknesse arrived as though he had been here only yesterday. The look on his face was immediately a plain indication of several matters: one (in his first greeting) that no other voice could match his for volume and sonorous elegance; two, my dress – for my purple cloak (for warmth) and smartest waistcoat (to cheer me) put his attire (worn out in battle) to appear exceedingly dilapidated. He made apology and begged my pardon for interrupting "the recitation of Shakespear or similar work" – for which unintentional compliment I forgave him everything else – and then he explained his "grievous disappointment" at failing to arrive a week or so earlier to speak for me at the trial:

'I have been, as you may imagine, fully occupied with a necessary journey to the Indies followed by a short stay in France. And there, by the by, I had good recommendation of your character – not that I needed any further report of that – but it was with regard to your kindness to an unfortunate gentleman by the name of M le Blanc, and . . .' he said, beginning by degrees of trial and error to find and occupy the least uncomfortable seat . . .'I should say also reports of an equally favourable nature the help you have given to friends of an American gentleman by the name of Franklin.'

Captain Thicknesse tapped the side of his nose, winked, and made a shushing noise before raising a salute in my direction that had more vigour than accuracy. Then he said without rising:

'I am at your service. The last time we met – I believe over the case of Lieutenant Nathanial Bunting in The King's Bench prison – I averred that you should always have a friend in me whatever your need might be. That need I learned when I landed at Dover. It is most dire. Have comfort, for you are a fine preacher – though less fine as a poet,'

The Captain smiled indulgently at me and in so doing, to my disappointment, now acknowledged me, not Shakespear, as the author of my declaimed verses. He returned to the subject of me as a preacher:

'You are a fine preacher and a benefactor to many of the poor yet are convicted of forgery.'

He shook my hand repeatedly so that I should know that I was to receive his support and congratulations for various matters and show, it seemed, that he did not despise me as much as I did now despise myself for the act of forgery.

Bulkley, who had been patiently waiting beside me, sensing that a breach in Thicknesses' flow of words might not be a frequent occurrence, now stepped in to introduce himself and Gascoigne to Weedon Butler and Mary, and then addressed me briefly before leaving:

'Dodd – despite the Captain's suggestion – I believe

you should declaim your verses aloud. We always said you were fit for pulpit or stage – and you will feel better if your voice is loudly heard. Apart from that, it will occupy your time while we look for measures that will improve your lot – and principally – if it can be done – to win you an appeal.'

Despite having the field clear for his own further pronouncements Thicknesse now left after several winking and nose tapping assurances to indicate that he would be back.

Whether my mood was dark or less than dark I was vulnerable at this time to all suggestions and willing and thankful to be sustained by the words and actions of my friends who, if that had been possible, would have taken all cares from my shoulders.

Mary did not leave my side but once, when depressed in health and timid as she was, on leaving Newgate and returning from Great Russell Street to the prison, she was pursued by a crowd of newspaper men, as a wounded deer fleeing the huntsmen. So my prison was now her sanctuary and she made no complaints about the unremitting din that filled it and she welcomed, too, the sound of me ranting my epics to the walls.

Even the nights were not left entirely to the silent moon, for St Sepulchre's mournful bell tolled midnight for the condemned who awaited death on the morrow. Frequently, at this doleful reminder of the fate which I may soon endure, I rose from my bed and by the economic light of one candle, wrote letters of appeal and verses for my friends and words of exhortation for the comfort and improvement of the minds of malefactors sharing their fate under the common roofs of Newgate – and I hoped perhaps in other prisons throughout the Kingdom.

If I needed any prompts to have me step down from lofty aspirations with the pen before the month of March was out, Captain Thicknesse brought unwelcome news from Great Russell Street – and more accurately – from the auction held there by John Barton of Covent Garden.

This sale of all my household contents spread over three days had been well – I say too well – advertised in the newspapers, and was being industriously presented by Mr Barton on the instructions of Mr Manley – that sly and smooth and treacherous toadeater who had not waited for the appeal in my case, but had acted – with a haste I thought indecent – to protect Fletcher and Peach and Sir Charles Raymond and himself by raising immediate cash on my property. How their interests were guarded and all mine exposed, was revealed by Thicknesse in a graphical account to me of the day preceding the public auction.

To accommodate the press of snoopers, viewers and would-be buyers, my home was turned inside out in disregard of rain, sleet, snow, frost and rain again. Furniture and ornaments, books, pictures, and curtains, kitchen-pots, ointments and balms from the toilet tables, two-light cut glass chandeliers upon their brackets (broken), pier glasses and girandoles, an assortment of rugs – two Persian and some others, historical prints (frames broken, glass cracked) *et cetera, et cetera* – was all spilled out of the house and onto the steps and pavement.

Amidst this scene Manley had heaved a locked and bound chest – in which many of my private documents and letters had previously been kept safe – broken open the lock and with the chest supported on two neat Indian chairs, and he standing on a third, plucked out letters and read out what he considered savoury tit-bits to a band of people gathered around. Once the papers were, in Manley's view, delivered of all their interest or the audience was becoming bored, he let the leaves flutter to the ground or into the greedy hands stretched out to catch them. So was lost a poem of mine – *Lines to My Lady Hertford* – said Thicknesse. But he and an older man – who by the Captain's description was my sister's husband, Porter – snatched and retrieved what letters they could before they dragged the chest back into the house and bound it up again.

Thicknesse was not clear as to whether he had bought the chest by private treaty then, or at the auction, or not at all. In any event as soon as he had finished his account his interest waned and he looked at me, as he said, "for another piece of work" to which he might give his attention.

The object of such attention was not far away. The room next to mine had occupants at least one of whom Thicknesse deemed more fair than he hoped to find in a prison, and he bribed a keeper and paid the prisoners to be allowed admission to them. Mrs Thomas – a plain French woman without money, had married an equally improvident Welshman and in an effort to repair temporarily their damaged financial state, Mrs Thomas had forged a money order with the signature of a clergyman. He refused to witness against her as he was "an interested party". She left all arguments about this to her prison partner, Miss West, a famous pickpocket known to her many friends and to the newspapers, as "Jenny Diver".

Here, according to Captain Thicknesse, was a different set of petticoats with a sharp mind above them – although some doubted that sharpness, seeing the very fruitful bulge within the petticoats – until they recalled that there might be some leniency shown in the court room if her gravid state conquered hearts as powerfully as did her voluptuous charms. Mrs Thomas at least was won over to Miss West at once and became her chamber maid and promised to be her mid-wife too.

Thicknesse had, it appeared to the gaolers who commented widely upon it, a very physical interest in these two women and rolled his eyes and kissed their hands on his arrival and departure. Gascoigne, consulted by him on legal matters pertaining to the two women, had a much more thoughtful interest – which partly allayed my annoyance that he now, as well as Thicknesse, spent more time with Mrs Thomas and Miss West than with me.

Gascoigne read the newspapers with very great thoroughness – whereas of which papers he now brought me I read only the columns where my name was mentioned – he followed all legal reports closely. He said that The Reverend Mr Tutte, whose signature was forged by Mrs Thomas, had stood to be himself a loser – as the money order was made against him – and so "had an interest" and could not be a witness against her. Some newspapers, Gascoigne reported, gave charity as Mr Tutte's only reason for refusing to witness against Mrs Thomas and thereupon Gascoigne enquired more deeply into the case to discover if the law that applied to the Reverend Mr Tutte might also be applied to The Earl of Chesterfield; but found no good news from it since it was a fact that the Earl did not have to bear a loss – Fletcher and Peach and Sir Charles Raymond carried the risk of loss – and therefore the Earl was right in law to have taken the stand and to have witnessed against me.

There was no comfort in this for me and my anxiety thereby was increased as I awaited the appeal. Thicknesse attempted mollification by telling me that Miss West and poor Mrs Thomas asked him if the unfortunate Doctor Dodd was preaching sermons all day long in his room, and if they might be admitted to hear him – for to miss such a famous clergyman would be the greatest disappointment. When Thicknesse told them, 'No, Doctor Dodd recites poetry,' they replied that it was a bitter shame it was not sermons being preached because they would have made a little entertainment in a place that was short of even slight and passing pleasure.

Of a certain, there were few pleasures for me while I awaited a decision from the Twelve Judges. If I slept – head drooping over my arms on the desk – it was only to awake to horrors and to have my imprisonment mocked by the cooing of stock doves and the twittering and flashing of goldfinches in the sunlight beyond the window bars. With my mind so much turned inwards, it were a marvel that even these birds caught my attention – and would not have done so I am sure if they had not been such potent reminders of my beloved West Ham.

Weedon Butler tried to cheer me by bringing affectionate greetings and money from his fellow clergy – all like he in the lower orders and saving pence and yet being as generous with their pence as the crowds at Galilee who offered loaves and fishes. No Bishop, no higher clergy or any of the well beneficed, responded to Weedon's requests – indeed a few of these allowed themselves to be quoted in the newspapers, giving unfavourable comments on me and the crime that I had committed. Yet as the public clamour grew in my favour, the newspapers printed more letters and ballads that put me in a good light so that Butler and Gascoigne and Bulkley and Thicknesse were encouraged to raise petitions and persuade others to the same purpose and to write to the newspapers on my behalf. Released debtors were the first publicly to recognise the good that I had achieved in founding their Society.

"Four thousand debtors," the newspaper's wrote, "have been set free from prison so far and should not then also their deliverer The Reverend Dr Dodd be spared?" I had cause anew to bless West Ham when their parishioners drew up a petition and commanded newspapers to tell that the congregations of West Ham and Plaistow recognised the true worth of the "unfortunate Dr Dodd who is a preacher beyond excellence for the good of all congregations."

The Society for the Release of Debtors took up a cry again listing the numbers of debtors released each week of my imprisonment: "fifteen mechanics restored to their families and to public utility in the first week, and twenty-five the next." The weekly tally continued, and as Thicknesse said as he brought in newspapers to me:

'The Morning Chronicle, The London Chronicle, The

A CROWDED CHAPTER

Morning Post, The Gazetteer and The Gentleman's Magazine – they are all stoking up each other to make the largest blaze there has ever been for one man – and he a parson, which is extraordinary; look at this . . .'
Thicknesse tore out a page reporting an appeal from *The Humane Society for the Resuscitation of Persons Apparently Drowned,* and read:

'Thousands have been saved from a watery grave by your efforts Reverend Gentleman,' before saying, 'It matters not that this is hyperbolical, you should rise from your miseries Dr Dodd and be grateful for the newspaper gentlemen. What is fact – is known that: 127 people were snatched from the grave by the methods of the Humane Society between May '74 and May '77.'

As April had turned to May my friends asked me to find others – but greater names than they recalled – to speak on my behalf, to write letters or appeals in court or sermons that I may have printed and circulated under my name; for my friends said that in my present state I was not the best ambassador in my own cause.

It was Bulkley in particular who lauded my performance as preacher and as an actor, yet limited his praise for my written words and recommended a Mr Cumberland who had written something for the Perreaus at their trial to write an appeal for me. Such a suggestion caused me to think harder and Dr Johnson came to mind. Bulkley, of course, thought this not to be a good idea: calling to his memory only the height and weight of a man, whose numerous ticks, popped-out-sideways eyes and booming voice lent a strange character to his performances regularly made outside theatres when criticising the players within. No, Bulkley would not recommend such a rival to his own ill behaviour and did not comprehend the least part of Dr Johnson's intellect. He agreed at length, however, to speak to Mr Allen a printer known to us, who lived in Boult Court next door to the great lexicographer himself.

Dr Johnson not remembering our slight acquaintance many years before and making no mention of my successes with the pen – nor The Literary Club's disagreeable failure to grant me admission – Dr Johnson immediately, as soon as asked by Mr Allen, put his vast talents at my disposal.

I shall not dwell on all he wrote and did for me in speaking to others and bending them to my cause, since always he gave freely the words he put into my mouth, and bade me never to name him as the donor. Had I been his equal he would have told me straight his opinion of my transgression and shown me none of the pity that he spent on me.

My desperate state grew worse as the month of April had progressed, for word was sent by an officer of the Court that the Twelve Judges had made their decision on the legality of Robertson's admission as a witness – but that the decision itself, the Tipstaff said, was to remain a secret closeted with the Judges until next they met for the May Sessions at the Old Bailey. At my distress, Weedon said that he thought the Court's intention was benign and was to reassure me that my case was not forgotten but for me this further fragment in my uncertainty drove me more furiously into the mental turmoil which my friends were at a loss to alleviate. They then redoubled their efforts to aid me.

Weedon asked Mr Wesley to come again to pray with me. Gascoigne wrote letters to the newspapers and Thicknesse appealed in every coffee house and tavern and at every table where he had secured an invitation. Mrs Cornelys was one of these and persuaded the company to raise petitions or put their signatures to others. My woeful circumstances were told on every tongue in town, while Dr Samuel Johnson devoted all his energies now to swaying opinions towards me and pleading my case still more fervently wherever there were eyes to read or ears to hear.

Bulkley, my dear friend, was also earnest in making endeavours on my behalf. He was at first at a loss to know how he might do so. Then in not knowing how, he hit upon the very business that was to give me such encouragement for an instant – and he hoped possibly in later times would ease countless others who were victims of a barbarous justice.

Bulkley, it appeared, had not been amused by the new playwright Sheridan's *The School for Scandal*. In truth, Bulkley maintained he had been dealt a double disappointment on this first night, for he could not remember any comedy that had offered him so little at which to laugh and yet was not so disagreeable that he was forced to rise from his seat and bellow disapproval to the stage. Had the playgoers been less silly in their laughter and applause, Bulkley swore he would have slept through the entire play. He therefore vowed to leave theatres alone for a space.

However by a connection not obvious to his friends, Bulkley decided that a seat in Parliament might suit him better. Thus to survey this scene, of what he was certain would be further triumphs for him, he visited that august establishment the following evening.

He was mightily impressed with the simplicity of the setting and, I believe, only prevented from an outburst of applause at the speeches by the very solemnity and subtlety of the arguments he strained to follow. A Bill had been brought in to make it a capital offence to set fire to any ships or warehouses – only the King's ships and yards being so far punishable by death. It was clear amongst the majority in the House that to put another capital offence in the statute book was to make a fine and honourable piece of legislation.

Sir William Meredith rose to oppose. He found no exception in the Bill, he said, if he could be persuaded that death was at all useful in the prevention of crimes, but this he questioned. The grisly toll at Tyburn grew every year; the more crimes were punishable by death, the more those crimes were committed. Even so, only one in twenty convicts was hanged, the rest escaping by exploiting legal technicalities. As it was, the law was despised, whereas with a lesser number of crimes carrying the penalty of death, the law would be feared and obeyed. Sir William piled up the arguments and I do not know how Bulkley was held back from cheering him to the rafters when, as he said, he had drawn such warm conclusions from the speech. As the Member of Parliament left the chamber Bulkley detained him and begged him to intercede for me. Sir William acknowledged the debt he owed to my sermon on hanging which he had heard and read, and for that reason alone he was determined to review my situation; he said he thought the law hard on me and said he would also continue his battles in the House, but had no other powers to help. Although I asked Bulkley to be clearer in his account and to expand the arguments for me and to press Sir William again for help. His only response was to say that one day the law would change and such as I would no longer be trapped by it.

Bulkley said he was quite enamoured with the idea of a seat in Parliament for it had "more dignity than the theatre and was never trivial," and he left me unvisited for several days while he pursued his intention in this direction.

However, Bulkley and Gascoigne and Thicknesse were about when early on the morning of 14th of May I was taken to a side room at the Old Bailey where the Twelve Judges were to deliver their verdict.

Weedon Butler had been sent for and arrived to stand with me while Sir Richard Acton told me with great tenderness that Robertson's evidence – however obtained – was legally had, and thereupon I was convicted according to the law.

'This decision is told you now so that you may be prepared for the consequent sentencing at the end of the Session.'

His voice and Weedon's face revealed the truth even if Sir Richard's words themselves had not been understandable.

'I thank your Lordships,' I replied. 'I am obliged for your candour and submit to your judgement.'

There was nothing more I could say for feelings rose in my chest to cut off breath and the power of speech. Neither did Weedon speak as he helped me from the stand and with my gaolers took me back to Newgate. So early in the morning there were few onlookers to see me but a Crier making his way home called out encouragement to me and enquired of a gaoler what the verdict and when the sentence, to receive the reply, 'Guilty and to be sentenced the day after tomorrow.' The gaoler quickened his steps, hurrying me stumbling into Newgate. As I entered my room I heard a baby crying in the next, and the voices of midwife-felon Mrs Thomas and mother-felon Miss Jenny Diver making happy cooing sounds above it.

Mr Allen the printer brought next day a speech written out by Dr Johnson that I "might find of purpose when before the court for sentence." The good man said he supposed it was to be too great an occasion to call out the best eloquence in a speaker and that I might more easily read it out or otherwise make use of such parts of it as would bend the hearts of the court to mercy. I did all day and night make efforts to commit the speech to memory but for all the repetition and thumping at my head, only snatches of Dr Johnson's lines stayed fixed. Was this to be my lot tomorrow – whatever the sentence passed – my memory, most prized possession, shattered into a thousand fragmental pieces? How these and other thoughts of my brain's decay intruded. There was no peace; I did not pray for fear the time so spent was lost in learning; I ate nothing and drank nothing and was too mad to weep, so that when daylight came the gaolers found me grounded in a corner as rigid as the walls and it took the force of both men heaving at me to fetch me to my feet and then had I been free to grip the door posts the gaolers could not have fetched me out except for dear Weedon coaxing me like a child and saying again and again, 'God is merciful. God is merciful. All is not yet lost. All is not yet lost,' and 'Outside the prison see this crowd – this tumult is for you, they are praying for you and surely their God and ours will hear and be merciful.'

Forgive me, forgive me, I doubted. I doubted that there is a God. I doubted that this great crowd was here to hope for any sentence other than death.
And so it was.
The day was warm.
Doors and windows in the court were opened. The Clerk of Arraigns stood.
I stood.

'Dr William Dodd, you stand convicted of forgery. What have you to say why this court should not give you judgement to die according to law?'
Now trembling and then with great effort holding myself erect and then again stooped and overcome with humility, I took Dr Johnson's speech clumsily from a pocket and holding it at first still folded, spoke:
'My lord, I now stand before you a dreadful example of human infirmity . . .'
I spoke and sometimes read, mumbling so softly that only by watching the uncertain movements of my lips could the court know that I was speaking; and each person leant forward to hear as if towards a child in distress. I could not say how long the speech – how long the court's attention – but there was no move to stop me. I sensed the sympathy of the court was due to me now since I had only a short time to claim an audience.

So quiet I spoke, few can have heard my sorrow at the weaknesses and failings of my life, nor been reminded of the charitable works that I had done.

But I raised my head at last and looked to the judge and begged,

'for a little life be allowed me – for time to repent and obtain mercy from that other and Omnipotent Judge who distributes to all according to his works.'

Finally I humbly implored that I should be recommended by his lordship to the clemency of His Majesty, 'for even amidst my shame and misery I yet wish to live.'

I remained standing and Weedon came to stand by me.

There was a long silence:

'You are contrite and repentant but your application for mercy must be made elsewhere. You must now declare your detestation of your offence and should not attempt to make little of it – for so doing would add to the moral harm done already by your bad influence.'

There was another silence and then:

'I am obliged to pronounce the sentence of the Law which is that

you, The Reverend Dr William Dodd, be carried from hence to the place from which you came; that from thence you are to be carried to the place of execution, where you are to be hanged by the neck until you are dead.

And the Lord have mercy on your soul.'

From the mouths in the court room and out through the windows and doors of the Old Bailey to the crowds around it, the one word "Death" took its leaden flight; and as Weedon and four of his clergymen friends accompanied me back to Newgate the people all parted to make a pathway and looked on us and the gaolers in silence.

I do not know if I felt anything of reality as we came close to Newgate prison – I was numbed and yet not frightened, and had begun to deny to myself the possibility of being hanged. I assured myself that I was to be reprieved; there was no reason why I should not be spared the gallows, for forces far greater than courts of justice would grant me a reprieve. His Majesty the King who knew me as his Chaplain – and Charlotte his Queen whose attendance at my Chapel had so often marked her approval of me – these two if no others, would secure my release. I looked into the crowd to see if there was even at that very moment a familiar face from St James' Palace who would tell of my urgent need. There was no such person, but within a pace of Thicknesse by the prison gate was a woman I thought I had seen just hours ago at the Old Bailey. She was dressed in drab – as was Mary when she had wished to avoid pursuit – and this woman's eyes were eyes that I had seen before – soft, blue, luminous yet empty and looking beyond me. Now she stepped forward, put her arms about me and laying her cheek on my chest moaned, 'O my beloved! O my husband, O my love.'

Thicknesse loosened her arms, 'Come Mary, you shall be with Dr Dodd later. Come now and I shall take you home.' He looked at me with a nod and a wink which being such common gestures from Thicknesse I was not astounded by it nor the circumstances. The gaolers took me into the prison alone and they, although I protested that I should be taken up to my room not down, took me below and said that they knew their business, that they were ordered – since I was sentenced and in their special charge – to put me straight away into the condemned cell.

That cell had no refinement but my desk, a bed and small space for visitors if they came. At first I did not care that any should break into my solitude and argue against my belief that a reprieve was near at hand, but no man can withstand the visits and solicitations of his friends.

Mary came crying and saying that she could not any longer bear the injustice done me nor the death announced, and she returned quickly to her lodgings on Ludgate Hill, commenting only absent-mindedly that frequently she saw another woman who appeared to come and go at the same time as she but in a contrary direction. Mary was ill, doubting her own ability to sustain an ordered mind, but kept up her visits as often as she could, and on one of these she carried with her a faded manuscript – loosely tied between boards – and laid it on my desk. Held in the ties was a note from Mary:

'I bring this volume begging for your forgiveness and hoping that it may give you occupation.'

Mary burst into tears, weeping over my father's death and how she had promised him to keep it safe to return to me one day if it were ever thought to be of use. That my father had paid £120 to buy it back from Mr Jolly – actor-manager at The Haymarket – and given it to Mary to hold for me, was the cause of her most bitter tears as she remembered happier times.

On seeing the title *Sir Roger de Coverley,* I kissed her and thanked her.

Before she left I was already seated with it and rewriting lines that had lost their meaning. As *Thoughts in Prison* was finished and also T*he Prison Director for the Instruction and Comfort of Malefactors under Sentence of Death* – my collection of exhortations and prayers – I lost no time in sending for Mr Allen the printer that he might publish these as soon as possible to raise an income for Mary if I should not survive. I advised Mr Allen that to these I would add a polished improvement of *Sir Roger de Coverley* before June was out.

So, with my head bowed over my desk, I was a little distracted from the terrible torture – between hope and fear worse than a thousand deaths – that wrenched my mind and soul in and out of terrifying moods and temporary deceiving calms.

Neither Mary nor my friends were here to comfort me when Mr Ackerman, the Keeper of the Gaol, brought report that the King had, in a few words, spoken to his Privy Council and said:

'The law is to be allowed to run its course.'

No more, no less, no words of explanation, no messages of sorrowful regret; the hand that the King might have stretched out in mercy was withdrawn in defiance of the crowds whose petitions attested to my worth. Mr Ackerman, realising the evil done to me by the King, spoke tenderly and looked for advantages to ease my unhappy state and raised no difficulties in allowing my door to be opened to whomsoever I wished, and when he saw Mr Allen entering with proofs of *Sir Roger*, he withdrew and not until later returned to chill me with the news that Friday 27th June was fixed for the hanging. At this I fell upon my knees and asked God to have mercy on my soul and swooned upon the cold flagstones.

Time is a commodity more easily appreciated if it is plentiful but if in short supply diminishes further in wasted hours of indecision. Therefore, I did not mark down passages of time for particular purposes but determined in the short interval before death to exert faith, perform obedience and exercise repentance – remembering that God willeth that every man should be saved and that those who obey his call, however late, shall not be rejected. And if I could not repair the injuries I had done, I reminded myself that to will sincerely, is to do, for in the sight of Him to whom all hearts are open our deficiencies are supplied by the merits of Him who died to redeem us. A few days later I preached in this way to those convicts in Newgate who were about to share my vision of eternity, and so strengthened my faith and I pray theirs also, for when the prospect is of death, each mind must concentrate on itself to the utter exclusion of present vanities.

And yet, all this while I continued in the belief that I might be saved by temporal powers and had no need for a while longer yet to call upon that ultimate salvation which alone grants entry into heaven. Foolish man to entertain such fancies! But they were raised to a white heat when I was told of the last and greatest petition of all:

The Petition from the Gentlemen, Merchants and Traders, inhabitants of London, Westminster, and the Borough of Southwark.

It was signed by twenty three thousand people. Their marks covered thirty seven and a half yards of parchment which was carried to the Palace by two dozen or so men – including that fighting parson The Reverend Sir Henry Bate Dudley, whose battles were fought in the columns of his own newspaper – *The Morning Herald* – and Thomas Sheridan – father of the playwright – who had been recruited by Bulkley on his return to the theatre when his recent ambitions towards parliament dwindled. And came Bulkley himself, still sweating from the exercise in hurrying to Newgate to tell me about the petitions. Shortly after that he rushed back to give the happiest shout of all that the Prince of Wales had turned the King's opinion in my favour – a reprieve had been granted!

Barely able to settle to the task, I corrected the printers' errors in *Sir Roger de Coverley* and returned the proofs to Mr Allen.

For two days then I was in impatient states of ecstasy rising above all other thoughts – and then how cruelly it was dashed by Bulkley himself admitting humbly that he had been grossly misled by a rumour which he thought to be a certifiable fact. There was to be no lifting of the law, but word now – from Mr Allen at Boult Court where Dr Johnson had enquired of a friend who knew several of the Privy Council – that the King was at first minded to allow a pardon but was cut short by Chief Justice Lord Mansfield. He referred to me as "a scoundrel who should receive his deserts" and was joined by The Earl of Sandwich who had never wished me to prosper after Mary became my wife, and Lord Bathurst who as Lord Apsley had cooked my goose over the matter of simony and Lord

Hertford who like Jenkinson (Lord Hawkesbury) craved the ear and the opinion of the King on all occasions. All these had their private reasons for wishing me ill.

These betrayals and my plunge from a pinnacle of glory to a desert of despair were followed hard on by my gaoler – who knowing nothing of Bulkley's latest information – handed me *The Morning Post* with a letter in it from Ignatius Sancho, the Black Grocer I had many times seen in my congregation and who was admired by Sterne and Garrick and many others. In the letter he said:

'. . . I have often been edified by the graceful eloquence and truly Christian doctrine of the unfortunate Dr Dodd . . . who as a divine has my love and reverence . . .'

He spoke of his hope for Royal clemency with the practical suggestion that given a reprieve:

'Dr Dodd could be of infinite service for example as Chaplain to the poor convicts on the river.'

How I loved the man despite that his words with their would-be-healing vinegar put more acid disappointment into my wounds.

Everything that I felt now was worse than the sentence of death itself and I took days in rage and mourning for myself which might have been better and more quietly continued in real repentance.

Weedon came regularly to see me. He was deeply impressed with my tragedy and moved slowly as though his solemnity bound his limbs by invisible bonds. He asked to pray with me to give me consolation although more of that consolation was sought and needed for him whose genuine distress matched Mary's. But to him I could only offer speech in consolation. He called my attention to another sad case. He told me that in a condemned cell a little way along the passage from mine, a fifteen year old boy called Joseph Harris convicted at the June Assize of stealing two half-sovereigns and some silver, had been sentenced to death and was to hang on the same day as I.

Poor Joseph – as I learned in the hours I spent with him – had no religion and no one to petition for him; he, a common criminal was unable to cite any virtues in himself or actions he had performed for the common weal. His offence he laid at the door of a cousin who had disappeared when the constables arrived, but admitted to me that his mother and father had put him to thieving as soon as he was old enough to walk and carry. I wrote letters as if from Joseph to both King and Queen and to some of the nobility whom I hoped may intercede on his behalf, and I sat with him in his cell and talked of the love of Christ and how he need not be fearful of the Kingdom of Heaven. The religious hopes that I inspired in him were less fervent than his desire to have some loosening from his chafing shackles and when this was accomplished – through the kindness of a turnkey I sent to him – he cried out loud enough for me to hear in my cell:

'Thank you, Dr Dodd. Thank God for me, Dr Dodd . . . Amen.'

I told Weedon of this step towards conversion in the boy he had referred to me and advised him, if he should so wish and had the strength, to spare time for Harris. But I was wrong to ask as much, for Weedon's own misery was now fathomless, and yet he dragged himself away to see Mr John Wesley and, if possible, to prevail upon him to visit me one last time. The Reverend James Villette – the ancient Ordinary of Newgate – was an infrequent visitor to my room –"the condemned cell" – he called it with mournful elocution and a lowering of his eyes to hint at my forthcoming dissolution, and furthermore to suggest the uselessness of my denying him a "little request". This favour was always to the same end. He would begin by admiring some words of mine – such as my sermon (Johnson's text amended by me) – which had, he said, such an effect upon my "brethren felons". Then he would crave a copy of the thing he wanted – wishing me to suppose that he could then learn it off by heart and spread my work amongst a larger audience. If I should deny him – or even for a moment hesitate – the chaplain's features, already morose and withered, would sag even more until he looked the very image of a drapery-faced hound while I, always tender hearted before a creature in distress, would give way to Mr Villette and put the sermon or letter or verses that I had written into his proffered hand. I was fully aware that such literary trifles were to be turned by him into sixpenny tracts – even before my dissolution – and were I to die with exceptional dignity or drama, or in any way that was particularly extraordinary – I ventured to believe that he would reprint everything and anything that had my name upon it; and would embellish it with his own name and opinions and put it on the streets for sale.

In the beginning as now, the Chaplain spared me his prayers and catechisms and I was glad to grant him what he requested just for the pleasure of seeing him leave.

Into the anxieties and yet the peace of my Christian contemplations the martial entrance of Captain Thicknesse was a tolerated disturbance. He had appointed himself to mount and lead a campaign of rescue – to lift me from confinement in Newgate and set me free in a New World – the Americas – that in his view being a country where freedom once gained might be enjoyed in perfect security. He would not listen to my protestations. He outlined the plan which he said found first place in his favour. At Thicknesses' command, a woman noted for the making of wax effigies, had already begun to make a likeness of me, which, when finished to his satisfaction, was to be rested on my pillow in the pose of sleep while the gaolers were distracted. Meanwhile I – dressed in gaoler's clothing that he would provide – was to make my escape from Newgate.

Thicknesse inclined his head to one side and asked if I did not think this was a plan of great subtlety and bound to succeed. I replied that yes, it was, but I would not have any part in it; and when the good Captain expressed disbelief in this discourtesy and at the dull-mindedness of my response, I spoke to him on a text in the sixteenth chapter of The Acts of the Apostles. This was the lesson read at evensong on my departure for Cambridge in 1745 – that year Lammas Sunday falling on the festival of St Peter in Chains. I quoted:

"And suddenly there was a great earthquake, so that the foundations of the prison were shaken; and all the doors were opened: and everyone's hands were loosened. And the Keeper of the prison wakening out of his sleep, and seeing the prison doors open, he drew out his sword and would have killed himself, supposing that the prisoners had fled."

I said that just as Paul, I would not leave, for here in Newgate Ackerman the Keeper was a good man who had shown great kindness to me. He did not deserve the disgrace of losing a prisoner – particularly one much in the public eye and who was about to be hanged. Captain Thicknesse raised his eyebrows and heaved his shoulders and pointed a finger to my head to give the clear impression that he thought me mad. However, undaunted by my obduracy and lunacy, he gave an outline of another scheme, which involved escape from the procession on the way to Tyburn and which to succeed would call up the aid of "a substantial crowd of heartfelt sympathisers." But, to his annoyance, I deemed such a crowd would be a mob, a riot and call down the wrath of greater powers than we could resist.

Finally, then Captain Thicknesse so far thwarted in his plans and regarding me as being almost too sanctimonious to warrant rescue, said that he would not divulge any further schemes to save me from the hangman's rope – which hemp I seemed so much to desire, but would hope that if in God's mercy I were to be saved at the last, I would not deny Our Saviour any opportunity for mercy, and would not ask the hangman to swing upon my legs to stretch my neck "until it cracked and its wrenching nearly separated head from body".

I was so appalled by the picture Thicknesse conjured up for me that I did not press him for details of his latest plan. Looking upon me as an ingrate, he huffed and puffed up the steps to daylight, there to join the company of more rational beings. I prayed to God to remove from my mind the images he gave me of my death.

Thus, the eve of Thursday 26th June arrived. Bulkley and Gascoigne came early in the morning – early they said to leave me full time in the day for spiritual contemplation and for them to embrace me in a last farewell while they still had the strength, for as the day wore on they said they were bound to be weakened by unutterable grief. They promised me that they and brave Weedon Butler would be at the prison on the morrow if permitted entry, to support me and to accompany my carriage on foot to Tyburn.

In the afternoon Mr John Wesley came. He stood with Mr Ackerman at the head of the steps leading down to my dungeon room where the door was left open as usual.

'How quiet it is here,' Mr Wesley's voice was lowered to an echoing whisper, 'as quiet and still as a college chapel. It appears that even your felons are unwilling to disturb Dr Dodd.'

'Sir,' said Mr Ackerman, 'of all the prisoners that have been in this place, I have not seen any such a one as Dr Dodd. I can trust him in any part of the prison, and he has even gained the affection of those wretches my turnkeys as well as the felons.'

There was warm sunshine in the yard above and the turnkeys, assuming that I was constantly at prayer and they confirming their inclination to idleness, went about soft footed to reach the yard and sit lazily by the door leading to the stairs, soaking up the sun.

Mr Wesley conversed with me for an hour and judged, I believe, that I was no longer kicking against the pricks of

503

dreadful fate, nor still tenacious of worldly opinions and aspirations, and certain that hope had no more dominion over me. He therefore prayed with me until Mary came. She came and sank sobbing to the floor and I lifted her into my arms and laid her on my meagre bed – for she was so depressed by grief that she had no more strength in her.

Then Mr Wesley left, saying to me:

'At this finality, I am persuaded that God has seen that this is the best, if not the only way of bringing you to God.' I nodded my assent and chose this moment of extraordinary peace to kiss my beloved and take a farewell of her that was witnessed by God only, and to whose love I entrusted her until we were to be united by death.

Towards five o'clock in the evening Mr Ackerman came down to tell me that I was to be allowed all the privacy I wished for but for a guard outside my door through the hours of darkness. Meanwhile, Sam – the turnkey who was to fulfil that function – was summoned to shave me and cut my head hair to stubble that my wig might be glued fast down against all usual disturbances. He brought new mourning clothes for me and a splendid full-bottomed wig all of which he laid out on the floor in the shape of a recumbent body. He took a smaller suit and wig, new white stockings and buckled shoes to Joseph Harris. The latter could be heard crying pitifully above the hammer strikes as his shackles were removed entirely and I called out words of encouragement to him – to be brave and to accept the mourning clothes and wig and stockings and buckled shoes that my friends – now his – had brought so that upon the morrow he cut no worse figure than me, and told him that the Almighty was with us both and had forgiven our sins. Joseph's whimpering died out before the bolts were shot on his door.

I prayed that he slept.

Mary rose to leave. Her body was without a mind, an automaton. I kissed her cheek. Gently steadied by a gaoler as though she were a clock that must be moved without stopping its tick, she walked up the steps and out of my life: for the last time.

At eight o'clock when the sun was slanting between the window bars, Captain Thicknesse came back with Mary – not my Mary, my wife – but that other "Mary" whose luminous eyes were now tear stained and touched with a little wildness. Thicknesse put hands on our shoulders and drew us together:

'Mary, embrace your good unfortunate Dr Dodd, the husband who has risen above his tragedy to provide for you again.'

She did so and kissed my cheek lightly but kept her arms tight around me until Thicknesse drew her away:

'I must take her to her carriage,' he said 'for all Mary's parts in these events are ended and she sets off tonight for a secure and peaceful haven.'

I had only the smallest inkling of what Thicknesse meant, and in the effort again to separate my mind from earthly things I bowed to them both and pulled the door to as they climbed the stairs – "Mary" with her hood pulled about her face and her body hunched in misery.

Sam, the turnkey, gave me lighted candles and a jug of water, shut the door and shot the bolts and locked it, and having dragged a rough stool down the steps sat and leaned his back against the door, wishing me goodnight and promising to respond to my requests happily and be speedy in the commission.

I wrote letters for an hour or more. I prayed, first on my knees and then sitting in my bed. I reviewed my wasted life. I prayed for Mary. The bell of St Sepulchre tolled midnight. I prayed and did not hear the next hour called.

I woke to the sound of a bell and thought the hour was three. I got upon my knees and prayed and stayed awake until the night watchman came that I might know the hour for certain. It was four o'clock.

A CROWDED CHAPTER

I rose from the cold flagstones and drank water and passed my waters into the chamber pot thinking that that function might be for the last time on earth for me and thereupon sat for the last time too and prayed again – not to review my life or reconcile me to death but to recite lines and benedictions and prayers to shut out each image of the scaffold as it jolted into my head.

At six o'clock Sam Turnkey opened the door for two more of his kind.

They smiled as they saw me wash my face as thoroughly as if I were setting out to meet my bride and smiled again when I took time to smooth my brightest waistcoat beneath the blackness of the mourning coat and to adjust the tabs of my calling. The turnkey's smiles turned to laughter when I had them three times fix and glue and re-fix my wig until it was set to my satisfaction.

To communion at eight. I looked back into my cell as the gaolers led me out. Sam Turnkey had begun to clear it out and soon I thought would be as bare of me as was the world I was leaving. The chapel was cold. I took communion.

Afterwards while waiting in the Vestry, Mr Ackerman brought to me a man condemned for attempting suicide. I listened to him and ministered to him until Joseph Harris and his gaolers joined me. Here the withered Ordinary gave Joseph a blessing with a withered hand before taking a bundle of freshly printed tracts from a pew and leading us out towards the prison yard. "*A last letter from The Reverend Dr William Dodd and Words to his Brethren in Newgate Prison*" the headings said, "*prepared and printed for The Reverend James Villette, Ordinary to the Prison.*" The Ordinary saw me twisting my head to see the titles and shuffled the bundle under his arm so that the Bible he carried was given greater prominence being held in front.

The breath of prison is foul.

At nine o'clock we came into the clear skies and bright

sunshine of the yard. Prisoners put newly into the condemned cells called out through the bars for a blessing from me and hands reached out and some I touched and I spoke to those felons I could not reach. And Joseph began to weep again so I put my arm around him until the carriage for the procession came to the gates. Then my hands and Joseph's were bound – his behind him – mine as a privilege in front, which I did not wish for, but the guards insisted that I should have that courtesy.

The gates were opened and guarded by an army of constables holding back the mass of people who would have entered. The crowd hissed at those who kept them back. I walked towards the mourning coach and showed the people around that I was not suffering and when I spoke to give them a quiet blessing a sea of black hats rose in the air and stayed as they would be raised on either side of the procession for the entire three miles to Tyburn – half a million men and women and children I should gauge – at first standing and then walking slowly with the procession until the press of the crowd ahead made no more movement possible.

At the head of the procession were Mr Sheriff Thomas in his carriage and the City Marshall on his horse, and then came the mourning coach that my friends supplied wherein The Reverend Weedon Butler, dear much afflicted man, already sat and beckoned me to sit beside him.
Opposite me, facing the prison, the Under Sheriff and The Reverend James Villette. Next behind us was a cart bearing the hearse and coffin designated for me – and all these vehicles were pulled by black plumed horses – and the cart for Harris was covered with black baize. In this, the boy sank weakly to the floor and laid his head in his father's lap who wept silently and seemed to see nothing but his son.

First amongst the followers on foot I glimpsed Bulkley and Gascoigne. There was no sound but the noise of iron-clad wheels on earth and broken stone and shortly in my coach the droning voice of the Ordinary reading the fifty-first Psalm.

At St Sepulchres the great bell tolled and the procession halted while from the steps the Rector gave an exhortation to repentance and young women of the parish joined by Magdalens gave nosegays into each carriage.

Faces in the crowd.

Again and again they bore likeness to faces familiar to me over the years of my life – my mother and father and sisters and brothers – even a baby Jacob held upon his father's shoulders, Warden Drake, The Reverend Mr Griffiths of Clare, Warden Semple, Lady Hertford, Bishop Sam Squire, Madame Brodeau and a dozen others forcing their way into my imagination; but one held my inner gaze – Miss Aphrodite.

Therefore, I looked away from the people and cast my eyes to see if Miss Numerus was here. And could not see her for her imagined face was another covered face – the Mary that Thicknesse had brought to me yesterday.

So little time was left to me, I could not linger on any one thought or scratch deeper at my memory.

Weedon opened his Bible as we passed onto the Oxford Road. Here the press of people was so great that our horses were able only to draw us forward inches at a time. Faces peered through the coach windows and as we for a moment halted, touched the glass with their noses. Weedon passed his wide brimmed hat for me to hide my face. Over the silence within the coach and around us, Weedon read from Paul the Apostle's Epistle to the Romans:

"Who shall separate us from the love of Christ? Shall tribulation, or distress, or persecution, or famine, or nakedness or peril, or sword?

Even as it is written for thy sake we are killed all the day long; we were accounted as sheep for the slaughter.

Nay, in all these things we are more than conquerors through him that loved us.

508

For I am persuaded that neither death, nor life, nor angels, nor principalities, nor things present, nor things to come, nor powers,

Nor height, nor depth, nor any other creature, shall be able to separate us from the love of God, which is in Christ Jesus our Lord.

Amen."

Motion had altogether ceased – our coach standing now by the turnpike a few paces from the Tyburn Tree.

Joseph Harris and his father were lifted onto the scaffold cart and when the rope was round the boy's neck the hangman signalled for our coach to draw up. Constables gathered round and lowered the steps down which I stepped firmly and looked neither right nor left and onto the scaffold. Harris turned to face me, attempting to put one leg out of sight of the other for a brown stain was growing through and spreading down his white stocking. He trembled, his teeth chattered and he wept.

I stood erect and looked upon this lad – smaller and younger than my beloved Lancaster – and pitied and loved him.

Now I remember no more after this.

CHAPTER 35
CHATEAU DE VOIRONS.

Voirons
1st November 1792

After the many lines written before these I am even more than usually exhausted. I am triumphant in my memory's detailed recollections of many matters. Yet there are gaps – events, names and even words – where there seems to be no prospect of return.

My left hand still regrets the one-time strength of the right hand to write and record without written fault. And it has me stain the page with tears of self pity. My disordered digestive and copious excretive powers are unreliable.

Oh! How I long for rest from all uncomfortable mind and body matters.

Alas! The hope of rest and ease was vanished by the appearance of Sir Philip Thicknesse two hours ago – but to my delight and proving her constancy – Lady Ann has accompanied him again. Her title, which she carries well, justifies his "Sir" however acquired – for she has a nobility and grace and beauty that clears and brightens the air she moves in. But when they came I was not ready for the bruising infliction that Thicknsesse's presence is so likely to put upon attendant company, and when at about teatime the rattle of carriage wheels – and no less than a pack of four hounds descended before him and began to bark and scrape at the Chateau door – I was overcome with a desire to be alone, suffering pains in my neck and other more intimate parts that demanded privacy. Quickly, I scribbled a note for Mary to give him:

THE HANGING OF WILLIAM DODD

Dear Sir,

I am just at present not very well and incapable of welcoming you or even having a rational conversation with you and beg you and your inestimable wife to excuse me until the morrow.

Yours in misery,

W.D.

By the time that Mary had delivered the note I had retreated to the safety of my chamber and locked the door and, like a practiced coward, pulled the bedclothes over my head – but sufficiently loose to hear loudly from the hall below:

Has he not yet found his tongue?'

Before I slipped into the delights of sleep, I was satisfied with myself and the results of labours with my pen over many days of this year and all the years at Voirons.

It is, as customary for me, an early dawn. Night's candles are burnt out and flaky darkness breaks within the east. At my desk all is familiar. On the right my father's Bible and *The Beauties of Shakespear* with ink blots on the Morocco binding. Also on the left, now well accustomed to my clumsy left hand's splashing, is the ink pot and rack for quills brought from Cambridge when I first set out for London.

Yesterday was Thicknesses' day and tomorrow he leaves. Mary wept last night saying that Sir Philip is bitter disappointed that I have not found my tongue and so is she. And Mary has fearful premonitions which she will not confide. But today is an early dawn for me. Through the windows the copper-coloured remnants of autumn gather on the lawns, one leaf fluttering now, and then another, reluctantly dropping from the trees.

It might be evening if just one grey moment of the day is captured, and certainly it is my evening. I know I am nearing the end of my life – it cannot be much further ahead

511

– surely it is almost finished now. I have lived it all, I have written it all. I have died once and lived again. There is no commentary by me on the subject of myself but only facts. Nevertheless, it is the history of my mind which could have been written by no other person. I have now at last no great regret that the power of speech is passed away from me – for however velvet tongued I once was, only a few people would learn my history by my talking and they would pass it on and garble it. I have written and told the truth – no more than that – for lies in print are spread about like locusts and hurt the teller and the told.

Lady Ann attached herself closely to Mary yesterday, the pair walking arm in arm to and fro before the chateau, sometimes deeply and sometimes lightly in conversation and sometimes silent.

Sir Philip has persuaded M le Blanc away from his microscope and could be seen in the distance demonstrating to him the dogs' obedience –which exhibition broke up into noise and disarray when a hare appeared out of long grass. After that the hounds and humans came into the study and gathered round Thicknesse who moved books to make space and spread his rump over a half of my desk. He called for the casket wherein was everything I had written and called for the key to open it – which he then returned to Mary. She sat in an upright chair working at a sampler; Lady Ann more comfortably on a sofa where – until silenced by her husband – she conversed with M le Blanc. Thicknesse lifted a bundle of papers from the casket and, turning it upside down like a wet nurse setting out to wind a baby, looked around imperiously at his audience.

'You have done well to complete your chronicle Dr Dodd,' said Thicknesse, 'but regrettably there are as yet no shocking discoveries here to bring speech tumbling and crying out from your mouth.'

He continued then for a while relating anecdotes from his own experience that illustrated the power of surprise in eliciting vocal responses from the nearly dead, the mute, the deaf and other deceiving knaves:

'Why,' he said, 'a soldier in my command in Jamaica with a sword wound in his throat, was as silent as the grave until I ordered him a whipping. By the tenth lash he was so far recovered he cried out loud and begged me listen while he thanked me for his cure.'

The women looked horrified: Mary lodged her needle in the sampler's fabric and drew her chair close beside mine; Lady Ann suddenly recalled to mind the dreadful state of her violoncello and solicited the help of M le Blanc to re-string that instrument immediately in the hall. I watched their departure and the shadow of irritation passing over Thicknesse's face while he ruffled pages and started at the end of my history and worked back to the beginning. He took each page in turn and held it like a dirty thing between his finger and thumb. If anything displeased him he let the page fall to the floor pronouncing loudly on its defects. So fell whole sheets of sermons and lines of my poetry.

'Ah! The hanging! You had a horrid eagerness to be there at last – and knew that the mob were amiable towards you for being the image of them – in liability to sin at least – and yet knew in this hour your courtship of popular applause was at an end.'

Thicknesse closed his eyes imagining the scene again.

'Yes you did step up to the scaffold quickly, erect and dignified. You took the hands of The Reverend Mr Butler and he talked earnestly with you and had plentiful tears flowing down his face mingling with the flurry of rain in the wind that took your cap off. The old Ordinary retrieved that and then found a secure place for some printed papers I presumed he brought to Tyburn for later sale.

'You spent a long while on your knees and the gentlemen and ladies who had paid guineas for a seat high in Mrs Carey's Pews – and other tiers of seats and boxes nearest to the scaffold – those people became restless. They silenced again when I dare say the noose was passed clear over the cap and head of your dear husband, Mary, and the knot put with deliberation high on his neck. Words passed between The Reverend Dr Dodd and the hangman. The whip was cracked which launched the boy Harris from the scaffold into eternity and then – it was said – with no covering for your eyes, the whip cracked again and put you, dear William, beyond the unreality of this world. You know the rest.

Mary, who had covered her ears up to this point, asked Thicknesse to tell me what happened to my friends. His knowledge was scant, he said, but that Bulkley and Gascoigne had kept up with the procession from Newgate, clutching the tail of the hearse as long as they were able. In the press on the Oxford Road Gascoigne's pocket was picked and he was injured in the scuffle and Bulkley lost his grasp and fell and was trampled upon until rescued by his friend. They neither of them recovered sufficiently to make headway towards Tyburn and turned back to give and take comfort at the Porters' house. Here the distress overwhelmed the household and rendered them all incoherent. Barbara, your sister, wept for us all and more so when she was told that for her own safety Mary had been entrusted to the keepers of an insane asylum near Colchester.

After the hanging, Weedon Butler had attempted to find Gascoigne and Bulkley but failed and within a few days he fell with a fever and a depression of his spirits so severe that it was only in recent years that he had recovered sufficient and had now opened a school in Chiswick.

Sturdy, your dear pupil and the betrayer of your crime, advanced in the service of King George – Ambassador to Spain, then Master of the Mint and now exercising the responsibilities of Post Master General, but, Thicknesse said, held in little affection by his betters or his peers.

Mary's appetite for knowledge of the lives of our acquaintances was insatiable. Sir Philip – she would never address him without his title – was pushed to recollect and therefore soon invented details to give his memory a good reputation. Tiring for once and only for a moment, Thicknesse paid close attention to the manuscripts in his hand and soon began to criticise and comment and give full flow to his opinions on every subject that arose – his pleasure increasing as his opinions grew more wild. Thus:

'Dodd, you are a dramatist resurrected in all you write but how fortunate the meagre income you derived did not depend on that meagre talent. Your sermons have a tincture of poetry in the language and I dare say you preached with energy and had something theatrical in your actions and so I must admit that you pleased generally – which is a happy circumstance – for one who does not, pleases nobody.

'In all this you have unwisely not entirely avoided deep philosophy – there is no money in it and it gains no notice by the press. You also in place of bad poetry had been well advised to turn out ballads which may sell well, but there was none to come to your rescue there.'

Two more pages were released to the floor and he began again,

'Of the Americas and Mme Brodeau you have said little except for a portion of regret – perhaps there are some matters there which stir up your conscience and seal your tongue? Patriotism and a dreadful consuming passion? Should I be the confessor to your sins and ease your malady?

> *"To cure the pains of love no plant avails*
> *And his own physic the physician fails."*

'But I should have understanding and would not censure you'

Thicknesse bent again to his task with quickening speed and more disdain.

By this time there were indications in my nose that dinner was cooked and other stomachs were loudly declaiming their need for food. Thicknesse attempted one more attack on my dumb state by turning pages until he found his own account of the revivification and adorned that description with more horrid detail – for his assumption was that I had never asked nor known about it and now my fright would be double in its effect. Mary, however, who had already taken up her sampler again, moved to go to the kitchens saying:

'Sir Philip, we are well acquainted with that part of dear William's history and are neither shocked nor instructed nor amused by any of your descriptions 'though we know what is your purpose. Come to dinner and help me with your friend William who is much fatigued.'

With the compliance of a small boy rebuked, Thicknesse did as bidden and Mary hushed him again when he said, 'There is one more thing that could provide the answer . . .'

Together they gathered all the papers in their proper order and returned them to the casket. I saw Thicknesse take two or three sheets of paper from his pocket and drop them slyly into the casket. I limped through on his arm.

Later that evening with curiosity denying me sleep I took the two sheets of paper from the casket. They were leaves of a letter written by him, addressed to me dated and dated 1st November 1792:

Dear Dodd,

I have spoken before about what I saw or did not see when I stood below the scaffold on that Fatal Hanging Day of June 27th 1777. I swore that I did not see the hanging. I hid that lie because I judged at the time that neither you nor Mary could bear to learn more detail of the last seconds of your life – which were inevitable had it not been for God and my own small endeavours.

It happened in this way and is etched upon my memory so: the boy Harrison had been dispatched and his legs pulled firmly to snap his neck. The sound of that fell like a fire cracker amongst the nearest crowd. He was taken down from the gallows' arm. His father bore him away.

Now it was your turn William. The crowd waited as
the hangman, with a look of authority, pulled you from
your knees. You appeared in a hurry to obey him and I
heard him introduce himself and say:

'You must cease your prayers for a moment now, but
soon you will speak to your God face to face. For they say
in eternity there is plenty of time for prayer, Sir.'
He smiled at you to soften his own harshness and smiled
all the time to himself in admiration of his own power over
you who had the manner of a man anxious to oblige and so
get the hanging done.

The hangman tied your thumbs behind your back,
pulling and twisting the cord tight until the pulps were
nearly bursting.

'Hood on,' he muttered to himself.

'Hood off! I will not look into a dark bag at my end.
All the people here are my congregation and will wish that
my eyes hide nothing of my love from them.'
A slight wind was herding grey clouds into a far part of the
sky.

'Noose on,' the hangman muttered.

'Noose off! And remove the hood and the noose as well,'
you giggled and shuddered.

The hangman has not heard for he is thinking hard, his
mouth fixed wide open to aid his mind's effort to make the
knot run free on the rope. He fails and is poking thick
fingers with broken black nails to scratch between rope and
your neck. He masters the knot and gives another smile of
satisfaction while the rope's stiff hemp fibres rub and jab
and pierce folds in the skin of your neck.

Your head is clamouring. Did you even now have the
desperate hope that you might be saved? Did you hear as I
did, the sound of distant galloping hooves? Perhaps the
King's reprieve? If the hangman heard he gave no hint of

it but adjusted the rope once more to be exact in the length of slack to hang you. I craned over the scaffold edge reaching to touch some part of you to give you courage, of no avail. I caught nothing but the hangman's breath escaping through manured teeth to stagnate in your nostrils.

The hangman explained his procedure as he would a dancing master to a dull child:

'You are to act like a gentleman,' he says, coaxing you even nearer to the edge of the cart.'Do not step back or lower yourself. I shall crack the whip once and the horses and we will make a neat business of the matter. Do not let this be a rehearsal. Let us do it just once and do it right.'

You mouthed something – agreement or a question that might make him delay and bring hope. You nod until the rope is so tight on your throat you must give up all speech. That was the longest and most grievous and non-ending-silence of your life Reverend Dr William Dodd.

The hangman turned away. You bent at the knees as low as you dared and fixed your head against the knot and stiffened your neck; eyes to the empty June sky from which no help came. Whip crack. You felt for the edge of the cart but it was gone. Tread air, no foothold, no earth, no air, no sound beyond you but the swirling of blood trapped in your head and screaming fibres in your neck, nerve and sinew and crushed flesh and bone in the skull behind your ear. Throat choked. No air in or out. How those near you saw your gross and swollen face and your member an obvious and a turgid swelling beneath the cloth of your trousers. You swung but slightly thrice and O God you were dead and your body hung slack.

I brought our cart near and, cutting the hangman's hemp, lifted you gently into the coffin and began the journey through the dragging crowds to Davies the undertaker in Gouge Street.

THE HANGING OF WILLIAM DODD

You know the rest dear Dodd. And you know from these few pages that you, like the boy Harrison, was never alone; that the cruelty of man to man, in these cases at least, was observed and preserved in memory. It is for all to read and speak and hear as you did in your sermon at The Chapel Royal before you had any thoughts of your death. The text you took was from Exodus XXv13 *"Thou shall not kill"* and in the printing of your sermon you subjoined some extracts translated from the Empress of Russia's celebrated *Code of Laws*. Of all that you quote I take but just one sentence which is from Article 210: "E*xperience demonstrates, that the frequent repetition of capital punishments hath never made men better".*

It will perhaps be remembered also Dodd that you, despite all that I say and do-down about anyone who may be lesser than I – you are a man of dignity, intelligence and worth.

Your obedient servant, Philip Thicknesse

Sleep was not to be obtained for me. I sat through the night putting pages in order, correcting and adding to, or subtracting sentences or words to make chapter headings complete.

Thicknesse and Lady Ann left early and suddenly this morning. I hope that I gave them both some indication of my affection for them, but they were much occupied in carrying their belongings out to the carriage and rectifying the dirt and damage done by their hounds.

So it was with brief embraces and prolonged waving, Mary and I and finally M le Blanc – they as dumb as I – watched the last tail of the last trailing hound disappear into the distance.

And it is also farewell to me in these pages.

CHATEAU DE VOIRONS

I will write no more.
Yet it is my fervent hope that soon I will in the company
of angels appear again in a new improved edition corrected
and amended by its Author,
Almighty God.
Amen

I closed and locked the casket.

EPILOGUE

Lady Ann Thicknesse
L'Hotel Maritime, Boulogne
8th November 1792

Dear Mary,

I address this letter and the package that goes with it particularly and directly to you because I hardly know what effect it may have on your husband should he receive it instead. You will, I am certain, have already discovered the loss of the casket and have suffered by it – even worse since you will have realized that my husband Sir Philip was the thief. Before I tell how this happened and to explain why I have not written before – and moreover to lodge a little pity in your heart – my husband is dead. I am just come back from the Protestant Churchyard where his body was buried today.

Oh dear Mary! I pray that you will again one day believe that Sir Philip was a good man, with a heart ever open to relieve the distress of others and to my knowledge, until this recent event, a man of strict honour and integrity.

On the morning after we arrived in Boulogne we set off on the first stage of the long journey to Italy where Sir Philip had determined – for the sake of economy, and after almost a full day's serious consideration! – that we should live for a year or two. We had hardly quietened the dogs and settled in our carriage when Sir Philip reached under his seat and brought out the casket and began immediately an attempt to break open the lock with a coarse penknife. I should not have spoken to him then while he was still angry and sweating from his exertions with the preparations for our departure. He expostulated angrily:

'Woman, damn me. Leave me alone. The loss of this to Dr Dodd is a small thing if it could be the very matter which restores his speech to him. And if, and if not, booksellers in London will pay a pretty sum for this.'

I made argument with him and pleaded tearfully and abused him roundly as I never have before and all the while he hugged the casket tighter to his chest, his face becoming purple and contorted, then deathly white and finally empty and he was dead. Dead. My husband dead.

The casket slid to the carriage floor and gaped open. And now I confess to theft also. As well as the bundle of papers one torn scrap of paper fell out loose, and on it written in your husband's hand were the words: 'If I do not see Sir Philip again in the morning, give him my heartfelt thanks for his efforts on my behalf and above all for his friendship, for I love the man.'

Mary, will you permit me to keep this sentiment which is so close to my heart and where it in fact lies now – with a painting of Sir Philip in a locket about my neck? All else is returned to you forthwith.

Please tell me that you forgive me and will write to me in Bath.

Your affectionate and honoured friend,

Ann Thicknesse

Mrs Mary Farrier

Chateau de Voirons, 12th November 1792

Dear Lady Ann,

If by the end of it this letter is tear stained, be assured they are tears shared and shed for you in your distress. Your letter and the package containing the casket and all that had been in it came today – the first I knew that there was anything amiss.

William took ill the day after you left. He lies without movement and his eyes pin-pointed to the heavens. I and M le Blanc – who as you know is very soft towards us –

and Cook, who says she has seen more of her family sicken and die in the same way, takes turns with us as we all share in our care for William. His bed is brought down to where stood his desk.

There is nothing for you to ask forgiveness – certainly, you may keep the torn off piece of paper – a "morning note" we call it but yours is more truly a "mourning note". But the sentiment still holds.

Oh dear Lady Ann, shall you come to see us ever again? I hope so and now I sign faithfully, yet with a forgery that both my William and your Sir Philip did always insist upon for letters out of France,
Your affectionate and true friend.
Mary Farrier

Lady Ann Thicknesse Bath
Christmas 1800 Post to Voirons

Mon Cher M le Blanc,
What great kindness to send me Mary Dodd's effects, and some relics of Dr William Dodd, and to trouble yourself with giving such a clear account of all the sadness that has befallen you over these last months.

In remembering the good that William did, I may remark in passing that the Lawyers here talk continually of the beneficial changes in the Penal Code – particularly the reduction in crimes punishable by death – more than one hundred up 'til now – which striking from the statutes has followed as a consequence of Dr Dodd's hanging and his sermons years before that. Now sometimes breaks into my sleep the dreadful thought that had the fact of his revivification been known none of the good he did in life and death would have been transmitted to us, for he certainly would have been hanged again. So bitter are the ways of some magistrates.

I understand that you wrote from the house of the l'Abbe de Prechamp and assume that he gave you shelter when your Chateau de Voirons was sacked and burnt by the same malcontents who destroyed most of the fine buildings in Paris and many great houses and chateaux throughout the land. Daily in my prayers I give thanks for my merciful flight from Paris when the aristocrats in that city suffered as did you at Voirons, That you have survived is perhaps a miracle – and one for which we all thank God.

We have some of your countrymen here in Bath – each one of them deploring the brutal excesses of *la revolution*, and the present triumphs of M Bonaparte. Should you manage to escape from your always *Belle France,* please give serious consideration to include Bath in your travels and to stay here for as long as you have the inclination. You may test our courtesy and kindness which have no limits and you will not find us wanting – particularly in the house of

Your friend and admirer,

Ann Thicknesse

The End

ACKNOWLEDGEMENTS

Firstly, sincere thanks are due to my family – Paula, Joanna & Richard, Emma & Adrian – who have patiently endured my absences while I have been with William Dodd and his friends for several years.

In chronological order rather than alphabetical order and each one with different skills and advice willingly given has become a friend. Here are the people to whom I owe much: secretarial, editorial and proof-reading: the late and brilliant Helen Hughes and the very living and talented Sylvia Funston. Willing at all times to share their knowledge: Dr Richard Hamblyn (Birkbeck, University of London), Professor Markman Ellis (Queen Mary, University of London) who read and gave constructive comment on the very first draft. A great friend and gentle critic the writer the late David Nobbs (creator of *Reginal Perrin*) commented on the nearly completed draft of *Dodd*. Phil Sadler has led me in and out and through computer territory so earning my admiration and gratitude. Terry Moore-Scott and Roger Grounds are individual friends and scholars who have given encouragement when it has been most needed.

The staff of libraries were always keen to help: Bourne (Lincs) Town Library, The British Library, Clare College, Cambridge and the University Library; The Bodlean Oxford Univerrsity, The Library & Museum of Freemasonry, London. The Hunterian   Museum at The Royal College of Surgeons, London; and Gloucester City Library.

These sanctuaries were almost as numerous as the churches having a Dodd connection where the vergers, wardens or the clerical incumbent   were sometimes surprised at a visit but always able to help. Only a few churches are mentioned here: City of London Churches or their sites,

.Out of London:The Abbey Church of St Peter and St Paul, Bourne, Lincolnshire; St Mary the Virgin, Chalgrove,

South Oxfirdshire; St Nicholas, Hockliffe, Bedfordshire; All Saints, Wing, Buckinghamshire.

A number of these places and others, and their people when available, made the author welcome – as their forbears did for Dodd many times and many years before this author broke into their peace.

ABOUT THE AUTHOR

Anthony Lynch studied history and philosophy at Cambridge (St John's College). Directed by a Tribunal for Conscientious Objectors to do humanitarian work, his two years National Service (1957-1959) were spent as a Nursing Assistant in East Dulwich at an emergency psychiatric unit for men. His book *Y Block* written in the nineteen-sixties and published in 2022, is an account of that time.

Lynch then held commercial manager/directorial posts in London for several years until he trained and qualified (MRCS LRCP, MB BS,) at The Royal Free, Hospital. After a range of hospital posts he set up his own GP practices in Gloucestershire.

Dr Anthony Lynch's leisure pursuits have always taken him deeply into eighteenth century medicine, art, and social and political history.

He is married with two daughters.

Printed in Great Britain
by Amazon

28407727R00294